C000213541

Parlatheas Press Titles:

The Cayn Trilogy:

Son of Cayn
City of Cayn
Blood of Cayn

Chronicles of Damage Inc.:

Phantoms of Ruthaer
Mask of the Vampire
Eye of Chaos*

Adventures of Roger V:

Thief on King Street
Message for the Devil *

* Forthcoming

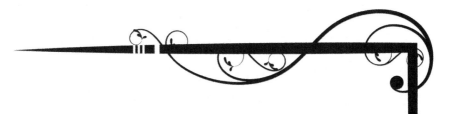

THIEF ON KING STREET

A ROGER V ADVENTURE

Jason McDonald
Stormy McDonald
Alan Isom

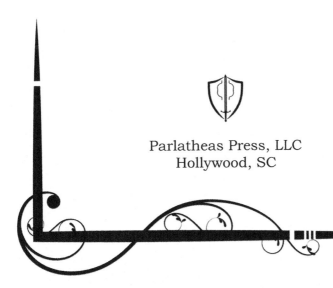

Parlatheas Press, LLC
Hollywood, SC

<u>Thief on King Street</u>
   Copyright 2022 by Jason McDonald, Melanie McDonald, & Alan Isom

Characters and Setting:
   Property of Alan Isom, Jason McDonald, & Melanie McDonald

All rights reserved. No part of this publication may be reproduced, distributed or transmitted in any form or by any means, including photocopying, recording, or other electronic or mechanical methods including information storage and retrieval systems, without the prior written permission of the authors, except in the case of brief quotations embodied in critical reviews and certain other noncommercial uses permitted by copyright law. For permission requests, write to the authors, addressed "Attention: Permissions Coordinator," at the address below.

Parlatheas Press, LLC
P.O. Box 963
Hollywood, SC 29449-0963
https://mcdonald-isom.com

Note: This is a work of fiction. Names, characters, places, and incidents are either a product of the authors' imaginations or are used fictitiously. All situations and events in this publication are fictitious and any resemblance to actual persons, living or dead, or to businesses, companies, events, institutions, or locales is purely coincidental.

Cover Image & Design: C. Jason McDonald
Title Page Design: MJ Youmans-McDonald
Title Page Border: Rebecca Read (Pixabay.com)
Interior Map: C. Jason McDonald

ISBN 978-1-958315132 (paperback)

DEDICATION

For everyone who dreams of magic
and traveling to other worlds.

ACKNOWLEDGEMENTS

The authors would like to recognize the language, culture, traditional medicine, and beliefs of the Gullah community of the South Carolina sea islands. We offer our deepest respect to the ancestors and keepers of the language and heritage of this rich community.

We would also like to give recognition to the following authors and organizations whose work informed and inspired this story:

Geraty, Virginia Mixson. *Gullah Fuh Oonuh/ Gullah for You: A Guide to the Gullah Language (English and Gullah Edition).* Sandlapper Publishing Company, 1998

Gullah Geechee Cultural Heritage Corridor.
https://gullahgeecheecorridor.org
http://visitgullahgeechee.com/

McTeer, J.E. *Fifty Years as a Low Country Witch Doctor.* iUniverse, 2013

Montgomery, Jack. *American Shamans: Journeys with Traditional Healers.* Busca Inc, 2008

Orr, Bruce. *Six Miles to Charleston (SC): The True Story of John and Lavinia Fisher.* The History Press, 2010

White, John Blake. *Essays on Capital Punishment.* South Carolina Historical Society, Charleston, SC, 1834

There are so many friends who have helped us hone this story. Foremost, we'd like to express our appreciation to Dana Isaacson, our editor, and to Scott B., Jake M., and Brad W. for their technical assistance with police procedure. Last but definitely not least, we would like to thank our Beta Readers, who helped pick apart and polish our story: David B., Lacy B., Leslie B., Jimmy R., and for critical analysis and five decades of friendship, Ray W.

KERCH

ALBORG

SCHONGRA R.

WAIZENBACH R.

KIEL

GALLOWEN

KARLSRUHE

ALASHALIAN MOUNTAINS

TYDWAY

MARGATE

MANNHEIM

ROSTOK

ROWANOAKE

JONGAR

PORT REMLEY

SCHONGRA R.

ISURA R.

RUTHAER

YORK

TENBY PT.

LUBECK

CAROLINGIAS

WAIZENBACH R.

ZARAGOZA

ALDBOROUGH

ESSEN

BURGOS

SWANSEA

NIMES

MURCIA

MALAGA

LIMOGES

OVIEDO

TOULOUSE

BLANC R.

SANTANDER

CADIZ

AMIENES

MULHOUS

MAP OF THE DARK ONE'S
INVASION OF PARLATHEAS

Situation shortly before April 4208

———— Political Boundary
– – – – Major River

BACKSTORY

Their king assassinated and a magical plague running rampant throughout the land, the peasantry and bluebloods of Carolingias fight amongst themselves while an evil priest of the Dark One sits on the throne. Forced into hiding, the remaining Knights of Carolingias seek out the one person who can unite their country.

Hunted by dærganfae assassins, Ambrose, the last Battenberg heir to the throne, has found refuge in the arms of the rebel leader, Camber. Driven by hunger, the rebels have infiltrated the capital with plans to liberate the food rumored to be stored there.

On the far side of the city, Roger Vaughn, thief and master spy in service to the Highlord of Gallowen, must create a distraction significant enough to give Carolingias a fighting chance...

CHAPTER 1
DECISIONS

April 22, 4208, K.E.

5:50 am

*R*oger Vaughn peered over a frost-limned stockpile of ballast stones and watched stevedores move plague-ridden corpses from a flat-bottomed barge into a wagon.

Overseeing the task, a bald priest in a grey cassock gripped the wagon's traces. About the Sha'iry's neck, a thin chain supported a silver medallion embossed with a forked cross — the symbol of the Dark One. Originating in Zhitomir, the evil priesthood had recruited men from every country. Hungry for power, they had turned away from the Eternal Father and sold their souls to Sutekh.

The early morning shadows stretching across the sluggish waters of the Isura River thinned and receded as the sun crept above the tree line. Although careful to remain physically still and silent, Roger's thoughts never stopped moving. He reviewed the contents of the burlap sack at his feet, the tasks he had to accomplish this morning, and the timing of events in other parts of the city, all while keeping track of the dock workers' progress.

After the last body was loaded, the Sha'iry guided the blindered draft horses uphill into the warehouse district of York, capital city of Carolingias. The road held deep wheel ruts, a testament to the number of similar wagons that had traveled this path and the lack of care given in recent months.

Roger scooped up his sack and followed. Dressed in drab clothes and a cloak covered in strategically placed varicolored patches, he fell in behind a pair of men heading in the same direction as the Sha'iry. With smears of soot and gravel-dust covering portions of his tanned skin, he appeared to be as down-on-his-luck as his fugacious companions.

Laden with its grisly cargo, the wagon trundled through a maze of twisting streets and lanes. The warehouse district, once a thriving industry, held abandoned buildings that were boarded up and dark. Down several of the alleys, people in threadbare clothing hunted rats or scavenged amongst the refuse for food. Many made a quick sign against evil and kept their eyes averted, not wanting to attract the attention of the Sha'iry.

Roger steeled his heart. *How had it come to this?*

The wagon entered a gap in a limestone-capped wall. Beyond it loomed a red-brick warehouse.

He fixed a handkerchief over his nose and mouth, then pulled up the hood of his cloak, using its mottled colors to conceal him, and crossed the street. He crouched low and studied the forbidding structure. Thick smoke plumed from a pair of square, soot-stained smokestacks protruding five-stories above its rear corner. Grease and grime coated the row of arched windows, blocking all view of the activities within.

Stacks of rotten crates filled the yard, discarded when the Sha'iry took over the building. Desiccated tobacco leaves spilled from their sides. Using them for cover, Roger crept after the wagon.

Man and beasts stopped at the base of a wide ramp leading to the main entrance.

"Open up!" the priest shouted.

At the top of the ramp, wheels rumbled along iron tracks, and the broad wooden door slid open. Waiting on either side were a pair of Kem'eyu — Sha'iry acolytes — their faces and shaven scalps red and sweaty. A third figure, wearing a long, black swallowtail vest over leather armor, guarded the entrance. His hands gripped the hilt of a two-handed greatsword whose point rested on the floor between his boots. Twisted runic script writhed down a third of the sword's fuller, leaving the remainder empty. It was a symbol of his power and rank.

Roger swallowed against a sudden dryness in his throat. He hadn't counted on the presence of an Anshu — a Blade of Sutekh, one of the Dark One's warrior priests.

The interior of the warehouse glowed orange and red, giving Roger a glimpse inside the charnel house. His stomach turned at the macabre sight. Long rows of bodies were stacked like cordwood, making it impossible to estimate their numbers.

The wagon cleared the opening, and the warehouse door slid shut with an ominous boom.

During the last six months, Roger had seen numerous towns where wagons worked day and night, but it wasn't enough. Bodies still lined the sides of the road. People called it a plague, but Roger knew better: it was an attack by the Sha'iry, part of their strategic invasion.

Some, like Roger, were fortunate enough to be immune to the creeping death, but the vast majority lived in fear, clutching at every new 'cure' or 'preventative' concocted by apothecaries and snake-oil salesmen. He'd skirted remote villages where nervous vultures perched on roof gables and ridges, the dead still inside their homes, uneaten. Then there were the gangs of men whose greed overshadowed their fear of the disease. They looted manors while wearing elaborate masks with beaks filled with pungent herb blends purported to keep the user healthy.

Roger gauged the position of the rising sun. It wouldn't be long before Phaedrus began his speech. He wished he could be there to see the faces of both the Carolingians and their Sha'iry oppressors. The half-elven priest intended to convince the warring Carolingian factions to stand together.

His job this morning was to distract the Sha'iry. If all went well, they would retake Battenberg Palace and the city before day's end. He opened his burlap sack, double checking that his gear remained secure.

Now to get inside. Pulling his cloak tighter about him, he faded into the shadows.

"Open up!" a rough voice called.

The Anshu slid open the warehouse door. A burlap sack sat on the ramp. Taken aback, the grim priest scanned the debris strewn yard before stepping outside, sword at the ready. He stopped at the end of the ramp and prodded the burlap with the tip of his blade.

Silent as a wraith, Roger came up behind him. Clamping a hand over the priest's mouth, he shoved a long, silver dagger between the man's fourth and fifth ribs, piercing his heart. After sliding the body off his blade, Roger snatched his sack from the ramp and dashed inside. Darting to his left and into a deep pool of shadow, he waited.

One of the acolytes unloading bodies noticed the open door. His eyebrows rose when he spotted the slain warrior-priest. He called out, and three Kem'eyu followed as he cautiously made his way down the ramp.

Roger saw the Kem'eyu's lips move as he bent and took the greatsword from the Anshu's nerveless fingers. He raised the blade in a reversed salute, then plunged it into the fallen priest's chest.

Glistening obsidian flowed up the blade and spread over the young priest, transforming his acolyte's cassock into the armor and swallowtail vest of the Anshu. In its wake, a single rune remained upon the blade's fuller. The dead man lay shriveled and naked.

"Huor now serves at Sutekh's feet," the former Kem'eyu announced.

Not relying on his cloak to keep him hidden, Roger backed down the aisle and ducked behind an oak barrel bound in metal hoops. From its shadow, he watched the three acolytes drop Huor's corpse atop the other bodies.

The fourth pointed his new greatsword at the youngest of the others. "Zephrim, find Anshu Luther. Inform him of what's happened." Turning to the other two, he ordered, "Lock this place down and search for intruders."

"Do you think it's Camber's men?" Zephrim asked.

"How should I know? Now do as you're told."

"But, Gurth, they're supposed to be in town—"

Gurth pointed to the door. "Go! Now!"

"Yes, Anshu Gurth," the acolyte said with a nervous bow.

Roger smiled. *That's right. Bring more. Bring the whole lot of you.*

He looked around to get his bearings, and the smile vanished. Stack upon stack of corpses filled the vast space. Everywhere he turned, the bloated faces of men, women, and children stared out between twisted arms and legs marred by dark lesions. Roger's stomach lurched, and he rested his shoulder against the barrel. Swallowing back the bile rising in his throat, he reprimanded himself before opening the barrel's lid and casting a furtive glance over the rim. It was half full of lamp oil.

Scattered along the aisles were more barrels. He could only assume the clerics doused the bodies with oil so they'd burn faster. It certainly didn't cut down on the stench.

Despite the heat, Roger tugged his cloak tighter and moved closer to the corner of the warehouse where glowing furnaces fed the smokestacks. Sha'iry scurried about collecting bodies, but word of Huor's death had spread. Each one kept an eye toward the main door.

Roger avoided them as he veered toward a storage room stacked floor-to-ceiling with oak barrels. He found a secluded nook inside, reached into his burlap sack, and took out a glass bottle that held less than an inch of water. A finger-sized piece of waxy, yellowish-white phosphorus inscribed with magic runes rested on the bottom. Removing the cork stopper, he hid the potion deep inside a dark recess between the barrels. On the opposite side of the storage room, he picked another recess and repeated the process.

His brow creased as he recalculated the water's evaporation rate. When air hit the phosphorus, it would ignite, and the runes would magnify the effect. He wanted to destroy this warehouse and everything it stood for in York without killing himself in the process. Looking back out at the main warehouse, he could only hope for the best. After wiping the sweat from his face, he dropped the stoppers into his pouch and crept toward the furnaces.

A cleric maneuvered his loaded wheelbarrow down an aisle aimed in the same direction Roger wanted to go, so he crouched low and followed. The heat went from stifling to oppressive, and the stench of charred flesh filled his sinuses and coated the back of his tongue. Roger fought the need to retch and promised himself a stout drink when he had completed this expedition, along with new clothes.

At the end of the row, the roaring furnaces came into view. Four arched openings, each large enough to admit a pair of mounted horsemen, gaped hungrily. Inside, angry flames danced and cavorted to music only they could hear. Stacks of blackened bodies fed the fire, and Roger knew this was a portal to hell.

One cleric grabbed the arms of the topmost body in the wheelbarrow, another cleric grabbed the feet, and they swung it into the raging conflagration. A third presided over the sacrifice, offering up the corpse's soul to their dark god.

Moistening his parched lips, Roger searched around and found a half-full barrel at the base of a timber column. He knelt and placed an opened glass bottle between them.

Two more to go. With a predatory glint in his leonine eyes, he crept closer to the furnaces.

A restless crowd of peasants and merchants in patchwork tunics gathered in the frost-laden Square of King David. Many of them wore sashes of scarlet about their waists to proclaim their support of a new Carolingias — one where a man could have a voice in the government. Hidden among them were another faction — those still loyal to King David and the old regime. Persecuted by both the Dark One's clerics and the scarlet faction, the loyalists met in secret, recognizing each other by sapphire ribbons embroidered with a single dogwood blossom. Their detractors called them bluebloods, or simply blues, although not all among them were nobility.

Murmurs passed from one person to the next, rumors of a holy man come to end the city's suffering. The crowd surrounded the square's central pedestal and toppled statue of Carolingias' first king. Broken shards of bronze were all that remained of his patina-stained sword and crown. Beyond empty stalls and across cobblestone streets flanking the square, the remaining citizens of York packed the balconies and rooftop terraces of weathered, two-story rowhouses.

In the square's northwest corner, Ambrose Battenberg tugged her wool coat tighter around her body, pulled her hands inside the sleeves, and held the fabric closed in her clenched fists. Eyeing the Sha'iry among the crowd, she shuffled closer to the man at her side and whispered, "We shouldn't be here. This could be a trap."

Camber wrapped an arm around her waist. "Don't worry, Ambrosia, I'll keep you safe. No one will lay a finger on you — except me," he replied with a suggestive grin. "Besides, we're surrounded by my men, and I want to hear what this holy man has to say."

Ambrose tried to return his smile, but she didn't feel the same confidence he displayed. This morning, Camber had bound his ash-blonde hair in a tight braid with a scarlet ribbon before shaving and donning clothes they'd stolen from an abandoned townhouse. With the addition of his studded leather doublet, he looked like a wolf in dandy's clothing. The fighters who followed Camber loved him, both for his style and his daring. It's what attracted her to him as well.

A hush fell as a slim man wearing light blue, homespun

robes stepped out from between two market stalls guarded by men in drab brown cloaks. His bright green eyes reflected the morning sun as he made his way through the crowd to the pedestal. A soft breeze teased his pale blonde hair, exposing the pointed tips of his ears and his partial elven ancestry. Climbing the pedestal, he found a relatively flat spot near the edge and surveyed the people before him. Despite the Sha'iry law against it, a wheel-cross hung from a leather thong around his neck to rest prominently on the center of his chest.

"Carolingians, I wish to speak!" Phaedrus announced. The half-elf's voice travelled across the square, reaching every balcony, every rooftop. "I have watched you fight amongst yourselves. Why? What are you fighting for?"

"We fight for freedom!" shouted a peasant wearing a scarlet ribbon.

"Equality!" shouted another.

The half-elf acknowledged both with a nod. "Lofty and admirable goals, but why are you still fighting? King David was deposed a year ago."

Silence was their response.

"I say it's because you are scared. Who are you fighting? The bluebloods? Why them?"

"Their taxes were killing us!" a peasant shouted. "We didn't have enough left over to buy food or clothing."

"But they are your countrymen."

Shouts broke out as many of the peasants raised their fists. "They're not my countrymen!"

The half-elf held up his hand, waiting for the clamor to subside.

"I have heard it said those who support the bluebloods support the old regime — a government that is no longer operating. King David and his heir apparent are dead. The York you know has fallen!

"What do you have now? Barren fields you cannot till. Roads you cannot travel. Families that cannot live together. A plague that kills by the thousands. And while you fight amongst yourselves, you have foreigners ruling your home. Is that what you want?"

Phaedrus looked at Ambrose, as if the question was meant solely for her. She tucked her chin, letting her long, auburn hair spill forward to hide her face. Her darting gaze searched the crowd for anyone who might recognize her. She couldn't afford to be called out as a member of the deposed royal family. Not here. Not now. As far as she knew, the citizens of York believed the Battenberg line was dead. If the Sha'iry learned the truth of her identity, not even Camber's army would be able to save her from public execution. No, it was far better for everyone to believe she was a common strumpet who'd slept her way through the Red Camp and into Camber's tent.

Ambrose didn't want to listen to anything else Phaedrus had to say. "Camber, let's go," she hissed.

Camber's arm around her waist tightened. "Not yet, Ambrosia. I want to know what Phaedrus is stirring up this morning."

The crowd's murmurs faded, and Phaedrus spoke again, but Ambrose ignored him. She'd heard it all before. The talk of peasant freedom and the justifications people made for slaughtering each other, when it all boiled down to fear — fear of hunger, the plague, and death. What none of them understood was there was no such thing as freedom. Not really. There were always rules and responsibilities. Work of one sort or another to do. Not even outlaws were free. She'd seen firsthand the amount of planning and work it took to keep Camber's troops fed and outfitted.

Shouts rang through the air, decrying the indifference of King David and the nobility toward the plight of the people, while others extolled the virtues of the Sha'iry with their gifts of food.

"You have food?" Phaedrus responded. "Oh yes, the wagon trains. Food supplied by the black dogs to keep you going just long enough to destroy the merchants and nobles, but did you know this food is spoils of war from the south? From Espia, where food can no longer be produced! How much longer will it last? Or should I say, how much longer will it be provided for you?

"When the last of those willing to stand against Maa'kheru Bolezni and the forces of the Dark One fall, the black dogs will move north to Gallowen and Tydway — leaving you with barren, untillable fields, and no food. Leaving you to starve.

"Then where will you be? Free? Yes, but dying or already dead! That is not an answer for those who enjoy life. So now what?"

Again, silence washed over the Square of King David. The Sha'iry slowly drifted away from the crowd.

Ambrose was surprised they didn't pull Phaedrus down from his pedestal. Though she was only halfway listening, it seemed obvious where the cleric's speech was heading.

"Let me step back a moment. Why are you rebelling now?" asked Phaedrus. "Because of tyranny? Because of a hard life? Why did you not rebel five years ago? Or ten? I say it is because life was not so bad under the old regime. I am not saying it was perfect. Certainly, you deserve better. What I am saying is you did not hurt until King David was deposed."

Ambrose couldn't help herself. She turned her gaze north, where barren dogwoods lined a wide lane paved with sheered river rocks. A few short blocks away, an ornate stone arch and wrought iron gate marked the entrance to the palace grounds. To either side of the archway, low stone walls topped with sharp spikes ran east and west for several blocks before turning the corner. Soldiers in burgundy livery and mail armor guarded the gate with barbed pikes.

Fifty yards beyond the stone arch rose the three-story behemoth of Battenberg Palace with its copper roofs topped by a forest of chimneys. Grand blocks of fitted quartzite enclosed the ground floor. Above, two rows of dark windows with limestone cornices stared toward the city.

Although she couldn't see it from where she stood, Ambrose knew the lane from the square turned into marble bordered by granite pavers beyond the gate. It continued north through the flagstone concourse to a barrel-vaulted gatehouse, wide enough for eight soldiers to march abreast. Resting atop the entryway, six fluted pillars with blue and silver veins soared two-stories high to support a limestone entablature and pediment embossed with a shield bearing a dogwood tree on a low hill. It overhung a cantilevered balcony that once bore flags of state.

Now, the forlorn balcony overlooked a concourse filled with timber X's. Each held up by a diagonal kicker, the rough crosses bore the limp forms of men, women, and children taken by the Sha'iry. Ambrose had made the mistake of passing too near the palace once. The groans and cries of despair she'd heard still haunted her nightmares.

"King David was deposed by those black dogs!" The half-elf's shout snapped Ambrose's attention back to the square in time to see him point a finger at one of the Sha'iry. The crowd parted, leaving the acolyte exposed.

"Yes, I am pointing a finger of guilt, but at whom am I pointing? At the bluebloods? No! At the reds? No! At the black dogs? As the Eternal Father lives, YES! Can I make it any clearer? The Hounds of the Dark One lie at the heart of your problems!"

The Sha'iry fled, and a shadow seemed to lift from the square.

"So, what can you do?" asked Phaedrus. "Let me tell you about the great battle that occurred just beyond the western mountains. A vast orcnéan army travelled south through the plague-weakened lands of Rhodina and Trakya – lands just like yours. Killing. Burning. Looting. Raping. Destroying everything. Never had those lands seen such army. Their troops numbered like the leaves in the forest — uncountable. Nothing seemed to slow them. No one could defeat them. With only the sick and dying to defend them, town after town, kingdom after kingdom fell. The few remaining Glaxons and Detchians could not put aside their differences. They argued and bickered as you do now. There was no united stand against these evil forces. At the western edge of Gallowen, disparate troops struggled against the invaders instead of a united army, and they were pushed back. Nay, they were defeated!

"What I am telling you today is that you cannot stand alone! No more of this tribalism. You must unite against the invaders. Only then will you triumph."

Ambrose felt the crowd's mood shift and the excited tension building in Camber. Phaedrus was inciting a battle, and there was nothing she could do to stop it.

"Get rid of your sashes and your hate!" shouted Phaedrus. "Join together under one color and stand side by side as Carolingians!"

Many of the peasants in the crowd raised their knives, their pitchforks, whatever they had in their hand, and shouted. The clamor grew louder, spreading to the merchants and hidden aristocracy. As one, the crowd drew closer to the pedestal. The half-elf raised his hands and waited.

"Camber," called Phaedrus. His eyes sought those of the rakehell. "It is a well-known fact that brave men need a brave leader, and daring men need a daring leader. What say you, sir, will you join us in our fight?"

The leader of the reds stepped forward, despite Ambrose's protests. "If we do this, do things go back to the way they were?" he asked. "There has been too much blood spilt to let bygones be bygones."

"Sir, whom do you serve: the reds, or the black dogs?" His bright green eyes settled on Ambrose. "Or, perhaps, do you serve Carolingias?"

"Phaedrus, I serve my people," replied Camber.

"Then serve them!" the half-elf exclaimed. "You know there is a path forward. Join us and fight one last time!"

Just then, the earth shook. Ambrose felt a series of hard thumps in her chest as the brick smokestacks at the tobacco warehouse exploded.

CHAPTER 2
THE ORDER OF CAROLINGIAS

April 22, 4208, K.E.

7:23 am

*T*he crowd in the square stood stunned, many open-mouthed, as a billowing cloud of white smoke blanketed the western edge of the city. The heavy cloud hung low to the ground as it drifted their way. Here and there, people threw off their shock and pushed their way through the others and out of the square. As more noticed the approaching mass, the hurried flight of a few turned into a desperate stampede.

Dropping their brown cloaks and donning their visored helmets, the eight knights who'd protected Phaedrus before his speech now chased the Sha'iry down the tree-lined lane. Each knight wore a blue and silver surcoat over steel plate armor, which glinted brightly in the morning light. They wielded cruciform swords and bore kite shields emblazoned with a silver dogwood issuant from a mount vert on an azure field. Pushing their way through the crowd, the squad stopped at the edge of the intersecting cobblestone streets just outside the palace gate.

Two more explosions rocked the city. In the yard outside Battenberg Palace, several Kem'eyu slapped a hand on the crucified prisoners, eliciting screams of pain. The prisoners shriveled and became grey husks of flesh and bone, all traces of life gone. Yelling at the guards to open the gate, the acolytes raced westward down the street toward the explosions. In the far distance, gouts of flame shot heavenward.

The pall of white smoke wove through the crowded streets toward Battenberg Palace. Sir Cerdic Uth Aneirin brought up his sword and bowed his head. "Please, Eternal Father, be with us in this time of need. By ourselves, there is no hope. Only through you can we achieve victory over the Dark One and his minions."

He held his breath and clenched his eyes shut. Even so,

the smoke stole the moisture from his nose and irritated his skin. Tightening the grip on his sword, he waited for the signal from Lord Alfonso.

A gentle breeze kissed his cheek.

"Now."

With the smoke cleared, the knights charged across the street. Throwing all his weight against the wrought iron gate, Cerdic shoved it open with his shoulder and slammed his shield into the first guard. He heard the man's nose crunch as blood spattered his armor. Turning abruptly, he smashed the flat of his blade against the side of another's head. Even with the protection of a mail coif, the guard went down.

"Sir Cerdic, you must kill them!" Lord Alfonso yelled over the din.

"Yes, milord," Cerdic replied, smashing his gauntleted fist into the neck of his opponent.

The eight knights formed an arc, standing shoulder to shoulder inside the shadow of the arch. Using both shield and sword, they mowed down the last of the gate guards. Blood and gore coated the marble flagstones, staining their greaves, sabatons, and spurs. As one, the knights stepped over the bodies and waited.

From single story barracks flanking each side of the concourse, palace guards wielding pikes rushed toward the knights. Behind them, eighteen Sha'iry streamed from the vaulted gatehouse in groups of three, each led by an Anshu bearing their distinctive two-handed swords. A vile, droning chant extolling their dark god rose from their ranks as the Sha'iry charged down the wide lane.

The palace guards formed up in two ranks. The ones in front held shields and longswords ready. The second rank snapped their pikes forward over the shoulders of the first with a defiant shout. Remaining behind the guards, the dark clerics continued to pray to their evil god.

Lord Alfonso raised his sword and shouted, "For the Eternal Father and Carolingias!" The eight knights surged forward.

Using his six-foot-four height and long reach to his advantage, Cerdic knocked aside a pike with his shield and drove his sword into the helmet of a guard in the front rank. Wrenching the blade free, he sliced the arm of the guard holding the polearm. With a swift push, he shoved aside the two men and plowed into the next. His blade was a blur as it plummeted down time and time again. Beside him, the knights gained ground and the line of palace guards faltered.

In response to the Sha'iry's foul prayers, a sickly green nimbus shrouded the dead soldiers at the gate. Their limbs jerked and spasmed. Slowly, the bodies climbed to their feet and shambled forward, their movements as clumsy as marionettes controlled by a child.

Rough hands clawed Cerdic's pauldron. He cast a glance backward and almost jumped out of his skin when he saw the dead guard pawing at him. It crashed against his armor, rocking him forward.

Planting his foot, he whipped around and chopped the undead guard's head clean off its shoulders. As he did, Cerdic heard a loud scrape along the side of his helmet from a well-placed pike. Before he could respond, the headless guard pounded Cerdic's back with both hands, driving him to one knee.

More undead guards clambered forward, blocking their retreat.

Cerdic lost sight of the other knights as he raised his shield to defend against the undead warrior. Spinning in place, he swept his sword across its legs, cutting down the creature like a stalk of wheat. The stench of decay filled the yard as the thing jerked and bucked.

The palace guards ganged up on the knight, jabbing and prodding his armor from every side in their search for weaknesses. Their strikes rained down like hail, and a din louder than a dozen blacksmiths working rang off the palace walls.

Cerdic continued his spin. "Pater Aeternum fortitudo nostra," he prayed. *The Eternal Father is our strength.* Clearing a path with his shield, he jerked up with all his might and sliced the nearest guard's throat with the tip of his sword. Bright blood gushed over rent chainmail links as the soldier fell.

The ferocity of Cerdic's attack shook the courage of his opponents, and they took an involuntary step back. Sunlight lanced down, and his dented armor glinted through his tattered and bloody surcoat.

The clang of sword on shield and the ring of sword on sword continued all around him. He couldn't tell how many knights remained on their feet, but he gave silent thanks to the Eternal Father they still fought.

A shadow fell across the knight's opponent, and he chanced a quick look.

Camber brandished a swept-hilt rapier and metal buckler. The scarlet sash at his waist fluttered like a pennant, and blood spattered his studded leather doublet. Behind the newly arrived soldier, others like him hacked the zombies in the yard into gory pieces.

"Where to, sir knight?" Camber asked as he feinted once, twice, and then stabbed a palace guard.

"There," Cerdic replied, pointing his sword through the line of guards at one of the Sha'iry.

"Lead the way," the Red leader said with a rakish grin.

Gripping his kite shield tightly, Cerdic charged directly into the shield of the nearest guard. Using no finesse, just brute strength, he bowled the man over in a clatter of chain and metal. Camber lunged beside the knight, nicking a pike bearer on the tip of his nose. With a flick of his wrist, he drove the rapier into the guard's open mouth. Faster than the eye could follow, he nicked another guard's nose.

"Why do you do that?" Cerdic asked as he kicked away the weapon of his prone opponent and turned to the next.

"Do what?" Camber said, nicking another guard.

"Cut their nose."

"They keep," Camber said as he slit another one, "sticking it out there."

It was like watching an Espian matador and an armored bull team up to kill the audience. For every swing of Cerdic's sword, Camber had three. Between Camber's skill and Cerdic's strength, the palace guards around them fell back, many dropping their weapons. The routed guards turned, only to face the Sha'iry.

Sword-tips pointing toward the knights, each clerical triad wove a combined prayer. Blue-black flames shot forth, engulfing the guards — even the ones who were still fighting. Their tunics turned to ashes, and their mail armor superheated, searing their skin and hair. They fell to the pavement, their screams underscored by the sizzling of flesh.

The flames roared forth and continued their path of destruction.

"Behind my shield!" Cerdic shouted as he crouched. A

foot in front of the knight, the flames hit an invisible barrier. Cerdic rocked back but held his ground.

Ducking behind the knight, Camber knelt along with several other soldiers, some with scarlet sashes and others in burgundy livery. In the face of true evil, all were welcome.

"Have at them, sir knight," Camber shouted over the deafening crackle of flames.

Sir Geoffrey and Sir Mortimer had fallen, leaving six knights to face the Sha'iry. They held their shields forward, protecting those behind them from the fury of the priests' spell. As one, the knights pushed against the fiery wall, and the flames licked at the edges of their shields. The six drew closer even as the eighteen Sha'iry poured more hate and misery into each prayer.

"Be ready!" Lord Alfonso yelled.

"What's going on?" Camber asked, his eyes wide. He glanced toward the open gate.

"Have faith," Cerdic replied.

All six knights lowered their shields and brought up their cruciform swords — points down — each with their mailed fist gripping their blade's ricasso. The individual knights' shields of faith became one and, in a flash of silvery light, turned back the flames.

The Sha'iry broke and ran. The lucky ones cleared the archway into the palace — others fell prey to their own raging fire. It engulfed their vestments and ate their flesh. Bloodcurdling cries of agony ended in wet gurgles as the evil priests were reduced to nothing more than greasy smears.

A shadow shifted on the presentation balcony, and an arrow streaked toward Lord Alfonso. It pierced his pauldron and plunged deep into his chest. The thick wooden shaft quivered from the impact. At the end, three pitch black buzzard feathers served as fletching.

The shimmering barrier snuffed out.

"Go!" Lord Alfonso ordered. Raising his shield, he staggered forward. His eyes on the balcony, he fell to his knees. "Finish this!"

"My Lord!" Sir Vergil said, moving to his commander's aid. More shadows shifted on the presentation balcony and two more black-fletched arrows streaked toward the knight.

They slipped past Sir Vergil's shield and punched through the armor protecting his collarbone. The knight spun, and his sword dropped from nerveless fingers.

"The Archer!" someone shouted. The very name sent a ripple of fear through Camber's soldiers, and they scattered as they sought cover.

With their shields angled at a slight cant, the last four knights raced forward, aiming for the second-story window to the left of the palace gatehouse.

Lying on his back beside the body of a rather husky pike bearer, Camber called, "Derrick! Where's Derrick?"

"Here!" said a stocky man with an oiled mustache and goatee. He had his short bow up, the arrow nocked and ready. Ten others, arrayed beside him, aimed their bows as they searched for a target.

"Shoot the bastard!" Camber yelled.

"We don't see anyone up there."

"I don't care. Shoot anyways!"

Their arrows flew across the yard. The eleven men kept shooting, chipping stone pillars and breaking the lead-paned windows filling the recessed wall behind the balcony.

"Camber, ye dog! Are ye restin'?" a Gael voice boomed from the gate. Camber groaned when he saw the tall, barrel-chested warrior draped in exotic furs over a belted plaid kilt of red, brown, and green. It was difficult to tell where the furs stopped, and body hair began. Until recently, the mercenary had been fighting for the Sha'iry. The sudden change seemed a miracle, but he couldn't help feeling it still wouldn't be enough. The Dark One's priests had a firm grip on everyone's hearts.

"Jongar, glad you could join us. I see you let your hair grow out," Camber said. Thick, curly red hair consumed the barbarian's face, circling his head and flowing over his shoulders like a raging wildfire. It matched his volatile personality.

The barbarian gave Camber a quizzical look, and stroked his beard, loosening a shower of crumbs. It took every ounce of Camber's self-control to stifle a smile.

"Is it too late ta join tha fight?" Jongar asked. "Ah brought friends." Eager Northmen, most wearing kilts like their leader, filled the street.

Camber rolled to his feet, careful to keep an eye on the balcony. "The Archer's here."

Hefting his heavy-bladed axe, Jongar said, "Let's get tha bastard."

Camber placed a restraining hand on the barbarian's arm. Jongar shrugged off Camber's caution. "Today is a good day ta die."

"There must be another way," Camber said.

"Coward."

Hand on his sword, the Red leader rounded on the barbarian. "No one calls me a coward."

Cutting through the building tension, a soft voice carried across the courtyard. "Right now, at this moment, you hold the hearts and lives of your men. The course of history is in your hands to steer."

Both men turned.

Kneeling, Phaedrus held Lord Alfonso's helmet in one hand while he closed the knight's eyes with the other. Laying down the helmet, he approached the two men. "Fight for what you know is right."

"Half-elf, I know the layout of the palace. It's a deathtrap," Camber said under his breath.

"Only one person need die today to win this battle," said Phaedrus.

"Priest, ye gab in riddles," Jongar said with a sneer.

"All I ask is you give the knights the time they need."

Camber gave a knowing nod. "All right, half-elf, we'll do it your way." Turning to the barbarian, he said, "Jongar?"

"Ah go where ye go, toothpick."

Phaedrus raised his wheel-cross and said, "The blessing of the Eternal Father be upon you. Kneel and accept it."

With a mighty roar, they charged the palace gatehouse. Behind them streamed their combined armies. Not stopping, they raced through the dark colonnaded passage with its barrel-vaulted ceiling. Neither of the two leaders questioned the raised portcullis at the exit or the abandoned murder holes.

Sunlight nearly blinded them as the Army of Carolingias burst into Battenberg Palace's Quadrangle. Ahead of them, row after row of palace guards stood waiting, their pikes and swords ready. Intermingled amongst them were Sha'iry.

Regularly spaced windows adorned the left- and right-hand wings of the three-story palace, each manned by a soldier armed with a loaded crossbow. Opposite the gatehouse, a portico with majestic blue and silver pillars shaded the marble steps leading to the recessed entrance of the Grand Hall. On either side, raised porches with low sloped copper roofs held more soldiers.

High above the Quadrangle, the caged bodies of the former king, queen, and crown prince hung from gibbets mounted to the palace wall. Impaled on rusty meat hooks that dangled from a short chain, their severed heads still bore gold crowns.

CHAPTER 3
A CHANDELIER IN PIECES

April 22, 4208 K.E.

7:42 am

With arrows flying overhead, the four remaining knights raced across the concourse into the sheltered corner on the gatehouse's left side. Pressing their backs to the palace and sheathing their swords, they propped their kite shields against the wall and removed their gauntlets and bascinets.

An eye fixed on the window, Sir Baldwin, a careworn knight with a long, grey mustache that drooped past the ends of his mouth, pulled aside a younger knight who wore a woman's lace scarf tied around his rerebrace. "Careful, Sir Julius."

Glass shattered above their heads, and a thick rope with regularly spaced knots dropped down.

"Climb up! It's clear!" a male voice called down.

Baldwin nodded to Cerdic. Behind the senior knight, Julius and Martyn gave him looks of encouragement. Taking hold of the rope, Cerdic climbed hand over hand. Only when he neared the top did he use the knots to help himself over the sill.

One of two guard rooms flanking the gatehouse, the room he entered held barrels of oil ready and waiting for someone to empty them into funnel-like murder hole inlets. A soldier lay on the floor, his throat slit. Beside his head, a pool of blood had congealed.

Roger stepped away from the window, giving Cerdic space. Despite the grim situation, the Gallowen spy's eyes were alight with mischief, and the man practically vibrated with suppressed energy. It made Cerdic feel old, despite being only a few years Roger's senior. The past months had been trying, to say the least.

"The Archer's on the balcony," Cerdic said. His matted black hair poked out from the edges of his mail coif.

"Not anymore. Lahar's chasing him."

His grim look changed to one of alarm. "Alone?"

"She can take care of herself," Roger said. The rope at the window shifted as the next knight climbed up.

"Which way did they go?" Cerdic asked, already moving toward the door with his sword drawn.

"Cerdic, wait."

"Which way?"

"Try the east wing. She was supposed to have it cleared out before the fight."

Cerdic cracked open the door with the tip of his sword and peered around the two-story room fronting the balcony. Arrows and broken glass littered the floor, but there was no sign of The Archer or Lahar. Stepping into the room, he hugged the wall as he worked his way around to the opposite end. Shouts from men charging the Quadrangle echoed through broken windows. He paused when he saw three guards face down on the floor. Dark stains marred their uniforms. "Pater Aeternum, dimitte militibus." *Eternal Father, forgive these soldiers.*

The door leading to the opposite hallway stood open. Gripping his sword with both hands, Cerdic passed empty parlors and sitting rooms. Tall windows afforded a clear view of the fighting within the Quadrangle, adding urgency to his steps.

He followed the corridor as it turned left and entered the east wing. The sounds of battle faded, despite several open doors filtering sunlight into his path. Rectangular patterns of light and dark marked where paintings or mirrors had once adorned the cracked plaster walls. Shapeless lumps of yellow wax marred hand-woven rugs positioned under dusty chandeliers with crusty candle tubes and overflowing drip pans.

His footsteps echoing heavily on the hardwood floors, Cerdic kicked open the first door on the left. In front of the window facing the Quadrangle, a guard knelt with his head pressed against the sash, his crossbow still gripped tight in his hands. Dagger wounds scored his back. Moving to the next room on the left, Cerdic found two more dead soldiers facing the window. He continued down the hallway, and in each room, found another dead crossbowman. While similar, each attack had subtle differences. In a room where a dead soldier sagged through a broken window, the knight found himself wondering if the man's wounds were a message of some sort, or if the assassin had simply grown bored.

The clamor outside grew as the fighting in the Quadrangle intensified.

He passed a series of private apartments on his right, pausing only long enough to be certain they were empty. At the end of the east wing, Cerdic stopped at a pair of double doors, each engraved with a four-petaled dogwood blossom.

"Hello stranger," a soft voice said. "Nice to see you without your helmet."

Cerdic turned to find a half-elf with long, mahogany colored hair beside him. Her dark, almond-shaped eyes took in the knight, lingering on his mouth. Black leather sheathed her long legs and lithe form. He noted the blood-stained longsword and dagger in her hands, each held in a reverse grip so that the blades lay along her forearms.

"Lahar, was that your handiwork?" Cerdic asked, gesturing back down the hallway. The tone in his voice came across harsher than intended, and the half-elf fixed her eyes on the door.

She wiped blood from her dagger on her pants before sheathing it. "If you mean the soldiers, yes."

"You killed all of them," Cerdic said.

"Would you rather I had left some?" she replied, turning to face him again.

"No, that's not what I meant."

"What did you mean?"

"Never mind." After a moment, he said, "Any sign of The Archer?"

"I caught a glimpse of him on the balcony, but he disappeared before I could catch up to him."

"It was foolish of you to go after him by yourself. You could have been killed."

"Is that concern for me that I hear?" Lahar purred in his ear.

Cerdic opened his mouth, then clamped it shut. His reddening cheeks elicited a melodic laugh from the half-elf.

Clearing his throat, he said, "We're wasting time. Camber and your lover won't survive the day if we don't find Maa'kheru Bolezni."

"Jongar is *not* my lover," Lahar shot back.

"Then you should not dally with him as you do," Cerdic said, his disapproval plain.

Her almond-shaped eyes narrowed, and her jaw clenched. She grabbed one of the door rings and yanked it open. Cerdic stayed close behind her as she strode down a short hallway. Even angry, Lahar was silent as a ghost — a shapely ghost whose swaying hips drew his gaze. Cerdic jerked his eyes up and away, silently reprimanding himself for his impropriety. When he dared look at Lahar again, she waited at the door leading to the Grand Hall, observing him with a feline smile.

A thump from the other side of the door stopped them cold. Lahar raised her slender longsword. Rumored to have been forged from a fallen star, strange colored nebulae flowed along the dark blade.

"How many?" Cerdic mouthed silently.

Lahar leaned closer to the door, listening. After a few seconds, she held up two fingers and gave the knight a wicked grin.

The knight bent his knees, pressed his shoulder against the carved wood, and held up his index finger. Lahar grabbed the doorhandle.

He raised another finger and tightened his grip on the hilt of his sword.

Three!

Lahar twisted the handle as Cerdic shoved with his shoulder. The door flew open and slammed into the guard on the opposite side. The other guard froze, and Cerdic plunged his blade into his chest. Before the guard hit by the door could recover his wits, Lahar slipped her sword into the fleshy part of his neck with a twisting motion. He died gurgling blood.

Up ahead, red light flared. Demonic shadows streaked across the walls and ceiling of the hallway as a piercing scream ripped through the palace.

Lahar placed a hand on Cerdic's breastplate as she listened to see if any of the guards had noticed them. Not hearing anything, she closed the engraved east wing doors, shutting off the last of the daylight. All sounds of the fighting outside vanished.

Open doors on either side revealed dimly lit drawing rooms. Lahar's elf vision picked out details in the shadows, and she made out empty bunks and abandoned tables. Motioning to Cerdic, they dragged the two dead soldiers into the righthand room.

The hallway opened out onto a gallery that partially wrapped three sides of the Grand Hall. Suspended from the vaulted coffered ceiling, a massive chandelier sparkled like crystalline star clusters, each pendant reflecting the ominous red light from below.

With Cerdic beside her, Lahar crept to the banister and peeked through the railing. Wide eyed, she stared down in shock. The once opulent heart of Carolingias had become the hellish home world of the Dark One.

Halberdiers lined the gold-trimmed walls. A wide, red runner led up three tiers of bluestone steps to the King's Rostrum then flared out and covered the dais.

Maa'kheru Bolezni stepped away from the cushioned throne. A sword-tipped stole of iron grey adorned his voluminous black velvet robe. Fiery runes twisted and writhed down the stole's embroidered fullers. The wizened high priest gripped a glowing red orb oozing black blood and raised it over his head. The viscous fluid ran down his arms and dripped from his sleeves onto the dais floor. Two Anshu, the Blades of Sutekh, flanked him, their greatswords held point down between their feet. Along the length of their fullers, the runic script matched that of their master.

Prostrate in front of the triumvirate, a Sha'iry had been stripped to his waist, his vestments shredded. Under numerous burns and bleeding wounds, his breath came in ragged gasps.

"You were supposed to keep the knights out of the city!" Maa'kheru Bolezni screeched, and his batrachian face twisted into a mask of rage.

"Maa'kheru, I'm—" His words became a scream of pain as a ray of light from the orb bored into his skin. The stench of charred flesh filled the three-story chamber. The flow of magic ended as abruptly as it began, and the Maa'kheru's cackles rose above the ragged gasps of the scorched priest.

A blur of movement to the right caught Lahar's attention. She grabbed Cerdic by the gorget and dragged him down. An arrow thunked into the oak railing where his hand lay a moment before. Pitch black fletching left no doubt that The Archer had found them. Another arrow whizzed by their heads, disappearing into the shadows at the far end of the gallery.

Together, they scuttled backwards around the corner beyond The Archer's reach.

"We have him trapped," Cerdic said.

"Are you crazy?" Lahar demanded. "The Dark One's high priest is out there!"

Cerdic's eyes filled with an anger so palpable it bordered on madness. "Throw something at him."

"Like what?" Lahar asked.

"A dagger. Anything. I don't care, so long as you distract him while I rush him," Cerdic said. "He assassinated Lord Alfonso."

"You *are* crazy." She took his head in her hands, and their faces almost touched. "I don't care about Alfonso or anyone else. If you go out there, you'll be killed."

Cerdic blinked, and his hazel eyes seemed to regain a bit of sanity. "I still have to try, with or without your help."

Letting him go, she swallowed her emotions and said, "Fine, but this is still stupid."

Lahar slipped a pair of throwing knives from her belt and followed the knight to the corner of the hallway. Cerdic crouched low and sprinted down the gallery. Holding the knives in her left hand, Lahar rocked back and snapped her arm forward, letting both go. They flipped once before the tips zeroed in on their target.

Down below, the priests and soldiers turned toward the noise and looked on with dumbstruck amazement.

At the end of the gallery, a lean, pale figure with jet hair and silvery, almond-shaped eyes glared back at the knight and half-elf. The Archer's long cloak revealed only an arm and a slender hand that held his recurved longbow with its nocked arrow. Fifty-eight inches tip to tip, the red cedar bow glistened as though wet with blood.

The Archer released the bowstring, clutched the edge of his cloak, and snatched it up between himself and the flying blades. The two knives struck the cloak but slid off, unable to pierce its inky fabric. His black-fletched arrow flew high, striking the wall an inch above Lahar's head.

Like a mad bull, Cerdic plowed toward the end of the gallery, sword in his hand. Moving faster than the eye could see, The Archer spun sideways, avoiding the blade by a hair's breadth. When he crashed against the banister, the gallery rail gave way with a loud crack.

The Archer tumbled backwards. In a desperate grab, he snatched a handful of Cerdic's surcoat. For a precious moment, the two teetered on the gallery's edge before both plummeted out of sight.

A guard looked up at the loud snap of wood over his head. He raised his arms wide, as if trying to catch the black-suited Archer. His eyes went even wider when he saw the fully armored knight also hurtling toward him.

A fistful of Cerdic's surcoat in one hand and his longbow in the other, The Archer fell into the hands of the waiting guard. They hit the floor with a loud clatter. Cat-like, The Archer rolled to his feet. His bow's upper limb dangled impotently, held together by a splinter and the string. Tossing it away with a snarl, he flared back his cloak and reached for his sword.

Surrounded by a milky red nimbus, Cerdic hovered over the fallen guard, six feet in the air. Lying flat on her stomach, Lahar gripped a rail post with one hand and reached over the edge of the gallery, her fingertips inches away from the knight's armor.

"Get her!" Maa'kheru Bolezni commanded, pointing at Lahar.

Three soldiers snapped to attention and raced up one of the pair of curved stairs at the south end of the Grand Hall, their halberds poised.

Waving off The Archer, Maa'kheru Bolezni faced Cerdic, who slowly drifted toward the triumvirate. The high priest raised the glowing orb higher and said, "A knight of Carolingias. I thought we finished off all of your order."

Struggling against the wispy bonds, Cerdic glared at Maa'kheru Bolezni and his pet Sha'iry in tight-lipped silence. The evil priest whispered words of magic, and misty tendrils constricted around the knight.

With the tenacity of an octopus, the tendrils probed Cerdic's armor. When they reached his head, they wormed their way up his nose, into his ears, and down inside the neckline of his armor.

"Give in, knight. There is no escape. After today, Carolingias will be mine."

Keeping to the shadows of the hallway, Lahar watched the three halberdiers ascend the stairs to her. She cast a nervous glance down below at Cerdic. His muffled gasps reached her as he struggled inside the red cloud. Turning back toward the soldiers, she readied two more daggers.

A loud thump reverberated against the south end of the Grand Hall. Obscured by shadows under the curved stairs' shared landing, she saw the outline of the twelve-foot-tall doors shiver. A thick timber set inside iron brackets barred them.

Light from the east wing blossomed on her left just as the halberdiers topped the stairs, exposing her position.

Swords flashing, Sir Baldwin and Sir Julius charged down the hallway, followed by a palace guard. She did a double take. The guard behind them was Roger in disguise, a roguish grin plastered on his face. "Come on!" he called as he raced past. "We're stealing back the country!"

The halberdiers dropped their weapons and fled.

Cerdic's face turned purplish red, and his veins bulged. He tried blowing through his nose, twisting his head, anything that would dislodge the tendrils, but they wormed deeper inside, filling his sinus cavities, and causing his eyes to water. The pressure grew, and he felt as if his head might explode.

"O, Pater Aeternum, custos carissime, cui me committit amor; Semper hic dies ad latus meum sit, in lucem et custodiam, ad regendum ac ducatum..." *Oh, Eternal Father, my guardian dear, to whom his love commits me here; Ever this day be at my side, to light and guard, to rule and guide...*

A tendril slithered its way down his throat, cutting off his prayer. Cerdic tried to retch, but the tendril remained rooted in place. He couldn't breathe. Spasms of pain wracked his body even as the specter of panic gripped his heart.

Maa'kheru Bolezni exulted in the knight's suffering. He knew his god was stronger than the Eternal Father.

"Maa'kheru!"

Something struck the south end of the Grand Hall, and motes of dust glinted in the red light.

"They're inside the palace!" one of his Anshu said.

Maa'kheru Bolezni quickly spotted the three halberdiers fleeing the gallery. Two Carolingian knights gave chase. Behind them, the she-elf who'd accompanied the captured knight ran beside one of his palace guards.

"Guards, to me!" shouted the high priest.

The throne room shook again, and a loud crack echoed in the vast chamber. Daylight gleamed around the edges of the double door at the end of the hall.

Following his orders, the halberdiers formed up, but the high priest noticed many looking over their shoulder to see if he was watching. He could see their loyalty wavering.

Maa'kheru Bolezni grinned as the two Carolingian knights raced down the stairs, but his expression faltered when they didn't stop. Instead, they attacked his line of guards.

The double doors crashed open, and sunshine flooded the Grand Hall. Camber and Jongar stood silhouetted for the briefest of moments before charging inside. In the Quadrangle, soldiers let loose a wild cheer as they surged forward like a tidal wave.

Releasing his spell and letting the captured knight fall, Maa'kheru Bolezni aimed the orb's ray at the two leaders.

With the knights and the two faction leaders leading the charge, the Carolingian army funneled inside the Grand Hall. The clamor grew deafening as the guards gave ground against the rising tide.

The death ray swung around until finding Jongar, leading his mercenaries. Smoke rose from the turncoat barbarian's hair, but instead of stopping or frightening the Gael warrior, he went berserk, chopping madly with his heavy battle axe. The fight shifted closer to the dais, and Maa'kheru Bolezni's ray struck the back of one of his own men.

What started as an organized regiment grew increasingly desperate, like cornered animals. The close quarters impeded the effectiveness of their polearms, and many dropped them in favor of short blades and knives.

Seeing his lines faltering around him, Maa'kheru Bolezni cut off the ray of light. He brought the glowing orb to his chest and stared deep into its center, where an oily, metal shard hung suspended.

Power pulsed in a full circle, striking all within the chamber — ally and foe alike.

The guards on the steps of the dais fell to their knees, coughing. Gouts of bloody phlegm flew through the air, spattering the faces of the men in front of them. Those men, in turn, dropped to their knees, and the disease cycle continued.

Maa'kheru Bolezni smiled as he watched the carnage progress from behind his two Anshu. The triumvirate had remained intact.

Rank after rank of men fell until only the two knights remained. They stood shoulder to shoulder; their swords held by the ricasso.

"Knights of Carolingias! This battle is over," stated Maa'kheru Bolezni. "You are simply too stupid to understand it yet. Kill them!" he commanded his two warrior-priests.

The Anshu brought up their weapons and edged forward. Sir Baldwin and Sir Julius split apart, each to face his own opponent.

Baldwin flipped his sword a hundred and eighty degrees. As he stepped over the bodies, he grabbed it by the hilt with both hands together and raised it in a quick salute.

Meeting the knight at the foot of the dais, the Anshu swung his sword. With his hands spread farther apart on the longer hilt, adding to his already substantial leverage, the priest's sword crashed down like an avalanche, and the knight's sword and upper body rocked from the impact.

Arms held in tight, the Anshu drew back his weapon but kept the tip aimed at the knight. His swallowtail vest seemed to lose its shape and floated around him like a stygian shadow.

Baldwin lost sight of his opponent's weapon until it scythed toward his head. The knight twisted at the last moment, and the priest's blade glanced off his coif. Baldwin jerked his blade, ripping a hole in the black garment.

Avoiding the writhing bodies on the steps, the Anshu jumped back and found a space clear of sick soldiers. Feet shoulder width apart, he grinned at the knight, beckoning him on with his weapon.

Clutching Cerdic's sword in his hand, Roger crawled toward the dais. He ignored the two knights who fought the Sha'iry and aimed straight for the throne.

Behind the Maa'kheru, Sir Cerdic Uth Aneirin slowly rose to his feet. His entire body ached. Each breath felt raw, like his lungs were aflame. He kept his feet moving, and his attention focused on the orb in the Maa'kheru's hands.

His armor clanked on the hard floor of the dais. Even with the din of the other two knights fighting the Sha'iry, the high priest heard him. The man turned, and his eyes filled with malevolence. "Still struggling to win. Good. Sacrificing you will be that much better." He thrust out the glowing orb, and its death ray shot forth. The lance of red light struck Cerdic's breastplate, and the metal brightened to a fiery orange.

Cerdic braced himself against the onslaught, steamy sweat pouring off his face. He took a tentative step forward, a prayer on his lips. The air around him shimmered, and pure white light flared to life on his bare skin. The beam widened and globs of molten metal dripped onto the red carpet, leaving a trail of flames behind the knight as he took another step toward the evil priest.

Maa'kheru Bolezni snarled a curse and urged more out of the orb. The air between him and the knight grew putrid.

The disease inside the orb became tangible, manifesting into a dark humanoid shape. It held its hands together as if carrying a weapon, but none was visible aside from a ripple in the air as something *other* bent the light.

"Cerdic!" Roger yelled. The cruciform sword slid across the slick carpet, stopping at the knight's feet.

Cerdic knelt and picked up his weapon. His breastplate, along with the rest of the armor protecting his upper torso, had melted away, forming a ring of fire around him, yet he remained unscathed by the searing heat.

"How?" the evil priest demanded.

"He has faith," Roger answered from behind him.

Turning toward the voice, the Maa'kheru found Roger holding a white cloth embroidered with silver runes. The priest swung the orb around and unleashed a blinding ray of red light.

The humanoid shape sprang forward with a flurry of strikes. Cerdic responded, his sword countering each one. The two flowed around each other in a violent dance. One moment they faced each other; the next they stood back to back. Spinning around, their weapons came together, crossed at the quillons.

Cerdic stared into the face of the dark form, not knowing if it was a demon or a construct of evil magic. He felt no breath. If not for the rotten stench surrounding it, he would have believed it was an illusion.

The two pushed away from one another. Striking high to low and low to high, Cerdic's blade flashed in the light. Dropping the tip of his sword, Cerdic rotated his shoulders, avoiding a lunge by the dark form. Reversing his grip, the knight sliced up with his blade, catching the thing across the arm.

The form stopped short, but Cerdic couldn't tell if he had hurt it or not. The thing seemed to weigh the knight. It swept up its aethereal blade in a crude salute, which Cerdic answered in kind.

Already tired from the orb's spell, Cerdic had the sinking feeling the dark form was only warming up.

Roger dodged to the left away from Cerdic and rolled as the searing red light cut its way across the carpet. Thankfully, Baldwin and Julius still kept the other priests at bay.

"You're agile," Maa'kheru Bolezni said, "but you cannot avoid the inevitable."

"Keep talking," Roger replied. Gauging distances, the nimble rogue dashed toward the dais steps, but he reversed direction when the death ray shot forth. Wide-eyed, Roger leaned way back, feeling the heat singe his nose hairs.

The ray kept traveling, and it caught the Anshu fighting Julius. The tail of his vest burst into flames.

Roger stared in open-mouthed incredulity. Instead of finishing the Anshu, the knight waited while the warrior-priest extinguished the fire.

"Are you stupid?" Roger shouted as he dodged another death ray. "Watch and learn!"

Holding the white cloth in one hand, he cast a quick glance up toward the ceiling before flinging a knife at Maa'kheru Bolezni's face. The ancient priest ducked, and the orb's death ray careened upward, striking the chandelier. The prisms captured and fractured the ray, filling the room with a rainbow-hued starburst. The chain holding the chandelier snapped, and it plunged to the throne room floor, shattering into myriad pieces.

Darting through the spray of crystalline shrapnel, Roger kicked the crouching priest in the side of the knee. Maa'kheru Bolezni dipped and wobbled as he tried to regain his balance. With a swipe of his hands, Roger swaddled the red orb inside the cloth as he snatched it from the priest.

Cerdic blinked away the bright spots obscuring his vision. He held his sword en garde, expecting another attack from the dark form at any moment. None came. When his sight cleared, it had vanished.

The two warrior-priests fighting Julius and Baldwin threw down their weapons and spread their arms to either side in surrender.

"No!" Maa'kheru Bolezni shrieked, his faced twisted into a mask of rage. Blue-black flames built around his hands as he wove an intricate spell and aimed it at Roger's back.

Cerdic stepped forward and threw his sword like a spear. The blade pierced the high priest's spell and bit deep into the evil man's chest.

Maa'kheru Bolezni tumbled down the dais steps and landed on his side, with the sword's hilt protruding from his robes, his sightless eyes fixed on the throne.

Roger spun around. His mouth opened and closed in a struggle to say something, but Cerdic merely clapped him on the back as he sauntered past. Pressing his foot against the Maa'kheru's ribs, he ripped out the bloody sword and wiped it on the black robe. Kneeling beside the dead man, the knight touched his sword to his forehead and prayed, "Pater Aeternum, dimitte obsecro perdidit vir." *Eternal Father, please forgive this lost man.*

Rising from his prayer, Cerdic scanned the Grand Hall. The soldiers were beginning to come around. Healers from the Quadrangle entered the chamber and worked their way through the wounded.

Roger pointed. "She's over there."

Cerdic's eyes followed the rogue's finger and found Lahar slumped against the wall. Blood pooled on the ground, and burgundy-clad corpses surrounded her.

Kneeling by her side, he wiped away a trickle of blood from her mouth and chin. A faint breath crossed his fingers. She lived! "Eternal Father, thank you," he whispered. He laid his hand over her heart and bowed his head in prayer. "Please heal this woman, Eternal Father. Please forgive her the wickedness she has done and guide her through these dark times. She is the world to me, and I could not go on without her."

Lahar took a ragged breath and her eyes fluttered open. Cerdic turned bright red. Before he could withdraw, she grasped his calloused hand and gave him a tired smile.

CHAPTER 4
ALL HAIL THE QUEEN

April 22, 4208 K.E.

9:00 am

*F*lanked by a pair of muscular guards in studded leather jerkins, Ambrose stopped in the shadows of the gatehouse. Injured soldiers filled the Quadrangle, their groans echoing off the palace walls. Most wore scarlet sashes about their waists like the men at her back. She searched the sea of faces, desperately praying she wouldn't find Camber's among them. In the center of it all, Phaedrus knelt with his back to her, ministering to the wounds of a palace guard.

The events of the past year raced through Ambrose's mind. Moving from place to place with the red army, raiding supply trains and abandoned estates — it was like stealing lightning from a wild storm. They lived outside in tents, and the cold nights had brought her and Camber together. She'd been content at his side. Under his protection, everyone left her alone.

Things changed when Roger Vaughn and Phaedrus showed up in their camp. She still didn't know how that pair of Gallowen spies learned she was King David's niece. It was only a matter of time before they reported her existence to their Highlord. Although Camber hadn't said so, Ambrose was certain they'd told him she was a Battenberg — why else would he suddenly insist she participate in his war councils?

With today's victory, she feared they would expect her to take her uncle's throne as Queen of Carolingias — a job she did not want. Her eyes drifted up to the gibbets with their carrion-ravaged corpses. Beneath them dangled severed heads wearing golden crowns. Her blood ran cold. She felt as if an executioner's cage was closing around her, too. She made to turn away, perhaps flee the city, but stopped short when she heard her name.

"Ambrosia! The day is won!" called Camber, leading soldiers out of the Grand Hall. They raised their weapons and shouted, "Huzzah! Huzzah!"

He wove his way through the carnage, occasionally sharing a word of encouragement with an injured warrior. As he drew closer, Ambrose raised a hand to hide her mouth. It wasn't the bloodstains on his armor that shocked her. It was the careworn lines and dark shadows around his eyes, marring that perfect face.

"Where's your smile? We won." Camber gestured toward Battenberg Palace.

Ambrose gave him a wan smile and took his hand. "Let's leave."

His face clouded with confusion, and he asked, "Ambrosia, what's wrong?"

Her eyes went wide in alarm when she saw three Knights of Carolingias heading toward her. "Now," she hissed, tugging on his sleeve. Relief unknotted the tension in her gut as his arm slid around her shoulders, but then he directed her toward the sunlight of the Quadrangle.

"No," she said, digging in her heels. "No! Camber, don't make me do this."

A wave of soldiers followed the three knights as they marched across the Quadrangle. Healers and the less wounded rose to join the throng, uncertain if some new danger approached. All eyes turned to Ambrose when the three knelt in front of her, offering their swords.

"Our Queen, York is yours," Sir Baldwin said, his eyes downcast.

A collective gasp rippled through the crowd. Across the battle site, soldiers and healers knelt and bowed their heads. Silence reigned in the yard. The city seemed to hold its breath.

Ashen faced, Ambrose glared up at her aunt and uncle in their cages. Pushing away from Camber, she took Sir Baldwin's sword by the hilt and tapped him on the right shoulder with the flat of the blade. Raising it over his head, she tapped him on the left shoulder. He rose and she kissed his left cheek. After giving him back his sword, she faced Sir Julius and repeated the ceremony.

When she turned to Sir Cerdic, she half expected to see him judging her. He knew she had hidden while assassins slaughtered her family. He knew the things she'd had to do to survive the harsh winter, and she had no doubt he'd heard the sordid rumors surrounding her relationship with Camber and the red army. Instead, he knelt like the others, his eyes downcast and his sword held out for her. She wondered if it was all a charade.

She took his sword and tapped him on his right shoulder. He looked up. There was no judgment, no subterfuge in his face. There was only raw honesty and trust. She felt the weight of what he wanted, and a tight fist clenched her heart as she raised the blade over his head. She tapped his left shoulder and he rose. Sir Cerdic leaned forward. She kissed his left cheek and gave back his sword. When he straightened, the other soldiers present erupted in a mighty cheer.

"Let it be known throughout the land!" Phaedrus said, raising his hands. "The Queen has returned!"

One of the smoldering logs split in the fireplace and bright sparks floated up the chimney. Fading sunlight filtered through the looped guardroom windows, painting rainbow-colored quatrefoils on the opposite wall. A spiral staircase at the far end led up to the third floor and the Queen's private chambers.

"Baldwin, is Martyn going to live?" Julius asked. He sat on a bench, wiping his armor with an oily rag.

Across the table, the elder knight mopped up the gravy on his plate with a piece of bread. "He's with Phaedrus. If anyone can heal him, he can."

Julius nodded and went back to polishing. After a moment, his head popped up, and he said, "I still don't know why we had to do that."

"Do what?"

"That ceremony in the Quadrangle. I mean, we've already been knighted."

"It wasn't for us. It was for the soldiers. They had to see her accept us as her champions," the older knight replied. "It's the first step in a long process that will end in her coronation."

"What about Camber? Will he be knighted? And what about Jongar?"

"That's up to the Queen. After her coronation."

A guard in blue and silver livery poked his head through the curtained doorway. "The Queen and her entourage have returned."

The two jumped up and followed the guard into the Queen's west wing office, where they took up positions on either side of her desk. Made from stout Glaxon oak, each of its panels represented the different regions of Carolingias, from the embossed Alashalian Mountains of the northwest to Fangpoint Lighthouse, representing the coastal plains. Separating the panels, dogwood blossoms, a delicate dimple decorating the tips of the four petals, wound their way around the sides.

Behind the desk, the exterior wall arched out in a semi-circle. Stretching from floor to ceiling, narrow, lead-paned windows looked out over the city through a copse of barren branches.

The door opened and Ambrose entered, followed by Cerdic and two elderly men dressed in ermine and sable-edged robes. Each wore a deep blue stole embroidered with a silver dogwood blossoms. "My Queen, you must decide what to do with them."

"Sir Cerdic, remove these men," Ambrose said as she flopped into her chair. "I don't want to see anyone wearing sashes."

"Yes, My Queen," Cerdic replied. His armor and surcoat replaced, he took a threatening step toward the two judges, holding out his hand. They quickly removed their stoles and gave them to the knight.

One of the judges said, "Now, My Queen, may we return to business? The prisoners must be dealt with, especially the foreign priests."

"I recommend you send them to the gallows," the other judge said. "The longer you wait, the more of a chance they have to regroup."

"Get out! Get out, both of you!" she shrieked. "I will not order anyone's death!"

The judges scurried out the door, casting withering looks as they left.

"That went well," Cerdic said as he shut the door behind them.

In response, Ambrose dropped her forehead to the desk with a meaty thud. She lifted her head a few inches and let it fall again. When she lifted it a third time, Baldwin slipped his bare hand between her and the desk. Her forehead smacked his palm. "I'm not a Queen."

"You are *our* Queen," Baldwin said to the mound of auburn hair. "As the last remaining Battenberg, you are the only one who can pull this country back from the brink."

"I can't be the last of my family. There must be another Battenberg somewhere. Why must it be me?"

"You know why. The aristocracy will follow you because your father was King David's brother, and Camber's people will follow you because they see you as one of them."

Baldwin felt his hand grow wet with her tears. "You are the Queen of Carolingias now," he whispered. "I know you don't want it, but this country will not survive without you."

At the other end of the desk, a soft huff escaped Julius. Baldwin looked up to see a disapproving frown on the young knight's face.

"Those two judges are just the beginning," said Cerdic, "and they're right. You need to bring them back and tell them what to do with the Sha'iry we captured in the throne room, and the villains who survived the fire at the warehouse."

"I know." She sat up, her face red and puffy. "I wish you hadn't taken me there. I'll never be able to unsee that warehouse, or what the Sha'iry did to those people in the streets as long as I live."

"Good," Baldwin said. "You're beginning to understand what this fight has been about all along. The quarrel between the Reds and Bluebloods — it was all a distraction from the true evil festering in this country."

The door burst open and Jongar strode inside with Lahar. Behind them, Camber and Phaedrus were arguing. The sentry in the hallway wore an apologetic expression on his face as if to say, '*I tried to stop them.*'

Cerdic's stern glare at Jongar softened as he turned to Lahar. He asked, "Did you find him?"

"No," she replied. "The Archer's still out there somewhere."

"An' Roger's stolen the orb! Ah knew we couldnae trust tha dodgy bastard," the barbarian exclaimed. "He'll be off ta Tydway afore we know it!" He carried a mug in one hand and his battle axe in the other. The reek of ale wrapped around his every word. "Everyone's gonna think you're a puppet o' the Highlord."

"Your weapon," Cerdic said with a hand on his hilt.

Jongar spat out his drink, some of it dribbling down his beard. "Ye better be prepared ta use that pigsticker."

Lahar traced a finger down the barbarian's arm. "Give it to me."

"What? An' be weaponless like a pansy priest?" Jongar grumbled with a nod toward Phaedrus. "No."

"I'm not asking again," Cerdic said.

Keeping one hand on his arm, Lahar grabbed the haft of the battle axe and slowly eased it from the barbarian's grip. "I'll take care of this for you," she said.

Jongar's eyes darted from Cerdic to Lahar, and he licked his lips. "'At's a real man's weapon. Ye sure ye can handle it?"

Tilting her head slightly, Lahar gave him a saucy smile. "I can handle anything you've got."

Jongar roared with laughter. "I bet ye can, lass." He released the axe and took another swig from his mug. Lahar headed toward the door, and he said, "Don't go far."

"Are you done?" Camber asked. "Or do you two need a room?"

"Tha' there is a braw hen, toothpick," Jongar said, admiring Lahar's backside as she walked out. "Show 'er some respect."

Camber shook his head. It was clear Jongar's definition of respect was different from everyone else's.

"You wouldn't know what to do with a woman if one dropped in your lap," Camber muttered.

Turning beet red, Jongar opened his mouth to respond.

"Gentlemen," Phaedrus said. "You are in the presence of the Queen."

"Ambrosia's not queen yet," Camber said with a sly grin.

"That may be true, but that doesn't mean bar-talk is any more acceptable here than in church," Phaedrus replied.

Ambrose rose from her chair. Even though she kept a straight face, her eyes sparkled with mirth. "Jongar, please, speak your mind."

"Lass, ye tempt me." The barbarian emptied his mug and said, "Ye must stop Roger from leavin' York with tha orb. It's a spoil o' war."

"And what would you have us do with it?" Cerdic asked.

"Do with it? Nothin' o' course. But lettin' it stray out o' 'ere is a sign of a weak leader." Jongar clenched his fist.

"Now's tha time ta be strong. Take no prisoners an' collect yer reward. That's whit ah says."

"Spoken like a true mercenary," Camber said.

"Whit would ye have 'er do, toothpick?" Jongar asked.

"Keep it, yes. But use it against our enemies. You saw what it could do in the hands of a priest. No one would question our sovereignty with that weapon. Even the Highlord would stop his meddling."

"It's not a weapon," said Phaedrus.

"Why should we listen ta you, priest? Ah don't recall seein' ye scrap. Or were ya too scared?" asked Jongar.

"He's a seeker of peace," Cerdic said. "Phaedrus does not fight."

Jongar waved a hand toward the priest. "For a seeker o' peace, he sure can stir tha pot an' get others ta scrap for him."

Cerdic stepped closer to the barbarian and said, "I speak for his honor. If you doubt him, take it up with me."

"Jongar is right." Breaking in between the two warriors, Phaedrus said, "I broke my vow of peace when I asked others to fight, but there was no other way to bring you together." His expression was grim. "The orb is a relic of the Dark One, and only evil can come of it. All of your mages are dead or have fled the country. This land is vulnerable. Giving the orb to the Highlord is the only way to be sure it doesn't fall in the wrong hands. There is no one else who can keep it safe."

"We should hae kept it," Jongar said. "Lettin' it go undermines whit we're doin' 'ere."

"Maybe, but you have no choice," Phaedrus replied. "Until this country controls its borders, magical and physical, you must rely on the Highlord."

"Bah! Who's runnin' this country? Him or her?" Jongar asked.

"We didn't fight for the Highlord, we fought for us," Camber added. "We fought for Carolingias."

"The people will return once word gets out. Guilds will flourish, and the ranks of our armies will swell," Baldwin said, "but it takes a leader. They need a Queen."

"Agreed," Jongar and Camber said together.

All eyes turned to Ambrose. She sat back down in her chair with a feeble smile plastered on her face.

"True. Word of your victory here will spread," Phaedrus said, "but there are things we must attend to first. We must bury our dead. King David, Queen Sophia, and Prince Bernard have been removed from the Quadrangle and conveyed to Westchester Hall, where they lie in state. Their funeral will take place on the twenty-fifth. Afterwards, preparations for the pre-coronation vigil will begin."

CHAPTER 5
THE HIGHLORD

April 23, 4208 K.E.

7:32 am

Slick with frost, the bronze statue of King David lay forlornly in the square. The people of York filed past it as if in a daze, their breath visible in the frigid air. Some looked toward the palace with hope, while others regarded the royal quarters with fear.

Unseen by the shuffling crowd, the Highlord of Gallowen stood near the statue's pedestal, one hand resting on the shoulder of his longtime friend and advisor, the Archmage Angus McHeath. It was Angus' power that kept them hidden for the time being, allowing the two men to observe the state of affairs in the Carolingian capitol.

Two soldiers with scarlet sashes about their waists manned the counters in each of the several stalls, rationing out flour, vegetables, fruits, and other staples. It occurred to the Highlord as he watched the crowd that, despite the civil unrest stirred up by the Sha'iry, for these people the war had long since stopped being about political power and had become one for survival. The spoils of this war were food.

A soldier in the nearest stall spoke to his companion. "Derrick, the dogwood blossoms are late. Shouldn't we have seen buds or something? They look dead."

"I don't know, Jimmy," Derrick replied, casting a worried glance toward the lane of barren trees.

Jimmy checked to see if anyone was near, then murmured, "Maybe Ambrose isn't a true Battenberg."

"Don't say such things! Not even a whisper, no matter what you might think."

"It's not just me."

"People have enough problems without worrying over those damn trees."

"Alls I'm saying is it's a bad omen."

A heavyset man wrapped in a fox-trimmed cloak slapped his hand on the table. Two gold coins glimmered between his fingers. "It's yours if you give me another portion."

"Sorry, milord. You know I can't do that. Until the roads reopen, everyone will need to tighten their belt. Queen's orders," Derrick said.

"She's not my Queen," the man shot back, grabbing up his coins and his one portion.

Two red-haired barbarians in belted kilts stepped forward. "Is there ah problem 'ere?" one asked in a thick Gaelic brogue.

The Highlord gently squeezed Angus' shoulder signaling the mage that he'd seen enough, and it was time for them to make their appearance to the locals.

Giving Derrick a disgusted look, the nobleman replied, "No. No prob..."

Blinding white light ripped the air apart, forming a wide circle near the pedestal. The dozen knights who'd been waiting for Angus' signal quick-marched out of the magical rift. Armed with spears and shields, each wore a bascinet and gold-tinted plate armor intricately fashioned with metal feathers to mimic the body and head of a great horned owl. Pinned at the shoulder, their mottled grey-brown capes fluttered in a slight breeze as they formed ranks, one on each side of the rift.

Stunned silence claimed the square. Using two fingers, Derrick motioned the barbarians toward the knights.

The barbarians stopped short when Angus stepped forward, seeming to emerge from the light. His dark eyes stared out at them from under the wide brim of his peaked wizard's hat. He wore the deep purple robes of a Gallowen Archmage and carried a long staff carved from mountain ash. Like forks of lightning, pale red hair streaked through his flowing white beard.

The Highlord took a moment to take in the looks of stunned awe on the nearest faces before he, too, stepped through the light and became visible. Behind him, the rift snapped closed with an audible pop. The gathered Carolingians gasped.

Despite his formal attire — a wool vest over a long-sleeved blue tunic, dark breeches, and black leather boots — his close-cropped black hair, rigid posture, and the bronze hilt of his broadsword bespoke a military man. A polished iron pendant on his chest winked in the morning light. He turned slowly, allowing those closest to recognize the crest on the medallion's face, a rampant dragon flanked by a tower and an owl. Like ripples on a pond, whispers swept the square. One by one, the people knelt.

Mothers hushed their children, and silence settled over the crowd. The Highlord surveyed the square. His chiseled jawline tightened as he saw the nobleman who tried to bribe extra food from the soldiers ducking into a shadowy alcove. "Who's in command here?" he asked.

"I am, Your Majesty," Derrick said.

"We seek an audience with your Queen," the Highlord said. "Tell her we'll wait here for her reply."

"Yes, Sir." Derrick turned on his heel and trotted toward the palace. People in the crowd shifted nervously as he passed.

"Good people of York, you may carry on your business," the Highlord proclaimed. He suppressed a smile when Derrick glanced back in time to see Angus produce two camp chairs out of thin air.

The annoying sound of someone knocking on her bedroom door jarred Ambrose from sleep.

"My Queen," Julius called through the door. Not receiving a response, he knocked for a second time. "Queen Ambrose, you have visitors."

She snuggled deeper under her fur blankets, hoping the knight would give up and leave her in peace. Nightmares of her uncle's crow ravaged corpse trying to place his crown upon her head had kept her tossing and turning most of the night.

A murmur of voices outside her room preceded the loud banging from a heavy fist.

"My Queen?" Sir Baldwin's deeper voice echoed through the door.

The door latch clicked, followed by the squeak of hinges. With the windows shuttered and the rich walnut-paneled walls bare, the clomp of heavy boots echoed, making the room seem cavernous. In truth, Ambrose's room was one of the smaller ones in the family wing. Despite the urgings of both Camber and Baldwin, she'd refused to sleep in the royal bedchamber — she could only imagine how much worse she'd have been haunted by the ghosts of her uncle and aunt had she tried to sleep there. Instead, she'd insisted on sleeping in the room she'd shared with her sister during visits to York. Its wide, canopied bed was a familiar comfort. Opposite the simple secretary desk, glowing logs smoldered in the fireplace, fighting off the morning chill.

The men invading her chamber separated, one coming to stand beside her bed while the other moved toward the windows. Ambrose remained still, hoping they wouldn't see the tell-tale lump of her hiding under the covers and seek her elsewhere.

"My Queen," Baldwin said in a measured voice, "the Highlord is here to see you." He was close, which meant Julius was across the room.

Stifling a sigh, Ambrose shifted, and the toes of her left foot poked out from the covers. Jerking her foot back under the blankets, she shivered and said, "Go away."

Julius responded to her command by opening the windows shutters and flooding her room with sunlight. Ambrose clutched at the bed furs lest Baldwin snatch them away. She had no desire to face the day or the view from her windows. Once, she'd loved York's western skyline and the riverfront along the Isura River. Now, the jagged remains of the tobacco warehouse towers turned it into an eyesore.

Julius threw open another shutter, admitting more light.

"Why won't the two of you leave me alone?"

"My Queen—"

"I swear, Sir Baldwin, if you call me that one more time, I'll have you beheaded."

Taking a deep breath, Baldwin said, "The Highlord is here to see you. He's waiting at the Square. What would you like for me to do?"

"Tell HIM to go away."

"Ambrose, I can't do that."

A protesting groan rose from the bed furs. She shifted again and sat up, pulling the blankets around so only her eyes were exposed. "Why is he here?"

"I don't know, but it's poor form to keep him waiting."

Ambrose heaved a resigned sigh. "Fine. Bring him to the palace. I'll meet with him in my study."

"Yes, my Qu... ma'am," Baldwin replied with a bow.

The Highlord marched north to Battenberg Palace with his personal guard arrayed behind him. Angus walked at his side. Together, they'd faced and overcome more enemies, more battles, than he cared to count, but none compared to the one they faced now. Followers of the Dark One had not moved openly across Parlatheas since the fall of ancient Korell. Their resurgence in the midst of this plague was no coincidence.

It was a new kind of war, which the free peoples of Parlatheas were losing. As if finding a cure for the Dark One's plague weren't daunting enough, the violent orcnéan horde pouring into the lands west of the Alashalian Mountains threatened to overwhelm them all.

The surviving Trakyans had retreated west, abandoning over half of their former territory. By all accounts, the Rhodinan and Detchian kingdoms were in disarray. Francesca, the Espian kingdoms, Carolingias, and his own Gallowen were under attack by an enemy who not only threatened their way of life, but literally robbed people of their very souls.

In the palace's concourse and quadrangle, a small army of men and women worked at removing battle stains. He shook his head when he saw the shattered door to the Grand Hall. As busy as it was outside, the throne room was thrice as busy with workers trying to remove the taint of evil left behind by the Sha'iry.

Their guide led them up a set of wide stairs and into the west wing. Another small army cleaned the hallway and rooms, their gaunt faces full of hope. The resilience of these people amazed him. He wished the fight was over for them, but he knew in his heart it was just beginning.

Leaving his men in the hallway, the Highlord and Angus entered the Queen's study. Inside, he was surprised by the grim expressions worn by the six men attending the Queen. He recognized Sir Cerdic and Phaedrus, but the other two knights were unfamiliar. Camber and Jongar, he knew by reputation. He focused his attention on the Queen-in-Waiting. Her midnight blue dress hung a bit loose, a mute testament to the country's dwindling food supplies. She was younger than he expected, standing behind her desk like it was a fortification, and he an invading army. Bright-eyed and stiff-backed, she held his gaze longer than most men.

"Queen Ambrose, may I present to you the Highlord of Gallowen," Phaedrus said, "and his advisor, Angus McHeath."

After Phaedrus completed the introductions, Ambrose walked from behind her desk and offered her hand. The Highlord took it, bowed his head, and brushed her knuckles with his lips.

Taking her hand back, she asked, "What brings you to York?"

"First, I wish to pay my respects to King David, Queen Sophia, and Prince Bernard and offer you my deepest sympathies."

"Thank you."

"Second..." He paused and studied the young woman before asking, "May I be candid?"

Ambrose cast a quick glance toward Camber and Phaedrus before answering, "Of course."

"Walk with me. I'd like to show you something."

Panic flooded her features.

"We won't leave the grounds," he added, as much to reassure the gentlemen in the room as their Queen.

She chewed on her bottom lip as she considered his request. To his surprise, she offered her hand again. "Lead the way."

"My Queen, I must insist you have an escort," the eldest of her knights said with a frown.

"As do I," Camber said.

She picked up the laced fan off her desk with her free hand and gestured toward Sir Baldwin. The knight snapped to attention before following them out of the room.

Tucking her hand into the crook of his arm, the Highlord struck off down the main corridor, took a nearby set of stairs to the third floor, and aimed for the south end of the palace.

"You seem to know where you're going. Have you been here before?" Ambrose asked.

"Many times with King David and, before that, I walked these halls with his father."

Ambrose asked, "How old *are* you? You don't look over thirty."

The Highlord smiled. "Old enough. Too old, sometimes. There it is," he said as he nodded toward a dusty alcove. Leading the way, he climbed a narrow set of spiral stairs and exited through a door to a secluded widow's walk.

Framed by brilliant azure skies, the sun drove away the shadows but didn't give off much heat. Giving her his vest, he asked, "Have you ever been up here?"

Wide-eyed, she shook her head.

They both turned when Sir Baldwin closed the door behind him and took up a guard position.

Wrapping an arm around her shoulders, the Highlord walked her to the deck railing and gestured toward the lines of people in the square.

"This is your city — your country — and as their Queen, you are responsible for them. Many in your position forget this simple but very important role, and things fall apart. Always remember, you serve them as they serve you. Men will go to battle for you, sacrifice themselves if need be. You must be willing to do the same."

Ambrose pulled away from him and said, "Who are you to lecture me? Where were you when my family was slaughtered, and the dark priests claimed York?"

The Highlord ran his fingers through his hair and replied, "The Rhodinans claim this plague started in the elven villages north of Michurinsk. Extremely reclusive, the elves there rarely traded goods or left their borders, so when they fell ill, no one knew.

"By the time Korol' Melikhov heard about it and recognized it for what it was, it was too late. The plague had spread to humans. At first, the disease seemed to target those whose lives were intertwined with magic — elves, all the fair-folk, arcane spellcasters. The more powerful they were, the faster they succumbed. However, trained mages weren't the only ones who contracted the disease. The malady afflicted anyone with the potential for arcane magic.

"As bad as those with an affinity for the arcane had it, the plague's true danger went unrecognized until the contagion exploded across the kingdoms. Priests and lay healers were helpless to save those who sought their aid. Their ministrations were useless against this new evil. It's only been in the last few months they've found a way to slow the plague's spread."

"But I already know all this. I've lived it," she said, the accusatory tone in her voice made it clear she blamed him.

Turning northward, he said, "What you don't know is the

plague has created a huge void. Driven by the Sha'iry, countless orcnéas have come down from the northern tundra and razed whole towns and cities. Too weak to put up any kind of defense, the Rhodinans, Trakyans, and Detchians have abandoned much of their lands along the White River. The western front has fallen.

"This vile disease has cleared a path for the northern horde — a path that leads to the heart of our kingdoms — yours and mine. With the Sha'iry sowing seeds of dissent, it won't be long before their army sweeps through Francesca and the countries of Peninsular Espia, by-passing the mountains altogether, and attack your southern border."

He turned to Ambrose and said, "You asked where I've been. My army and I have been in Detchia, fighting the invading horde of monsters."

He clenched a fist and struck the top of the railing. The memories of those he lost washed over him. "Not even the knights of the Iron Tower and Horned Owls can fight a war while looking over their shoulders, worrying about their families and homes. We had to retreat to the mountains."

Ambrose stepped toward him and laid a hand on his arm. His head jerked up, and he grabbed her by the shoulders. "But you. Your people have claimed a victory in this war. Our first."

"What do you mean?"

"Don't you realize it? The Sha'iry have fled York. Your people have killed their high priest and taken their orb — the very genesis of this magical plague. Even now, its affects are disappearing, melting away like snow under the first breath of spring."

Letting her go, he said, "Our remaining mages no longer have to hide, and we can bring them to bear. Now is the time to drive the Dark One's army back beyond the White River."

Ambrose glanced toward Sir Baldwin, then down toward the square. "You ask too much," she said, pointing to the food lines. "My people are barely surviving. I don't even know if I could muster an army that would fight under your flag."

"Queen Ambrose, that's not why I came here. I need Carolingias to be strong. I can't fight a war on two fronts, especially this one. Guard my back, hold your borders, and I swear I'll drive this horde into the ground."

"You're not asking for troops?"

"No. Yes. In a way."

Ambrose looked at him askance. "If you're not asking for troops, why are you here?"

"I want us to form an alliance. One similar to what King David and I had, and his father before him, but stronger. I want us to be a Confederation of Nations."

Roger Vaughn crossed the spartan, second-floor room of the Dogwood Inn and pulled aside one of the curtains. Two men talked with a shopkeeper across the street. From all appearances they were locals discussing the weather — except that he knew one of them: Alvaro San Miguel. The two had met in Tydway at the Winter Ball last year. Like Roger, he was a spy.

After the fight in the throne room, Roger had fled with the orb. Jongar and Camber's men pursued him, but he'd lost them in the crowd gathered at the square. It seemed everyone wanted to catch a glimpse of the new Queen.

His eyes scanned the people walking the street. He wasn't worried about Jongar or Camber or Espian agents, even though he knew they all wanted the orb. He worried about The Archer. The assassin was out there — somewhere — and he had soldiers, too.

Six months ago, when the Highlord and Angus sent Roger to Carolingias, the briefing he'd received had been just that — brief. The Archer and his band of assassins were dærganfae, a race of elf-like beings from a realm beyond Gaia. Unfortunately, little was known about them, other than they controlled a region of the Alashalian mountains the local clansmen referred to as the Haunted Hills. One thing Roger did know: The Archer had his own agenda, and it did not include defending Maa'kheru Bolezni.

Roger wiped sweat from his brow, thinking he'd made a mistake leaving the palace. At least there he could have counted on Cerdic, Lahar, and Phaedrus. Here, in this dilapidated inn, he was alone with the orb.

No, he had made the right decision, he assured himself.

Turning away from the window, he studied his room. Intricately carved base and crown molding framed the pine-paneled walls. It gave him the impression of an aged aristocrat more focused on his appearance than his bones. Wooden walls, wooden floor, wooden roof, he hoped the inn he had chosen would be a safe place to regroup. Of course, that's if it didn't collapse under its own weight first.

Still swaddled within the white cloth embroidered with silver runes, the orb lay dormant on his bed. He'd been careful to keep it covered, lest any of its magic escape. Beside it sat an empty wicker basket and some clothes he'd *borrowed* from an unattended wash line. The top of the dresser held an ad hoc alchemy lab, complete with a blob of melted caramel-like substance resting on a trivet.

Downstairs, the front door slammed shut, and the whole building shook.

"You'll never believe who I saw — the Highlord!" he heard a young voice exclaim. "And he's meeting with the Queen!"

"Christopher, is this another of your tall tales?" a woman's voice responded. Roger pictured her behind the bar, wiping the counter with a soapy rag.

"No! The Highlord is really here! He came through a magical portal with a mage and a dozen golden knights."

"Golden knights? Really."

"I'm going to be a knight one day," he said.

"*Mmm hmm.*"

"No, I'm serious," he insisted.

"Well, Serious, there's a bale of hay with your name on it. Take it to the square and sell it."

"*Aww*, Mom."

"If you hurry, maybe you'll get to see the High..." Loud footsteps drowned out the rest of what she said.

Roger smiled despite himself. She was right. The Highlord would probably leave the same way he arrived. The only question was how long he would stay in town.

"Excuse me, young man, can you direct me to the Square of King David?"

The teenager started at the voice. Christopher put down his small hay bale and pointed down the crowded cobblestone street. "It's that way, sir. About two blocks."

He dropped his arm when he realized the old man had a grimy bandage wrapped around his eyes. A mud-stained cloak partially covered his ragged leather armor, and the boy could only guess he had been a soldier, once. The old man waved a long stick in front of him and kept tapping it on the pavement.

"What's in the basket?" the boy asked.

The old man shifted his burden into the crook of his arm and said, "Never you mind. Just tell me which way I need to go."

Christopher grabbed the old man by the arm and aimed him north. "It's a straight shot from here."

"Thank you, lad."

The boy watched the veteran totter down the road for a bit longer before picking up his bale of hay. Giving the old man one last look, he noticed he had veered left and entered the busy intersection at a diagonal. The crowd jostled as he cut through them. People who'd seen the veteran and boy together, now gave him a reproachful look. Someone yelled out, "Boy, look to your grandfather before he gets hurt!"

Christopher opened his mouth to protest but closed it when he saw the veteran had walked straight in front of an approaching horse and two-wheeled cart covered with a tarp. Throwing down his bale, he raced through the crowd and grabbed the old man, pushing him forward a few steps, out of the horse's path. To his surprise, the old man swung about with his long stick as if to attack him, missed, and struck the horse full on the flank.

"Hey!" the rider shouted, pulling back on the reins. The horse reared up with a scream and side-stepped several paces, causing the cart to careen wildly. For a precious moment, it teetered on one wheel before tipping over and spilling half-rotten potatoes. At the sight of the food, the fearless crowd swarmed like locusts from all directions.

Weaving their way through the mob, man and boy dove into a shadowed alley.

"Old-timer, you are nothing but trouble," the boy said, catching his breath.

"Name's Roger," the old man said, removing the binding from his bright leonine eyes. "Thank you for saving my life." Resting his stick between his neck and shoulder, he held out his hand.

Confused, the boy shook it. "Christopher."

"Nice to meet you, Christopher. Hold this," Roger said, handing him his stick and wicker basket.

Peeking over the boy's shoulder, he wiped the dirt and sweat from his face with the bandage.

"Maybe they didn't see us."

"Who?"

"Them," Roger answered with a nod.

Christopher turned and followed Roger's gaze to two frustrated, olive-skinned men trying to force their way through the crowd.

Roger flipped his cloak inside out, revealing a rich blue velvet. After making a few adjustments to his armor, it transformed into a gold-buttoned, satin coat with white lace jabots at the sleeves and neckline. Last, he produced a leather hat with a matching blue band, erasing all traces of the grizzled veteran.

"Who *are* you?" the boy asked.

"Roger," he answered. "I thought we already established my name. You're not dense, are you?"

"No. No, sir."

"Good." Roger laid a hand on the boy's shoulder and said, "I have an assignment for you. In return, I promise you and your family will have food. There may even be a knighthood in it for you."

When warriors in belted plaid kilts arrived to disperse the crowd, Roger whispered, "Now."

With the white bandage wrapped around his forehead, Christopher sprinted into the intersection. He stiff-armed his way through the crowd, the wicker basket tucked into the crook of his elbow. Shouts and grumbles followed in the wake of the nimble youth.

"Stop, thief!" Roger yelled, pointing to the white bandage. The two warriors dropped the cart, spilling more potatoes, turned toward the commotion, and gave chase.

Roger kept to the edges of the crowd, eyes alert, and worked his way north of the intersection, where the street wasn't as congested. Three men with scarlet sashes around their waists charged past him. He maintained a steady pace toward the square although every voice inside his head told him to run.

Just stick to the plan, Roger. Stick to the plan.

The warriors closed on the wicker basket and white bandage left abandoned in the middle of the intersection.

There was no sign of the boy. Roger kept a neutral face when a tongue of bright flame licked out from the basket. Cursing, the warriors jumped back. The flame flashed and sputtered, replaced by a plume of greyish-white smoke. There seemed to be no end to the low-hanging fumes that spewed from the burning basket, filling the street, and engulfing the entire area.

Remembering the white smoke from the previous morning, panic erupted as people sought to get away. Many held a hand over their mouths to keep from coughing or rubbed at irritated eyes. Soldiers from the square pushed through the exodus, but they stopped when the smoke became too thick to see through.

"What's going on here?" asked a stocky soldier with an oiled mustache and goatee.

"Black magic," a kilted warrior answered, making a sign to ward against evil.

Catching sight of the smoking basket, the newcomer shook his head. "That's nonsense. Keep this crowd moving while we search for the culprit."

Roger rode the wave of people all the way to the Square of King David, where they spilled out like waters from a ruptured dam. They flowed past the stalls and filled the yard, mingling with the food lines. The soldiers who guarded the different wares fingered their hilts with itchy hands.

Roger gave a silent prayer of thanks. In retrospect, he wished his plan hadn't worked quite as well as it did. The people had provided the necessary cover, but at the same time, the Highlord could be five feet away and he'd never know it. Holding the swaddled orb tight under his cloak, he aimed for Battenberg Palace.

Shrill screams erupted from the northern part of the square. The flow of the crowd suddenly shifted, and Roger found himself fighting against the current.

His blood went cold when he spotted a lean, pale figure dressed in a long, black cloak jumping from balcony to balcony of the rowhouses, a recurved longbow in one hand and black fletched arrows in the other.

The Archer.

Three pale figures, also wrapped in black cloaks and carrying bows, leaned over the rooftop parapets along the east side of the square and shot into the crowd.

Roger swore under his breath. "He's trying to drive me away from the palace. And what happens when he clears the crowd?" he muttered to himself.

For a brief moment, Roger glimpsed the golden armor of a Horned Owl under the boughs of the dogwoods. Arrows with black fletching riddled his body. Just as quickly, the crowd closed about him again, and Roger felt himself swept away.

Instead of moving directly against the current, he aimed west then east in a zigzag. For every step forward, he took three sideways. At least he was making progress. Sort of.

Along the west side of the square, a line of Gael warriors kept the crowd moving. To the south, soldiers ushered people down a side street, emptying the square as quickly as possible.

"Awright, ye! Stop richt thare!"

Recognizing the Gaelic brogue, Roger found Jongar staring straight at him. Would he dare attack with the Highlord here? He didn't have to wait long for an answer. The barbarian and his warriors pushed toward him, brandishing axes and two-handed swords.

The crowd thinned, leaving him by himself at the pedestal with the remains of the king's statue. Where was the Highlord?

Like streaks of black rain, arrows struck the ground at Roger's feet. Four of The Archer's dærganfae were on the ground, moving toward him with longbows, arrows nocked.

"Glaxon!" The Archer shouted from the balcony. "Hand over the orb!"

Behind Roger, the stocky soldier with an oiled mustache and goatee shouted, "No! Give us the orb!"

"Tha orb is ours!" Jongar bellowed.

With everyone closing in, Roger raised the shrouded orb. "Stand back or you're all dead."

Jongar held up a clenched fist, and his mercenaries halted their march. To the south, the stocky soldier did the same.

"You're the one who's dead!" The Archer shouted, firing an arrow with two more behind it.

With all his strength, Roger smashed the orb on the granite pedestal. The explosion that followed shredded the embroidered cloth around the orb and tossed Roger to the ground like a ragdoll. A brilliant hemisphere of blood-colored magic rolled across the square, throwing down everyone in its path. Passing through the dogwood grove, it slammed into the windows along the south face of Battenberg Palace, shattering the glass into countless shards.

Roger's eyes fluttered open to find the world a blur of light and shadows. A smudge of blue and a second one of purple leaned over him, flanked by others who seemed to glow in the sunlight. Fearing he was under attack, Roger fought through the pain and tried to reach for one of his long daggers, but his body didn't respond.

"Don't try to move." Phaedrus' gentle voice was barely audible over the ringing in Roger's ears. The priest laid a hand on Roger's forehead, and the air turned soft azure.

When the light receded, Roger found he could see and hear a little more clearly, but his paralysis remained. The figures of the Highlord and Archmage Angus McHeath came into focus. The Highlord stood with his sword in hand, broad shoulders tense, and ageless grey eyes scanning the crowd. His clothes were dirty and torn. It looked as though he had fought a pack of barghest.

"Whit happened?" demanded Jongar. The mighty barbarian stumbled to a stop, axe gripped in one meaty fist, and blood trickling from his ears. In his wake, more Gaels and several of Camber's men gathered.

"The Archer's dærganfae ambushed us inside the palace," the Highlord said.

"The Queen?"

"She's fine," the Highlord answered.

"My spells were useless against them," Angus muttered as he tightened a bandage around Roger's leg.

"The orb," Roger said in a low, rough voice. His throat was raw, and he was having difficulty breathing.

"Don't talk," Phaedrus said, laying a hand on his arm. "We need to get you to the palace."

"No. The Archer," Roger croaked. Darkness clawed at the edges of his vision.

"Hush now," Phaedrus soothed.

"Ah wouldnae worry yourself about tha Archer. He an' his men are dead. Look." Jongar pointed.

Those around him turned, and Roger strained to follow

the barbarian's pointing finger. Four splotches of blackened earth marked where dærganfae bodies should have been.

"The orb did that?" asked the Highlord.

"So it would appear," Angus said.

Derrick turned to the soldier at his side. "Grab anyone who's able and search those rowhouses. Make sure the dærganfae are gone."

"Yes, sir," the soldier said before dashing off.

Camber's second in command gave the square a long look. Bits of shattered glass lay scattered about the pedestal. "I guess that's it for the orb."

Angus stood up and said, "Yes. The orb is destroyed, its magic dead."

"Dead or set free?" Jongar asked.

The Highlord and Angus shared a quick look before the mage answered, "What does it matter? It's gone. Nobody can use it now. The plague's source is no more."

Second by second the heavy weight grew in Roger's chest, and he gasped for air.

"Bring him to the palace," Phaedrus said, a worried look on his face. "I'll run ahead and ready a room."

Jongar gave him a curt nod and motioned for two of his men to help. "You're right, priest. Clan comes first."

One of the mercenaries leaned over Roger and undid the clasp on his cloak. The last thing he remembered was being lifted before he slipped back into unconsciousness.

The Highlord and one of the Horned Owls carried a wounded soldier in a makeshift litter. Leading the way, Angus cleared a path through the milling crowd with his staff. Derrick ran up to them from the rowhouse. In his hand, he carried a broken arrow shaft. At the end, pitch black vulture feathers ended in sharp points half a finger-width from the arrow's nock.

"Where did you get that?" the Highlord asked.

"From the balcony, Sir," Derrick replied.

"Appears we haven't seen the last of The Archer after all," said the Highlord.

Once they entered the palace grounds, the Highlord handed his end of the litter to a soldier and took Angus aside. He asked, "Did anyone see you take the shard from the orb?"

"No, I was very careful," Angus replied. "I'll take it back with me to Tydway and hide it at the Academia until I can figure out what it is and how to destroy it."

"Good."

Angus gripped the Highlord's shoulder. "Artos, be careful. By destroying the orb, Roger has split Moirai's thread into multiple strands. Until a path is chosen, I am blind to your future."

"And that troubles you, my friend?"

"Aye, it does," Angus said, the concern adding lines to his already wrinkled face. He dropped his hand, but his eyes never left those of the Highlord. "Only one path is true. All others lead Gaia to the Winds of Chaos."

With a smile, the Highlord said, "Cheer up. It's about time we controlled our own destiny."

"Of course, you would say that," Angus said. "Ignorance must be bliss."

"At least I get to sleep at night."

"*Hmmph,*" replied Angus. "What about you? Do you plan to stay?"

The Highlord cast a quick glance over his shoulder. Jongar and Camber's men worked together when they had a common cause. Let that cause end or falter, and they squabbled like siblings.

"Yes. Tell the Highlady I'll return as soon as I can."

CHAPTER 6
MANY GREETINGS

April 24, 4208 K.E.

8:26 am

*R*oger woke in a narrow bed covered with thick furs. His senses catching up, he blinked at the hearth with its glowing embers. There was just enough light to see the heavy drapes covering his only window, and a dresser and mirror where someone had piled his gear, along with a fresh set of clothes.

Watching him from the foot of his bed was a grey tabby cat with blue eyes. It stretched, jumped off the bed, and exited his room through the partially opened door, flicking its tail as it went.

Barefoot, he crept across the room. A bar of light from the door stretched across the floor. Stopping at its edge, he eased the door open farther and scanned the hallway beyond. Under a dim wall sconce, Phaedrus slept in a plush chair, his head propped against the plaster wall. Soldiers lying on pallets lined the hall, many with bloodstained bandages wrapped around a leg, an arm, or across their torso.

At the far end, a tonsured priest in green and white robes held a wheel-cross in his hand and knelt beside a wounded soldier. The blue nimbus surrounding them winked out. Head bowed, the priest laid a hand over the soldier's forehead. Phaedrus started, as if coming out of a bad dream. He sat up, rubbed the sleep from his eyes, and joined the priest.

Roger snuck to the window and lifted the edge of the drape. A bright beam of morning sunlight illuminated his room. He let out a sigh of relief when he recognized the view from Battenberg Palace.

Letting the curtain fall, he moved to the low dresser and his change of clothes. He faced the mirror and stared at a man who had spent most of his twenty-seven years hiding. Someone had washed away his powders and creams, leaving his tawny skin exposed. He took in his leonine colored eyes, broad forehead, and square face — Islander features handed down to him by his great grandmother. He gave himself a mental shake. *Time to go to work.*

He was pulling on his boots when there was a gentle rapping at the door.

"You're awake," Phaedrus said, pushing the door open farther.

"What happened?" Roger asked.

"The Archer attacked the palace. He must have found a secret entrance into the throne room. A dozen of his dærganfae appeared out of nowhere. They ambushed the Highlord and Sir Baldwin outside the Queen's chambers."

"Cerdic? Lahar?"

"They're fine. Ambrose, too, though she's a bit shaken up."

"The Highlord?"

"He's well, despite bearing the brunt of The Archer's attack. It was a fierce battle, but short. They fled before I arrived with the guard."

"You got lucky."

"How do you feel?" asked Phaedrus, taking Roger by the head with both hands. He turned him one way then the other. "Breathe for me."

"Sore, inside," Roger replied, rubbing his chest. He sucked in a deep breath of air and slowly let it out.

"You had me worried. Dærganfae coat their arrowheads with a nasty paralytic toxin," Phaedrus said letting him go. "Be glad the Eternal Father likes you."

Walking to the window, Phaedrus opened the curtains wide and let sunlight stream into the room. "I must say, things are coming together. Priests from the nearby towns are here to help repair the cathedral. And have you met Sir Jeffrey Beauchamp, the Lord Steward? He and the surviving members of his family have moved back into the palace. It's hard to believe, but I think everything will be ready when it's time for the coronation."

"How long have I been out?"

"About twenty-four hours." Phaedrus gave his friend a wry smile and said, "I think you angered everyone with that stunt you pulled."

Roger grinned. His stomach grumbled and, after giving his midsection a serious look, he asked, "Do you have any food?"

"A little. Wait here, and I'll ask Thomas to find you something," Phaedrus said.

"That's alright, just point me to the kitchen," Roger said, stretching. "I need to get out and move around anyways."

Brilliant bands of red, orange, and yellow streaked through jagged fragments of glass and into a second story room of the palace as the sun approached its zenith. Roger held a board in place while he nailed it across the broken window. Retrieving another from a pile of cut lumber in the middle of the room, he set it above the first. A chuckle from the doorway behind him stopped his hammer mid-swing.

"Your father thinks you're a hopeless lay about, and here I find you doing manual labor. Your mother would be appalled," the Highlord commented.

Roger turned toward his liege and gave him a short bow. "They want me to be a *barrister*," he said. "I'll gladly bear the weight of their disapproval in exchange for being one of your Rooks, Majesty." He turned back to the window and resumed nailing the board in place.

"You don't have to do this," the Highlord said, picking up a board and starting on the window next to him.

"I know, but I feel responsible." Wiping the perspiration from his forehead with the back of his arm, Roger said, "Why must there be so much glass in this palace?"

The Highlord laughed over the banging of his hammer.

"Are you staying for the funeral?" Roger asked.

Shaking his head, the Highlord replied, "Everyone seems to be worried about when I'm leaving. Jongar and Camber want me gone. Phaedrus wants me to stay, and I have no idea what Queen Ambrose wants — other than to be left alone."

"This place would have fallen apart if you hadn't arrived."

"Maybe, but did it occur to you that by being here, I escalated events?"

"What do you mean?"

The Highlord picked up another board and held it in place. "Perhaps The Archer wouldn't have attacked the palace, and you wouldn't have destroyed the orb."

"Sire, you may have affected the timing, but not the events. Those things would have happened anyways — or worse, The Archer may have gotten his hands on the orb and assassinated Ambrose. Either of those two things happen, and Carolingias falls."

"We walk a precipitous path," the Highlord mused.

The shrill cry of a clarion pierced the room. Both men peered through the gaps in the wood and spied a bright glow in the Square of King David. An olive-skinned standard bearer marched out of a magical portal, his flag a crimson cross quartering an argent field.

Next through the portal was a raven-haired woman wearing an ankle-length cassock of purest white. A gold and green stole was draped about her neck. On her head, she wore an embroidered mitre edged with silver tufts. Beside her walked an unbearded man in a crimson and argent tabard.

Two rows of six monks in brown cowls and tunics marched out behind her. A heavy mace set into a loop hung from the knotted, silk rope at each of their waists. Their armored feet clanked heavily on the river-rock lane.

"Archbishop Letizia Trastámara of Peninsular Espia and her nephew, Don Cipri Trastámara, Ambassador from Zaragoza. Which means Burgos and Malaga won't be far behind," the Highlord said.

"Aren't we all supposed to be friends?" Roger asked.

The Highlord didn't answer.

Another clarion called out, and another portal opened. The first man to appear seemed to be a commoner. A blacksmith's leather apron covered his red tunic and breeches, and a leather skullcap encased his bald head. He bore a standard emblazoned with a gold tower with three turrets all on a red field. Contrasting with the lowly standard bearer, the second person through the portal wore onyx and gold plate armor that glinted in the sunlight, giving it a shimmering halo. Statuesque in his physique, he seemed to pose with every step.

Marching next through the portal were a dozen olive-skinned women with long, dark hair that flowed freely over tight-fitting scale armor the deep blue of lapis lazuli. Cut above the greaves protecting their shins, their intricate scale tunics shimmered like water. They carried long ranseurs with a sparkling sapphire embedded at the intersection of the spearhead and the crescent-shaped blade.

"Don Esteban Ramos y Medina, Ambassador from Malaga. What a pompous ass," the Highlord said.

"You know, some people say the same about you," Roger said.

"Maybe."

"The way I heard it, you were escorted by golden knights. A dozen Horned Owls in their parade armor. That must have been quite a sight."

The Highlord laughed. "You may be right. We could all use a lesson in humility."

Down in the square, the lines of people waiting for food became a semi-circle of spectators. Camber's men worked the crowd, making sure they gave the visiting parties plenty of room.

A third and final clarion call rang out, and another portal opened. This standard bearer carried a red flag with horizontal gold stripes. The emissary from Burgos wore a sleeveless, forest-green doublet embroidered with gold sequins over a white camisa. His high-waisted, forest-green pants stopped below the knees, exposing pink stockings. He wore black, flat slippers secured with a matching bow on his feet, and a black, knitted hat, with bulbs over each ear.

A light-skinned man and woman stepped out behind him. Dressed similar to the standard bearer, he wore a short promenade cape and carried a longsword on one side and a triangular-shaped short sword on the other. She wore a wispy, green gown that brushed the ground and held a long staff of white oak engraved with silver runes. A delicate, gold circlet adorned her forehead, holding back long, black hair that reached her waist.

The portal winked out with no other soldiers or escorts forthcoming.

"Priests, warriors, and a sorceress. All we need now is a thief," the Highlord said, giving Roger a sly look.

Roger raised his hands, a mock look of hurt writ across his face. "Who, me?"

"Come on, thief. Time to get ready."

Sir Jeffrey, the Lord Steward, struck the throne room floor with the butt of his dogwood staff and announced, "The Highlord of Gallowen and Roger Vaughn, son of Earl

Wolverton."

Passing under the second-floor gallery, Roger entered with the Highlord and two of his Horned Owl knights. Being the last to enter, they turned the heads of the Espian representatives already present.

At the far end of the Grand Hall, the throne remained empty as did the bluestone dais around it. One step down, Camber and Phaedrus stood to the left, while Sir Baldwin and Sir Julius stood stiff-backed to the right.

Roger followed the Highlord as he positioned himself between the dignitaries from Burgos and Zaragoza, both of whom had also brought two of their knights — all unarmed.

"Archbishop Letizia and esteemed ambassadors, welcome to York and Carolingias," Sir Baldwin said with a gracious bow. "Please forgive the construction. We are recovering from our recent battle."

"We demand to see the Queen," Señor Ramos said. "Where is she?"

Sir Baldwin replied, "As you may be aware, Ambrose has not been officially coronated. Until that time, we are acting in her stead."

"I see," Señor Ramos said with a slight nod of his head. "We heard about the battle here at the palace and mourn the loss of King David and his familia, but we have urgent business that cannot wait any longer."

The Sorceress of Burgos took a step forward. When she spoke, her contralto voice wrapped the throne room in a sensuous blanket. "Knight, let us speak openly. Our people are starving. The food your people took from the Sha'iry is rightfully ours, stolen from our fields."

"I don't recall seeing your people here when we defeated the Sha'iry," Camber said.

"Hechicera Antonia," Sir Baldwin said, cutting off Camber, "the food from the Sha'iry trains is the only food the people of York have. You cannot expect us to just give it to you."

"I expect you to do the right thing."

"*We* expect you to do the right thing," Archbishop Letizia echoed.

"Sir Baldwin," the Highlord said, facing the knight. "I have seen the storehouses of the Sha'iry here in York. I cannot believe the entire crop from three countries is housed here. There is some, but what about the rest?"

The Sorceress of Burgos' eyes flashed. She brandished her white staff, punctuating every word, as she asked, "What are you saying? Our food has disappeared?"

"Espians are starving!" Señor Ramos exclaimed. "The stores that carry us through the winter are empty."

"What about your neighbors, Cadiz, Murcia, and Santander? Have you approached them?" asked Camber.

"We shouldn't have to," Señor Ramos sniped. "Our crops are here."

The tension in the throne room built, and Roger gripped the hilt of a dagger under his doublet.

"Make no mistake. The Sha'iry are not defeated — only driven back into the shadows," the Highlord said. His calm voice cut through the chaos and tension. "The food they left in York was meant to flame a civil war, not feed the masses. If you want your food, find where the Sha'iry have hidden it."

"Ladies and Gentlemen," Phaedrus said. "York and Carolingias have been a battlefield. It is up to you to decide if you are the carrion that feeds upon the dead, or the healer that tends the wounded."

The Espian representatives seemed frozen in varying states of shock and outrage, and Roger wondered if Phaedrus was on the verge of inciting another battle.

The Archbishop recovered first. "Half-elf, you seem more a mischievous duende than a priest. What is your purpose here?"

"Your Grace, I am a fool who has been asked to give the king a drink of water."

The throne room descended into a cacophony of arguments and threats. Ambrose watched wide-eyed from the shadows of the western gallery, her hand over her mouth.

"Phaedrus could have handled that a bit better," Sir Cerdic whispered behind her. "You really should be down there with them."

Her eyes glistening, Ambrose replied, "I cannot do this. There must be someone else."

"My Queen... Ambrose, look at me." When she turned, he said, "No matter how much you deny it, you are a Battenberg. You are King David's niece. There's strength in your blood, a gift from the Eternal Father. Have faith in him, and the rest will work itself out."

His eyes bore into hers. They shined with fervent adoration, and a slow dread filled her. He didn't really see her — none of them did — not Camber, Jongar, or the Highlord. They saw only what they wanted to see. They didn't see the turmoil inside her, the stark fear. Plastering a smile on her face, she wiped her nose with her sleeve and asked, "Why did Phaedrus speak to Archbishop Letizia that way?"

Cerdic looked over her shoulder at the priest and replied, "He and the church hierarchy don't get along. They want him to stop roaming and settle down in an out-of-the-way village of their choosing, but he refuses. It's a sore spot for them both."

"Why doesn't he obey? Seems that's what priests are supposed to do."

"He's always done things his own way, I guess. Made his own path. One day, he'll gather his flock and build a church, and when he does, it will be a sight to behold."

"I have another matter! One that may make this argument unnecessary!" the Ambassador of Malaga shouted over the din in the throne room below, drawing Ambrose's attention back to the visitors. Without looking, he half-turned and held out a hand to the knight behind his right shoulder. In response the woman placed a thick roll of parchment on Don Esteban's palm. "If I may approach the throne."

Sir Baldwin maintained a neutral expression as he stepped down onto the main floor. "Please, step forward."

The Ambassador handed the scroll to Sir Baldwin and announced, "These are my patents of nobility. If you look, you will see that my grandmother was a Battenberg. We are cousins, you and I." Don Esteban gave Sir Baldwin a predatory smile. "Have your scribes verify my legitimacy. They will tell you I have a claim to the throne of Carolingias."

"We have reviewed his patents," Hechicera Antonia said, "and Burgos supports his claim."

"As does Zaragoza," said Don Cipri.

"Rey Odón of Malaga supports my claim as well," added Don Esteban. With his chin set firmly and chest puffed out, he stared intently at Sir Baldwin. "Carolingians would do well to have me as King."

Red in the face, Camber pointed a finger at Don Esteban. "Carolingias will be ruled by a Battenberg, not a Ramos."

Sir Baldwin cleared his throat. "The Queen has been chosen by the people."

With a slight tip of his head, Don Esteban spread his arms wide. "I only offer an alternative. Considering her behavior in the wake of her family's deaths, Ambrose may decide to abdicate or, heaven forbid, an accident may befall her between now and her coronation."

"Is that a threat?" Camber asked.

"No, rakehell, just the voice of a concerned kinsman."

Taking a deep breath, Sir Baldwin replied, "Ambrose will be Queen." He had a deadly calm about him that cut through the air.

Esteban looked the knight in the eyes and said, "You have seven days to bury your dead and crown *your* Queen. If, at the end of that time, she has not taken the throne and resolved the matter of our countries' stolen food, I will take it — by force if necessary."

With that, his entourage turned their backs on the throne and stormed out. Behind him, the representatives from Burgos did the same.

As Archbishop Letizia turned to leave with her nephew, Phaedrus asked, "Where does the church stand on these matters?"

"You should know," she replied, fixing the half-elf with a meaningful gaze. "You are, after all, a part of it. Or have you forgotten?"

There was a bitterness to his voice when he replied, "No, I have not forgotten. These people have suffered much at the hands of the Dark One. They need our help."

"The Church will assist its flock, as always, but when it comes to politics and feuding governments, we remain a neutral arbiter." Archbishop Letizia faced Sir Baldwin and said, "The Espian representatives will await your response. In the meantime, the cloister at Daventry Cathedral will host the ambassadors and serve meals to the faithful. You are welcome to join us." She leveled a pointed glare at Sir Baldwin. "See that your absentee Queen represents her family with the dignity expected of a Battenberg."

CHAPTER 7
FUNERALS

April 25, 4208 K.E.

1:13 pm

*B*agpipers playing a mournful dirge marched past Westchester Hall, a grand stone edifice with arched stained-glass windows and an imposing sixty-foot-tall bell tower. Citizens of York crowded the streets to view the young Queen, her four knights, and the foreign dignitaries.

Behind the musicians, the Archbishop set a solemn pace with her dozen monks flanking her. She wore a white surplice over a purple cassock and carried a tall crosier with its curved shepherd's crook. Her mitre headdress stood tall and proud.

After Archbishop Letizia and her entourage came three horse-drawn biers. The first bore a gilded coffin with a wax effigy of the king lavishly dressed in fur-lined robes. Its gloved hands gripped the bejeweled hilt of his sword. The second bore the queen. Decorated with sparkling rings, a necklace, and earrings, her effigy wore an elaborate dress and clasped her hands together in prayer. Prince Bernard's polished armor, draped with his royal tabard, rested atop the final coffin. Twenty-four pikemen wearing black tunics marched alongside.

Wearing a full-length black mourning cloak with the hood pulled up, Ambrose walked alone behind the horse-drawn biers. With her head bowed and hands lost in the folds of her sleeves, she seemed more a specter of the dead than one of the living. Three steps behind her were Sir Baldwin, Sir Cerdic, Sir Martyn, and Sir Julius. They wore silver, green, and blue checkered tabards and carried their swords in front of them with gauntlet-covered fists clenched on the weapon's ricasso.

Next came Sir Jeffrey Beauchamp, the Lord Steward, with his family and the surviving heads of state from the local municipalities, as well as the envoys from Gallowen, Malaga, Burgos, and Zaragoza.

Ambrose felt the heated glares from the Espian

ambassadors on her back. After the debacle in the throne room, she had hidden away in her room. In her stead, Sir Baldwin met with each party, offering what solicitudes he could, and managed to assuage Archbishop Letizia by letting her lead the funeral procession. He was a better politician than she could ever be.

Her older siblings and cousins had trained in statecraft from an early age, each bound for one position or another to support King David and, one day, their cousin Bernard when he assumed the throne. As one of the younger children in a large family, Ambrose had managed to avoid many of those lessons and responsibilities. However, it had come with a price. Often ignored, her parents never seemed to heap upon her the same affection as her siblings. Her thoughts wandered back to her visits at the palace and warm hugs from her aunt and uncle. Now they were all dead. Her entire family gone, most fed to the Sha'iry's furnaces.

The music stopped, and the procession halted. Ambrose blinked back her tears.

Braced by a series of mammoth flying buttresses, the cross-shaped Daventry Cathedral spread four hundred feet in the long direction and two hundred feet in the short. Facing west, its central spire, topped with a wheel-cross, soared over a hundred and fifty feet high. Two smaller spires flanked it, each with a pair of grotesque gargoyles that leered down at them. Between the spires, wooden planks filled recesses where rose windows once decorated the facade. White foundation stones gleamed in the sunlight, revealing hasty repairs. Above the granite water table, the facade was damaged and, in some places, covered with graffiti — scars from the Sha'iry occupation.

Four tonsured priests in white cassocks with black stoles waited within the pointed arch framing the entrance. At the foot of the steps, Camber and Jongar, along with twenty-two other pallbearers, crossed the sandstone plaza to collect the coffins.

A lanky wolf in a funeral tabard, Camber caught Ambrose's eye and gave her a quick wink. He led seven pallbearers to the Queen's coffin. Forming two lines at the rear of the bier, Camber and his opposite grabbed the nearest coffin huckle. Two by two, the pallbearers lifted it off the bier, backed up several steps, then followed Jongar and the king's coffin inside the church. The remaining men bore the prince after his parents.

His sword sheathed, Sir Baldwin offered Ambrose his arm. "Your Highness."

Letting the ceremony guide her, she rested her hand and forearm atop his.

The cathedral took her breath away. She had forgotten the elegant beauty within its walls. Supported by proud pillars, thin stone ribs met in a pointed arch a hundred feet above the nave. Through cracks in the boarded over stained-glass windows, thin streamers of sunlight spilled onto oaken pews and the tiled floor with its alternating bands of ivory and onyx. At the intersection of the transept, the tiles wove an intricate pattern that culminated in an octagonal labyrinth with a medallion at its center.

The vast chamber smelled of beeswax and lye.

At the eastern end of the sanctuary, long, narrow windows set into seven polygonal apses gave the altar a radiant glow. The largest apse held a wheel-cross suspended above a cloth-covered altar table and tabernacle, borrowed from a nearby parish.

In front of the altar, the coffins rested on stout tables. Behind them, Archbishop Letizia took her place at the altar with the priests serving as her assistants. Ambrose bowed her head as numbness seeped into her soul. Her vision narrowed as she fought to put one foot in front of the other.

Sir Baldwin guided her down the central aisle and stopped at the front row of pews. She stood beside him, unwilling to take those additional steps to pay her last respects.

Ambrose felt more than saw Camber take her arm and lead her the rest of the way to the altar. The wax effigy of her uncle bore a slight sheen, giving her the impression the thing was sweating. Curly locks of real human hair framed a gaunt, sallow face. Its unseeing glass eyes and thin red lips held no vigor — none of that spark her uncle had had during life. Visions of his head dangling from the meat hook swam before her, making the room spin.

"Uncle, I'm so sorry." She clutched at Camber as her strength failed and blackness overtook her.

"Her conduct was dishonorable," declared Archbishop Letizia. "She will never be Queen."

Careful to keep her breathing controlled, Ambrose lay tucked against the wall on a low divan with thin cushions that held a faint aroma of sandalwood. The last thing she remembered was standing before her uncle's coffin in the sanctuary with darkness clawing at her sight. They must have taken her to one of the priests' private chambers.

The Archbishop paced back and forth across the bare room. Sir Baldwin stood with his back to the divan, his arms crossed. Even though she couldn't see his face, she felt his suppressed anger.

"Your Grace," he said, "give her time. She's a Battenberg."

"I think you put too much faith in a fragile bloodline."

"It's not just her lineage. Phaedrus says the people will follow her."

"Do not speak to me of that meddling duende," Archbishop Letizia said with a swipe of her hand. "By joining Camber, she rebelled against her family. For all we know, she may have even had part in their deaths."

"There is no evidence, not even rumor, that Camber or his people had anything to do with slaying the royal family, Your Grace. Everything points to dærganfae assassins. I don't believe she would have—"

"Caballero, she's weak. Camber could have done whatever he wanted — and he probably did — and she wouldn't have raised a finger to stop him. She would have followed him, no matter what."

"I was there in the courtyard. She knew what had to be done when she accepted us as her champions." Sir Baldwin stepped forward, his fists clenched at his sides, and said, "Archbishop, Camber and Jongar support her, the aristocracy supports her, and I support her. She will be Queen, and if you don't like it, then to hell with you."

Archbishop Letizia regarded the knight with a deep frown. "Very well, Caballero, I will not interfere, but mark my words, she will disappoint you. That will be her legacy."

"Your Grace, you're wrong," Sir Baldwin replied as he escorted the Archbishop to the door.

"I hope, for your sake, you are right."

Outside, Camber and several others waited in the hallway. The buzz of their conversation came across harsh and discordant with Ambrose's name being mentioned multiple times. The knight shut the door, letting out a deep sigh, and walked back to check on her. She leapt up from the divan and wrapped the grizzled knight in a tight hug. After a slight pause, he returned it.

"Thank you." She leaned her head against his chest and squeezed tighter.

"My Queen," he replied, "I thought you were asleep." With a gentle push, he held her at arm's length.

Ambrose met his gaze and said, "Sir Baldwin, I promise you I will be the best queen I can."

"That is all we can ask of you."

The door cracked open, and Camber burst into the room. "Ambrosia? Archbishop Letizia said you were still asleep."

Letting Ambrose go, Sir Baldwin said, "Camber, please let everyone know to prepare the sanctuary for her vigil."

A sly look came over the rakehell, and Sir Baldwin said, "The vigil is a time for prayer — not whatever it is you have in mind."

The young man began to protest, but Sir Baldwin stopped him short, "No. This is something she must do *alone*. She must begin her journey to be Queen on the right foot — free of distractions."

CHAPTER 8
VIGIL

April 25, 4208 K.E.

6:33 pm

*L*it candles surrounded the circular room, giving it a warm glow. Leaning over the edge of a low stone wall, a nun poured scented water from a ceramic jug into a round pool. Her white coif and headdress hugged a round face that held a perpetual smile. She wore her black tunic pinned up in the front. Behind her another nun held a sponge.

Water sluiced through Ambrose's long hair as she broke the surface. She spread her arms, letting it wash away her tensions.

After leaving the priest's chamber, Sir Baldwin had led her arm-in-arm across the alley into the convent where everything was orchestrated down to the smallest detail. Every step, every word had a meaning and an origin steeped in time. Even the robe she was to wear during the vigil had been worn by King David's mother and her great, great grandmother before that.

Maybe after all this, Camber would agree to be her consort. She grinned, remembering the disappointed expression on his face when she left him standing in the hallway. Maybe they could slip away and...

Think pure thoughts. Think pure thoughts.

Her mind wandered again, and it dawned on her that the sisters had never introduced themselves. "What's your name?" she asked.

"Shush, My Queen, you're supposed to be praying," the one with a round face said.

My Queen. The words stuck in her head. She frowned as she thought about the events that led her there: the murder of her family, the skirmishes between the reds and bluebloods, the battle at the palace. She felt more like flotsam swept along with the tide than a future Queen.

"It's time," said the nun behind her.

Ambrose stepped over the low wall. Goosebumps spread over her bare skin. They dried her off with oversized, coarse towels and slipped a plain white robe over her. While one tied a braided rope about her waist, the other produced a chair and bade her to sit. Working in silence, they dried her hair and combed the tangles from it. Then, they bent and dried her feet before giving her a pair of sandals. After a quick onceover, they led Ambrose back into the cathedral.

The brass sconces affixed to each of the pillars shimmered in the candlelight as if surrounded by an aura of magic. High above, the windows were dark mirrors reflecting the light from below.

As above, so below.

Moving in single file, they followed the path of ivory tiles as it wound back and forth through the south transept. When they reached the labyrinth mosaic inlaid at the cathedral center, the two nuns stepped aside.

"My Queen, there is only one true path to heaven," said the sister with the round face. Crossing their arms with their hands inside their sleeves, they watched her progress like silent sentinels.

Ambrose marveled at the intricate bands of onyx and ivory. At its center, an octagonal medallion held an ornate wheel-cross with Korellan writing inscribed along each edge.

Taking a tentative step, Ambrose entered the labyrinth. She traced the paths with her eyes until she found the correct one and took it. Her footsteps echoing hollowly in the sanctuary, she turned this way and that, aiming toward the center, but somewhere along the way she made a mistake. She found herself at the beginning with the nuns. Confused, she retraced the path — this time with her finger extended. Where had she gone wrong?

Trying again, she stepped into the labyrinth. She followed it a few paces, traced the path, and moved forward. She continued this pattern, certain she had found the correct route this time.

A dead end.

She stomped her foot and turned around. Had the pattern moved? The sisters remained standing at the entrance to the labyrinth. The sconces and windows hadn't changed. The narthex lay to the west and the altar to the east.

Third time's a charm. She started to retrace her steps but stopped when she felt that it wasn't just the two sisters watching her.

No longer amused, she asked, "Has anyone ever *not* made it to the center?"

Their pervasive silence left a void inside her that filled with fear. What if she didn't make it? The Archbishop had said her bloodline was fragile, weak. Maybe after all was said and done, she was an imposter. How could she ever be Queen?

Free of distractions. Sir Baldwin's words came unbidden.

On the night of his vigil, her uncle had stood here, faced with the same choices — the same obstacle. What would he have done?

The thought of it made her stomach clench and throat tighten. It had been so long. Taking a deep breath, she closed her eyes, picturing the labyrinth in her mind, and prayed to the Eternal Father.

At first, her prayers were childlike, asking the Eternal Father to reveal the path to the center of the stupid maze, as if he were a genie in a bottle who granted wishes. Her prayers evolved, and she prayed for peace, her family, and her uncle. The more she prayed, the more the words became an introspection.

Thinking back to when the dærganfae had come for her family, she remembered being paralyzed with fear. She had hidden inside the hollow seat of an elm chair in the hall outside her parent's bedroom. With swords and knives, her father and brothers fought the dark-haired elves not a foot from her. The harsh clang of steel on steel resonated inside her hiding place, deafening her. The fight shifted, and someone fell against the chair, jarring it. She slapped a hand over her mouth to keep from crying out.

The death cries of her father and brothers, followed by the screams of her mother and sisters being dragged out of their rooms, still rang in her ears. Clenching her eyes shut, she fought the despair and self-loathing that had driven her to Camber's bed. She had disowned the Battenberg name, disowned that life, even came to hate it. And now...

"Eternal Father," she prayed, "please forgive me. I have no excuse for what I have done; no excuse for what I have become. The people of Carolingias deserve better than me, but if it's your will that I be Queen, please give me the strength to serve them." Opening her eyes, she found herself kneeling on an ivory tile. Instead of the circuitous route from before, a clear path lay directly ahead of her. A faint glow emanated from either side. Rising to her feet, she followed the path to the labyrinth's center and stepped onto the medallion.

The glow spread to the octagon framing the labyrinth's center. A thin lip formed then grew deeper, and the medallion slowly lowered into the floor, taking Ambrose with it. The long onyx shaft ended at the peak of a ribbed vault, where it opened into the crypt. As above, candlelit sconces cast a warm glow, illuminating rows of rectangular sarcophagi nestled between thick stone columns.

The medallion floated a foot above the undercroft floor, and Ambrose stepped off it. Relieved of her weight, the labyrinth's center rose back into the shaft.

Broken statuary lay about the floor, surrounding plundered sarcophagi. Atop, many of the stone effigies representing kings, queens, or the queen's consorts bore hands broken at the wrist. The priests had done their best to put everything back in order, but she still caught glimpses of tattered cloth and bone through cracks in the walls. With all the wanton destruction, the fresh sarcophagi holding her aunt, cousin, and uncle looked out of place.

Ambrose should have been frightened but, instead, being alone with her ancestors comforted her. She remembered playing down here as a child once and being admonished for it when they found her. Her mother's strident voice, once grating, now brought a smile to her lips.

In an alcove, a lit candelabra rested on a prie-dieu with a cushioned kneeler and slanted shelf. Behind it, a wheel-cross hung from the wall. Kneeling, Ambrose clasped her hands and bowed her head.

The staccato of multiple explosions shook the crypt, causing dust and debris to rain down. Ambrose looked up from her meditation, her movements slow and lethargic. Iron-shod footsteps echoed loudly within the vault as Sir Baldwin ran toward her. The front of his steel breastplate gleamed brightly. "My Queen! The Archer's men are trying to break through the sanctuary."

Behind him, Derrick positioned eight soldiers at various columns and sarcophagi. When finished he asked, "Is there another way out of here?"

"No," Sir Baldwin replied, pulling Ambrose to her feet.

Facing the only entrance, Derrick swore under his breath and drew his weapon.

"Where's Camber?" Ambrose asked.

"Defending the door, with Roger and Sir Cerdic," Sir Baldwin said, brandishing his sword.

Another explosion, stronger this time, shook the crypt and smoke filled the vaulted ceiling. Before Ambrose realized what was happening, Sir Baldwin shoved her inside the nearest sarcophagus. "You'll be safe here," he said as he replaced the lid.

No, not like this.

Ambrose wanted to scream, to fight, anything else, but she didn't dare. Instead, she watched Sir Baldwin through the narrow crack in the wall and waited.

A sickening gurgle marked The Archer's entrance to the crypt. Someone shouted and the clash of arms ensued.

The dust settled, and the candlelight from the prayer bench silhouetted Sir Baldwin in his plate armor. The picture of confidence, he gripped his sword with both hands, feet apart.

An inky black cloak blotted out the candle, and the strident ring of metal on metal sent tremors through Ambrose, as if she were the one holding the sword.

The tall, pale form of a dærganfae ran at the knight with an elegant longsword raised above his head. Right hand at the base of the quillon, Sir Baldwin met the dærganfae's blade with his own, dropping the tip of his sword into a hanging parry.

Soldiers rallied around the knight, engaging the dærganfae. A second dærganfae leapt from the shadows. Sir Baldwin pivoted and swiped left to right toward his opponent's shoulder. The dærganfae brought his sword around in a quick block, then blocked again as the knight pressed his attack.

Sir Baldwin kicked the dærganfae hard in the groin. Doubling over, the dark fae fell back, pain wracking his features.

The first dærganfae rushed at the knight. Sir Baldwin

stepped back and, with a violent slash, disemboweled his foe.

Leaping over their fallen comrade, a third and fourth dærganfae engaged the knight. With a twist of the wrist, Sir Baldwin made a diagonal swipe at his third opponent from low right to high left. The dærganfae jumped back, evading the attack, while the fourth lunged forward and drove his blade into Sir Baldwin's exposed side. Bringing his sword crashing down, Sir Baldwin cleaved his opponent's head in two.

Ambrose gasped, and the two remaining dærganfae turned toward her.

Beyond them, The Archer raised his longbow, a black-fletched arrow aimed at the knight. With a *twang*, the arrow shot forth and impaled him in the base of the throat. Sword still in hand, Sir Baldwin blinked twice at The Archer before falling backwards.

Dærganfae raced toward Ambrose's hiding place. She scrabbled around, searching for a weapon, anything she could use against them. One slid the lid of the sarcophagus aside, letting it fall to the floor with a loud thud, while the other reached inside. He grabbed a fistful of her hair and yanked.

Gnashing her teeth, she bit the dærganfae on the forearm. With a shout, he released her hair, but his partner caught the fabric of her sleeve, ripping it.

Her desperate fingers wrapped around a long bone, even as her other hand found a thin round object embedded in a crack in the floor — a coin. A simple phrase jumped into her head. It was an odd phrase that demanded her attention.

The dærganfae reached farther into the sarcophagus, trying to pin her down.

Releasing the bone, she held the coin with both hands and said, "Assayer, take me home." The coin flashed a bright golden light once, twice, thrice.

Once their vision returned, the two dærganfae frantically searched through the bones and bits of cloth.

The Archer approached, wearing a frown. "Aimsitheoir?" he asked.

One of the fae leaned back, his silvery eyes filled with confusion. "Father, she vanished."

CHAPTER 9
TIGHT SPACES

April 26, 4208 K.E.

4:36 am

"What a mess," Roger said, crossing the plaza in front of the cathedral. Dried blood trailed along his hairline, and dust caked his clothes and boots. Beside him, Sir Martyn, a bandage wrapped tightly around his ribs, held a bright lantern.

The iron-bound doors to the sanctuary lay smoldering inside the narthex. He ran his hand along the cratered doorjamb. Craggy pits marked the location of each hinge and the anchorage for the timber used to bar the door. At least the archway above his head had held.

Four soldiers caught by the dærganfae spell remained where they fell, their bodies twisted at odd angles. In the nave, two nuns sprawled in a pool of blood.

Roger shook his head. They'd expected an attack by the Sha'iry, prepared for it. The only condition was that Ambrose couldn't know. She had to be alone for her vigil.

Camber had positioned a score of soldiers inside the cathedral, and Jongar had an equal number outside. It hadn't been enough. A few well-aimed spells, and the dærganfae cut through them like chaff.

Dærganfae attacking Daventry Cathedral! It seemed inconceivable.

Most of the north transept lay under a mountain of rubble. While the first attack had targeted the front door, the second focused on the flying buttresses at the corner of the transept and nave. The buttresses and supporting piers had crumbled, toppling arches and roof over the crypt entrance. Like falling dominos, the collapse spread to the opposing piers, tearing apart portions of the exterior wall.

Frantic shouts and a heart-stopping groan from the building seized Roger's attention. The last of the north transept crashed down with a thunderous boom that rocked the cathedral. Chunks of masonry fell atop the already buried entrance to the crypt. An army of carpenters worked feverishly to brace the sanctuary walls with ropes and temporary shoring, their hastily built scaffolds lit like a Yuletide tree.

"Did you find anything?" asked Cerdic.

"Nothing we didn't already know," replied Roger. "Phaedrus, Archbishop Letizia, and the rest of the priests are tending to the wounded and dead across the street in the cloister. Jongar and his men are still searching the surrounding area, but they haven't found any signs of Sha'iry or dærganfae so far."

While they talked, Camber climbed the mountain of rubble. Covered in a thick layer of plaster dust, he began throwing chunks of debris into the nearest aisle.

"Camber, you need to wait," Roger called, pointing to the shored buttress. It seemed to teeter with every breath they took despite the carpenters' efforts. "You don't want to bring that down."

"Ambrosia's down there," he croaked, as he strained under the weight of a hefty piece of stone. Cerdic joined him, and together they dumped it in a waiting wheelbarrow. They both looked as if they had been dragged behind a galloping horse.

In addition to Camber's soldiers positioned at the entrances and various windows around the cathedral, Roger, Camber, and the four knights had guarded the only entrance to the crypt. Behind them, a ramp checkered with bluestone and slate tiles had passed through corbeled archways cut through the flying buttresses before curving into the undercroft. After the first explosion, Sir Baldwin and Derrick took half the men down into the crypt, thinking The Archer might use magic to gain access to Ambrose.

Roger swore. The Archer had used magic alright. He blew up the church, dropping a ton of stone on them. All things considered, Roger felt lucky to be alive. Six of Camber's men hadn't made it. They still lay buried.

"I don't understand why The Archer destroyed the entrance," Sir Julius said, returning with another wheelbarrow. "I mean, now no one can get to her."

"Who knows what was in that fae's head?" Camber replied.

"There may be a way through!" Sir Cerdic called, shoving aside a piece of cornice. He stood near the peak of the mound, a dark hole at his feet. They climbed up, and Sir Martyn raised his lantern, giving everyone a good look inside.

"Maybe," Roger said, scratching his chin, "but none of you are going to fit."

"I'll go," Camber volunteered.

Roger raised one eyebrow and studied the other man speculatively. "Were you a mountaineer in your previous life?"

"What? No. I was... a highwayman."

Roger shook his head. "Then you don't have the proper training to climb in there. Hand me that light." Kneeling, he peered down into the jagged shaft. A musty current of air wafted out. "It might go all the way through," he mused.

Overhead, one of the ropes snapped and the looming buttress gave an ominous rumble. Men scurried about, shouting for more rope and wood.

"We should probably wait," Sir Julius said.

"We'll be here all day if we wait for the carpenters to say it's safe," Camber griped.

"I hope I don't regret this," Roger muttered, giving his belt and pair of long daggers to Cerdic. In return, the knight handed him the end of a coiled rope.

While Roger prepared, Sir Julius acquired a handheld candle lantern from one of the carpenters. It looked like a perforated beer stein with a conical top. "Good luck," he said.

Cerdic gripped Roger's arm. "Yank three times to let us know you live. If we don't hear from you, we're pulling you out — or coming in after you."

"Got it." Slithering like a snake, Roger bellycrawled down the hole. The rope knotted about his waist played out as he took off at an angle. Careful to avoid random glass shards, he passed through a window frame, under a heavy timber beam, then squeezed by a leering gargoyle head. He tried to remember all the architectural terms, but many escaped him. Capitals, dripstones, gablets, pieces of tracery — they all surrounded him in a jumble.

Behind him, the rope bent and twisted so much Roger lost all hope anyone would be able to pull him out if he did get stuck. Setting his lamp on a sill, he tugged the rope three times in quick succession.

Rewarded with a faint tug at the other end, he let out a brief sigh. At least he had a backtrail through this maze of debris.

The shaft opened, and he adjusted his position. Now standing, he used crockets for hand and footholds as he climbed down an inverted pinnacle.

Suddenly his world lurched, and the spire rolled. Still clutching the lantern, he wrapped his arms and legs around the carved surface like a cat on a swaying tree trunk. Chunks of stone cascaded down around him. The rope about his waist became taut and rode up his torso, snagging him under the armpits. He let go the lantern. It clanged as it bounced down the pinnacle, and the light snuffed out, enveloping him in stygian darkness.

Ducking his head, Roger reached for the knife in his boot — he had no desire to be ground into paste or to be left dangling in the dark. Fighting to hang on to the pinnacle, he sawed on the taught rope. Faster than he expected, the rope popped, releasing the tension, and the frayed end slid past him.

Once the mound of debris settled, he took stock of his situation. Going up was probably not an option. Swallowing his panic, he felt his way down the spire. With each slow, methodical step, he felt around in the closest debris, hoping to locate the lantern. He stopped when the toe of his boot landed on a flat surface.

Crouching, he groped for the lantern and found it half-buried in the rubble. He sighed with relief and retrieved flint and steel from a pocket hidden inside his sleeve. After a few strikes, candlelight flared. He wanted to shout for joy.

Not two feet away, the pinnacle's finial gouged the tiled ramp like a spearhead. Roger worked his way around the spire and crockets. Ahead of him, irregular pieces of debris blocked the lower ramp and created a honeycomb of tunnels. The air from each felt stagnant, and he didn't know which to pick.

Taking the candle out of the tin lantern, he held it before each one. Three of them in a tight cluster caused the tiny flame to flicker. Crawling into the largest, he followed the obstacle course until it ended at the base of a corbeled arch.

Deep, jagged cracks dominated the masonry foundations supporting the buttress high overhead. He stepped over the contiguous piles of mortar dust and crushed brick that ran from one side of the ramp to the other, hoping the remaining brickwork above his head would hold.

Roger continued down the checkered ramp, lantern in one hand and knife in the other. With only the candle to light his way, he trod cautiously and listened for signs of movement. At the bottom of the ramp, shadows shifted and slid over evenly spaced columns that supported ribbed vaults. Affixed to massive octagonal pillars, bronze wall sconces with curved arms held a pair of unlit candles.

Aligned with the cathedral transept, sarcophagi filled the spaces between columns. Except for the ones that held couples, most were about three feet wide by seven feet long by three feet high, and each held a thick stone lid and an elaborate stone effigy. From their number, it seemed every Carolingian monarch and their spouse had been interred here.

There was no telling the age of the undercroft. Some said it predated York and they had built the cathedral over it. All Roger knew for certain was that The Archer had somehow managed to get inside.

Taking a moment to get oriented, Roger spied Derrick's body sprawled across a recumbent effigy, cold and lifeless. A ragged gash ran across his chest.

Distant, flickering light cast a dim glow on several more bodies. Hoping to find survivors, he headed toward it.

Sir Baldwin lay flat on his back, still clutching his bloodied sword. Rushing to him, Roger noticed the black-fletched arrow protruding from the knight's throat. Dead soldiers surrounded him, some with puncture wounds, others with long slashes. The Archer must have retrieved his arrows — all but the one.

Roger knelt beside the knight and closed Sir Baldwin's eyes. The older knight's death would be a blow to Sir Cerdic. Despite Roger's training in the Brotherhood of Rooks — Gallowen's elite cadre of spies — to not become attached to his assignments, Roger had developed a friendship with the paladin. Angry over the pain inflicted on his new friend, Roger swore that The Archer was going to pay for this day.

Lighting the wall sconces as he went, he followed the ebb and flow of the battle. Roger found eight soldiers in total, plus Derrick and Sir Baldwin, but no dærganfae. No Ambrose.

He checked the prie-dieu, tipped it over, and looked

under the tilted shelf and kneeler. He lifted the wheel-cross off its hangar and felt along the wall for a hidden catch. Nothing.

Turning to the nearby sarcophagi, he found one with the lid slid off to the side. It was directly across from the prayer bench and bore cracks that gave furtive glimpses of the interior. Inside, someone had scattered the remains of the ancient occupant. He dug in the corner where most of the bones lay in a pile and found a dusty piece of white cloth — part of Ambrose's vigil robe.

More cracks ran along the bottom of the sarcophagus, but no matter how long he stared at them, none gave him any indication where she had gone. He was faced with the real possibility the dærganfae had taken her. Roger frowned. The Archer never took prisoners.

Something crashed onto the crypt floor, sending up a cloud of dust. Light streamed down, and voices echoed off the stone.

Roger raced to the apex of one of the vaults where a knotted rope dangled from an octagonal hole centered in the ceiling. Camber was the first one down, followed by Sir Cerdic and Sir Julius.

"You look healthy for a dead man," Sir Cerdic said, clapping him on the back. "We thought for sure we'd lost you. It took the priests forever to tell us there was another entrance. Too bad we had to smash the labyrinth medallion." His smile faded when he took in the bodies scattered about the crypt.

"Cerdic, Camber, I'm sorry," Roger said.

"Where's Ambrosia?" demanded Camber.

"I don't know," Roger replied. He led them to Derrick first, where Sir Cerdic and Sir Julius both said a funeral blessing. Then he moved to Sir Baldwin.

Kneeling, Sir Cerdic bowed his head and placed a hand on the knight's forehead. "Requiescat in pace, amicus meus."

"What do we do now?" Sir Julius asked, emotion adding a quiver to his words. "Sir Baldwin's dead, the Queen... Sir, the dærganfae never —"

Sir Cerdic surged to his feet and grabbed the young knight by the shoulders, stopping his words. "First, we're not going to panic. The Queen is not here, therefore she is not dead."

"Yes, sir."

"I want you to climb back up and put guards in the sanctuary. No one — and I mean *no one* — is to come down here."

"Yes, sir," Sir Julius replied with a nod. Sir Cerdic watched him as he ran off with a purpose and shinnied up the rope.

"Did you check everywhere? She's got to be here somewhere," Camber said. The normally cocky wolf seemed paralyzed.

"Yes, I was very thorough." Roger held up the bit of Ambrose's vigil robe. "Camber, she's not here. From what I can tell, it looks like The Archer and his fae have her."

CHAPTER 10
TWO COINS

March 13, 1969 C.E.

8:00 am

When the light faded, Ambrose kept her eyes squeezed shut and tensed, waiting for the dærganfae's death blow. She clutched the silver coin in her hands, afraid to let it go.

A songbird trilled overhead.

She cracked open one eye. A dusty grey slab hovered an arm's length above her face. Confused, Ambrose raised her head and studied her surroundings. She lay on cold, hard-packed dirt. Past her feet, the slab ended, allowing standing room between it and a pair of narrow wooden doors. Daylight shimmered around their edges and revealed long cracks at the vault corners. The cool brick walls to her left and right and the one near her head made her feel like she'd been tucked away on a merchant's shelf.

Must not be top shelf material.

Scooting out, she climbed to her feet, but dizziness overtook her. One hand on the stone shelf, Ambrose fell back to her knees. When her head finally stopped spinning, she spotted another silver coin half buried in the dirt where she had lain — the same size and shape as the one in her hand.

Ambrose picked it up and gripped the two coins, not sure of their significance. Somehow, they had helped her escape the dærganfae.

She was inside a cramped vault with a barrel ceiling. Built to house four coffins, it now stood empty. Pushing open the doors, she stepped outside.

Bright sunlight hit her like a physical force. She jerked her head, letting her hair spill over her eyes. Wiping away her tears with a grimy fist, she focused on the arched brickwork and the crumbling parge coat. Marble letters set within the gable read, RECEIVING TOMB.

The coins had brought her to an expansive garden cemetery with ornate mausoleums, tall obelisks, and statuary. Bearded oaks with sprawling branches shrouded well-trod paths that wound between gravestones and meandered past the marsh-laden shores of a tidal creek. Beyond the marsh, a grey river sparkled.

"Hey! You're not supposed to go inside. If they catch you, they'll kick you out," someone called.

Squinting, Ambrose turned toward the voice. A slender woman with golden-brown hair reclined on a weathered stone sarcophagus. She wore a blue dress with a bright floral pattern and held a thick book one-handed. Tinted spectacles with large round lenses hid most of her face.

"And sitting on tombs *is* allowed?" Ambrose asked.

The woman closed her book, swung her feet around, and dropped into a pair of thong flats. "Not really, but the caretakers don't say anything." She tilted her head to one side. "You aren't from around here, are you?"

Ambrose stood stunned. Voices screamed at her from inside her head. They told her to run, hide, find a way back home.

Book in hand, the approaching woman carried herself with confidence. Older than Ambrose by several years, she wasn't a peasant, yet she wasn't royalty. Maybe she was one of the troubadours that roamed the countryside. It would explain her strange accent. However, she had a carefree air that drew Ambrose to her.

Taking off her glasses, the woman regarded her with sapphire-colored eyes. They widened in alarm. "What happened to you?"

Ambrose looked down at her white robe covered in dirt, cobwebs, and grave dust. The garment had been her grandmother's. She swiped at it but only succeeded in smudging the fabric. Somewhere along the way she had ripped her sleeve and lost her sandals. Her bare feet were grimy.

"Oh, honey," the woman said, brushing away dirt from her hair.

Emotions boiling over, the young queen flung herself into the stranger's arms and wept. Thoughts of her aunt and uncle, the screams of her family in the hallway, and Sir Baldwin's death in the crypt fed the despair welling inside her. Her gut twisted when she realized she could still taste dærganfae blood.

Ambrose had tried to stay strong, to be the queen

Camber wanted. Now, she felt like a little child. If only she could wake from this terrible nightmare.

She let the woman lead her away from the river. They followed a circuitous path to a four-wheeled, metal chariot parked on the side of a dirt road.

Trimmed in shiny steel, the seafoam green and white machine was longer in the front than the rear and lacked any sharp edges. Near the middle rose a pilot's cabin, enclosed with crystal clear glass windows affixed to a hard white roof. Ambrose had never seen anything like it.

In the distance, another, larger four-wheeled chariot bounced down the road with a guttural hum, propelled by an unseen force.

"Where am I?" Ambrose asked, her eyes growing wider. Sunlight reflected off the curved tops of white silos towering north of the cemetery. Heart pounding, Ambrose tried to breathe through her nose. The world began to spin, and the woman held on to her until it passed.

"I need to get you to a hospital." The stranger opened the door and guided her to a pale fabric bench seat for two. On the opposite side, what looked to be a small ship's wheel projected from an elaborate control panel.

"No. I don't need a healer," Ambrose replied. "Give me a moment to catch my breath."

Ambrose sat down even as the woman reached around her and collected paper wrappers from the floorboard. Dropping them on the tiny rear seat along with her book, she said, "Sorry about that. I wasn't expecting company."

The woman sat on her haunches and said, "Okay, let's start with something simple. What's your name?"

"Ambrose," she mumbled.

"Nice to meet you, Ambrose. My name is Bryony, but my friends call me Brie. Second question: where do you live? I can give you a ride home if you want."

"York."

"That's a long way from Charleston. How did you get here?"

It was an easy question, but Ambrose knew there was no easy answer.

Rising, Brie put her hands on her hips. "You escaped from juvey, didn't you?"

Ambrose gave her a questioning look. "Juvey? No. I

don't even know what that is."

"Tell me something. Otherwise, I'm getting the police."

"You won't believe me."

"Try me."

Ambrose opened her hand, revealing the two silver coins. "These brought me here."

"What?"

"Two men attacked me, and somehow these coins saved my life. I don't know how or why, but here I am."

Brie picked one up by the edge, using her thumb and forefinger. The coin was roughly an inch and a half in diameter. Illegible inscriptions surrounded a crusader cross that divided the center into four parts. Worn lions and castles diagonally opposite one another filled the quadrants. On the obverse were two pillars over waves. The other coin was identical. Every worn surface, irregularity, and symbol matched exactly.

Ambrose stared at the twin coins. She remembered clutching the coin in her hand just before the golden flash.

"Here," Ambrose said, handing Brie the other coin. "You keep them. I don't want them anymore."

Brie tried to give them back, but Ambrose folded her arms, refusing to even look at them.

"Did you steal these coins?" Brie asked, accusingly.

"No, I didn't steal them. I found them," Ambrose replied testily. "Actually, they found me."

"And two men attacked you."

"Yes."

"But these coins saved you. The coins *brought* you here."

"Yes."

"From the other end of the state?"

The question hung in the air. Ambrose turned to face Brie and said, "State? No, York is in the center of the Kingdom of Carolingias."

"Kingdom? Wait... do you mean you're from Great Britain?"

"No. I told you. I'm from Carolingias."

Brie worried at her lower lip as she took a nervous step away from Ambrose.

"I knew you wouldn't believe me."

"It's not that. What you describe sounds more like a bad acid trip. I really should take you to the hospital."

"Give me one of the coins," Ambrose said, holding out her hand. Brie dropped it in her palm. "Go stand under that tree and place your coin on top of that gravestone."

"What're you gonna to do?"

"You'll see."

Ambrose could tell Brie thought she was crazy, but to her credit, she took her coin and walked to the tree. After entering its canopy, she placed her coin on the marker, turned around, took a few steps back, and waited.

Sitting on the bench seat, Ambrose gave the silver coin in her hand a hard look. Fear clutched her heart. She wanted to prove herself, but she didn't know if the two coins would decide to take her back to York instead of performing a parlor trick.

Ambrose closed her eyes and clutched the coin in her fist. She felt the weight of Brie's eyes staring at her, and doubt wormed its way into her heart. Her thoughts drifted back to when she escaped the dærganfae. "Assayer, take me home," she said. Emotion swept through her as it did in the undercroft, but it didn't feel right. The coin wasn't responding. She cracked open an eye and relaxed her hand. The coin sat there, glinting in the sunlight.

"Was something supposed to happen?" Brie asked.

"I was trying to get them to reopen the portal. Show you I'm not lying," Ambrose replied. She rose, holding the coin between her thumb and forefinger, and shook it vigorously.

"What are you doing? That's not how magic works," Brie said.

"How would you know?"

"I read books," Brie replied. "Here. Let me try." She picked the coin up off the marker and studied the engravings. In a commanding voice, she said, "Assayer, take me to the other coin."

Ambrose gasped when the coin flashed, and Brie suddenly appeared not two feet from her.

"How?" Ambrose asked.

"I don't know," Brie answered, her face filled with wonder. "It just pulled me into it." She gave the coin to Ambrose. "Does that mean one of the coins in the Receiving Tomb?"

"Yes. I found it half-buried in the dirt."

"I wonder how long it's been there."

Ambrose shrugged. "How far did they bring me? What country is this?"

"You're in the United States."

Ambrose shook her head. "I've never heard of it. Is it on Parlatheas?"

"Parlatheas?" asked Brie. "Is that part of Europe?"

Realization dawned. If Ambrose hadn't been sitting, she would have collapsed. "This isn't Gaia, is it?"

"Gaia? I've never heard that name outside of my Greek mythology class."

"What do you call this world?" Ambrose asked in a tiny voice.

Brie tilted her head quizzically. "This world? Oh my..." Her voice trailed off, and her eyes grew wide. When she finally found her voice, she said, "You're on planet Earth, but a lot of the books I read refer to it as Terra."

One hand beside her left knee and the other between the seat and the door, Ambrose held onto the fabric bench of the chariot with a death grip. Wind rushed in from the open window, blowing her hair across her face.

"Sorry about that," Brie said. "You can close the window if you want, but it'll get hot in here."

They passed through an open wrought-iron gate supported by white pillars. Crossing the intersection, Brie shifted a lever on the steering column, and the engine's hum deepened. At the end of the road, she shifted the lever again. The chariot slowed to a complete stop. The way clear, the engine's hum grew louder as she turned the cabin's wheel to the left. Following Brie's direction, the chariot accelerated onto Meeting Street.

Ambrose gaped at the clapboard houses packed close together under the shadow of a sprawling, serpentine bridge. Larger than anything she had ever seen, the bridge seemed to stretch forever.

Another chariot charged straight toward them, and Ambrose gripped her seat tighter as it came closer. She cast a fearful glance at the woman beside her, then back at the road and noticed the painted marks delineating lanes. As the other vehicle roared past, she realized Brie had been talking to her the whole time.

"My dad fixed her up for me. She's a '58 Metropolitan.

Eleven years old. She's not much, but at least she gets me around town. I wanted a Mustang or a Cougar, but my dad said, *if you want a real car, get a real job.*" Her voice dropped as she imitated her father's tone.

Ambrose relaxed a little and settled into the seat.

"I guess I should be happy my car doesn't have torpedoes on it. You see, my dad works at the Naval Yard. I'm studying anthropology at the College of Charleston. Maybe get a job at the museum. If all goes well, I should graduate this time next year."

Turning right, the little car whizzed down Huger Street and traveled under the sprawling bridge. On the opposite side, short trees draped in bearded moss lined the road. Ambrose fought the lethargy gripping her. The drone of the engine and Brie's voice worked against her, and she stared out the window with heavy-lidded eyes.

The car lurched to a stop, waking Ambrose with a start.

"We're here," Brie said, rolling up her window with a hand crank. Ambrose found a similar lever on her side and did the same.

"My mom's home, so we'll have to be quick," Brie said. "Once we get you cleaned up, I'll let you meet her, but we need to get our story straight."

"Our story?"

"We can't tell my family you're from another world," Brie said.

"Why?"

"My parents are..." Brie sighed. "They're very *normal*. If we tell them the truth, they'll think you're crazy, and my father would probably call the police."

Ambrose shivered. "What do you think we should say?"

Brie chewed her lip for a moment, then grinned. "We'll say you're a Mennonite. It'll explain why you're unfamiliar with technology and modern ways."

"Mennonite," Ambrose said slowly. "Are they a clerical order?"

"Not quite," Brie said with a smile. "Come on. Let's get you cleaned up, and then I'll tell you about them."

Ambrose stepped out of the car. Overlapping boughs covered in vibrant green leaves arched overhead. Shifting shadows played on the grey surface of the street as a cool sea breeze swept through the foliage. Nestled behind the trees, a row of quaint houses lined the righthand side.

"It's this way," Brie said.

Following a short concrete walk, they approached a one-and-a-half story, cross-gabled brick residence with a detached carriage house. A hedge of dark green shrubs with deep pink flowers hugged the house on either side of the front stoop. In the yard, an engraved wooden plaque read, "The Tylers."

Near the peak of the upper gable, a narrow window with lace curtains stared out toward the street. Underneath, red-brick steps led to an off-centered front door with a scalloped window. A few feet to the right of the door, white shutters flanked a rectangular picture frame window.

"Hey, Mom!" Brie called out as she entered. She ushered Ambrose across the living room and up narrow stairs. The whole house smelled of warm bread.

"Brie? What are you doing home?" answered a woman's voice from another part of the house.

"Go upstairs and wait for me," Brie whispered. "Mine's the room on the left. The bathroom is at the top of the stairs."

Ambrose raced up the steps. The second floor was bigger than it appeared from the street. Her new friend's bedroom was unlike anything she'd ever seen. Colorful images of bards in outlandish costumes covered the wall space between two lace-curtained windows. Multi-colored books filled shelves flanking a narrow bed and spilled out onto the hardwood floor. A pile of shoes lay in a corner. Hanging on the wall were several gold medals embossed with archers in various poses.

"Mom, I hope you don't mind, but I brought a friend over," Brie said from downstairs.

"A friend? From college? It's not a boy, is it?"

"No, Mom."

"Well, where is she? I'd like to meet her."

"You will. She fell and got dirty. I sent her upstairs to get cleaned up. If it's okay, I told her she could borrow some of my clothes."

Leaving Brie's room, Ambrose found the *bathroom*. Glossy black and white tiles checkered the floor. Tiny animal images covered the walls, drawn on some type of paper. Tucked in the corner was a white tub opposite a porcelain sink and short table. A louvered door led to the water closet. Above the sink, a mirrored metal cabinet reflected a filthy teenage girl with scratches down her cheek and dark circles around her eyes. Like her vigil robe, she felt torn and out of place.

Light bloomed inside a round half-dome affixed to the ceiling. Startled, Ambrose turned from the mirror and found Brie in the doorway, bearing a bright red, short-sleeved shirt and a pair of blue shorts with a thin white belt. Laying them on the table, Brie said, "I hope these fit."

Ambrose stared at the scandalous garments. "You... you expect me to wear those?"

"What's wrong with them?"

"I'd be practically naked!"

Brie pursed her lips and took in the long robe Ambrose wore. "*Hm*. Would you prefer pants, or a dress?"

"A dress, I suppose," Ambrose said with a shrug.

"I think you'll be too hot in any of my winter dresses. You'd better come take a look and see what suits you."

Ambrose followed Brie to her bedroom closet. None of the brightly colored dresses inside extended below her knees. If only her mother could see them! She broke into a half-smile when she imagined wearing one in the Grand Hall during her coronation. "This one," she finally said, choosing a short-sleeved gown with clusters of multi-colored flowers.

Back in the bathroom, Brie opened a narrow door between the water closet and tub and pulled out a large towel and a small towel. "Here you go."

Taking them, Ambrose gave her a blank expression.

"You really aren't from around here, are you?"

Ambrose shook her head.

Brie turned on the water in the tub and tested the temperature with her fingers. "It takes a little while for the water to warm up." Pointing to each bottle, she said, "That's soap, that's the shampoo, and that's Cam's conditioner."

After checking the water one more time, Brie put a stopper in the drain and let the tub fill.

"Turn the knobs to the right to shut off the water when you have enough. Once you're done, come downstairs. I want you to meet my mom."

CHAPTER 11
SMOKY IMAGES

April 26, 4208 K.E.

10:00 am

*C*leaned up and mostly refreshed, Roger sat cross-legged in front of the open sarcophagus where he had found part of Ambrose's vigil robe. Bright wall sconces illuminated the crypt, but it still held its secrets like a miser.

After removing the last soldier's body from the undercroft, Cerdic and Camber had gone to meet with Archbishop Letizia. Carpenters had stabilized the flying buttresses, enabling workers to begin clearing away the mound of brick and stonework piled in the cathedral. Even now, he could hear their muffled shouts.

"Why would you take the Queen?" Roger asked aloud. "What are you planning, Archer? You've never shown interest in ransom before."

A shadow crossed the hole in the ceiling. The knotted rope jerked, and a pair worn leather shoes appeared, followed by legs in patched canvas pants. A bulky haversack obscured the climber's face, but Roger recognized the bag and his young assistant's clothing.

"Christopher, over here," Roger said as he rose. "What took you so long?"

"Sorry, sir, there's a crowd gathered outside, and it took some doing to get through them."

Taking the haversack off the young teen's shoulders, Roger asked, "Did you get everything?"

"Yes, sir. I cleaned out your room like you asked."

"Good. Now hold this," Roger said, handing Christopher the haversack. Opening it, he retrieved a hardened leather pouch with wide straps and set it aside. Reaching deeper, he came away with an ivory box.

"What are you going to do with this stuff?" asked Christopher.

"Alchemy, my boy, and, perhaps, a touch of magic," he replied with a sly wink.

Inside the pouch, six glass vials with different colored

powders sat in a cloth-lined wire tray. As he arranged the items, he asked, "Did your mother get the food?"

"Yes, sir. Thank you."

Roger knelt in front of the sarcophagus, took out a glass vial with dark blue powder, and sprinkled a thin line along the base.

"You see, most of the writing and artwork has worn away, and this one has no effigy. It happens with the older ones." Taking out another vial, this one with white crystals, he tapped the end a couple of times. "So, it helps to see who was interred. Gives you context."

Blue smoke wafted up, filling cracks and crevices in the sarcophagus walls. It spread inside the stone coffin and formed the smoky image of a man in funeral robes. Two coins lay over his eyes, each bearing the symbol of a cross with diagonally opposing lions and castles in each quadrant.

"Can you read the name and dates?" asked Roger as he studied the image inside the sarcophagus.

"Yes, sir. Captain Tho..." The boy paused, muttered to himself, "Thorn, maybe," then started again. "No, it's Captain Thomas Richards. I can't make out the date."

"Thomas Richards..." Roger mused. "He was one of the eight founders of Rowanoake, a city at the mouth of Hadlee Bay, north of the border between Gallowen and Carolingias." Roger turned to Christopher and explained, "Interestingly enough, during his latter years, he left Rowanoake, moved to York, and insinuated himself amongst the nobility. He didn't die of natural causes, though. Oh, no. The history books say he lost a duel with the Highlord and was beheaded in 4075. Even so, he was wealthy enough to be buried here, like a king."

Christopher peeked over the side of the sarcophagus.

"You see those coins?"

"Yes, sir."

Opening the ivory box, Roger took out a pair of whalebone spectacles joined by an iron rivet.

"Antonio de Erqueta, the esteemed assayer, made eight twins. Each founder of Rowanoake was given two identical silver reales to pay the ferryman. Rumor has it there was some kind of bond between the twins. Something that wouldn't allow them to be separated."

Roger adjusted the spectacles to fit his nose. His eyes

seemed to swim inside the thick lenses. Christopher hid his smile behind his hand, but he couldn't hide the mirth that lit his face.

"These things make me look silly," Roger said, "but they work." He mixed the contents of two vials and poured it into the sarcophagus. Indigo smoke billowed over the side and onto the floor.

Through the spectacles, Roger watched the smoke coalesce. Two vaporous shapes ran toward the sarcophagus of Lord Thomas: Dærganfae. One slid the semi-solid lid aside while the other reached inside, grabbing for something.

Roger leaned in closer as Ambrose's smoky image struggled with the fae. She held something pinched between her fingers. It flashed a bright light, amplified by the lenses, and Roger raised a hand to block it.

When his vision cleared, Ambrose had vanished. The shapes of the dærganfae loomed over the sarcophagus. A smile spread across his face when he realized the dærganfae didn't have her. She had escaped.

His smile faded as he mused, "She wasn't supposed to have anything with her, and all these tombs have been plundered."

Before the smoky dærganfae dissipated, one pulled something from the sarcophagus. It was small and flimsy like cloth or hair, but with only the smoke as a medium, it was hard to tell what it was.

Taking off the glasses, Roger stared down at the jumbled pile of bones. He motioned to Christopher and said, "Let's put Lord Thomas back together."

With a nod, Christopher placed the skull at one end while Roger took the larger bones and arranged them back in their original position as best he could.

"Any luck?" the Highlord asked, walking toward them.

Scrambling out of the stone coffin, Roger said, "Sire, I was wrong about the dærganfae taking her."

Christopher stood dumbstruck for a moment before dropping to a knee.

"Rise, son. You don't have to be formal down here." The Highlord ruffled the boy's hair and grave dust went everywhere. Turning to Roger, he asked, "What happened?"

"Queen Ambrose hid in Lord Thomas' tomb. The dærganfae found her and tried to pull her out, but she managed to escape them using magic. I think she opened a portal."

"A portal? Really?"

"Yes, sire."

"Then she could be anywhere," he said. He peered into the thickest shadows of the crypt as if willing her to be there.

"She left us this." Roger pulled part of Ambrose's vigil robe from his pouch.

The Highlord held it in his hands and rubbed it with his fingers. "Do you think The Archer knows where she is?"

"I would count on it."

"Then it's a race to see who gets to her first."

"I'm afraid so."

"No offense, but we need a mage."

"What about Angus?" Roger suggested.

Still looking at the cloth, the Highlord pursed his lips in thought. "No. I can't pull him away from what he's doing. It's just as important, maybe more so. Even though the plague's source is gone, it has left us handicapped."

"There's one other mage we can ask."

"We can't ask the Sorceress of Burgos."

"No, I meant the pilot of the *Morningstar*."

"Lahar's ship?" the Highlord said. "We can't ask that bunch of pirates for help, either. They'd as soon kidnap Ambrose and hold her for ransom than hand her over to us."

"Sire, Lahar will help us if Cerdic asks her."

"No," Cerdic said. He paced across the chancel floor, his armor clanking with each step.

"You have to," Roger said. "It's the only way to find Ambrose."

Cerdic flushed bright red, pulled Roger behind a silk screen, and whispered, "You don't know Lahar like I do, Roger. Her friendship with Phaedrus is the only reason she agreed to come to York."

"I don't believe that."

"Regardless, she will never agree to help the Queen."

"Yes, she will."

Cerdic turned toward the altar. The look on his face made it clear he was asking the Eternal Father for guidance.

Standing beside the knight, Roger said, "The Archer

probably knows where Ambrose went. If you don't do this, we've lost her."

There was a subtle shifting in the armor, and Cerdic's broad shoulders slumped. "Roger, I'm scared."

"Of what? *Lahar*? You've fought fiery demons and creatures that should only live in people's nightmares. How can you be afraid of her?"

"I don't know. I just am."

"Well, grow a backbone, paladin. We need Lahar and her mage."

Cerdic and Roger crossed the Square of King David, then passed through a narrow alley between rowhouses.

"Remember, do it like we practiced," Roger said as they walked.

Cerdic breathed heavily, and a bead of sweat crept down his temple. He swiped his cheek with the back of his hand and gave a sharp nod.

After several twists and turns, the pair entered a grassy field filled with tents surrounding a pavilion. They wound through a maze of ropes, tent pegs, and campfires. Outside the pavilion, a red, brown, and green plaid banner flapped from a tall pole. Emblazoned in the middle, a fist holding an argent file rose above the words, "Ferrum Forti". A pair of men in belted plaid kilts with two-handed swords strapped to their backs guarded the pavilion entrance.

"We're here to see Lahar," Cerdic said. His deep voice carried through the park, turning heads.

"*Ach,*" Jongar called through the tent flap. "Come in. Welcome ta mah humble abode."

The barbarian rose from his stool, a jeweled goblet in his hand. The vessel tilted slightly, and beer sloshed over the rim, adding another stain to the bearskin rug under his feet. A redhaired woman in an ankle-length tartan skirt found two more stools.

"Hae a seat."

"Is Lahar here?" Cerdic asked. His eyes scanned the lavish interior of the pavilion.

"She's behind you," Lahar purred in his ear. The knight jumped and half-turned, his face bright red, but Lahar moved with him, remaining close behind his shoulder. Taller than most elves, the top of her head came just above his nose.

"You like doing that, don't you?" Cerdic demanded.

Laying a hand on his armored shoulder, she slipped past him. The sound of her clothes brushing against his armor seemed to fill the air. "What can I do for the mighty knight of Carolingias?"

"We..." Cerdic started but stopped when Roger nudged him. "I need your help."

"Really?" Lahar said with a sly smile that lit up her dark eyes. She pressed her leather-clad chest against his armor. The blush that had been receding rushed back up his neck, turning his ears scarlet and his cheeks splotchy. Lahar laughed as she stepped back.

Jongar flopped back onto his stool and took a long drink from his goblet. "How's tha Queen?" he asked.

"She's missing," Roger said quietly.

Jumping to his feet, all traces of drunkenness gone, Jongar demanded, "Whit happened to her?"

"All we know for sure is that The Archer did not get her."

"Who's runnin' th' country?"

"Camber, with Phaedrus' help."

"Toothpick, eh," the barbarian said with an approving nod. "Whit about tha ambassadors?"

"Archbishop Letizia knows, and I'm sure the others will find out soon enough."

"What do you need from me?" Lahar asked.

Cerdic looked down at his feet. Taking a deep breath, he straightened and took her hand. "Can we talk in private?"

Her hard, angular features softened, and she said, "Of course. Jongar, may we use your room?"

"Aye," he said, waving toward a furred wall. "Ye have mah leave."

The three entered a small area partitioned off by multi-colored furs and exotic animal skins. An unlit oil lamp sat on the corner of a scarred table. Stabbed into the center, a single-edged knife with a bone handle stood at attention.

Whipping around, Lahar cocked her hip to one side and gave Roger a dark look. "You put Cerdic up to this didn't you? Spill it, thief."

Roger took out the torn fabric and handed it to Lahar.

"We need use of your pilot," said Cerdic.

"No."

Roger pointed to the fabric. "That's part of Ambrose's vigil robe. She's out there somewhere, frightened, and alone. Your Mister Cavendish is the only mage in York, possibly the country, that we can trust. He can find her."

"I don't give a damn about that little strumpet," Lahar said, practically throwing the fabric in Roger's face. "She gave up on this country, and you know it. She doesn't want to be Queen. For all we know, she ran away."

"She didn't run away," Roger said.

"I say let someone who wants to run this country, run it. It doesn't have to be a precious Battenberg. Let Jongar do it."

This elicited a choking fit from the other side of the furred wall, followed by a loud cough.

Lahar turned back to the thief and said, "Roger, you're not asking me to have my pilot cast a simple spell. You're asking for my crew and my ship to take you to her. To fight for her and, if necessary, die for her. This country will burn before that happens."

Roger threw his hands up and said, "I can't talk to her when she's like this. Cerdic, maybe you can talk some sense into her."

Cerdic watched Roger leave before turning back to Lahar. She stood with her hands on her hips, her normally pale skin flushed with anger.

He waited for some of her color to fade before he said, "You didn't have to do that."

"Are you going to lecture me on my manners now? Should I have offered him tea? Been all pleasant and smiles before kicking his arse out?"

Cerdic grinned as he imagined Lahar doing just that. "You've always been one to speak your mind," he said. "I don't think Roger's used to honest speech."

Lahar gave Cerdic a sidelong glance. "Maybe not, but that's no excuse. I've never marched to anyone else's drum, and you know it." The angry flush returned to Lahar's cheeks. "You tried to play with my emotions. Worse, you let Roger use you to manipulate me."

Cerdic spread his arms in an apologetic gesture and said, "But I wasn't playing." He stepped toward her.

Lahar's eyes narrowed. He knelt on one knee, his head bowed. "Please forgive me."

He felt a tug on his pauldron and climbed back to his feet. Lahar was inches from him.

"We really need your help."

"We?" She shifted a fraction closer.

"I need your help. I want my Queen back."

Lahar backed away. "Why do you want her to sit on the throne? She's not your Queen — she's Camber's concubine. Cerdic, you're better than her or that popinjay, Don Esteban. You're better than all of them. It should be you sitting on that throne."

Cerdic shook his head, his expression making it clear he couldn't believe Lahar would dare make such a suggestion. "It *has* to be a Battenberg."

"That's a load of pig manure and you know it. Every member of the Order of Carolingias prides themselves on being able to trace their lineage back to the first king of Carolingias. For as much as you might deny it now, you, Sir Martyn, and Sir Julius are of royal blood. Let The Archer kill Ambrose, I'll dispose of Don Esteban, and the throne is yours by right."

Shock turned to anger, and Cerdic growled, "That's treason."

"No, it's not. This isn't my country. I'm only being honest and practical."

"It has to be her," Cerdic said.

"Are you sure? What if you succeed, and she rips this country apart?"

"That is up to the Eternal Father, not me."

"Now you're hiding behind your religion. You don't know what's going to happen. You're reaching blindly for something that may not be there."

"That's called faith."

"You're impossible," Lahar said, folding her arms.

"Will you help us?" Cerdic asked.

Lahar grabbed him by the front of his armor, her face so close he felt her breath on his skin. "I'll do this for *you.* Not Roger, not Ambrose, not Carolingias — just you. But, Paladin, there's a price."

"Wh... what do you want?" Cerdic stammered.

She gazed into his eyes and said, "You'll owe me a favor."

Lahar backed away, and Cerdic found he could breathe again.

"Don't be surprised if Ambrose refuses to return," Lahar said as she exited the room. "King Cerdic... I like the sound of that."

CHAPTER 12
DINNER GUESTS

March 13, 1969 C.E.

4:45 pm

Sitting on Brie's bed, Ambrose thumbed through a thick hardback book. On the cover, white lettering proclaimed it to be, "A Pictorial Encyclopedia of American History – Years 1776 to 1966." Underneath, as she understood it, were the flags of fifty states displayed in a circle.

Brie lay beside her, arms behind her head, and her feet crossed. "How is it you can read or even understand the words I'm saying?"

"I don't know. Where I'm from, our language is called Glaxon. Our alphabet is almost the same as your English. There must be a common root — some common connection between this world and mine."

"Which one came first?" Brie asked.

"How should I know?"

"Come on, your mages had to know. What with all their magic and all."

"Mages don't know everything," Ambrose said. "Many of them died during our latest war."

"How horrible," Brie said, sitting up. "What happened?"

"Plague. War. Famine. The peasantry revolted against the aristocracy — Reds against the Bluebloods. Assassins killed my family, and Carolingias fell."

"Assassins? Ambrose, who is your family?"

"My uncle was the king," she whispered.

"So you... you're a princess! Holy cow, Ambrose. Does that mean you're in line to be Queen?"

Ambrose thought about Camber and the people in York. They had counted on her to hold it all together. "Not anymore. I left."

"When those men attacked you," Brie added.

"Yes, but I'm not going back. I'm not sure I could, even if I wanted to."

"It sounds amazing," Brie said wistfully. "I sure would love to see it one day."

"Amazing?" Ambrose said. "What about all the things you have here? Automobiles, trains, and these flying machines. What did you call them? Airplanes. *That's* what's amazing. And you can drive anywhere you want. No one tells you what to do or what to wear."

"Knights in shining armor, castles, and dragons," Brie countered. "Sorcerers who can create anything you want with a single word. Elves and dwarves joining you in your epic quest to save the world. You were so lucky."

A door slammed downstairs, and someone yelled, "Brie! Where are you?"

With an involuntary gasp, Brie shot out of bed and bolted down the stairs. "Cam, I'm so sorry. I completely forgot about picking you up."

"I waited for an hour."

Ambrose followed, then stopped midways on the steps. Downstairs, Brie stood before her sister, Cam. Where Brie was all flowers and bright colors, Cam was trim and neat in a pair of no-nonsense white pants and beige blouse. With her golden-brown hair wrapped in a pale blue scarf, she looked older than Brie.

"You skipped your classes again, didn't you? Wait 'til Father hears about this."

The wide picture frame window facing the street revealed a broad-shouldered man with close-cropped hair walking back to his car.

Brie grinned and said, "And Nate happened to be in the area."

Cam folder her arms and tried to look down on her sister. "Yes. Lucky for you." She spotted Ambrose on the stairs and her scowl morphed into surprise. Both sisters turned toward the stair.

"Ambrose, this is my twin sister, Camelia. Cam, this is Ambrose."

Ambrose straightened and glided down the stairs like her mother had taught her. She faced Cam and curtsied.

Stunned, Cam stood rooted in place.

"I'm afraid it was my fault," Ambrose said as she raised her head. "Brie has been helping me, and we lost track of the time."

"Isn't she a dear?" Mrs. Tyler said, exiting the kitchen. She wore a white apron over a knee length dress. The spicy aroma of garlic and herbs followed her through the dining room, teasing Ambrose with random whiffs.

"Helping you?" Cam asked.

"Yes, she's a Mennonite," Brie said with a sparkle in her eyes. "We learned a little about them at school. She's had very little contact with the outside world. So, I decided to educate her."

"We call it Rumspringa," Ambrose said, hoping she had pronounced it correctly. "It gives us a chance to see what we're missing. To dress English."

"And your family's okay with you hanging out around complete strangers?" Cam asked.

"Yes," Ambrose said. "It's expected. It's our rite of passage."

Cam frowned and said, "I could never do that."

"I could," Brie said.

"Oh Brie," Mrs. Tyler said, with a sad quiver in her voice.

"Mom, I didn't mean it like that. It's just that I crave adventure — something that will never happen if I stay here in Charleston. I want to see the world."

"The world is what you make it, Brie," said Cam. "Remember Jeremiah 29:7. 'Seek the prosperity of the city to which I have sent you.'"

Brie scowled at her sister. "First Corinthians, 7:21, Cam. 'If you can gain your freedom, do so.' I intend to live a life of freedom."

"That isn't what that verse means, and you know it!" Cam shouted.

"Girls!" Mrs. Tyler admonished. "Don't fight, especially not in front of company."

Ambrose felt as if she'd stumbled upon an old argument. While Mrs. Tyler lectured her daughters, she gazed about the living room, admiring the plump cushioned green couch and matching chairs. However, instead of facing the room's center, they all faced toward a wood paneled box with one side made entirely of smoky glass. It sat on a short table with stubby conical legs. An oil painting of a white heron hunting in the marsh hung on the wall behind it.

"Ambrose, I hope you like spaghetti," Mrs. Tyler said.

"I've never had spaghetti," Ambrose replied, carefully enunciating the strange word, "but it smells delicious."

Mrs. Tyler gave their guest a radiant smile. "I'm glad you

think so. Mr. Tyler should be home any minute now. Brie, why don't you and Ambrose help finish making dinner? Cam, did you want to invite Nathan?"

"Yes, ma'am. If that's okay with everyone," Cam said, looking at Ambrose.

Ambrose gave the sister a quick nod. "That's fine with..." Cam didn't wait for her to finish before dashing off to the kitchen.

"Nate lives around the corner," Brie whispered to Ambrose as they followed. "He's a policeman. They've been dating for almost five years. He proposed this past Christmas. The wedding is next year, after Cam graduates."

"He's a fine man," Mrs. Tyler said behind them. "A lot like your father."

"I bet he doesn't smell of diesel when he comes home," Brie said, wrinkling her nose.

A dreamy smile matching the faraway look in her eyes, Cam talked into a glossy orange, handheld object tethered to a matching box mounted on the wall by a curly cord. Cam kept her voice low and turned away from them when they entered.

Mrs. Tyler pulled down a bowl from one of her cabinets and handed it to Brie. "You and Ambrose, go in the backyard and see if any of the strawberries are ripe."

Ambrose followed Brie outside through a screen door. Unlike the tree-covered front yard, the backyard was open to the sky. Recently cut, the grass tickled her feet as she walked to the leafy garden that fought for dominance with a cedar privacy fence.

Holding out the bowl, Ambrose knelt while Brie shifted the dark, heart-shaped leaves in search of red berries. Many were still green. She took her time, inspecting each plant.

"You have a nice family," Ambrose said.

"Thanks," Brie said as she pulled another ripe strawberry off a plant and dropped it into the bowl. "Wait until you meet my father."

As she said it, a car door slammed, and someone walked into the house.

"Should I be worried?" Ambrose asked, turning toward the noise.

"No. Come on. I think that's all we're going to get," Brie said taking the half-filled bowl.

Washing the fruit in the sink, Brie started when her mother said, "Brie! Ambrose! Your feet are filthy. Did y'all walk out to the garden barefoot? Go upstairs and get cleaned up. We'll eat as soon as your father gets out of the shower."

The two rushed out of the kitchen. Cam gave them a disapproving frown as she and Nate circled the dining table with ceramic plates and silverware.

Ambrose caught an acrid odor that wove through the smells coming from the kitchen. Her gut twisted as she thought about all those starving people in York, and here she was about to have a casual dinner with strangers.

Brie grabbed her by the wrist and said, "Come on. It won't take him long to get ready."

The two raced back down the stairs and huddled together at the door to the dining room. Everyone else, including Brie's father, stood at their chair, waiting.

Each place at the table had been meticulously set with a tented cloth napkin on a round plate and silverware set to one side, all on a frilly placemat. To the upper left of each setting, a clear glass held cubes of ice. At the center of the table, a large bowl of noodles covered in red meat sauce steamed. Another bowl held salad with tongs sticking from it. Beside it, a basket held cloth-wrapped sticks of bread.

Holding Ambrose back with a firm hand, Brie said, "Permission to enter, sir."

Tall and lanky, her father eyed them both with the same disapproving stare Cam had given them earlier. Except for his receding hairline that held streaks of grey in otherwise black hair, Ambrose could see traces of Brie and Cam in his features. Like Nate, he wore a white dress shirt and black tie.

"Permission granted," he replied, and the two hurried to their chairs.

Mr. Tyler took his seat and clasped his hands in front of him. Everyone followed suit, and he said a quick prayer.

Ambrose watched curiously as the family crossed themselves and said, "Amen," at the prayer's end. She caught sight of Mr. Tyler's arched eyebrow and quickly ducked her head, repeating the strange word.

Starting with the salad, Ambrose got lost with the flurry of passing dishes. All too quickly, she had a bowl with lettuce and tomato covered in some kind of orange-colored sauce, a plate of spaghetti with garlic bread, and a glass of *sweet* tea.

"So, Ambrose, where are you from?" Mr. Tyler asked.

"Oconee County, sir."

"Mildred says you're a Mennonite."

"Yes, sir," Ambrose replied. She hated lying to him, but she and Brie had come up with a story that they hoped would stand up to scrutiny.

"I met some Mennonites from the upstate. Nice people," Nate said.

"Tell us a little bit about yourself," Mr. Tyler said.

Ambrose raised her tea. The ice clinked in the glass as she took a swallow. Her taste buds practically screamed with joy as the cool liquid washed over them. Everyone at the table, including Brie's father, gave her an amused look.

"Sorry, this is the first time I've had iced tea."

"I'm sure you're experiencing a lot of firsts," Cam said.

"You have no idea," replied Ambrose. "Where I'm from, we don't have any of this. Horse and buggy is the extent of our technology."

"What about your family?" Mrs. Tyler asked.

"They died last year. The community has taken care of me."

"I'm sorry to hear that. I guess it's a good thing you have people you can count on," Mrs. Tyler said. "It does seem strange that they would let you wander so far from home, though. Especially with nothing but the clothes on your back."

"It's our custom."

"Seems dangerous to me," Nate said. "You know, I have a classmate from the academy that moved to the upstate. If you want, I can reach out to him. He can let your minister know you're safe."

"No," Ambrose said a little too quickly. "Don't do that. This is something I have to do alone."

"Well, not alone," Brie added. "You can still have help."

"That's right."

"What are your plans?" Mr. Tyler asked between bites.

Brie answered, "We were hoping she could stay here for a little while. At least for a few days."

Mr. Tyler put down his fork, and it clattered on the plate. "Mildred, what do you think?"

"Robert, I like her," she replied. "I think it will be fun to have a new person in the house. Plus, Brie really wants her to stay."

He scrutinized his daughter and said, "I don't want her hanging around your hippy-dippy friends."

"No, sir."

"And you both must adhere to the rules of this house. If I have to call you to the *Green Table*, she's back out on the street."

"Yes, sir."

Cam asked, "What about tomorrow?"

"She needs clothes. If it's okay, I was going to take her shopping and give her tour of the college campus."

After supper, Ambrose watched as Nate and Cam began clearing away the table and putting away the leftover food, what there was of it, in what the Tyler's called a refrigerator.

Approaching the double basin sink with the dirty dishes stacked neatly on one side, Mr. Tyler rolled up his sleeves and stuck his tie through a gap between the buttons of his shirt. He turned on the water, added soap, and let one of the bowls fill. Beside him, Mrs. Tyler prepared a wire rack. The two bumped hips and leaned into one another. It was a subtle familiarity that stemmed from their time together, and it had Ambrose thinking of Camber.

Brie pulled a fresh towel from the drawer and handed it to Ambrose. "You dry while I put them away."

Ambrose took the coarse cloth, unsure of her place in this assembly line.

"Your station's the dish rack," Brie said.

Mr. Tyler washed a plate and handed it to Mrs. Tyler, who rinsed it with hot water and placed it in the wire rack. The two repeated the process, quickly moving through the dirty dishes.

"Don't let them get backed up," Brie said, motioning to the dishes in the tray. "Dry them with the towel and hand them to me."

Picking one, Ambrose wiped it down and gave it to Brie. She developed a rhythm, and she thought about how everyone had a job, a responsibility. You could tell Mr. Tyler was the head of the house, but here in the kitchen, Mrs. Tyler took charge. It was on a much smaller scale, but a person could run a country this way.

The last plate slipped through Ambrose's fingers just as she was about to hand it off. It landed flat on the floor and broke with a loud crack.

"Ambrose! Watch what you're doing," Mr. Tyler said.

His voice came across gruff, and despite knowing his comment wasn't meant to be personal, fat tears streamed down her face. She looked down at the pie-shaped pieces, but there were too many. Embarrassed, she wanted to run away and hide.

Soft hands gripped her arms, and she found Mrs. Tyler staring at her. "Don't move. You may cut your feet."

Behind her, Brie began sweeping the floor with a broom. Kneeling, Cam had the dustpan ready.

Producing a handkerchief, Mrs. Tyler dabbed at the steady flow of tears. "It'll be alright. Accidents happen. Besides, that's what families are for."

Leading with her heart, Ambrose wrapped Mrs. Tyler in a tight hug and cried harder.

CHAPTER 13
FLIGHT OF THE MORNINGSTAR

April 26, 4208 K.E.

6:00 pm

*R*oger, Cerdic, and the Highlord followed a wide road down the hill. In the distance, the waters of the Isura River glimmered like fire in the sunset.

Swords at their sides, they wore tunic and breeches that blended with the few dockworkers who still had jobs. Of course, Cerdic balked at leaving his armor, but Roger had made it clear they couldn't draw attention to themselves.

Turning left, Roger ducked into a side alley between two warehouses. At the next street, he turned right and waited. No one seemed to be following them. Falling behind a group of stevedores, he aimed for a two-masted brigantine.

"Tell me again," Roger said. "How did you convince Lahar to help?"

Cerdic swallowed audibly.

The Highlord and Roger gave the knight a quick glance. His ears had turned scarlet.

"She said I'd owe her a favor."

"What kind of favor?" the Highlord asked.

"She didn't say."

"Well, what *did* she say?" asked Roger.

Cerdic swallowed again. "Something about me being King of Carolingias."

The Highlord and Roger stopped midstride, while Cerdic kept walking. They both hurried to catch up. When they did, Roger asked, "How's that again?"

"We didn't go into specifics," Cerdic mumbled.

"Uh-huh," Roger said.

"Should I be worried?" the Highlord asked.

"We should all be worried, Your Majesty," replied the knight.

Over sixty-five feet in length and a beam slightly under twenty feet wide, the brigantine seemed huge anchored in the sluggish river. Captured by webbed shrouds, the square-rigged foremast had three sets of yards. Behind it, the taller mainmast held a furled topsail and long boom with a tightly furled mainsail. A sailor used ratlines tied between the shrouds to climb to the crow's nest and relieve his shipmate. More sailors walked the main deck and aftcastle, preparing the ship for departure.

As Roger drew closer, he noticed the furled sails had an unusual coppery sheen. Mounted at each end of the yardarms, an unlit glass lantern encased a copper rod, topped with a metal torus, and set in a base of spiraled copper tubing. But the sails and lanterns weren't its most unusual feature. Rather than the natural browns and shining brass of typical ships, every inch of the masts, freeboard, and railings on the vessel were mottled shades of blue and grey.

At the prow of the ship, the robed figurehead of a muscular man, holding a bolt of copper lightning, peered ahead.

Shouts and curses drew the group's attention to the broad dock protruding into the water. Rugged men in tarry breeches hauled back on thick ropes wound through block and tackle and loaded cargo into an open hatch.

At the base of the gangplank, Roger yelled, "Permission to come aboard?"

A short, barrel-chested man, wearing a striped tunic over bright-colored pantaloons tucked into worn leather boots, doffed his tricorn hat in greeting. "Permission granted!"

As the three approached, he gave them a wide, toothy grin, only slightly hidden by his bushy beard and mustache, and held out his hand. "Evening to you, sirs. I'm Mister Smeyth, the quartermaster. The Cap'n and Mister Cavendish are already aboard, waiting for you."

After shaking their hands, he turned to a lad at his side. "Master Andel, show these gentlemen to the Cap'n's quarters."

"Aye, aye, sir," the cabin boy replied. "This way, gentlemen."

The three followed Master Andel past two rows of long, one-foot diameter, black-iron tubes set in wooden frames anchored to the deck. Each tube had a hole, no larger than an index finger, in the capped end that faced midship. The other end, shaped like the open mouth of a fierce dragon, aimed toward a closed porthole in the bulwark.

The boy stopped at the louvered entrance of the aft cabin and waited for the three men to catch up. To either side, steep ladders led to the quarterdeck where a high-backed chair, engraved with arcane symbols, sat behind and to the left of the spoked ship's wheel.

Pulling open the door, Master Andel said, "Captain, they're here."

Silhouetted against lead-paned windows, Lahar lounged in a chair with her glossy black boots propped on a scarred table. A wide-brimmed hat with a grey ostrich plume lay next to them. Though her manner appeared casual, Roger noticed her almond-shaped eyes never strayed far from the Highlord.

Off to one side, a thin man with deep-set eyes and long silvery grey hair rose from his chair. He wore loose britches tucked into brown leather boots and an open tunic. Vibrant-colored sigils painted every inch of his exposed skin, and Roger suspected that extended to his whole body.

His first sea mage, the man did not disappoint.

"Did you bring it?" Mister Cavendish asked when Master Andel closed the door.

Roger handed him the torn fabric from his pouch. "Will this work?"

"It should," Mister Cavendish replied, setting the cloth on the edge of the table.

Lahar dropped her feet and slowly backed away. "You're not going to mess up my desk, are you?" she asked.

"No, mum."

Turning to the three men, he said, "You do realize that I can't find Ambrose using this, but I can find the robe she wore."

"It's the best we can do," Roger said.

Closing his eyes, Mister Cavendish waved his hands over the fabric, and the smell of the briny sea flooded the room. "*Reperio indumentum,*" he whispered. Wind flowed through his hair as if he stood on deck. He brought out a compass and laid it on top of the fabric. A magical spark lit the cramped cabin, and the needle spun around and around.

He opened his eyes, and the needle continued to spin. With a frown, he closed his eyes and tried again... with the same results. "I can't find the robe," he said finally. "It's hidden from my sight."

"What could cause that?" Roger asked.

"The item may have been destroyed."

"What if it's not here on Gaia?" the Highlord suggested.

"What do you mean?" Mister Cavendish asked. "Where else could it be?"

The Highlord turned to Roger and said, "She hid in Lord Thomas' crypt. What if she found something?"

"Those tombs were plundered. I know. I searched them myself," replied Roger.

"But what if?" countered the Highlord.

Lahar leaned forward and asked, "What could she have found that would have taken her off Gaia?"

"Lord Thomas and the founders of Rowanoake weren't from here. They were from Terra, a world that mirrors ours. However, magic waned there, and technology prevailed."

"I'm not familiar with Terra," said Mr. Cavendish.

"Few are," the Highlord acknowledged. "Ambrose must have found something in Thomas' tomb."

"The twin coins!" Roger said, snapping his fingers. "But I saw both of them. They covered his eyes."

"He had them when he was first buried," the Highlord said. "But the coins are relics from another world. They belong in Terra, and items like that have a way of finding their way home."

"How do you know so much about Lord Thomas?" Mister Cavendish asked.

"Thomas and his captains helped me overthrow the tyrants of Tirna Livádia and establish Gallowen in the year 4054," the Highlord said. "I gave them their town charter for Rowanoake the next year — much to my regret."

Cerdic's brow creased as he worked out the math in his head. "Sir, that was over one hundred fifty years ago."

The Highlord shook his head ruefully. "Some days, it feels far longer."

"That's all well and good, but how are we supposed to find our way to Terra?" asked Lahar.

Instead of answering, the Highlord pulled a knife from his belt and raised his left hand over the desk. He sliced into the mound at the base of his thumb, letting several drops of blood fall onto the fabric before closing his fingers over the wound.

Cerdic reached for his hand. "Your Majesty, let me heal

that for you."

The Highlord waved him off, then wiped his hand and blade with a handkerchief. The wound had closed without a trace. "Try your spell now."

Mister Cavendish waited for Lahar's approval before turning back to the fabric. Again, he waved his hands and the smell of the sea washed over them. This time, the compass floated above the fabric, magic sparks dancing all about. The needle spun so fast it became a blur, and a magical sphere took shape around it. Inside, strange images of glass and brick buildings played across its surface.

The compass fell to the table when Mister Cavendish cried out, pain wracking his features. He grasped the table edge with both hands, trying to catch his breath.

"I know where her robe is," he gasped. "The Highlord was right."

"That means she's safe," Cerdic said. "I mean, no one can reach her there."

Roger shook his head and said, "The Archer knows, and I bet, like us, he's doing everything he can to find her."

"Mister Cavendish," Lahar said, "can you take us to her?"

"Aye, Cap'n."

"Good. Have Mister Smeyth ready the *Morningstar*. We leave tonight."

Cerdic stood aside to let the mage pass and made to follow.

"Where are you going?" Roger asked.

"If we're leaving tonight, I need to be properly outfitted," he replied, patting his clothes.

"No armor," the Highlord said.

Cerdic's face paled, and he looked as if he'd been struck. "Sir?"

"Where we're going," he said, "magic and your armor will draw unnecessary attention."

"Yes, Sir," Cerdic replied, the disappointment clear in his voice.

"You're from Terra, too," Lahar said. "Aren't you?"

"Let's just say, I have a long history there."

"What should we expect when we arrive?" Lahar asked.

"It's a world like ours: oceans to sail, land to walk, and air to breathe. However, they persecuted their sorcerers and witches, killed most of them, and scientists and engineers took over. If we go in there with flashy magic and suits of armor, their constabularies will hinder us. It's best if we don't attract attention to ourselves."

"Then how do we find her?" Roger asked.

"Mister Cavendish found her robe. We start there."

Lahar frowned. "What about my crew? My ship?"

"They'll have to stay out of sight."

"What about The Archer?" Cerdic asked. "Won't the dærganfae have to abide by the same limitations?"

"Maybe," the Highlord answered. "But I wouldn't count on it."

"I wouldn't count on it either," Roger agreed. "We have no way of knowing how they'll get there. Hell, we don't even know how they got behind us at the church or inside the palace."

"Why didn't you use your smoke from the crypt?" the Highlord asked. "Wouldn't that have told you?"

"I wish," Roger said. "We use the smoke's enchantment to find graverobbers. It only reacts with grave dust and has a limited area of affect."

Lahar grimaced and said, "I'm sure there's more in that crypt you can use. Scoop it up and sprinkle it around."

"You can't do that," Cerdic said. "Those are the Kings and Queens of Carolingias."

"Cerdic's right. Besides, it doesn't work that way," Roger replied. "The smoke is tied to both the grave dust and the tomb. Its best if the person was interred and allowed to decay naturally. The older they are, the stronger the bond and the better the picture. So, killing someone and burning their body to ashes would only give vague impressions as opposed to what we saw at Lord Thomas' tomb."

"You're no help," Lahar said.

An uncomfortable silence settled in the cabin. Outside, the quartermaster shouted an order, and it was answered by the metallic squeal of block and tackle.

"How long before we sail?" Roger asked.

"We'll be ready within the hour, but I'll wait until nightfall."

"Good. I'm going to town to get my pack."

"I'll come with you," the Highlord said.

"Me, too," Cerdic said.

Roger shook his head. "Stay here and help. We won't be

long."

Lahar narrowed her eyes at Roger and the Highlord. "You think I'll leave without you?" she accused.

"The thought crossed my mind," Roger said.

Lahar stabbed the air with her finger. "Let's get this straight, right here, right now. I agreed to help, and I will. You'll have your precious Ambrose — even if I have to tie her up and throw her in the damn brig."

Lahar leaned over the table. The bloodstained fabric still lay at the edge. Roger and the Highlord had left, leaving her alone with Cerdic.

"They don't trust me," Lahar said. "Even after all I've done."

"Maybe it's because of what you've done," Cerdic said. "No one really knows where your loyalties lie."

"Is this about me and Jongar?"

Cerdic's silence was answer enough for her.

"Do you remember us sitting around this very table before entering York? *'Let's steal back the country,'* Roger said. You, he, and Phaedrus insisted your plan hinged on me convincing Jongar to join our side. He turned. What more did you want?"

"Yes, we wanted Jongar, but we didn't want to lose you in the process."

Coming around the table, Lahar said, "You haven't lost me."

"What about Jongar?"

"What about him?"

Cerdic stared down at his feet. "You're always at his side. You stay in his camp, eat his food."

Lahar gently touched the paladin's chin and raised his eyes to meet hers. "My loyalties never changed. Not once."

From the quarterdeck, Roger watched sailors wearing fur-lined jackets unfurl the strange sails. They billowed and caught the wind with a taut snap like canvas, but emitted a soft chime as they moved, like distant bells. Curiosity got the better of him, and he reached up to touch the underside of the mainsail. Instead of being cloth, the sails were woven from fine strands of copper wire. He jerked his hand back when he felt a slight tingle in his fingers.

The *Morningstar* let the current of the Isura carry it downriver. As the sails bellied out, they gained speed and were soon out of sight of York.

Brilliant flashes of light blazed inside the lanterns at the ends of the yardarms. Inside them, forked lightning danced and cavorted about the copper rods, and an ozone fog wrapped itself about the hull. Roger felt a lurch, and the ship slowly lifted from the water.

Mister Cavendish sat in the high-backed chair near the ship's wheel, eyes rolled back into his head so only the whites showed. A tattoo on his upper chest glowed green, illuminating his left hand as it continued working the traveling spell. His right held the compass, the needle guiding the way. Wearing her wide-brimmed hat, Lahar stood with one hand on the ship's wheel.

Roger wondered what they would find in Terra. From what the Highlord described, it would be both wonderful and terrible. He glanced at the black-iron tubes. Same as here, he guessed.

The ship rose above a bank of clouds, and icy wind ripped through his tunic, eliciting a shiver. Stars dotted the evening sky, so crisp and clear they were almost painful to look upon.

"Shorten the mainsail, Mister Smeyth," Lahar ordered.

"Aye, aye, mum," the quartermaster replied from the main deck.

Lahar adjusted the wheel and the ship aimed toward a blue-green star that held constant. It grew brighter and brighter until all others seemed to fade away.

Standing next to Roger, the Highlord murmured, "Second to the right, and straight on 'til morning."

CHAPTER 14
AN SAIGHDEOIR

April 26, 4208 K.E.

11:00 pm

*M*oonlight illuminated the circle of menhirs connected by horizontal lintels. Dust clouds from the barren fields surrounding them floated in the air. A purplish glow appeared on the surface of the westernmost standing stone and out stepped The Archer. He scanned the area and found a Sha'iry in leather armor and a swallowtail vest waiting for him. The long hilt of the priest's two-handed sword cast a shadow over his bald head.

"Saighdeoir," the Sha'iry said with a slight bow.

"Anshu Jezra," The Archer said in Glaxon, returning the bow. "You requested my presence?"

Jezra faced the moon and said, "I must say that I'm disappointed. Not only did you let the Highlord's thief destroy the orb, but you also let the last Battenberg slip through your fingers."

"In all candor, Maa'kheru Bolezni underestimated the Order of Carolingias and the Highlord."

"Bolezni was a fool. He reaped what he sowed. Do not let his mistake be yours," Jezra snapped as he turned toward The Archer. "A Battenberg... alive. You said you had killed them all, every last one of that wretched family. It was she who united the Carolingians. It was she who they rallied around."

"My apologies, Anshu Jezra. We believed the girl was dead. Who could have known she hid within Camber's camp?"

"Don't make excuses. It appears everyone knew she lived; everyone except you. And here she survives another one of your attacks. Saighdeoir, if I didn't know better, I would think you wanted her to escape."

"If you doubt my loyalty—"

Jezra cut him off with a swipe of his hand. "Perhaps all is not lost. Despite the Highlord's sorcerer hiding the Shard of Ka'Sehkuur from our sight, there is still a way for us to win this war and for me to become Maa'kheru. You must capture the Carolingian Queen. She must live — at least for a little while longer."

"That is not part of our contract," The Archer replied, gripping the hilt of his sword. "We do not take prisoners. You know that."

"I don't care if it's in your contract or not." The Sha'iry turned back toward the moon. "Our contract was for you to kill all the Battenbergs. You failed."

The cleric's words left The Archer with a bitter taste in his mouth. Failure meant he and his team would forever be slaves of Sutekh, a *sclábhaí*. He knew it, and his dærganfae knew it. He glared at the Sha'iry, regretting he'd ever made this bargain with him. Now, he felt he was on borrowed time — at least until he could get his hands on the last Battenberg.

Coming back to the present, he asked, "Where do we find her?"

Jezra faced The Archer with a vicious smile. "She has fled to a remote realm called Terra."

"Terra," The Archer repeated. "It is an ancient place. Our people once traveled those lands, but the Secret Ways are now sealed."

"Not all of them," Jezra said, clenching his fist. "She is alone with none to protect her. I want her alive, Archer."

"You don't expect to use her to bargain for the Shard?" The Archer asked, unable to keep the incredulity from his voice. "The Highlord would never agree to that."

"I have communed with Sutekh. He has revealed the Highlord is going after her, personally. No, Archer, I do not plan to use her to bargain with the Highlord. I plan on you using her as bait."

"Anshu, if what you say is true, then Gaia is free of the Battenberg line as requested. To ensure it remains so, let me kill this girl who would be Queen. In less than a year's time, she and her family will be a distant memory," said The Archer. "Besides, going after the Highlord was never part of our deal."

"I'm changing the deal," the Sha'iry said with a feverish gleam in his eyes. "Now is our chance to rid Parlatheas of the Highlord, once and for all."

"It's a fool's quest. The Highlord cannot be killed."

"Yes, here on Gaia he is immortal, but Sutekh has shown me the way. On Terra, the Highlord will be like any other man. There, he will be vulnerable."

If there was any truth to dærganfae legends, the Highlord and his Lady had been a bastion against the forces of Sutekh for three millennia, if not more. There was a mystery about the two of them. No one knew where they hailed from or even their real names. The Archer could understand Jezra's fervor. "A new bargain, then. We will capture the Queen as you request."

Jezra tossed a buckskin pouch on the ground. A gold skeleton key poked out the open top. Encrusted with fiery diamonds, it glimmered and sparkled in the moonlight. "Use it to open the Ways. It will take you to the city where she is hidden."

The Archer ignored the key at his feet. "I want the last Battenberg and her knight," he said.

With a piercing stare, Jezra replied, "After you capture the Queen and assassinate the Highlord, you can do with them as you please. Your contract will be complete, and you and your team will be free."

CHAPTER 15
THE MARKET

March 14, 1969 C.E.

9:30 am

"That looks nice," Brie said when Ambrose pulled a blouse off the rack. Both in tie-dyed sundresses and white tennis shoes, they perused the wares of the only clothing vendor in the low timber shed. A cool morning breeze brought with it the smells of nearby restaurants preparing for the lunch-time crowd. Next to them, a middle-aged man in a straw hat arranged pastel-colored knick-knacks on a wooden table. Each had "CHARLESTON" written across the top in fancy script.

Four city blocks long, the open-air market housed over sixty merchant stalls. It was set up in two rows with local farmers lining the sides of the shed and displaying baskets full of produce. This time of year, most were wan, flavorless hot house versions of their in-season selves grown in the bright summer sun. However, a few were stocked with seasonal crops that looked to have been picked that morning.

Clusters of housewives of all shapes and sizes meandered past them, filling the market with laughter and constant chatter. Farther down the narrow building, hawkers competed for attention. Across from them, a dark-skinned woman, wearing a bright yellow dress, hunched in a metal folding chair and wove strands of sweetgrass together. The table in front of her held various sized baskets, some woven so tight, they could hold water.

Ambrose put the blouse back and pulled out another, reading the price tag. The paper money Brie loaned her was tucked inside a pocketbook. It was strange to not feel its weight. Back home, a money purse had a comforting heaviness and clinked when you walked. Of course, Brie had shown her their copper and silver coins. She had explained that the government had stopped using real silver five years ago and gold coins were for collectors — not for the general public.

Out of the corner of her eye, she spotted two fae in black

suits and fedoras walking toward her. Framed by long black hair, their pale faces held sharp angular features that sent a shiver down her spine. She felt the intensity of their gaze even though their eyes were hidden behind dark spectacles Brie had called *sunglasses*. Turning her head, she saw two more coming from the opposite direction.

Heart in her throat, she grabbed Brie's arm. "We must go. Now!" She shoved the rack of clothes into the central aisle and dove under the vendor table. Shouts from the crowd erupted as the fae charged.

Ducking under the lattice that hung from the eave, Ambrose and Brie leapt out the wide opening between brick columns and ran south, down Market Street toward where Brie had parked the car.

Another fae in a black suit stepped into their path. In his hand, he held a thin-bladed dagger. The two did an abrupt about-face and raced the other direction.

Screaming, hysterical women fled the market, driven forward like a herd of cattle by the four fae in black. They filled the street between the market and a row of one and two-story brick buildings with glass storefronts.

Fighting their way through the crowd, Ambrose heard Brie gasp, and she spun around. One of the fae must have lost his sunglasses in a scuffle. Silver, almond-shaped eyes swept the crowd, searching for them.

"This way," Brie said as she shot down State Street. Nearly yanking Ambrose's arm from its socket, Brie cut down an alley that doubled back at an angle. Surrounded by the odd miasma of biscuits and raw fish, they ran hand in hand. In the distance, sirens wailed.

From behind the corner of a building that advertised cold storage, the two watched the crowd thin. A sixth fae stalked the open market with a subtle grace that belied his violent intent. Taking something from his pocket, he held it up and turned until he faced them.

"Damn," Brie swore. "How did he spot us?"

"No time to figure it out," Ambrose replied. "Let's go."

Two more converged behind them.

"Who are they?" Brie asked, her eyes wide with fear. The fae closed in from all sides. Their steps were unhurried, confident they had them trapped.

"Dæ'rganfae," Ambrose whispered.

"What?"

"Dark elves."

"Elves? Really? I thought they made toys and stuff."

"Not these."

Rounding the corner at the far end of the market, a wailing police car raced down the street. Another screeched to a halt at the end of the market closest to them, blocking the intersection. A policeman wearing a dark blue uniform and silver badge sprang out of the passenger seat while his partner spoke on the radio.

Ambrose and Brie ran toward him, waving their arms. People spilled out of the shops lining the street. They shouted over each other, trying to tell the policeman what they saw. When Ambrose turned back toward the alley, the dærganfae had disappeared.

The two young women drifted along the edge of the growing crowd. At its center, the policeman pulled out a notebook.

"No, Officer, nothing was taken," Ambrose heard a merchant say.

"But they were after something," said an elderly woman. "That one with the dark glasses pushed me down." She pulled up her sundress and displayed a scraped knee.

"How many were there?" the police officer asked.

"I counted four in the market," a man said.

"That's not right. There were only two," the elderly lady said in a shrill voice.

"You're both wrong. There were at least six of them," said another woman, pushing her way to the front.

"Everyone! Please step back," the officer ordered. "I'll take your statements one at a time."

Ambrose scanned the crowd. She wasn't sure if it was some type of glamour, but no one seemed to be able to describe the dark elves. The only point of consensus was they wore black suits.

"Brie!"

She spun around and saw Nate jogging toward them. His patrol car sat behind him, the light on top still rotating. He looked sharp in his crisp uniform and peaked hat and carried himself with an air of authority.

With a cry of relief, Brie caught him in a tight hug. "I'm so glad you're here. Men in black suits chased us."

"Brie, calm down," he said, trying to disentangle himself. "Were y'all hurt?"

"No, we're fine," Brie said.

"Good. What happened?"

"We were shopping when these men in black suits seemed to come from nowhere. They had silver eyes, pasty white skin, and pointed ears like that guy on that tv show you watch."

Nate held up a hand, fingers splayed. "Slow down, Brie. You're not making any sense."

"I swear, Nate, those men chased us into the alley. I don't know what they would've done if you hadn't shown up."

"Take a deep breath," he replied. "You're safe now."

Brie let out a long sigh. "You sure got here quick. Was the mayor's wife shopping today?"

"No," Nate said with a short laugh. "The city gets upset when there's trouble at the market. I think they're planning to put this place on the Historic Register."

"Uh didn't see nobody," said a brawny police officer as he approached. "If dey was anyone here, dey gone now."

Ambrose took an involuntary step back. Well over six feet tall, the dark giant of a man had a broad nose set under sharp eyes. He gave her a wide smile that struck her as more intimidating than reassuring.

"Brie, Ambrose, this is my partner, Corporal Middleton," Nate said.

Nate's partner held out his large hand. "You ladies can call me Tee."

Unsure, Ambrose took the offered hand. Thick callouses covered his fingers and the pads of his palm. There was a power to his grip that went beyond the physical. She felt it course through her and tried to jerk away.

Without dropping his smile, Tee held her in place. His pitch-black eyes searched her face. She tried to look away, to look anywhere else, but his gaze trapped her like an insect in tree sap. Finally, he said, "Oonuh long way fum home, missy."

"Please, mister," Ambrose said, using her other hand to pull away. He let go and she retreated behind Brie, rubbing the palm of her hand down her dress.

"What in blazes, Tee?" Nate said, adjusting his hat.

"She been cussed," Tee said. "She should see a root

doctor tuh take off de root."

"A root doctor? Really?"

"Jis' because you don't believe, don't mean it ent real."

Nate's expression grew pained as he explained, "Brie, Ambrose, I'm sorry about this. Tee's family is from the sea islands."

Brie's eyes grew wide. "You're Gullah, aren't you?"

"Yaas, ma'am," answered Tee.

"I'd like to meet a real root doctor," Brie said.

Behind her, Ambrose frowned as she shook her head. "I don't think that's a good idea."

"I agree with Ambrose," said Nate. "Why don't y'all head home. Where did you park?"

Taking Brie to the side, Tee told her, "Yo friend needs help. Uh dark cloud folluh'n her."

"Do you know someone?"

Tee looked around, his face dour. With reluctance, he said, "Go to de county co'thouse. Find Doctor Wampus. Tell'em Tecumseh sent you." He held up a cautioning finger. "Jus' be careful. De Doctor folluh his own rules."

CHAPTER 16
DOCTOR WAMPUS

March 14, 1969 C.E.

10:00 am

*I*n the passenger seat of the Metropolitan, Ambrose chewed her bottom lip. "Brie, what's a root doctor?"

"A sort of healer who uses traditional medicines — herbs, poultices, that sort of thing, but some people believe they use magic. That they cast and remove curses, exorcise ghosts, and can tell the future."

"I don't want to see a root doctor."

"Come on, it'll be fun," Brie countered as they pulled onto East Bay Street and headed south.

"I don't think your idea of fun and mine are the same," Ambrose griped, staring out the window at the buildings and pedestrians.

"Yes, it is. You just don't know it yet," Brie replied with a quick grin.

"What kind of name is Doctor Wampus, anyway?"

"Maybe it's this root doctor's spirit animal. I think wampus is a Cherokee name for a kind of monster — maybe a panther — that roams the south. One of my teachers called it superstitious folklore nonsense, but we still hear rumors of them from time to time. I think there must be a grain of truth in there somewhere." Stopping to let a family cross the road, Brie turned to Ambrose and said, "Those dark elves..."

"Dærganfae."

"Whatever. Those men. Were they the same ones who attacked you?"

"Yes."

"Then, I think the question you *should* be asking is how did they find you?" A horn blew behind them, jolting Brie. She released the clutch and stepped on the gas, easing the car forward.

"How should I know?" Ambrose said. "Bad luck maybe."

"That's wishful thinking if I ever heard it. If they found you at the market, they can find you anywhere."

Ambrose let out a deep sigh. "I know."

"Hey, snap out of it! You're in real danger here."

"You think I don't know that? All I want is to be done with wars, magic, and everything else from Gaia."

"I get it. You're scared," Brie said, "but you're not alone."

"The dærganfae killed my entire family, and now they're trying to kill me," Ambrose said in a meek voice.

"Not if I can help it."

Glancing at Brie, Ambrose felt a swelling of affection. The feeling abruptly turned to fear when Brie cut the corner onto Broad Street, driving way too fast.

Hanging on to her seat, Ambrose gaped at an ornate two-story building, flying four flags from a raised entrance. With arched doors and windows, limestone cornices, and pediment, the colonial building held a quiet dignity. Ambrose wasn't sure if it was the architecture or the events that took place inside and around it that gave the building its character.

She whipped her head back around and faced a wide street flanked by granite curbs, bluestone sidewalks, and palm trees. Shoulder-to-shoulder, the sheer faces of limestone and brick multistory buildings stretched as far as the eye could see. Signs, hung from cast-iron brackets, dangled over the doorways.

"Do you think this Doctor Wampus can help me?" Ambrose asked.

"Maybe. The Gullah are as close as we get to a traditional African culture here in America. It's really an amalgamation of over a dozen West African tribes, blended together during the slave trade before the Civil War. Unlike the Creole, which has ties to Roman Catholicism and all their saints, Gullah is more Protestant based. Learned that in school."

"I read a little about the Civil War in your history books. The defeat of the South freed the slaves?"

"Yeah, but it's only been in the past fifteen years or so that there's been real changes in civil rights."

"What do you mean?"

"There have been all kinds of protests, speeches, and court cases. Congress passed the Civil Rights Act a few years ago outlawing discrimination, but we still have a long way to go before we're anywhere close to being governed by the ideals of peace and love. Don't get me wrong. The doors are slowly opening, but in this modern world we live in, it's still an uphill climb for anyone who's not a white male to break through those socio-economic barriers."

"You learned that at school, too?" Ambrose asked, trying to work her way around the unfamiliar words.

"Sorry. Yes. Take Tee, for example. He's only one of a handful of black police officers who work at the city. He's breaking through those barriers."

Brie pulled over onto the side of the road and parked the car. Turning to Ambrose, she said, "I'm not sure what to expect from Doctor Wampus, but I'm hoping he can remove your curse."

"I'm not cursed," Ambrose said.

"Well, take off your root then."

"I don't have that either, whatever it is."

"C'mon, Ambrose, you can't deny there's something going on with you. Those elves found you. Hopefully, Doctor Wampus can give you a charm or something to stop them from finding you again."

"Did it occur to you that it's not a spell? They found me because they know I don't belong here."

"What kind of talk is that? Of course, you belong here."

Ambrose stepped out onto the bluestone sidewalk and waited at an open wrought iron gate that guarded a shaded park with a granite obelisk at its center. Men and women with children in tow crisscrossed brick pavers to read the plaques on the various monuments.

"This way," Brie said.

Falling in with a group of men in suits and ties, the two headed toward the busy intersection of Meeting and Broad Streets. The buildings on three of the corners represented different levels of government — Federal, State, and City — while the building on the fourth corner was a white church with stained-glass windows and a steepled bell tower.

"The Four Corners of Law," Brie said. "You can get married, taxed, divorced, and go to jail all at the same intersection. Maybe even on the same day."

Ambrose took it all in with wide-eyed wonder. She began to feel underdressed as she watched people entering the three-story courthouse. Trimmed in white marble, the front along Broad Street, with its grand columns and entablatures, bespoke authority that reminded her of Battenberg Palace. "Are you sure they'll let us inside?"

"Don't worry," Brie said with confidence.

At the crosswalk, a pinprick of pain blossomed inside Ambrose's gut. Clutching her stomach, she scanned the crowd and spotted a long-haired dærganfae gliding toward her, gaze unwavering. Cold sweat dotted her forehead as spasms shook her, and she doubled over. It felt like snakes twisted inside her body.

Brie grabbed her by the upper arm and helped her cross the street. "Are you alright?"

"*Ugh.* No, let's get inside." Jaw clenched, Ambrose let Brie guide her. The moment the heavy door closed behind them, the pain eased, and Ambrose took a deep shuddering breath.

Lit by bright overhead lights, the lobby's stark white walls glowed. Wide, polished wood stairs led up to an open balcony above, where the images of stern men in a variety of clothing styles stared down from gilded frames. Brie followed a line of men across the glossy marble floor to the guard desk. At their approach, the deputy met them with a slight frown. Younger than Nate, he had short-cropped hair and serious eyes. At some point, his nose had been broken and not set properly, resulting in a somewhat squashed and pugnacious appearance.

"Excuse me, Officer," Brie said.

"Yes, ma'am."

"Can you tell us what's on the docket today?"

Still frowning, the deputy said, "Are you here to spectate? Judge Gregory doesn't take kindly to protestors."

"It's for a class project," Brie replied in a sweet voice.

"*Ohh,*" Ambrose groaned. Outside the door, the dærganfae stared at her through the crowd.

"Ma'am, are you alright?"

"She overexerted herself," Brie said quickly. "May I take her in the ladies' room and rinse her face before we go into the courtroom?"

The deputy nodded and pointed to a door partially hidden behind men in dark suits. "There's one case today: the Solomon case. It's that way. The women's restroom is over there. You'll have to hurry. Counsel wrapped up their opening arguments a few moments ago, and the judge called for a recess. Once they start calling witnesses, they'll reclose the doors."

"Thank you," Brie said, flashing him a smile.

Ambrose clutched the edges of a sink and rested her forehead against its cool, porcelain lip. Beside her at the next sink, Brie held a wad of paper towels beneath a stream of water.

"What's wrong?" Brie asked. After turning off the faucet, she wrung out the towels and spread them over the back of Ambrose's neck.

"Stomachache. Like everything is writhing inside. It hit me all of a sudden."

"Do you think you got yourself all worked up about seeing a root doctor?"

"No, it's not that," Ambrose said, wiping her face. "There was a dærganfae outside the door."

"They can cast spells on people? Do they know what we're doing?"

"At this point, anything's possible."

"Well, let's see if we can find this Doctor Wampus."

Taking a seat at the back of the gallery, Ambrose and Brie were amongst a dozen or so spectators. There was no sign of the doctor, but the bailiff at the doors hadn't closed them yet.

Oak paneling wrapped the room and reflected the recessed lights, giving it a natural glow. Partitioned off by low walls, each space within the courtroom had a distinctive function. Speaking in a low murmur, Brie pointed to each area and explained their purpose.

Near the front along the side, sixteen seats for the jury remained empty. On the other side of the room opposite the jury box, a single witness fidgeted in his seat. Raised above everyone else, the judge's bench stood empty at the head of the courtroom. Between the judge and jury was the witness stand. On the judge's other side, at a desk bearing a machine Brie called a stenograph, sat a mousy lady with thick glasses. Bailiffs stood at each of the far corners of the room, flanking the judge's bench.

Studying the courtroom's layout, Ambrose began to understand the architecture. Like the throne room in Battenberg, everything was positioned to establish the proper hierarchy.

The prosecuting team of attorneys sat at their table, facing the judge's bench. One shuffled through files of papers, pulling out some and replacing others. When finished, he tapped them on the tabletop, straightening them, and gave them to a distinguished gentleman with short, silver hair. Parted off-center on the left, his hair swept toward the back like feathers.

At the table across a central aisle, the single counsel for the defense sat beside a young black man, Solomon Wright. The accused wore a new suit that hung loose about his emaciated frame. He stared down at his rawboned hands, clasped together as if in prayer.

Ambrose had overheard the men outside talking about how he had beat up a white kid. Assault and battery with intent to kill, they'd said. The family of the kid who had been beaten sat at the front of the gallery, behind the prosecution team.

As the bailiff moved to close the courtroom doors, a tall, gaunt man with pitch black skin pushed them back. Slightly hunched, he wore a white linen suit with a lavender silk tie and dark purple glasses. Taking off his short-brimmed straw hat with its lavender band, he sat down in the gallery two rows behind the defense's table. Mumbling words that Ambrose couldn't make out, he took out a bit of crooked root and stuck it in his mouth.

Led by another bailiff, the jurors filed into the room from a rear door that blended with the wood paneling. The bailiff moved to a predetermined spot and announced, "All rise! The Court of the Second Judicial Circuit, Criminal Division, is now in session, the honorable Judge Richard Gregory presiding."

The judge entered from a different rear door and settled in as everyone retook their seats.

"The State versus Solomon Wright is reconvened. Is the prosecution ready?"

The attorney with silver hair stood up, said, "Yes, Your Honor," and sat back down.

"Is the defense ready?"

"Yes, Your Honor."

"Prosecution, you may call your first witness."

The distinguished prosecutor approached the judge's bench. "Thank you, Your Honor. I call to the stand, Mr.

Jessie Daniels."

The witness was about the same age as Solomon. For all Ambrose knew, they could have been friends as easily as rivals. She watched with interest as the witness glanced at the man in the white suit before placing his hand on the bible. Out of the corner of her eye, the man leaned back in his seat and started chewing the root. His eyes never left those of the youth.

"Do you swear to tell the truth, the whole truth, and nothing but the truth, so help you God?"

"I do."

As soon as the witness sat down, it was apparent to Ambrose something wasn't right. He began to fidget in his chair and sweat beaded on his forehead. The prosecutor opened his mouth to ask his first question. The fidgets turned into full convulsions. Crying out, the witness spasmed and fell sideways out of his chair. His eyes rolled back into his head and foamy froth bubbled from his mouth.

A woman on the jury shot to her feet and screamed.

The man in the white suit kept his eyes fixed on the witness, who jerked and writhed on the floor as if possessed.

"Someone, call an ambulance!" the judge shouted, leaning over his bench.

Two bailiffs rushed forward and knelt beside the witness, trying to grab hold of him. They wrestled him out the rear door, slamming it shut as they went.

"Well," the judge said, resuming his seat. "Tom?"

The prosecutor ran his fingers through his silver hair, staring at the door.

"Tom?"

"Uh, Your Honor," he replied, "I must ask for a continuance. He was our only witness."

"Granted," the judge said. Turning to the defense attorney, he said, "Mr. Carver, you and Tom meet me in my chambers after this to reschedule."

"Yes, sir."

Striking the bench with his gavel, the judge announced, "Court is adjourned."

"All rise!" a Bailiff said.

As the judge left the courtroom, Brie turned to Ambrose and nodded toward the man in the white suit, who started to leave. "That must be him."

Before the root doctor reached the door, Tom, the silver-haired prosecutor, called out, "Doctor Wampus!" He crossed the courtroom with long strides and threw open the gate separating the gallery from the rest of the courtroom. The attorney looked as if he were going to punch the doctor.

Hat in hand, Doctor Wampus turned to face him. "Mr. Battles, we meet a'gen unduh unfortunate circumstances." His deep voice seemed to resonate, as if it carried the weight of his power.

"You won't get away with this," the attorney said, jabbing the air with his index finger.

"Suh, even if oonuh could prove dat I done enyting to yo witness, dey is no law in Sout' Ca'lina a'gens me g'ven dem de root."

The attorney turned three shades of red before getting control of himself. "We'll see, Doctor. We'll see." With that, he stomped back down the aisle to rejoin his team.

The doctor gave the retreating attorney a chilly grin before donning his hat and leaving the courtroom.

"Doctor Wampus!" Brie called as she ran to catch up to the man in the white suit. "Doctor Wampus, we need your help. Tecumseh sent us."

He stopped and a wide, bright-toothed smile spread over his face. "Tecumseh, huh. Wuh kin I do fuh two purty young gals?"

Ambrose felt as though his sharp gaze pierced her innermost thoughts. A feeling of fear swept over her. She wanted to go back into the courtroom. She cast a quick glance at Brie, but her friend didn't seem to notice.

"Someone's put a root on my friend," Brie said. "Can you take it off?"

"Leh we go outside tuh discuss yo situation."

Ambrose grabbed Brie's arm and shook her head. "We can't. They're out there."

"Who?" the doctor asked, taking off his purple glasses. His cobalt blue eyes narrowed at her with a keen interest.

Ambrose stood mesmerized.

"Who?" the doctor repeated.

"Men," Brie said in a low voice. "They're trying to hurt us."

Replacing his glasses, the doctor turned to leave.

"We're serious. There really are men trying to hurt us."

"What fuh all two of ya come tuh me? Dis is sump'n' fuh de police."

"She can't go to the police. They wouldn't understand," Brie said. "Please. At least take a look at her."

He eyed both of them for a moment, as if weighing them, and then said, "Tecumseh, eh?"

"Yes, sir."

"Awright, leh we see wuh Tecumseh done brung me."

They followed him to a deserted corner of the lobby where he took off his purple glasses and slid them into his jacket pocket. He took Ambrose by the hands and trapped her with his unblinking gaze. His blue eyes bore into hers. She felt the snakes inside her squirm in response and tasted her breakfast trying to come back up.

Fighting the nausea that threatened to overwhelm her, she wrenched back, and the doctor let go. Ambrose barely noticed that Brie held her. Spotting the door to the women's restroom, she jerked away and raced across the lobby, dashing inside. Pressure erupted in her gut, and bile rose in the back of her throat.

The root doctor appeared beside her, holding her head over a toilet in one of the stalls. Tears streamed from her eyes as she felt the snakes crawl their way up her throat.

He whispered in her ear, but his words weren't meant for her. Ambrose fought against him, but his grip held her like a vice. Dry heaves shook her. She wanted to throw up. No matter the cost, she had to get the snakes out.

Just as she thought she couldn't take it anymore, the feeling faded, and she slowly relaxed. Damp with sweat, she stared at the empty toilet bowl unsure what had happened.

Brie knelt beside her. "Are you okay?"

Wiping her mouth with the back of her hand, she took stock of her body. Whatever it had been was gone. She stood on weak knees, leaning heavily on Brie. Doctor Wampus washed his hands at the sink and pulled a paper towel out of the metal bin.

"What did you do?" Brie asked him.

"I tu'n'um back," he replied.

"Turned what back?" Brie asked.

Instead of answering, he took a bit of root from a burlap pouch and placed it under Ambrose's tongue. It tasted bitter, and she wanted to spit it out.

"Don' swalluhr'um. De conjuh-man won't t'row no spell 'pon oonuh as long as ya hold'em in yo mout'."

Ambrose felt her strength return. She gently pushed away from Brie, taking tentative steps.

She exited the restroom and saw a crowd had gathered at the entrance to the courthouse. Along the side of the lobby, women rested on several benches, fanning themselves. Overwhelmed by the amount of chatter, Ambrose pushed her way to the door with Brie behind her.

Outside, a writhing mass of slimy, black snakes lay in a pile. A bloody trail led to a pale figure in a black suit sprawled on the sidewalk. Dead, the fae's jaw gaped at an unnatural angle.

CHAPTER 17
WE'RE PRIVATEERS

March 14, 1969 C.E.

10:00 am

Sprawled on the quarterdeck, Roger woke with a start. Sharp pain lanced through his skull, and the burning heat of the morning sun beat down on his back. The scent of brine competed with the pine pitch used to seal the deck boards. Overhead, a seagull cried, and he felt the brigantine rise and fall as it rode a passing sea swell. Surrounded by a boundless ocean, the *Morningstar's* copper sails drooped and hung limp.

He cast about with bleary eyes and discovered the Highlord and Cerdic, like him, fighting to get to their feet. Lahar leaned against the ship's wheel with her head bowed. Behind her, Mister Cavendish slumped in the pilot's chair, unconscious but alive. A trail of dried blood ran from his nose and left eye. Roger winced when he noticed the burnt sigil on the mage's chest and the singed skin around it.

The last thing he remembered was Lahar giving the orders to make the *jump* — and jump they did. The whole ship had risen as if riding a tidal wave. He'd gripped the rail and braced himself. Others did the same.

All except Captain Lahar. She stood at the wheel, her wide-brimmed hat with its grey ostrich plume rippling in the cosmic winds.

His heart in his throat, they plummeted into the wave's trough, but they never hit bottom. Instead, they flew faster and faster until the stars in the sky became bright white lines.

Suddenly, the whole universe seemed to bear down on them. The ship reeled, and its seams began to pull apart. His long silver hair streaming as if in a hurricane, Mister Cavendish had shouted out a spell, and a magical glow from the pilot's chair enveloped the *Morningstar*, holding her and her crew together.

Roger had blacked out, not knowing if they had broken through the barrier. Wiping sleep from his eyes, he rose to one knee. The world swam, and he fought back the rising queasiness.

"Everyone! On yer feet!" Mister Smeyth yelled from the main deck. "This isn't the King's ship. Here, we work for our meal!"

"Quartermaster, can we do that again?" asked a scrawny youth with a shock of blonde hair.

"Mister Cryst, glad to see you're enjoying yourself. Make yourself useful and take the crow's nest."

"Aye, aye," the young man replied, dashing up the ratlines.

"Has anyone seen my spleen?" asked a brawny sailor with a bald head and bare chest. "I puked it up around here somewhere." Laughter broke out in the crowd around him.

"Stow that language, Mister Bekke," Mister Smeyth said. "Miss O'Brien! Where's Miss O'Brien?"

"The gunny's below, sir, checking the fireboxes," someone responded.

"Mister Marston, when O'Brien finishes, get all hands on deck."

"Makes you wonder how many times they've done this," the Highlord said as he watched the crew.

Roger raised a hand. "Help me up, Sire."

Once on his feet, the sharp pain became a dull ache and the cobwebs inside his head began to clear. The Highlord stood beside him, favoring his left arm. A dark green and yellow bruise spotted his wrist.

"Sir, you're hurt."

"I'm fine. Don't worry about me. Worry about Mister Cavendish," the Highlord said, with a nod of his chin.

Laying a hand on the pilot's shoulder, Cerdic whispered a healing prayer. A dim blue glow emanated from the sea mage, and a feeling of peace mingled with the sea breeze. Lahar watched from the other side of the pilot's chair, the magical compass gripped tight in her hand. Lines of concern creased her forehead.

When Cerdic finished, he straightened and said, "That's all I can do for him. The rest is up to the Eternal Father."

"Cerdic, you must do better," said Lahar. "We need him awake."

"I healed his physical injuries. They are not the problem.

He channeled a lot of magic bringing us here, and it took a toll. He needs rest."

Turning to the youth at the edge of the quarterdeck, Lahar said, "Master Andel, prepare Mister Cavendish's cabin."

"Aye, aye, Captain."

At the head of the ship's ladder, Mister Smeyth made room for the youth.

"Cap'n, everyone's accounted for. A few minor injuries amongst the lot, but otherwise the ship is ready and willing."

"Have a couple of men carry Mister Cavendish to his quarters."

"Yes, mum." The quartermaster stared openly at the pilot. His eyes mirrored the concern they all felt. Not only was the pilot a longtime member of the crew; he was their only way home.

Lahar straightened her hat and scanned the horizon. "Everyone is to remain at general quarters until we find out where we are, Mr. Smeyth."

With a curt nod, he replied, "Yes, mum."

Turning to the Highlord, Lahar said, "Majesty, get that wrist looked after. Mister Huff, our surgeon, works wonders with his poultices."

"Shouldn't that have healed by now?" Roger asked, thinking back to the Highlord's knife wound that had closed without the aid of a priest.

The Highlord gazed up at the azure skies and took a deep breath. There was a bittersweet edge to his voice that seemed out of place when he said, "I'm home."

"How long has it been since you've been to Terra?" Roger asked.

"Seventy years on Gaia, but time flows differently here, so it's hard to say."

"Let me see your wrist," Cerdic said, stepping forward.

"Healing prayers don't work on me."

"Perhaps on Gaia, but here you appear to be like the rest of us," Cerdic said, gently taking his arm and murmuring a prayer.

Blue light reflected in the Highlord's eyes. At first, they remained stoic but slowly softened as the bruise faded. A smile crossed his face as he wiggled his fingers and rotated his wrist. "Nice work, paladin."

"It wasn't me, Sir."

Lahar gently leaned into Cerdic and said, "Don't get him started. He'll start preaching."

Cerdic turned away. "I'll check on Mister Cavendish and see if your Mister Huff needs help with the crew."

A confused expression crossed Lahar's face as she watched him disappear down the ladder.

"Boat off the port bow!" Mister Cryst cried out from the crow's nest.

Lahar grabbed a spyglass from a nearby stand and aimed it in the direction Mister Cryst pointed. Roger shaded his eyes with his hand and spied a glint on the horizon.

"Have the ship come about, Mister Smeyth!" she said and held out her spyglass.

Roger took it and zoomed in on a white vessel with a blue stripe down the hull. Forty feet long, it had a wide foredeck, an open wheelhouse, and walkaround side decks lined by bright mahogany toe-rails. With neither sails nor oars, it cut through the swells and headed straight towards them.

Shaded by a bright blue canvas, a deeply tanned, bare-chested man leaned over the rail of the flybridge and gestured. Next to him, a man wearing a peeked cap with a gold trimmed visor sat in the captain's chair.

A stiff breeze swept across the deck as the *Morningstar* swung around. The copper sails billowed with a snap and came to life.

"Cap'n! She's comin' fast!" Mister Cryst yelled.

"Mister Mitchell!" Lahar called.

A gangly man with leathery skin and a gold nipple ring scrambled up from below. "Here, Cap'n." Starting at his left shoulder, the tattoo of a voluptuous woman with four arms extended the length of his torso. He drew closer, and it became clear just how well-endowed she was.

"Take the chair, Mister Mitchell."

"Yes, mum," he said with a nod. He leapt up the ship's ladder and sat down.

Lahar gave the wheel a gradual turn, adjusting their course. White caps broke against the hull and threw scintillating sprays of water into the air.

"Um, Lahar," Roger said, gaze darting between the two vessels.

"Not now," she replied.

"But you're... you're heading straight toward her. Shouldn't we run away?"

"Roger, the *Morningstar* doesn't run.   We face our problems head-on."

"Besides, we're pira—," Mister Mitchell started.

Lahar cleared her throat and gave the Highlord a pointed look.

"Right. We're privateers — 'cause anything else would be wrong."

"There's no profit in it," Roger said under his breath, answering his own question.

"Exactly," Lahar said with a fierce grin. The captain of the *Morningstar* adjusted the wheel and the nose of the ship aimed to the right of the approaching vessel.

"Port side, Miss O'Brien! Prepare the long nines!"

"Aye, Cap'n," an ebony woman responded as she crossed the deck to the iron dragon closest to the quarterdeck. Long dreadlocks cascaded down her back, bound by a scarf of red silk. She wore a simple leather vest and a kilt of green and blue plaid. In her hand, she carried a delicate ruby rod marked with nine thin white lines. She shoved it into the rear of the tube with the flat of her hand. Glowing red lines swirled about the iron shaft, coming together at the iron cap.

Down the length of the main deck, five other iron dragons along the port side flared to life. Beside them, crewmen tugged on short ropes, opening the portholes in sequence.

"We're ready to shoot our load!" O'Brien said. White teeth gleamed in the sunlight as she knelt with her right hand on the tube and her left hand in the air. "Give the word."

"Mister Mitchell?" Lahar asked.

The new pilot closed his eyes and whispered, "Aichmiró máti."

A pulse of power thrummed in the pit of Roger's stomach, adding to his fears. "Lahar, you can't attack that vessel."

"Mister Vaughn," she said with a hard edge to her voice, "there is one captain on this ship, and you aren't it."

"But..." Roger said, looking around. The Highlord maintained a neutral expression but stepped closer to Roger.

Eyes pinched shut and brow furrowed with concentration, Mister Mitchell said, "Their boat is powered by some strange device. I detect no magic."

"Weapons?" Lahar asked.

"Not that I can see."

"They'll probably have a small handheld weapon or two on board," the Highlord said. "The bigger worry is their radio — it uses waves in the air to talk to other radios. As long as we don't do anything suspicious, we should be safe. If we threaten them, they'll call the authorities, who will try to detain us."

"There are four people aboard that boat," Mister Mitchell said. "They're curious about our ship. No signs of hostility."

"Can you see these radio waves, Mister Mitchell?" Lahar asked.

"No, mum."

"They're invisible," the Highlord said.

Nodding toward the other vessel, Lahar asked, "Do they pose a danger to this ship? I need an answer, now."

"No," the Highlord said.

"No, mum. I don't think so," Mister Mitchell replied.

"Suggestions."

Thinking quickly, Roger said, "I say let them be curious. Maybe even invite them on board."

After considering it, Lahar gave Roger a grim smile. "Miss O'Brien! Stand down." Turning to the quartermaster, she said, "Mister Smeyth, have Mister Marston ready with the rigging. If this goes bad, we'll need all the wind we can muster."

The smaller vessel drew closer, and Roger spotted two attractive women on the foredeck, one blonde, the other brunette. Lying on their stomachs, feet swaying in the air, they watched the brigantine through the bars of a metal rail. They each wore nothing more than two tiny swaths of brightly colored fabric, revealing a shocking amount of bare flesh.

Lahar adjusted the wheel, and the ship slowed even more. A shrill whistle erupted on the main deck followed by bouts of laughter.

"Miss O'Brien, don't get distracted!" the quartermaster shouted at the gunny, who stood beside her iron dragon.

"But they're such tempting morsels, sir, presented practically on a platter." Miss O'Brien's reply evoked more laughter and several salacious remarks.

"We're here to parley."

"That's exactly what I plan to do, Mister Smeyth." She motioned with her arm and said, "Go down there and parley with those two women. Assist in foreign relations."

"You sure you can handle them?" Mister Bekke asked from the ratlines. A broad smile stretched across his face.

"I can handle them, alright," she said eyeing the two women.

"Both of you!" the quartermaster growled. "Back to it!"

The boat made a wide circle around them. Bright blue block letters across the stern proclaimed, "*NeverLand* Yonges Island, SC."

The Highlord chuckled. "An auspicious name. Here's to hoping they're friendly."

Letting Mister Mitchell take the wheel, Lahar approached the deck rail and called out, "Ahoy!"

Down on the main deck, the crew of the *Morningstar* worked at looking busy, all the while keeping one eye on the other craft.

The second circle tightened, and the vessel came up alongside them. Overshadowed by the sails, the flybridge was about the same height off the water as the main deck of the brigantine, giving everyone a clear view of the newcomers and vice versa.

"That's an amazin' tall ship!" the other captain replied with a drawl. He was a big-boned man with meaty hands and the hefty build of a fighter gone soft. A beige bandage braced his left knee. With one hand on the wheel, he gazed at them through mirrored spectacles. "I've never seen a blue one with copper sails."

Next to him was a middle-aged man with a hairy chest. Deep lines scored his face, giving him a perpetual frown. The two women had moved to the aft deck, where they waved at the burly men in the rigging.

Roger shook his head in dismay. *If they only knew.*

"She's a fine lady, that's for sure," Lahar responded, running her hand down the railing. "What about yours? I love the lines."

The captain beamed with pleasure and said, "It's a Chris-Craft Corinthian. Got her last month. With the weather being nice and all, thought we'd take her out for a run and see if the fish are biting."

"Is there a port nearby?" asked Lahar, glancing at the compass in her hand.

"Charleston's to the north of us. That's the closest one. Where are you out of? I don't see a flag or anything."

"Across the sea. We hit rough water last night and lost some of our rigging," replied Lahar. "Unfortunately, our flag went with it."

"Did you have any damage?" the other captain asked. "I can radio it in if you need help."

"Actually, we need a place to berth," Lahar said. "Does Charleston have a pier large enough to accommodate my ship?"

"I don't think so. Most everything there that size is for commercial traffic only, but my family owns a towing company with a deep-water pier. You can use it."

Lahar turned to the three men behind her and asked, "What do you think?"

The Highlord rubbed his chin. "I guess Southern hospitality's not dead."

"Southern what?" asked Lahar.

"I met a gentleman from this region, once. He used to say, 'there are no strangers, just friends we haven't met yet,'" the Highlord replied. "He was a good fighter, but politeness and hospitality were just as important to him. It appears that still holds true."

Roger laughed and said, "That, and who'd suspect us of being exactly what we are — a bunch of pirates. No offense, Lahar, but that boat can literally run circles around us."

"I know. That's what has me worried," Lahar said, eyeing the smaller vessel. "If a civilian craft can do that, what can their military ships do?"

"A lot," the Highlord answered. "The last time Britannia called me home, it was toward the end of a terrible world war that covered most of Terra. One that used technology to fight on land, sea, and in the air. Looking at that boat, they've come a long way since then."

"Cap'n, I recommend we take them up on this southern hospitality," Mister Mitchell said. "I'd like a closer look at this area before going after the Queen. Besides, it may give us the time we need for Mister Cavendish to recover."

Lahar took a deep breath before facing the *NeverLand*. "Captain, I accept your kind offer. If you lead the way, we'll follow."

CHAPTER 18
GOOFER DUST

March 14, 1969 C.E.

10:50 am

*B*ehind the wrought iron fence surrounding Washington Square, The Archer watched the crowd gathering across the street. Dressed in matching black suits, hats, and dark sunglasses, the five remaining dærganfae stood behind him. The wail of a siren pierced the air.

"Father, we don't know what happened," Aimsitheoir said. "Cailleach only meant to make her sick. Limit her movements."

"Cailleach got what she deserved," The Archer replied. "The same will happen to you, Aimsitheoir, if you kill the girl before it's time."

"I swear to you — we did not intend to kill her."

Fists clenched, The Archer turned on the younger fae and snarled, "What happened? The Queen cast a spell on her?"

Aimsitheoir bowed his head. "Yes, Saighdeoir."

"It's true," an older dærganfae said. Though similar to the rest, his translucent skin exposed tendons and faint blue veins that pulsed with each heartbeat.

Struggling to keep his tone respectful, The Archer said, "Saoi, that's not possible."

"Obviously, it is. She reflected Cailleach's curse," Saoi said.

"Not only did she reflect it, she returned it tenfold," added Aimsitheoir.

The police arrived and began dispersing the crowd. Soon after came a red and white, low-slung automobile with a whirling red light atop its extended cabin. Men in white jackets stepped out of the front, opened the wide door at the back, and slid out a wheeled stretcher.

The Archer swore when the men hoisted Cailleach's body. It wasn't the first time he had regretted working for the Dark One's priest. Squaring his shoulders, he put aside those thoughts. His dærganfae, his son, had all signed Jezra's contract. They had no choice.

Turning to Saoi and Aimsitheoir, he said, "Take the team. Follow the Queen like the reaper. Go where she goes, see what she sees. If an opportunity presents itself, take her, but do not kill her. Not yet. We await Gallowen's Highlord."

"Gadaí," The Archer said, "find us a place to hide the Queen. Someplace that can be defended. Someplace where we won't be bothered by these... humans."

"Yes, Saighdeoir," a short dærganfae replied. He bowed and his suit coat pulled back, revealing the hilts of his many daggers at his waist.

"Saighdeoir, what will you do?" Saoi asked.

"Retrieve Cailleach's body before those men dishonor it."

Ambrose and Brie hurried to catch up to Doctor Wampus. Heading east on Broad Street, they passed Washington Square and their parked car.

His white suit shimmered in the bright sunlight. Those on the sidewalk gave him a wide berth even as they cast furtive glances in his direction.

"Gal, what for oonuh folluh me?" he asked, rounding on the two girls.

"We need your help," Brie said.

"Uh awready helped yuh."

Desperation guiding her every move, Ambrose grabbed the doctor's sleeve and said, "Those fae know how to find me. They'll kill me."

Doctor Wampus grinned. His skin stretched tight against his skull, giving him a ghoulish appearance. "What's it worth tuh oonuh?"

Ambrose tilted her head to one side. "I don't understand."

"Uh don't work fuh free."

A grey cloud blotted out the sun, throwing a shadow over them. Brie and Ambrose dug in their pocketbooks and pulled out what cash they had.

He looked at it briefly and laughed. "Oonuh sho' hol'um cheap if tha little bit be all yuh offuh."

He was about to turn away when Ambrose said, "Here. It's all I have." She held out her hand. In her palm was the pair of silver reales.

"No, you can't give him those," Brie said. "They're what brought you here."

Doctor Wampus snatched up the coins and studied them. His purple glasses reflected the pillars and waves. Dropping them into his pocket, he said, "Folluh me."

They continued down the sidewalk and turned left onto Church Street. At a three-story building with a gravel parking lot, Doctor Wampus climbed a set of exterior metal stairs to the second floor. Above the door hung a simple wooden placard with a haint-blue hand, its fingers splayed. Centered in the palm was a single eye with a red iris.

Ambrose didn't know what to expect. Inside a quaint foyer, four-foot-high wainscot accented cream-colored plaster walls. In the corner between a velvet chair and leather couch, shallow wire shelves displayed thin books with garish pictures on the front. Behind the couch, an encaustic painting of concentric blue and yellow circles on a red field dominated the wall. More books covered an oval table in the middle of the room. There was a faint scent in the air, reminding Ambrose of vanilla and fresh cream.

A thin receptionist with light brown skin and a halo of thick black hair stood up from behind her walnut desk. A blue telephone sat at the edge. "This came for you while you were out" she said, handing the doctor a plain envelope filled with a wad of cash.

The doctor tucked it away inside his jacket and said, "Mary, uh gwine be busy fuh while."

"What about Widow Jackson?"

"She'll haffuh wait."

"Yes, sir."

"Come on back," Doctor Wampus said. He motioned toward a narrow hallway and the corner office at the end.

Compared to the foyer, the doctor's office was positively spartan. The wainscot and cream-colored plaster continued around the perimeter, but no decorations hung from the wall. Heavy drapes covered the two windows. Glossy hardwood flooring reflected the harsh light from a bare bulb in the ceiling fixture. A plain wooden table and spindle chair rested off-center. Against the wall were two more spindle chairs. The floor felt uneven underfoot, as if one side of the room was lower than the other.

The doctor took a seat and laid his glasses and hat on the table. His cobalt eyes followed them as they pulled up their chairs and sat down. A slight smile teased the corners of his mouth. "Not wuh you expected, iz'um?" He reclined back and asked, "Now, tell me yo names."

"I'm Brie, and this is Ambrose. Thank you for what you did at the courthouse. I don't think we would have made it out of there alive."

"Tecumseh sent all-two uh you tuh de courthouse tuh fin' me?" he asked.

"Yes, he thought you could help us."

"Help oonuh o' she?" the doctor replied, nodding toward Ambrose.

Ambrose glanced quickly at Brie before she said, "Tecumseh said you could help me. The fae at the courthouse was one of the ones who chased us at the market. They seem to always know where I am."

Leaning forward, Doctor Wampus steepled his long fingers and said, "Uh don't normally see de fae in dese parts, but that one was real 'nuf. Wuffuh you draw its attention?"

Looking down at her hands in her lap, Ambrose said, "I ran away from home."

Brie shifted closer to her. "You didn't run away. You were brought here."

"Either way, they're here to kill me... just like my family."

Doctor Wampus stood and walked around the table. Hunching over, he placed his hands on the sides of Ambrose's head. He closed his eyes and whispered an incantation. When finished, he straightened and said, "You have a mighty skrong cuss cast 'pun you."

"Is there any way to get rid of it?" Brie asked.

"Maybe." He stepped back, rubbing his chin in thought. "Dey's no root tuh take 'way, but I t'ink I can cut de knot dat bind'um. I jus' can't do it here."

"What do you mean, you can't do it here?" Brie asked. "This is your office, isn't it?"

Doctor Wampus grinned and spread his arms wide. "What you t'ink? Me have conjuh potions and ole tomes on de shelf? Or maybe uh smoky lab like dem shows on de TeeVee? Hoodoo don' work dat way."

He turned his head toward the door and yelled out, "Mary! Call Vie. Tell'um me bringing fr'en's."

"Yes, sir," she replied.

When he faced back toward them, Brie said, "I guess, I half expected you to have voodoo dolls and a wall full of potions and herbs.   Maybe a few shrunken heads or something hanging from a mantle."

Doctor Wampus laughed. "Now, dat would be 'gainst de law. You see, I can't give anyone homemade med'sin. No matter if'um cure de cuss — leastways not b'dout a license."

"But you can put a root on someone."

"Funny how dat work, ain't it?" he replied, a glint in his eyes. "Before dey can come after me for puttin' de root on somebody, dey haffuh accept dat Hoodoo is for true. Until den, dey'll dismiss wuh I do as hooey."

"How did you put a root on that witness?"

"Do wuh?"

"You made that man fall out of his chair, didn't you?" Excitement laced Brie's words as she continued, "I can't believe that in our modern age, spells and curses still exist."

Ambrose said, "Brie, stop asking him so many questions. I'm sure the doctor wants to keep his secrets."

Doctor Wampus knelt. His intense eyes captivated them both, and he replied, "Is no secret dat yo *modern age* don' stop somebody like me or de fae from puttin' the root on people. Because people today are eddycated and all-time look fuh de rational explanation, it's mo' easier. Dey don' recognize wuh done happ'n until it's too late.

"Yuh see, deep down, everybody believes in magic. It's de part of de mind cain't nobody control, jus' like dey dreams." He extended his index finger and tapped Ambrose on the forehead. "Dat's de part of yo mind de conjuh-man touch."

The knock at the door made Ambrose jump. Through the door, Mary said, "Doctor, Charles has your car ready."

Doctor Wampus swept up his hat and glasses as he stood. "T'engky, Mary. Tell'um we be dey dey."

Downstairs, a muscular man wearing a black hat with a shiny visor loomed beside a sleek, black Cadillac. Matching the car's formal elegance, he wore a crisp suit, tie, and patent leather shoes. As soon as he saw the doctor on the stair landing, he stepped around to the car's rear door and opened it.

"Doctor Wampus, where are we going?" Brie asked.

The doctor stopped at the bottom of the stairs. He gave them an evil grin as he said, "To me smoke and shadduh lab with de shrunk heads 'pon uh shelf."

Lost in the deep backseat of the Cadillac, Ambrose rode in silence. She kept her eyes on Charles, fascinated by the meticulous way he drove down Broad Street. The smooth stops and starts, the gliding turns. It was vastly different from Brie's Metropolitan.

Doctor Wampus rode in the front beside Charles. Leaning back, the doctor sat very still with his fingers steepled in front of him.

Ambrose thought about the curse the dærganfae had cast upon her. It seemed so surreal to have the fae follow her here to this world. She found Brie's hand and held it. Brie gave her a reassuring squeeze in return.

They drove past the courthouse and turned right. Various sized cars and trees crowded the street, but somehow Charles managed to maneuver the Cadillac without sideswiping something or losing a side mirror. Beyond wide sidewalks, the pastel-colored homes were built sideways, with their colonnaded piazzas facing narrow drives.

They crossed Queen Street, where the neighborhood transitioned to long strips of two-story buildings separated by lanes and alleys. Remarkable for their uniformity and efficiency, each had brown brick veneer, white sashes, waves of brown clay tile on their gabled roofs, and regularly spaced chimneys.

At the end of the block, a five-foot high wall bordered a larger property. Inside loomed a dull grey, three-story building with crenelated battlements and an octagonal tower. Behind rusted bars, dark windows brooded with unconcealed menace. Vertical cracks connected lintels to sills, and portions of the parged skin had peeled away, revealing blood red brick. Ambrose shivered. Even from the backseat of the Cadillac, the place felt haunted.

A sharp right curve led the street around the dilapidated eyesore. As the car turned left onto a new street, Ambrose twisted in her seat, unwilling to have the building at her back. On this side, square, four-story towers flanked the arched brownstone entrance, barred by an iron gate.

"The Old City Jail," Brie whispered. "Built in the early 1800s, some say over ten thousand people died there. The Housing Authority owns it now, but they can't get anyone to do anything with the place."

"Why not?"

"They say it's too expensive, but I think the real reason is the jail holds too many bad memories."

Near the end of the street, Charles pulled the Cadillac over against the sidewalk and helped everyone out. The sounds of children playing echoed from courtyards where their mothers hung clothes out to dry.

At the street corner, Doctor Wampus waited for everyone to catch up. Charles stood behind them, scanning the area for trouble. Across the way stood a two-story, clapboard building whose paint had weathered to a pale, greyish blue. Glass storefront stretched across the first floor and let plenty of sunlight into a salon. Fancy script on the glass door proclaimed, "Queen Bee Hair and Makeup."

Inside, two women lounged in leather chairs against the right-hand wall, reading thin books with paper covers. Shiny domes covered their hair. On the back wall, a twenty-something woman reclined in an orange chair and rested the back of her head in a sink. A short, round woman wearing an apron poured shampoo from a bottle and worked it into the woman's hair. Beside them, two more chair/sink combinations sat empty.

Doctor Wampus opened the front door, and a brass bell jangled. An elderly woman with dark-brown skin and beaded cornrow braids watched them from behind a counter. A beige cash register sat next to her. Behind her, various tonics, soaps, relaxers, and shampoos filled shelves built along the triangular wall that served as the interior support for steep stairs leading to the second floor.

"Masio, it's been a while," she said coming around the counter and giving him a hug. "You been doin' okay?"

"Been good, Bee," Doctor Wampus said, returning her hug. "Oonuh?"

"'Bout de same," she replied. She tried to give Charles a hug, but her arms only reached partway around his girth. "Charles, do you need a haircut? I'm sure Vie would be happy to give you a hand. She needs a good man to look after her."

"Bee, where Vie got off tuh?" Doctor Wampus asked.

The elderly lady frowned at Brie and Ambrose. "She's upstairs. Do you want me to get her?"

"Da's awright," the doctor said, taking the envelope from his jacket. He handed Bee a couple of greenbacks. "We need her fuh de afternoon."

While Charles remained in the salon, Brie and Ambrose followed the doctor up rickety stairs and down a short hallway. He knocked on a door at the far end.

"Yes?"

"Vie, leh'we in."

The door opened and an attractive woman with dark eyes and lustrous black hair peered out. Upon seeing the doctor, she smiled broadly, revealing a perfect set of pearly white teeth that contrasted with her honey-colored skin. She wore a simple forest green dress cut low in the front. Her feet were bare.

"Doctor, come in."

Delineated by gold-colored shag carpet, her living room had a couple of padded chairs that faced a couch across a low coffee table. Colorful posters and oil paintings covered the walls. A paperback book lay on the couch with a bookmark a third of the way in. On the right-hand side of the living room, an open door led to her bedroom. On the left-hand side, olive cabinets wrapped around the refrigerator, porcelain sink, and stove — all tied together by a smoky grey counter that took up most of the exterior wall. The cabinets and counter stopped near an open window that overlooked the rear of the property. Under it was a round dining table with two wooden chairs.

Brie stepped forward and said, "Hi, my name—"

Vie shook her head. "No names. The less I know about you, the better." She asked the doctor, "Need anything?"

"Not yet." Doctor Wampus laid his hat and glasses on the coffee table and turned to Ambrose. "Still got de root I give 'em?" he asked.

Ambrose nodded.

"Good. Go 'head and swalluhr'um." He picked up one of the wooden chairs and slid it into the kitchen with the back toward the sink. "These fae hab folluh oonuh a long way.

Dey hab dey fingers deep in yourself. De root will tek'care de inside, but dat only part uh de conjuh."

"Seddown," he said motioning Ambrose to the chair. "Vie, we need uh couple uh wash pans. Fill one wid saltwater. Run it thru she hair uh few times. Get'um soppin' wet."

Vie reached up and pulled out a bag of salt from one of the cabinets. "Anything else?"

Ambrose felt queasy, sitting there watching the two work. The doctor draped his jacket over the back of the other wooden chair and rolled up his sleeves. Reaching into his pocket, he pulled out a leather pouch with a rawhide drawstring and untied it. "You hab a small bowl?"

Standing next to Ambrose at the sink, Vie pointed to the counter near the window. "Bottom shelf."

With one hand on her forehead and the other underneath for support, Vie leaned Ambrose's head back and let her hair spill into the pink wash pan resting at the bottom of the sink. Vie ran her fingers through the auburn hair, loosening it.

"You okay if I let go?" Vie asked. Ambrose gave a quick nod.

Using a plastic cup, Vie poured saltwater over Ambrose's head and massaged it into her scalp. The brine was cold and felt prickly against Ambrose's skin. After the third cup, her hair grew stiff and crusty.

"Relax, honey," Vie said, giving her an encouraging smile. Out of the corner of her eye, Ambrose saw the doctor hunched over the bowl.

"What's that?" Brie asked the doctor as he upended the bag and let yellow powder fall into the bowl. He used a knife to prick his thumb. He squeezed it, and three drops of glistening red blood fell into his mixture.

"Goofer dust," he replied.

Vie inhaled sharply. "What are you doing, bringing that stuff in my house?"

Brie asked, "What's goofer dust?"

"It's poison," Vie said with disapproval.

"It *can* be uh pizen," Doctor Wampus countered.

Vie stepped away from Ambrose. Her voice grew in volume as she said, "It's graveyard dirt. You use it to cast hexes."

Ambrose jerked up, and saltwater ran down her face.

"What are you going to do with that?"

Doctor Wampus narrowed his cobalt eyes at Vie. When she didn't flinch, he answered, "De fae got a lock of she'own hair. Dey use dat to cast dem cusses. We got tuh kill de root."

"But we don't have the root," Vie said.

The doctor focused on Ambrose's hair and said, "You're wrong. We do hab it."

Vie's features became pinched as she forced down her next words. She opened a drawer, retrieved a pair of scissors and a straight razor, and slammed it back with a clatter.

Ambrose stood frozen. "What are you going to do?"

"Cut your hair," she answered.

"Hold on," said Ambrose, raising her hands. "No one said anything about cutting my hair."

"Gots to," Doctor Wampus said. "It's de sho'est way."

Vie laid a gentle hand on Ambrose's arm and in a soft voice said, "I'm afraid the doctor's right. This person who's after you is using your hair against you. Without doing anything, it would take at least six months for your hair to change enough to render what they have useless. From the looks of it, you don't have that kind of time."

Ambrose's hand shook as she touched the tips of her hair. "How much do you have to cut?"

"All of it," the doctor said. "We haffuh get tuh de root."

"Wait a damn minute," Brie said. She stood with her hands on her hips, one foot forward. "You mean to tell me that these fae have a piece of her hair, and that's what they're using to follow her and make her sick?"

"Yes," Doctor Wampus said.

"So, you're going to shave her head?"

"Yes.

"What about the dust? What are you going to do with that?"

"Rub'um into she scalp en kill de root."

Ambrose's eyes brimmed with tears as she let Vie lead her back to the chair in front of the sink. "Is there any other way?"

"'Less you kin ask de fae for yo hair back, no," he replied.

"You said 'kill the root.' Does that mean her hair won't grow back?" Brie demanded.

"No," replied Vie. "It will grow back — eventually." She

ran saltwater through Ambrose's hair a few more times before picking up the scissors.

The *snick, snick, snick* of the shears filled the silence in the room, and something inside Ambrose broke. Her tears mixed with the brine, and she shook with each sob. Vie put the scissors down. Cool air kissed her scalp, and she felt different, her head lighter.

Brie knelt beside Ambrose. "It's going to be okay. Don't you worry."

"Now stay still," said Vie. "I don't want to cut you." Handing the cup to Brie, Vie said, "Take this. Keep pouring water over her head, while I get the rest."

Ambrose closed her eyes. Saltwater sluiced over her nearly bare scalp.

"Be careful tuh not git no hair on oonuh," Doctor Wampus warned. "Mek sho' it all go into dat pan een de sink."

The straight razor felt rough against Ambrose's skin. With each scrape, she lost parts of herself. No, not lost — the razor *exposed* parts of herself. Memories. She remembered her maid brushing her hair and weaving it in elaborate braids. Ambrose swallowed and fought back the welling emotions.

Vie laid down the razor, and she and Brie stepped away. Doctor Wampus took her place. He leaned in close and whispered in Ambrose's ear. Like earlier in the courthouse, his words were not meant for her. She tried to pick out one or two, but they slipped through her consciousness like smoke. His strong fingers felt gritty as they kneaded her scalp, and the doctor fell into some sort of trance.

The odor of rotten eggs wafted from the mixture. It grew stronger, and a burning sensation spread across Ambrose's head. The sensation delved into her skin, seeking the roots of her hair, and turned painful. She tried to twist away from his grip, but the doctor held her down.

"Hang in there. He's almost done," Vie said.

Sweat trickled down her spine as she gripped the edge of her seat. The pain grew searing hot. It felt like her brain boiled inside her skull.

"No more," she gasped, lunging up as Doctor Wampus lifted his hands. Ambrose half expected to see smoke coming from her. Dreading what she'd find, she reached up. The bare ridges of her scalp felt foreign to her.

"Do you have a mirror?" she asked in a tremulous voice. While Vie dashed off to retrieve it, Ambrose went to Brie. "I can't believe it's all gone."

"Oh, honey." Brie wrapped her in a tight hug. "At least now those fae can't find you."

The *pop, pop, pop* of gunshots rang out from the salon.

Ambrose and Brie both jumped at the harsh sound. Vie ran back into the living room and met Doctor Wampus at the front door. "That was Charles," she said, alarmed.

Down below, they heard glass shatter followed by a shriek. It sounded like Bee. Soon after, a loud roar erupted, and acrid smoke crept under the door.

"What do we do?" Brie asked.

"Out the back," Vie said, pointing to the open window.

Grabbing hold of Ambrose, Brie raced to the jamb and peered outside. Below the windowsill was a short jump to a wood awning.

Brie pushed Ambrose out onto the low roof. Ambrose scampered to the edge and dropped onto the pavement, Brie right behind her.

Dark smoke billowed from the first-floor windows and around the back door.

"Run!" Vie shouted. They both looked up. Someone grabbed Vie from behind and threw her back into the apartment.

Two dærganfae stood at the window. Their silver eyes quickly found Ambrose. One of the fae made a cutting motion with his hand. Something heavy struck her from behind, and her world faded to black.

Tongues of scorching flame licked around the windows and doors of the blue building. Thick black smoke roiled out, seemingly held down by the oppressive heat and humidity.

Saoi, the elder dærganfae, looked back upon their work and smiled. The Archer might not be happy about the attention they'd drawn, but at least they had the Queen.

He caught glimpses of humans dragging the dead and the injured beyond the reach of the growing fire. Spectators collected in the street, on the sidewalks, and amongst the apartment buildings.

The building's spine broke with a thunderous crack, and bright flames erupted from the roof. Dancing sparks floated in the air like hellish fireflies.

"Elder, we must leave," Aimsitheoir said.

Saoi nodded. Even though Terrans could not see them directly, there were those few who could — like the shaman. He motioned for the three dærganfae to follow.

Behind him, Trodaire held the unconscious Queen like a sack of grain over his broad shoulder with one meaty arm. At odds with his black suit, long- and short-bladed weapons hung from multiple belts. Their silver and gold filigreed hilts were well worn.

Next to Trodaire, File carried the Queen's companion. The dærganfae's lean figure and thin fingers held both masculine and feminine qualities that made it difficult to guess the scop's gender. Longbow in his hand, Aimsitheoir remained a few steps behind, constantly on guard.

"Elder, where are we going?" File asked.

"Gadaí has found a place to keep the queen," Saoi replied. "It's not far."

Skirting around the milling crowd, they walked to the other end of Wilson and stopped. In front of them, the abandoned City Jail loomed like a slumbering dragon. A sharp-featured dærganfae with a cunning glimmer in his quicksilver eyes waited under the arched gateway rising from the estate wall. He pushed open the barred gate and motioned them to hurry.

"The postern door is over there," Gadaí said.

Saoi studied the thick walls and barred windows. "Is this the best you could find?"

"Yes," Gadaí answered. "There are no humans here. I have a room prepared on the second floor."

Still, Saoi hesitated. "There is something here."

The wail of distant sirens filled the air, growing louder by the second. Out of time and options, the fae rushed inside with Ambrose and Brie.

The building shifted on its foundations, and shadows swallowed the dærganfae. No one remained to hear the door lock slam into place.

CHAPTER 19
CAPTAIN WALKER

March 14, 1969 C.E.

12:30 pm

*T*he *Morningstar* cut through grey ocean waters, her copper sails catching every ounce of available wind. Even so, the *NeverLand* raced ahead without effort.

Roger leaned against the rail and admired the bearded oaks marking the shores of lush barrier islands. Atop a cluster of bleached driftwood, a white heron eyed the muddy beach like a king surveying his lands.

Behind him, the Highlord paced the deck with his hands clasped behind his back.

"Your Majesty, you may be better served if you dove in the water and pushed," Roger said with a smile.

The Highlord paused. "Patience is not one of my virtues."

"I'm sure it doesn't help that we're at the mercy of the wind while that little boat runs rings around us."

"No, it doesn't."

Master Andel climbed the ship's ladder with a wooden bowl of fruit balanced on one hand. "Anyone hungry?" he asked.

Roger pushed himself away from the rail and picked out a shiny, red apple. "Sire?"

"No, thanks," he replied.

"You should eat something. Once we reach shore, there's no telling when we'll have another opportunity."

"Roger's right," Lahar said from behind her wheel. "Master Andel, leave the bowl and go tell Mister Huff I want everyone fed."

"Aye, aye, Captain."

"The *NeverLand*'s turning!" Mister Cryst yelled from the crow's nest. Up ahead, the boat swung wide and entered the mouth of a river.

The waters around them turned darker, and the *Morningstar* slowed as it fought the current. They passed between the first barrier islands, and cordgrass marshes replaced glistening beaches.

"Mister Mitchell," Lahar said.

"Yes, mum." The sea mage closed his eyes and took a deep breath. The lanterns crackled, and a faint glow spread throughout the ship. It flickered and faltered.

"Mister Mitchell?" Lahar said, concern making her tone harsh.

Brow furrowed with concentration, he mumbled a few words. The glow returned and grew brighter. Roger grabbed the rail when the ship began to rise. The sea mage lifted the *Morningstar* just enough to reduce the drag from the current.

"Maintain this speed, Mister Mitchell," Lahar said. She adjusted the wheel to follow the *NeverLand*'s path down the center of the twisting river.

A sea breeze followed them, carrying a slight chill. To either side, spots of solid ground broke through the marsh grass, and became more prevalent the farther in they went.

After forty minutes of traveling upriver, a commotion broke out on the main deck, with a lot of shouting mixed with bouts of nervous laughter.

Master Andel raced up the ladder and said, "Mister Cavendish. He's awake."

"Have him join us, if he's able," said Lahar.

With his pale skin and dark circles surrounding his deep-set eyes, Mister Cavendish looked more a corpse than the living. He stood straight with an effort and said, "Reporting for duty, mum."

Lahar's crew watched from the main deck.

"Glad to have you back, Mister Cavendish," Lahar said. "Mister Mitchell has the chair, but I'd like for you to remain. Tell me what you see."

"Yes, mum."

Down below, Mister Smeyth yelled, "Back to work, ya dogs!" and Miss O'Brien started barking.

Mister Cavendish lumbered forward and said, "I'm sorry about the jump. I don't know what happened."

"No need to apologize, Mister Cavendish. The crew survived, and we have a strong tailwind."

The sea mage's eyes darted about the ship and finally rested on Mister Mitchell and the chair. "Captain, we're bleeding magic."

"What?" Lahar asked.

"The ship. It's losing its magic."

"Can you make it stop?"

Mister Cavendish shook his head. "No, mum." He spread his arms and said, "It's this place."

Lahar adjusted the wheel, following their guide, but everyone could tell her thoughts were elsewhere.

"Can we get back?" she asked.

"Yes, mum. For now."

From above, Mister Cryst said, "The boat's pulling into port!"

"Mister Mitchell," Lahar said.

"Aye, Captain," he replied, and the ship dropped back into the water. He let out a loud sigh and wiped the sweat from his forehead.

"What do we do?" Roger asked. The thought of being trapped on Terra sent a ripple of panic down his spine.

"They're signaling us!" Mister Cryst said.

A glossy black craft the size of the *Morningstar's* longboats buzzed around the riverbend, trailing a spume of white froth in its wake. The boat's pilot cut sharp to avoid the brigantine, grazing the far bank as he passed. The *Morningstar* rounded the bend and aimed for the deep-water dock that lay along the east side of what appeared to be another barrier island.

Made of concrete and steel, the dock looked new. Behind it, a long metal-paneled building with high eaves and a flat roof ran alongside a gravel yard stockpiled with construction materials, old boats, and scrap metal. A half-dozen strangely shaped, dark yellow vehicles moved about the yard, their operators dimly visible through dusty glass windows. From the middle of the yard, steel rails with timber crossties disappeared into the choppy water. It was like looking at an alien landscape on some distant, inhuman plane, not one that was supposed to be similar to Gaia.

Farther north, past charred pilings, the landscape turned more familiar. Grassy lawns sprawled between fishing piers and wooden houses raised up on slender columns. To the left was a tree-shrouded brick building with limestone arches over the windows. South of that, more elevated residences peeked through the leafy branches.

A dangerous calm settled over Lahar. "Mister Smeyth!" she said. "Make ready."

"Aye, Cap'n," he replied.

Lahar turned the wheel, and the ship drew closer to the port. Once the mooring lines were tied off and the ship safely docked, Lahar said, "Mister Mitchell, Mister Cavendish, I'm going ashore. Find me a solution."

"Aye, Captain."

As she stalked past Roger, she leaned in close and hissed, "This expedition of yours stinks."

Arms at his sides, Roger stared after her, unsure what to say. Lahar joined Cerdic on the main deck where he helped the crew position the gangplank.

Coming up beside Roger, the Highlord said, "We'll need transportation."

"I don't see any horses or carriages," Roger replied, scanning the yard. "Please tell me we don't have to use those evil-looking yellow conveyances."

The Highlord slapped the thief on the back and pointed to several box-shaped vehicles similar in size to coaches, but much closer to the ground. "That's our transportation."

Outside the brick building, a man dressed in a dark coat and hat entered one of the four-door vehicles. A mechanical purr cut across the gravel lot as it backed up, moved onto a blacktop road, and zoomed away.

"Well, you don't see that every day," Roger said.

"Here, you do," the Highlord replied. "Did you notice the way he was dressed?"

"Yes, no weapons."

"Lahar's not going to like you."

"What do you mean?" Roger asked. "I'm already afraid to turn my back on her lest she plant a knife between my shoulders."

"You're the one who gets to tell her she can't carry her sword."

"Oh, no," Roger said, shaking his head. "I think that particular job should go to someone with more clout than me. Someone who, say, runs a kingdom."

The Highlord watched the crew finish with the gangplank. Cerdic walked amongst them, talking and smiling. "Knighthoods and lordships carry no weight on this ship."

"What about out there?" asked Roger.

"My friend, we are about to enter the Dark One's

playground: a land run by politicians and bureaucrats."

Lahar had surrendered her longsword to Mister Smeyth without much of a fuss, which only served to fuel Roger's suspicions. Touching the hilts of various knives and daggers tucked away about his person, he realized he couldn't say anything. Of the four, it had been Cerdic who put up the biggest fight.   In the end, he'd acquiesced to carrying a hunting knife on his belt.

Walking with a slight limp, the burly yacht captain met them on the dock with his hand extended. "Bo Walker," he drawled.   Roger found himself liking the easygoing and friendly captain.

Shaking his hand, Cerdic said, "Cerdic Aneirin. This is Lahar, our captain. This is Roger Vaughn, and this is—"

"Arthur," said the Highlord, shaking Bo's hand in turn.

Behind Bo, the man and two women from the yacht approached them.   The captain stepped back, his gaze lingering on Lahar's almond-shaped eyes. "Lemme introduce you to my wife, Cindi, my brother, Frank, and his girlfriend, Sam."   Bo spoke in a relaxed way, adding syllables and drawing out his words as he went.

After shaking everyone's hand, Frank glanced up at the crew of the *Morningstar* and said, "Y'all look like a bunch of pirates. What do you do? Dress up like buccaneers and cruise the coastline?"

"Something like that," Lahar replied.

Bo whistled and said, "That's some ship. Love the copper sails. Never seen anything like it. Have you, Frank?"

"Can't say that I have," Frank said, lighting a cigarette. He took in a deep drag as he studied the hull with a critical eye. "Y'all said something about damage earlier. You need any supplies?"

"No, thank you," Lahar replied, flashing the brothers a quick smile. "Giving us access to your dock is more than we could have hoped for. Would you like to come aboard?"

Like a child given a free piece of candy, Bo's whole face lit up. "I'd love that."

After the tour, Frank and the two women thanked Lahar and headed ashore. They didn't mention anything about the various cutlasses, daggers, and blades the crew wore, though it did seem to quicken their step.

Remaining behind, Bo knelt and admired the iron dragons. Like an overprotective mother, the gunny stood right beside him with her arms crossed.

"O'Brien? You don't look Irish," Bo said, rising.

The crew laughed, and one said, "We call all the gunny's, O'Brien."

The Highlord waited for the laughter to subside before he said, "Captain Walker, it'll take a little while for the crew to finish their repairs. Would it be possible for you to take us into town? We'd pay you for your time."

"Sure, where do ya need to go?"

Lahar held out her compass. "That way."

Bo laughed and said, "That's funny." He peered closer at the compass and abruptly stopped. "Hey, your compass is broke."

Sliding a gold coin from his pouch, the Highlord said, "It's not broken. It just doesn't point north."

Bo looked from the compass to the gold coin and then back to the compass. "Hey, now. I won't do anything that's against the law."

"We're not here for that," Roger said.

His features hardening, Bo studied them. "What are you here for?"

"We're here to find a young woman," the Highlord answered. "She ran away from home, and we're worried she's in danger."

"And you followed her to Charleston on this tall ship, using that compass?"

The question lost on them, the four looked at each other in confusion.

"It was the quickest way," said the Highlord.

"Uh-huh," Bo said. "Do you know how ridiculous that sounds?"

"It's the truth," Cerdic said.

"You got me. Where's Allen Funt?" Bo chuckled, looking about. "There must be cameras hidden all over this ship."

Again, the four looked at each other, trying to make sense of the yacht captain. Bo laughed harder. "I'm on Candid Camera, aren't I?"

"Captain, we're here to find my Queen," said Cerdic, his tone dead serious, "and we need your help. That magical compass is our only means of finding her before assassins do."

Bo swallowed and wiped his eyes with the back of his hand. "You're looking for your Queen with a magic compass? I can't believe what I'm hearing."

The Highlord jangled his money pouch. "We can make it worth your time."

Bo took another look at the ship and the hard faces of her crew. He turned to Lahar and said, "Just where are you people from? Y'all sound European, but you look half Asian."

Lahar's jaw clenched, and her hand strayed toward her weapon belt.

Roger flinched. A child born of violence, Lahar was touchy about her lineage. Seeing that things were about to turn ugly, Roger stepped forward. "We're most recently from York, Captain Walker."

"England?" Bo exclaimed. "You are a long way from home."

"No," Cerdic replied.

At the same time, the Highlord said, "Yes."

Bo looked from one man to the other, his suspicions growing. "I didn't see your registered port displayed anywhere on the bow or aft."

The Highlord sighed. "We didn't sail here from England. What do you know of English and Scottish legends?"

"You mean King Arthur and Camelot?"

"That," the Highlord nodded, "and legends of the people under the hills. Avalon. The Sidhe. The Seelie and Unseelie courts of the fae."

"You trying to tell me you're from fairyland?"

"No. Just wondering if you're familiar with the premise of portals to other worlds and races other than human."

"This is too much!" Bo exclaimed. "You expect me to believe you're from some magical otherworld because you're dressed like pirates and have a broken compass?" He laughed. "Pull my other leg while you're at it."

Roger sighed. This was taking too long, and they were short on time. "Lahar, perhaps a demonstration by Mr. Mitchell is in order."

Lahar frowned at Roger before turning to the sea mage. "Mister Mitchell, if you please."

Bo seemed to grow worried as the mage approached.

Mister Mitchell wove his hands in an intricate pattern and said, "Gíne fílos mas, Bo Walker."

Instantly, Bo stood dumbstruck.

"Captain, please provide him something to focus on. Something unique to you," Mister Mitchell whispered out of the corner of his mouth. "It'll complete the charm."

One eyebrow twitched upward. Wordlessly, she removed her hat and shook back her mahogany hair, exposing the points of her ears.

Bo's eyes grew wide, and he stumbled back. Cerdic grabbed him by the elbow before he bumped the rail. "Captain, you're amongst friends."

"Is this some kind of trick? A costume, or something?"

"No, Captain," Lahar replied. "I am an elf."

Fascinated, Bo reached up as if he meant to touch Lahar's ear, thought better of it, and shoved his hands in his pockets. "You only need a ride into town?" he asked, his eyes meeting each of theirs.

"That's all," the Highlord said, handing Bo three more gold coins.

Weighing them in his palm, Bo asked, "Who's going?"

"Just the four of us."

"All right. Let me tell Cindi and Frank, and I'll pull the truck around."

Cerdic let the captain go, and all four watched him leave.

"Can we trust him?" Roger asked.

"Captain Walker is a good man," Cerdic replied. "There was no need to cast a spell on him."

"You believe there's good in everyone," Lahar said, tilting her hat so the brim shadowed her eyes. "That does not mean they're trustworthy. Besides, Mister Mitchell's charm was quicker."

"He would have helped us," Cerdic replied.

"You don't know that," Lahar said.

"Just because you don't see the good in a person, doesn't mean it's not there."

"Oh please," Lahar said. "If everyone were as good as you, the world would be a boring place."

"Would you prefer a world in chaos?" Cerdic asked.

"No, I prefer a world that's balanced. Every thinking being has the capacity for both good and evil. In the struggle for survival, all a person can hope is that, in the end, they've done more good than bad when the Eternal Father does the final tally."

"Excuse me, do we have to have this discussion now?" the Highlord asked. "Captain Walker should be back any minute, and we need to prepare."

Inside the captain's cabin, Roger and Mister Smeyth stood with Lahar as she conversed with the two sea mages. Cerdic and the Highlord were below gathering their gear.

"We have 'til morning. After that we're dead in the water," Mister Cavendish said. "The ship needs to go back."

Lahar slapped her hand on the table and said, "Why the hell didn't you tell me this was going to be a problem before we jumped?"

"My apologies, mum, we didn't know. Travel between Gaia and Terra was... complicated."

"So, if we don't find this precious Queen and return here by tonight, we'll be forced to give up on her altogether. What a waste of time."

"Actually Cap'n," Mister Mitchell added, "based on our calculations, we have eighteen hours before the chair loses all its magic. We'd need to leave a couple of hours before then. I'd say sunrise at the latest."

"Can we put some men ashore, send the ship back to Gaia, and come back for them later?" Mister Smeyth asked.

"It's possible," Mister Cavendish answered, "but I'd have to find someone who knows the correct sigil. And as we saw, if it's the least bit wrong..." His face became pained, and his eyes grew distant. "I don't know how long it would take. We could be talking days, or years."

"Damnit," Lahar said. "With the Espians threatening war and the Dark One's army looming, Carolingias doesn't have days— much less weeks or years."

Roger stepped forward and said, "We know the Queen is here. Let's go and bring her back. I mean, how hard could it be?"

Lahar narrowed her eyes at Roger. "You should know better than to ask a question like that, thief."

Forging on, Roger said, "Do you get a sense of distance with that compass? Or just direction?"

Lahar held up the compass and faced the same direction as the needle. "Feels like she's close, but that's as the crow flies. Not sure how far it will be by road."

"See? She's just around the corner. How long would it take for this ship to fly, say, ten leagues?"

"With a steady wind, less than three hours," Mister Cavendish answered.

"Plenty of time," Roger proclaimed.

Lahar looked at each of the four men. She stared the longest at Roger, seemingly to test his resolve. Roger nodded back at her and winked. "This will work."

The cabin door opened to admit Cerdic and the Highlord, the former with Roger's haversack slung over his shoulder.

"Were you able to find everything?" Roger asked.

"Yes, we got it all. I like this thing. It holds a lot but only weighs a few pounds," Cerdic said, adjusting the pack higher on his shoulder.

"I'm glad you like it. You can carry it," Roger said with an impish smile.

The Highlord said, "Captain Walker's outside waiting for us. You ready?"

Lahar pressed both her palms against the tabletop and said, "Gentlemen, the ship is bleeding magic. We have less than eighteen hours before it's drained, and we're stuck here. It's imperative that we don't dally. If all goes well, we find the Queen, and Captain Walker brings us right back."

"And if it doesn't?" the Highlord asked.

Lahar straightened. "If it doesn't, then we retreat to the ship and leave Queen Ambrose here in Terra."

Cerdic opened his mouth to protest, but Lahar cut him off with a stern glare. "Make no mistake, my ship and the lives of her crew come first. If we fail to return by sunrise, Mister Smeyth will take the *Morningstar* back to Gaia without us."

CHAPTER 20
THE TYLERS

March 14, 1969 C.E.

2:15 pm

Captain Walker had changed out of his swim trunks and into denim pants and a short-sleeved shirt. He sat in the driver's seat of a metallic green truck with rounded fenders and a short, recessed step between the cabin and the rear tires. He leaned over and pushed open the passenger door.

"I'm afraid I only have room for one up front. The others will need to ride in the back." Bo jerked his thumb toward the truck bed.

Standing in the gravel lot, the Highlord held the truck door and motioned for Lahar to take the seat inside the cab. She eyed the metal beast with suspicion. "I'll ride in the back, thank you."

"You have the compass," the Highlord reminded her. "Captain Walker will need you to guide us."

Cerdic and Roger climbed into the truck bed and gave her smug grins.

"I hate you," she said to both of them. Lahar removed her hat and placed it on her lap as she took her seat. The Highlord slammed the door and hopped in the back.

"Where to?" Captain Walker asked.

Lahar held up her compass and showed it to Bo.

He studied it a moment before saying, "Let's start by heading to Charleston. I can always turn around if we pass her."

"Sounds good, Captain," Lahar said.

"You can call me Bo," he replied, turning the key. The truck grumbled to life. He shifted it into gear as he stepped on the gas, and they sped down the street.

Roger leaned back against the vehicle's cabin with his knees bent and feet planted shoulder width apart for balance against the buffeting wind washing over him. Flowering marshes filled with lush tropical growth rushed past, along with the occasional opposing vehicle. Despite being jostled at every bump, he enjoyed the experience. He quickly learned the art of leaning into the turns and using his arms and legs to keep from sliding.

Sitting opposite one another on the humps outlining the vehicle's rear wheels, Cerdic and the Highlord kept the haversack between them. Ever vigilant, they scanned the horizon for trouble. Of course, at the speed they traveled, they'd easily outdistance wayward trolls or anything else that might threaten them.

Roger readjusted his two-inch wide leather belt, making it more comfortable. Along its length were a mixture of horizontal and vertical pouches with terracotta grenades affixed between them. Bulbed at one end, intricate runes worked their way around the pipe-like shapes.

His gaze drifted toward the sky, and he wondered what it would be like living in a place such as this, not having to fear something evil lurked beyond every horizon. Everything seemed so peaceful.

He jerked himself awake.

Looking at the faces of Cerdic, the Highlord, and even Lahar, he realized that was the true danger of this place: complacency. With The Archer also searching for Ambrose, a false sense of security and dropped guard would get them killed.

White-knuckling the door handle, Lahar stared out the open window of the cab, occasionally checking the compass to see if the needle moved.

Beside her, Bo said, "My family's been here for generations. Before any of these roads were paved, you used to have to take a carriage or go by horseback."

"Must have been horrible," Lahar muttered.

"Oh, it was," Bo replied with a smile. Out the window, long stretches of woods followed open spaces where sunshine sparkled on the frothy, brown waters of a tidal creek. "There really wasn't a good way to get from Edisto Island to Charleston. Using his boat, my grandfather traded with the farmers along the river and took their goods to the market. Cabbage, beans, taters, you name it. I still remember him wearing his vest and captain's hat."

"What does your family do now?"

"Barges. We haul freight all up and down the East Coast."

"Run into any pirates?" Lahar asked.

Bo laughed. "No. Last time there were pirates in these waters would have been after the War of 1812." He thought for a moment and said, "George Clark. That was his name. Don't remember the name of his ship, though."

Turning right at an intersection, the truck aimed east. The compass needle pointed straight ahead.

"What happened to George Clark?" Lahar asked.

"They hung him and his crew."

Bearded boughs overhung the road ahead, giving it a timeless quality. Afternoon shadows dappled the pavement. Lahar could easily picture oxcarts and carriages traveling toward the city. Was it so different in Gaia?

"What about you?" Bo asked. "Captain of a tall ship?"

Lahar shifted in the front seat and said, "It's a long story."

"It's a long ride."

She sighed and said, "I was serving as the quartermaster of the *Morningstar* at the time. Captain Dutton was in command. He was a skilled seaman, better than any I had seen, but it was his luck that was his legacy.

"The *Kerberos,* a Gastrian brig, had blockaded the port of Oakenhart, the capital of a small island country east of Carolingias, and demanded ransom from the merchants. One they weren't willing to pay. As luck would have it, the *Morningstar* put into that very port for repairs a week earlier. By the sixth day of the blockade, we were anxious for action.

"Captain Dutton persuaded the mayor to lend him a cutter and twelve volunteers. With two other boats, Dutton planned a night raid on the ship guarding the entrance. He took me along with six other crewmen, which made 20 men in total.

"Striking out ahead, the captain reached the *Kerberos.* Heavily outnumbered, we were beaten back twice by the Gastrian crew, but on the third attempt we boarded the *Kerberos* and killed every one of their officers. Then, with the help of the other two boats, we towed the brig to shore. The expedition was a success, but luck had turned against our captain. During the fight, Dutton got caught up in a trawlnet and had a pike driven through his chest. Several of the men were wounded, including me, but it was the captain who didn't live to see the next morning. Before he died, he handed me his sword and named me his successor. I've been captain ever since."

Bo shifted gears and the truck merged onto a busier road with wide lanes. Fields of cordgrass flanked each side, and the pungent odor of the marsh flooded the cab.

Shaking his head, Bo said, "It's hard to swallow that you're from a different world. Brick and mortar I can handle, but magic ships... if I hadn't seen it, I never would have believed it. I do know one thing. You've got a good crew, and they respect you. You can tell a lot about a person by the people who follow them."

Lahar nodded, not sure how to respond.

"What's the story with the guys in the back? I mean, you're an elf. Shouldn't you be with other elves?"

Bo's open candor made it hard for Lahar to take offense at the question. "They're my... friends," she said simply.

"And this Queen. Is she your friend, too?"

Lahar stared at the compass. She felt the distance closing, like a subtle pressure clenching her chest. Searching her feelings, she questioned herself. Why was she risking everything for this tramp? Her ship, her crew — all twenty of them. All for what? She glanced at the men in the back, using the rearview mirror. Her gaze rested on Cerdic, taking in the passing scenery with innocent eyes.

"Oh, I see," Bo said with a smile.

Lahar straightened. Her compressed lips formed a thin line as she mentally berated herself.

"I take it he doesn't know how you feel," he said. "Being around Cindi and her friends gives me a little insight into a woman's head. Not much, mind you, and mostly it gets me in trouble, but I know enough to keep my mouth shut, if you know what I mean."

The marsh disappeared behind bearded oaks, and roads to their left and right became more frequent.

"Keep going straight?" Bo asked.

Lahar looked down at the compass and replied, "Yes."

They slowed as more cars filled the road. Various types of buildings lined the sides. Some were hotels, others were businesses advertising services or wares. There was even one calling itself a Drive-In Theater.

Lahar felt it. Ambrose was less than a mile ahead.

After passing a couple of churches, the needle shifted. "We passed her. She's back that way," Lahar said, turning her head to the left.

"Got it." Bo pulled into the center lane marked off by solid yellow stripes and drifted to a stop. Cars flew past them going both directions. "Welcome to the Idiot Lane."

Bo turned left, and the needle aimed due west. He turned left again, driving slowly.

"Anything?"

Lahar looked around at the houses and cars lining the road. There were so many. "Keep going," she said.

The road ended at a street called Parish. Multiple houses stared back at them. Bo stopped the truck and turned to her. "How about now?"

She looked at the needle, still pointing due west. "It doesn't feel right. Is there another street behind those houses?"

"Yeah, hang on."

He pressed down on the gas and turned left. Exiting back onto the highway they came in on, he turned right and turned right again onto Moore. They crept past the church and the needle moved as they did.

"There," she said pointing to the next street. Bo turned the wheel, and they eased past a couple of driveways. Lahar grabbed his arm, and the truck slammed to a stop.

Overlapping boughs arched overhead. The needle pointed to a one-and-a-half story, cross-gabled brick house nestled behind the trees. In the yard, a thick wooden plaque had, "The Tylers," carved into its surface.

"What do we do now?" Bo asked, glancing at the brown sedan parked in front of the detached carriage house.

"We find Cerdic's Queen," she replied.

The four got out and stretched their legs.

Lahar leaned in the passenger window and said, "Wait here. We shouldn't be long."

Bo reached over and opened the glovebox. After some digging, he found a wool watch cap and said, "Leave that fancy hat here and wear this. It won't attract as much attention."

The four crossed the lawn toward the redbrick steps that

led to the off-centered front door. Voices could be heard from within the house, and it sounded like whoever was inside was upset.

The Highlord said, "Stay back. Before we go barging in, let's see who lives here first."

The three waited at the foot of the steps while the Highlord knocked. A tall man with broad shoulders and a close-cropped haircut opened the door. He wore a dark blue uniform with a silver badge above his left pocket. At his waist was a holster on one side and a truncheon on the other. He stared at the four with open suspicion and asked, "Can I help you?"

"We're looking for Ambrose," the Highlord said. "Is she here?"

The tall man seemed taken aback and didn't respond.

"Nate, is that Brie?" a woman's voice asked from within.

"No," he replied over his shoulder. "It's some strangers asking about Ambrose."

"Well invite them in," another woman said. "They're Mennonites."

"They don't look like Mennonites to me, Mrs. Tyler."

A woman wearing a white apron over a knee length dress pushed Nate aside as she said, "What do you know about Mennonites?" Turning to face the Highlord, she stopped short. Her gaze swept across the four people in front of her.

"Milady, I apologize for this intrusion," the Highlord said with a short bow. "Let me introduce myself. My name is Arthur, and we've been sent to collect Ambrose. Is she here?"

"Wow, this Rumspringa thing is a lot different than what you read in the papers," she said. "Come in, come in. Let's talk inside."

Lahar glanced at Roger, who was as confused as she was. She mouthed, "What's going on?" He shrugged and followed the Highlord through the door.

As they entered, the woman said, "I'm Mildred Tyler, and this is Nathan Stone— he's a police officer." That last part was spoken in a conspiratorial whisper. "Please take a seat. My husband should be home shortly."

A third person, another woman, sat stiffly in a padded chair. She rose and said, "I'm Cam, Brie's sister. You said you're here for Ambrose."

"Yes. It's time to take her home," the Highlord said. His

ageless, pearl grey eyes surveyed the living room and the other parts of the house visible from where he stood.

"She ran off," Cam said, curtly. "We don't know where she went."

Her eyebrows knitting together, Lahar looked down at her compass. "She's supposed to be here," she told the Highlord.

"Well, she's not," Cam said, crossing her arms.

Roger peered around the room and up the stairs. "But she *was* here?"

"How do we know you're really Mennonites?" Cam asked. "Do you have any identification?"

"Cam, there's no reason to be rude," Mrs. Tyler said.

Nate stood between Cam and her mom. He raised his hand toward the four and said, "Let me see some ID." His voice deepened as he tried to exert some authority.

The Highlord replied, "We don't have any. You'll have to trust us. Now, where is Ambrose?"

"Arthur," Lahar said, "she's upstairs. I'm sure of it."

"I think you'd better leave." Nate laid a hand on his weapon belt. It was an obvious gesture that no one missed.

"Young man, I suggest you relax," the Highlord said. "We're not here to cause trouble." He nodded at Roger and Lahar and leaned his head toward the stairs.

Nate fumbled at his holster. In one swift move, the Highlord grabbed his wrist. "Easy, boy."

Lahar raced upstairs, Roger right behind her. She followed the compass to a bedroom with various-sized books covering the floor. Glancing around, she knew Ambrose had to be close. Her gaze rested on the bed. Kneeling, she shoved aside a pile of books and peered underneath the bedframe.

"It was hidden under a bed." Lahar held the soiled remains of Ambrose's vigil robe as she walked down the steps.

Cerdic and the Highlord faced the young policeman. Their eyes became hard and held a steely edge.

"What did you do with her?" the Highlord asked, wrenching Nate's arm behind his back.

"Mister, let him go. We didn't do anything to her. Other than invite her in," Cam said.

"Where is she?" the Highlord asked. "If you've hurt

her..."

"She's with my sister."

The Highlord looked around at their faces. Something was wrong. Letting Nate go, he asked, "Where's your sister?"

"She went downtown," Nate replied, rubbing his wrist. "I saw her at the market. She was going on about pale men with silver eyes and pointed ears. She wasn't making any sense. I didn't think anything of it, but then someone reported one of those silvered-eyed men dead outside the courthouse. It's got the whole precinct talking. And not an hour ago, I got a call that Brie's car had been found abandoned on Broad Street." He paused, taking in the expressions on the newcomers' faces. "You know these silver-eyed men, don't you?"

The Highlord rubbed his chin and began pacing. He eyed Lahar's borrowed cap and asked her, "Would you mind?"

Making a face, she removed her cap. "I'm getting tired of being put on display." She ran a hand through her hair and tilted her head so everyone could see her ears. "There, you happy? The next time we do this, you men are going to have to do some revealing."

The Highlord gestured toward Lahar and said to Nate, "Like those?"

"Yeah. Brie said they were pointed like a Vulcan's."

"I'm not a bloody Vulcan, whatever that is, " Lahar said. "I'm an elf."

"Are they real?" Nate asked. Like Bo had earlier, he raised his hand slightly as if he wanted to touch them.

"Hell, yes, they're real," Lahar said, backing away.

Mrs. Tyler gasped.

"Watch your language," Nate demanded. "No swearing."

"I've got to keep busy," Mrs. Tyler said, ruffling her apron. She avoided looking at Lahar when she asked, "Does anyone want tea?"

Nate patted her on the shoulder and said, "Yes, please. Bring some for everyone."

When Mrs. Tyler left, Cam implored, "Is my sister in trouble?"

"Yes," Cerdic replied. He and the Highlord turned their backs toward Nate and Cam, then leaned close together as they whispered. "It has to be The Archer. This complicates things."

"I know," the Highlord replied.

"Do you think he's already killed her?" Cerdic asked.

"Excuse me." Cam tapped the Highlord on the shoulder. "What's going on? I know you're not Mennonites, so who are you?"

Nate stood behind her, his face a mixture of concern and curiosity.

The Highlord studied them a moment before he said, "Although I doubt you'll believe me, what I'm about to tell you is the absolute truth. We — and Ambrose — are not from your world. We're from the *other side.* Beyond the stars."

"You're aliens?" Nate said.

"No. Maybe. It depends on your definition. We're from Gaia, a mirror world of your Terra."

"It's a world like Earth?"

"Similar. But it's a world where magic prevails — not technology."

"Look, I've seen a lot of crazy stuff, and I like science fiction, but this..." Nate said, scratching his head. "It's hard to take in."

"And these silver-eyed men, they're from Gaia, too?" Cam asked.

"No. The dærganfae are from a world *in between.*"

"How did they get here?"

"We don't know," the Highlord replied.

"For that matter," Nate said. "How did y'all get here?"

"A ship."

"A spaceship?" Nate asked, the doubt in his voice thick.

The Highlord replied, "No. A sailing ship."

"What a load of crap!" Cam threw her arms up. "You're a bunch of lunatics who've read too many fairytales. I bet your Ambrose had Brie believing all this nonsense."

"Cam, wait. I didn't listen to Brie earlier, and now she's gone missing," Nate said. "I want to hear what they have to say."

"It's not nonsense," Roger said. "Your sister is in real trouble."

Mrs. Tyler came out of the kitchen with a tray laden with glasses and a pitcher of tea. "Anyone thirsty?"

CHAPTER 21
TIME FOR TEE

March 14, 1969 C.E.

3:15 pm

*I*n the back of the house, a door opened, and a harsh chemical odor crept into the living room. Despite Roger's alchemical pursuits, the scent was unfamiliar and made his eyes water. His stomach turned over and threatened to rebel.

Perched on the edge of the couch, he placed his glass of tea on a coaster and reached for one of his daggers.

"It's still hard to believe you served aboard the *Seawolf.*" Bo's relaxed drawl was unmistakable, and Roger suspected the captain's friendly manner had struck again.

"I was transferred to the *Cerro* in '43."

"You know," Bo said, "that transfer saved your life."

"Mildred, we have company," a deep voice announced from beyond the dining room.

"Robert, I'm in here," Mrs. Tyler said.

"This is Captain Bo Walker. His family owns one of the barges that supplies the Base." Tall and lanky, Mr. Tyler seemed skinny compared to Bo's girth. Even so, he loomed in the living room's arched entry, giving the four unexpected strangers a disapproving look.

"Robert, these are the people I was telling you about," Bo said. "This here is Arthur."

The Highlord put down his glass as he stood, said, "Mr. Tyler," and shook the man's hand.

When Bo finished his introductions, Mr. Tyler said, "You forgot to mention they're buccaneers."

"Don't let their clothes fool ya. They're good people. Got a good crew. And those two," Bo said nodding toward Cerdic and Lahar, "are in love."

Cerdic coughed and turned three shades of red, while Lahar scowled at the captain.

Roger stepped back and retrieved his glass to hide his smile. He'd seen Lahar lash out at people for comments far more benign, and he didn't want her to see him laughing at her expense.

The Highlord laid a gentle hand on her shoulder. "Captain, he meant no harm."

Unamused, Mr. Tyler asked, "Nathan, what's this business about Brie missing?"

Nate said, "Sir, I'm sorry. I should have brought them home."

"Son, start at the beginning."

Nate did. He recounted the disturbance at the Market, mentioned the death at the courthouse, and ended with Brie's car being found abandoned. "It doesn't look good, sir."

"Brie's always gone her own way. She can take care of herself," Mr. Tyler said. "It's how we raised her."

"But, sir—"

"Nate, I'm worried, too, but what can we do?"

"Robert, there must be something," said Mrs. Tyler. "These gentlemen think she and Ambrose are in trouble."

Roger went through Nate's story in his head. Something was missing. He asked, "Why would Brie go to Broad Street? Is something there?"

Nate replied, "They were going to the courthouse. My partner, Tee, put them up to it. He mentioned something about them meeting a root doctor."

Wide-eyed with shock, Mrs. Tyler put a hand over her mouth.

"What business did my daughter have with a root doctor?" Mr. Tyler asked.

"It may be nothing," Nate said.

"Not that I hold anything against the Gullah," said Mr. Tyler, "but my daughter shouldn't be messing around with some shaman."

"I tried to stop her, but you know Brie once she gets something into her head—"

Roger asked, "Why would your partner think Brie needed a shaman?"

"Not Brie. Ambrose. Something about a root being cast on her. I never got the straight of it."

"Where's your partner now?" asked Roger.

"After our shift, he hangs out at King Billy's. It's a bar in the Neck."

"How far is that from here?"

"About fifteen minutes," answered Nate.

"Sire," Roger said to the Highlord, "let me do a little

digging with Officer Stone here — if he's willing."

"What about us?" the Highlord asked. "You want us to stay here?"

"Yes, Sire. It would be a lot less conspicuous if two of us went instead of five. Besides, this may be a wild goose chase, and I'd hate it if Ambrose returned, and no one was here."

Lahar interjected, "We don't have time for this."

"I say we make time," said Cerdic, gripping the hilt of his knife like it was a sword. "The Archer's a butcher. He'll kill his way to Ambrose. We have to stop him."

"You're after vengeance, not—" Lahar started.

The Highlord held up his hand and said to Roger, "Go, but be quick about it. Time is against us."

"Yes, Sire," Roger said with a slight dip of his head. Turning to the police officer, he said, "Nate, let's find your partner."

Nate had the look of a man swept away by rapids. Mr. Tyler laid a hand on the young man's shoulder and gave him an assuring nod. "Nate, we'll be all right."

"Yes, sir."

Cam gave Nate a tight hug and said, "Call us when you find them."

Roger kept to himself as he rode in the front seat of the brown sedan. He studied Nate's movements at the wheel and discovered the young man had great instincts. Somehow, he was able to find the proper street rhythm in the chaos of cars. They wove through the traffic and shot ahead.

Even with the radio volume turned down, Roger heard the constant chatter of policemen and dispatchers announcing different 10-codes and locations. After a while it turned into white noise and faded to the background.

Nate had changed out of his police uniform but had kept his gun. Taking advantage of the time, Roger had adjusted his attire to fit in better. Of course, if he truly wanted to blend, he'd have to go shopping. He could only hope the place they were heading would have limited lighting.

They crossed the Ashley River, turned north, and drove through a tree-shaded residential neighborhood with closely packed two-story houses. Nate turned right, passing more houses, then turned left onto King Street. Lined with a mix of old and new buildings, it traced a meandering path that seemed better fitted for horse-drawn carriages than two-way traffic.

Nate glanced at Roger. "So, what exactly do you do for Arthur?"

"I'm a member of his Confrérie des Freux or roughly translated, Brotherhood of the Rooks."

"Rook? Like the chess piece?"

"More like the bird, but, yes, sometimes like the chess piece."

"I'm not sure I understand."

"We steal information for him." Under his breath, he added, "And sometimes a country."

"You mean you're a spy?"

"Arthur prefers the term thief," Roger answered. "It's his idea of a joke."

"And that makes you qualified to find Brie and Ambrose?" Nate asked.

"Not exactly."

"Care to elaborate?"

"Officer Stone, I solve problems."

"What kind of problems?"

"Human problems. I understand people, and when necessary, I assemble parties for specific expeditions. Like the three people in Mrs. Tyler's living room right now. We are Brie's best hope."

Nate tightened his hold on the steering wheel. "I sure hope you know what you're doing."

"I do."

Leaving behind the shabby, unpainted homes of Charleston, they passed below a sprawling concrete bridge and entered a no-man's land that bore industrial scars. Serving as the gatekeeper, a twelve-story tall apartment building seemed out of place amongst the rail lines, crumbling cemeteries, and metal silos.

Nate pulled into a gravel lot and parked alongside a plain, white building with no windows. Painted on the wall, a canted gold crown encircled the body of a goat. "King Billy's" was written in faded letters above it.

Its inside was exactly as Roger had hoped: dark.

A black man sat in the far corner, strumming a soulful tune on a battered guitar. The sparse crowd was a mix of different-aged men, mostly manual laborers from appearances.   Backlit by shelves filled with spirits, the bartender, an obese man with drooping jowls, wiped the lacquered oak bar with his cloth.

Under the suspicious gaze of the other patrons, Roger followed Nate to the bar, where he took a stool next to a brawny man nursing a beer. He wore a high-collared shirt covered with clubs, spades, hearts, and diamonds that sprouted from ivy leaf and vine tracery.

"Can I get you something?" the bartender asked.

"Two beers, please," Nate replied and laid a couple of one-dollar bills on the counter. The two sat on metal barstools with seats that swiveled. When they did, the other drinkers turned back to their own murmured conversations.

"Tee, were you mugged by that shirt?"

"Naw, buh. Dis my Jimi shirt," Tee rumbled with a wide grin. "Nevvah seen you in here b'foe. Trouble with the missus?"

The bartender set the two beers in front of Nate and slid a bowl of peanuts closer to him.

"No, Cam's fine. Tee, this is Roger. He's a friend of Ambrose," Nate said. Roger felt Tee's sharp eyes sweep over him.

"Glad tuh meet oonuh," Tee said. "Name's Tecumseh Middleton. Buckruhs 'round here call me Tee. Kinda like the drink."

"Have you seen Brie?" Nate asked.

Tee shook his head. "Not since dis mawnin' at de Market."

Nate gulped down half his beer before asking, "Why did you send Brie and Ambrose to the Courthouse?"

"Dey needed tuh see de doctor."

"Tee, they're missing."

The man sat up and faced his partner. "Wuh makes you think dey missing? It's barely sunlean. Shoot. It's at least three mo' hours befo' sundown. Dey could be out having a good time."

"Man, I don't know. A feeling, I guess." Nate finished his beer and asked for another. "You heard the report. They found one of those silver-eyed men at the courthouse."

"Yeah, I heard."

"What if Brie was right, and those men were chasing them? We should have taken them home."

Tee laid an arm across Nate's shoulders and said, "It's not yo fault. We'll find 'em."

Roger leaned over and asked Tee, "You sent them to see a doctor. Why did you do that?"

"Brie's friend was cussed, and the doctor could take it away."

"Do you know where this doctor is now?" Roger asked.

Tee thought a moment and replied, "He got an office downtown. We'll start dey."

"Tee, no," Nate said. "We can't ask you to do that. It may be nothing."

"If you gwine see de doctor, I have tuh take you."

"Thanks, partner. I really appreciate the help."

Nate motioned for the bartender and flashed his badge. "I need your phone."

"Local calls only," the man said, slapping it down on the counter. While Tee paid his tab, Nate called the Tylers.

Heading south on King Street, Roger sat in back while Nate and Tee were up front. The two policemen seemed comfortable with each other — even complemented each other, though they probably didn't realize it.

Roger thanked the Eternal Father that Ambrose had found a good family here in Terra. Despite the trouble with The Archer, things could have gone a lot differently. He contemplated how much he should tell the two men and decided to keep quiet for now.

As it was, he felt they had already revealed too much. Everyone was distracted for the moment. Eventually events would slow down, and the Tyler's would have time to let their presence sink in. Even Nate and Tee. When all was said and done, would they think the four of them had escaped from a lunatic asylum? Would the two try to stop them from leaving?

The sun seemed to race westward as they wove through a confusing maze of streets, and Roger knew darkness would fall sooner than anyone wanted.

People in cars were heading home, most aimed out of town. There were older men in suits, younger men in short-sleeved shirts, and women, who wore a mixture of dress types. The younger the woman, the shorter the skirt. Roger found the variety refreshing. He tried to imagine his father,

Earl Wolverton, or his elder brother dressed in suits and smiled. Their father only wore state robes or riding clothes. His mother, brother, and sister, on the other hand, always wore the latest fashions, especially when attending the Gallowen court.

"Turn lef' at Broad," Tee said. "Den go up Church."

"Got it."

On Church, Tee pointed to a gravel parking lot with a set of exterior metal stairs leading to its second floor. Above the door hung a simple wooden placard painted with a haint-blue hand, its fingers splayed. Centered in the palm was a single eye with a red iris.

"He's dey."

They got out and climbed the stairs. At the top, Tee knocked on the door and tried the doorknob. It was open.

"Mary," Tee called out, as he entered the waiting room.

"Where is everyone?" Nate asked, peering down the hallway to the corner office.

Tee searched Mary's desk. She still had her sweater jacket draped over the back of her chair.

Roger crept down the hallway. The spartan office was empty except for a bare table surrounded by uncomfortable chairs.

"I got sump'n'," Tee said. He held up a notepad. A stylized QBEE covered the top page. In the middle of the Q was tomorrow's date and a time.

"It looks like an appointment," Nate said.

Tee studied the cryptic note and said, "Maybe Queen Bee? She runs a salon dis side of town."

Nate leaned in next to him and asked, "Didn't we hear that a salon burned down earlier today?"

Worry and concern filled the room like a clammy blanket. Nate stared down at the blue phone. His hand hovered above the receiver.

Roger pulled it away and said, "Not yet."

"He's right," Tee said. "Let's check it out first."

"Did they mention any fatalities?" Nate asked.

"At least two, I t'ink," Tee answered, "but dey sent a bunch tuh de hospital."

At the top of the stairs, Tee locked the door behind him and made sure it caught. Roger and Nate leaned with their backs against the car and watched him.

"It had to be those silver-eyed men," Nate said.

"Dærganfae don't care who gets in their way," Roger said. "Cerdic's right — they're ruthless."

"How do we stop them?"

"One step at a time. Let's find Ambrose and Brie first."

Tee jogged toward them and said, "Sorry. Couldn't leave it open like dat."

"No problem," Nate said. "Let's go.

They continued down Church and turned left on Queen. Though he stared out the window, Roger ignored the modern marvels all around him. He kept picturing Ambrose burned alive. He shook his head to clear the vision.

Roger clenched his fist. How had The Archer found Ambrose so quickly? Did they have a piece of the vigil robe, too? No. If they'd had a piece of the robe, they would have attacked the Tyler's at their home. They had to have something else.

He wasn't a mage, but he'd tracked a few in his time. They could use hair, fingernail clippings, feces, anything that held a trace of the person. It paid to be careful when staying at an inn.

When they turned right on to Logan Street, Roger asked, "What did people do in this salon?"

"Get dey haircut and styled, mostly," Tee replied. "Maybe manicures and pedicures, I don't really know."

The street forked, and they veered left. Up ahead, yellow barricade tape surrounded the remains of the two-story salon. Still smoking, the roof and floor had caved. Portions of the exterior walls remained standing, braced by the debris. Shattered glass, sparkling in the fading sunlight, covered the street.

A police car sat outside with two uniformed officers in the front seat. They both held cups of coffee and looked like they were settling in for a long stay.

"Is that Chapman?" Nate asked.

"And Tucker," added Tee.

Nate pulled up behind them and got out of the car. Tee followed him.

"Hey, Chapman," Nate said. "They got you babysitting?"

Still holding his coffee, Chapman stepped out of his car.

He was an older officer with salt and pepper hair. Starched and creased, his uniform fit snugly over his barrel chest.

"Stone, what are you and Middleton doing here?" Chapman asked after taking a sip. "This is an active crime scene."

"What happened?" Nate asked.

Not waiting to hear the answer, Roger slipped out of the backseat. The pungent reek of charred wood tickled his nose, and he held back a sneeze.

Using the tree at the corner for cover, he stood at the head of Wilson Street and studied the burnt building. More trees lined the cracked bluestone sidewalks, giving it a worn but homey feel. Across Beaufain, there was a narrow lane that led to the rear of the salon. Roger crept to the other side and ducked down the alley.

From the soot stains on the adjacent buildings, it was apparent that Terran firefighting was a work of art. Yes, the primary building burned down, but the fire had been contained. Assignment accomplished, but it didn't leave much to work with.

He opened one of the hardened leather pouches at his belt. Inside was a metal vial and his ivory box. Opening the vial, Roger inhaled the contents. This time he really did sneeze. Replacing the stopper, he took out his pair of whalebone spectacles and adjusted them to fit his nose.

Squeezing his eyes shut, he waited for the vial's contents to take effect. He hated this part.

His stomach flipped, and his gut churned. A wave of dizziness swept through him, sending him stumbling to prop against a nearby building until his head stopped spinning. Slowly, the alley came back into focus, and the nausea receded.

Looking through the spectacles, Roger watched the ground. Vaporous footprints led away from the rear of the salon and back toward Wilson. Dærganfae — they had used magic to disguise themselves.

He didn't see any signs of Brie or Ambrose, but at least he knew who had burned down the salon.

CHAPTER 22
COLONIAL JUSTICE
March 14, 1969 C.E.

6:00 pm

*T*he Archer circled the old city jail, scrutinizing the dark windows and grey walls. Confident in his glamour, he took his time looking for a way inside. The doors were locked, and the windows barred. He called up his magic, searching the walls for a weakness, but found none. His survey ended where it began, back at the postern door near the front.

Where had Aimsitheoir and his team gone? This was where they had said to regroup. He tried the door again, giving it a hard yank. The lock refused to yield.

Every sign indicated his team had entered the building, but they hadn't left. No one had, not in a while. The dark building leered, mocking him as he stepped away.

A nagging sensation crept up his spine. The Archer ducked behind the wall and peered through the open gate. His eyes narrowed at a figure creeping down the sidewalk: Roger Vaughn. Walking in the edge of the evening shadows and wearing funny-looking spectacles, the human was following his team's footsteps.

The Archer flashed back to the Square of King David and the destruction of the orb. Events clicked into place, and he realized it had been Roger who had stood between him and his target this whole time. And now he was here, all alone.

A wicked smile spread across his angular features as he slipped his longbow from his shoulder and nocked a black-fletched arrow.

Roger kept to the shadows as he followed the vaporous trail down the bluestone sidewalk. Children watched him from across the street, some smiling and waving as he went by.

Turning the corner at Magazine Street, he gaped at the three-story grey prison flanked by two square towers with barred windows and battlements. A white wall with brick coping surrounded the adjoining grounds. Sure enough, the trail he followed crossed the street and disappeared beyond an arched gate.

Sensing more than seeing the quick motion, Roger acted on instinct, throwing himself onto the ground behind a tree.

The sharp sting along his side didn't register at first. Lying prone on the ground, he felt his tunic become wet and sticky. Searing pain soon followed.

Pushing his spectacles back onto his nose, Roger scanned the street. He slid his long, silver daggers from their sheaths and waited. To his left, a faint glow appeared beside the gated entry where the trail ended.

"Your aim's off, Archer!" Roger shouted. "Having a bad day?"

"It's the humidity. Makes the arrows drop faster. Stick your head out. I won't make the same mistake twice."

"No, thanks. Isn't there a limit to the number of times you can try to kill me? I mean, this makes it twice this week, doesn't it?"

The faint glow vanished.

Roger swore as he pushed himself off the ground. Feeling dizzy, he leaned against the tree and waited for it to pass.

Crepuscular light blazed up from a nearby bluestone paver. There was a rush of wind, and suddenly The Archer loomed in front of Roger. His silver eyes shimmered as he stabbed with his curved sword.

Daggers crossed in an 'X,' Roger caught it.

"Feel your heart beating." The Archer's voice was soft, barely more than a whisper. He pressed his blade against Roger's. "Do you feel your fingers growing numb? A tightness in your chest? Your blood is spreading my poison throughout your body. It's a matter of time before you lose muscle control. After that, darkness."

"Bastard," Roger growled. Desperate, he shoved The Archer's blade to one side with the guard of his righthand dagger and sliced with the other. The dærganfae leapt back but not before Roger scored him across the cheek.

The Archer hissed and slashed at Roger's neck.

Ducking, Roger rolled to the side. His pounding heart sent numbness into his arms and legs. He couldn't stand.

His daggers dropped from nerveless hands, as he tried to crawl away.

The Archer stood over him, triumphant.

"Freeze!" Nate shouted. He stood with his legs apart and arms forward, his gun aimed at the dærganfae. "Tee, grab him!"

Tee surged forward.

The Archer gave them both scathing looks. "Animals! Try to save him if you can," he said. A purplish light appeared on the surface of the bluestone sidewalk, and The Archer sank within its glow.

Tee skidded to a stop and made a sign against evil. The light winked out.

Nate holstered his gun and knelt beside Roger. "You're bleeding," he said, ripping open the tunic. Blood ran freely from a gash across Roger's ribs. Nate yanked off his shirt and pressed it to the wound.

"Can't... move," Roger gasped.

"Tee, call an ambulance."

"No... Cerdic..."

Ambrose woke with the putrid smell of rotting flesh assailing her senses. She inhaled through her nose to keep the taste out of her mouth as she lay on her side atop a bed of damp wood shavings. A blanket of oppressive heat and humidity pressed down upon her, making each breath an effort.

She opened a single bleary eye. A bloated corpse stared back at her with milky eyes, its fluids saturating the wood chips.

"*Ughh!*" she cried as she leapt up. Sporadic laughter broke out around her.

Ambrose found herself in a six-foot by eight-foot iron cage. Barefoot, she wore an ill-fitting white dress soaked with sweat. Heavy shackles bound her wrists and ankles. Grabbing the bars, she looked around frantically for Brie but didn't see her. She ran a sweaty hand over her head and felt the remains of the doctor's Goofer dust covering her bald scalp. The sensation grounded her and drove away the rising panic.

A scraggly man with long, stringy hair leered from the opposite end of the cage. Covered in suppurating sores and his own filth, he crouched low, his eyes filled with madness. Between him and her lay the dead man. Flies and maggots crawled about fresh wounds along its bare arms and legs where it had been gnawed upon.

In total, ten cages similar in size and shape to the one that held Ambrose filled the rectangular chamber. Stuffed inside, men and women wore little more than rags and pinioned shackles. Many bore brands on their hands, cheeks, or arms, depicting a stylized L, M, or other letter. Some had their noses or ears cropped. All bore open wounds from frequent lashings.

A twelve-foot-wide central aisle separated the cages, five to a side. A forged metal column rose from the center of the aisle, and near it, an ominous hook hung from the vaulted brick ceiling. Behind the cages, there was enough space for a person to pass between the bars and the thick grey walls.

Fading light from outside entered through narrow windows set with a rusted grid of cast-iron bars. At each corner of the room sat a soot-stained fireplace, now barren and lifeless. In the middle of the grey wall opposite the windows, a barred gate guarded an ironclad door. A dawning horror overtook Ambrose as she realized she was in the City Jail.

Keys jangled and the iron door creaked open. A jailor poked his head into a curved recess in the barred gate, allowing him to see into the room. Satisfied, he unlocked it and entered.

He wore a linen shirt, open at the collar. His faded trousers fed into the tops of scuffed boots. A short club hung from his belt. Two more came in behind him. One carried a box piled high with square pieces of cornbread and the other a bucket of water and ladle.

"Keep it orderly!" the jailor said, locking the barred gate behind him. He wiped his bearded face with a stained handkerchief, then adjusted his hat and scanned the prisoners with dead eyes. Taking out his club, he dragged it across the bars. There was a general shuffle and clanking of chains as prisoners, at least the ones who were able, stood at opposite ends of their cages with their tin cup poking through the bars.

Starting nearest the far wall, the three walked past the first row. One handed out the cornbread, while the other dipped the ladle in his bucket and filled the prisoners' cups. They came back down the central aisle, turned, and went up the next row, forming a double "u" pattern.

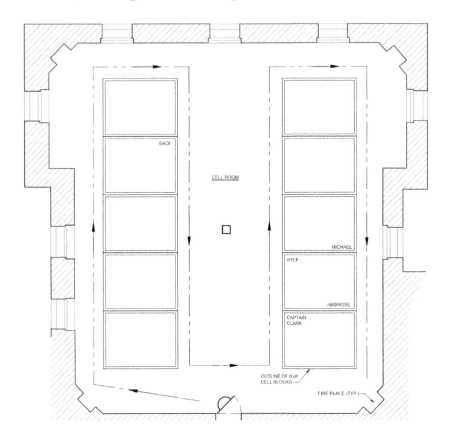

Ambrose watched as they wound around the end of her row. She was in the next to last cage with her hands down by her sides. The jailor stopped in front of her. His dead eyes came to life as he took in her shapely form.

"It's been a busy day," he said with a smirk. "You make seven."

Ambrose lifted her chin and said, "I demand you release me at once."

"Take your bread and water, girl," he replied. "Where's your cup?"

She looked around and found it half buried in the wood

shavings. Grimacing, she plucked it out of the filth and stuck it through the bars. Expecting them to clean it first, she frowned when the one with the ladle filled her cup. A thin sheen of slime rose to the top. Stunned, she stared at her piece of cornbread.

In the cage next to hers, a man with a boyish face and eager eyes asked, "You gonna drink that?"

Licking the crumbs from his parched lips, he reached toward her cup. She handed it to him, and he gulped it down. He was about to finish it but stopped. Instead, he set the cup down amid the wood shavings, a swallow at the bottom.

She took her eyes from the cup and broke open the cornbread. The insides were a brownish-red, and there in the middle was a bloodied fingernail. Shocked, she dropped it. "What kind of place is this?" she gasped.

"Welcome to Hell," said the man with the boyish face.

"This is the city jail, isn't it?"

A lucid look came over the man as he said, "Yes. It's the last bastion of Colonial Justice. Here, they don't try to reform you, they make an example of you. They strip away your humanity and hold you up for everyone to see what happens to criminals." The man's boyish face turned dark and sinister. He began to laugh maniacally. The laugh turned into a wail, and he pounded his fist against the cage.

"We're all mad here," the scraggly man in her cage whispered.

Wide-eyed, Ambrose realized the truth of what the man said. If she didn't get out of here soon, she'd go mad too. Picking up her cup with that last swallow of water, she downed it.

Out of the corner of her eye, she noticed that the door had been left open. Led by two guards, a woman wearing a long flowing gown passed their room. The procession had an air of repetition, and Ambrose's heart went out to the poor woman.

Everyone grew quiet when animalistic grunts echoed from the hallway. Ambrose gripped the bars of her cell and waited, but the guttural noises didn't stop.

Outside, the sun dipped below the horizon and cast a blood-red hue about the room. She tried to block out the sounds but found she couldn't. It became primeval, feeding the fear building inside her. The fear, in turn, tightened her throat and tried to steal her voice. Finding some of the reputed Battenberg steel, she rattled her cage and cried, "LET HER GO!"

The men and women around her went pale and waved their hands. "Shut up."

"THIS IS WRONG!"

"Bitch, what are you doing?" the scraggly man in her cage said, looking at her with murderous intent.

The jail grew quiet.

Unnerved, Ambrose put her back to the bars.

In the hallway, the procession of guards returned. Stiff and sore, the woman in white held her arms across her gut. She paused in front of their door and straightened as if pulling together the last vestiges of her dignity.

"Keep moving," one said, shoving her from behind.

Not long after they were gone, the jailor came back with two guards. Careful to make sure the whole room was clear, he opened the barred gate and aimed for Ambrose's end of the cell.

"You can't treat people like this." She spread her shackled feet as far apart as the chains permitted and raised her fists.

Spitting in her face, the jailor said, "Move back." He opened the cell, brandished his club in one hand, and said, "It's your turn."

Anger seared away any fear. She'd already lost so much — her family, her home — she'd be damned if she'd let these men have their way with her. Ambrose had to find Brie and get out of here.

Lashing out like a demoness, she scratched at the jailor's eyes and face. He tried to flee, but she managed to wrap her chains around the man's neck and rode him all the way to the floor. His companions' laughter ringing in her ears, she slammed the jailer's head into the woodchips until she found concrete and bashed him senseless.

Whipping around, Ambrose glared at the scraggly man who shared her cell. He prostrated himself on the soiled wood chips. All about them, inmates shouted and hooted.

Wearing sly grins, the other two guards held their clubs ready.

"What's going on here?" asked a hoarse voice. Like a

razor, it cut through the rancor and sent a chill through the swampy air.

Ready to challenge the newcomer, Ambrose stopped cold when she saw the creature at the barred door. Haggard and pale, it more closely resembled an articulated skeleton than anything remotely human. Deep black eyes, recessed into its skull, peered out. They burned with visceral hate that sent everyone cowering.

The nearest guard, one with a jagged scar down the side of his neck, grabbed Ambrose by the arm. "Come on, you sod," he said, jerking her closer.

Regaining her senses, she dug in her heels and struggled against his grip. The other jabbed her sharply in the gut with the point of his club. The breath knocked out of her, Ambrose collapsed in a heap. Together, they half-dragged/half-carried her to the creature at the doorway.

"Executioner," one said, "what do you want us to do with her?"

"Take her to the holding cell," the thing said, eyeing the cowed prisoners.

Taking a lantern from a wall hook, the guards hauled Ambrose from her room and past a set of concrete steps that accessed the third floor before letting her regain her feet. Each with a tight grip on her upper arm, they walked her toward the octagonal wing and entered the first door on the left.

Inside, spatters of blood decorated the hardwood floor and iron plating riveted to the walls. In the middle of the room, ropes dangled from a pulley attached to the ceiling. Below was a short chain with a clasp.

Ambrose cried out when the guard with the scar struck her across the kidneys and sent her to her knees.

Working together, they strung her up by her wrist shackles and chained down her ankles. After giving her restraints a quick tug, the one with the scar nodded. The other jailor, standing beside a crank, began turning it. The ropes creaked and grew taut as Ambrose was slowly stretched to her breaking point. She gritted her teeth and tried not to cry out.

The Executioner shut the door behind him with an ominous clank. His claw-like hand clutched a short, leather whip with lead balls sewn into the end. "Seven new prisoners in one day, and only one who can't see us. The devil must be smiling." He slowly drew back his arm. Disappointment and anger clouded his features when she neither cowered nor begged. He struck her with the whip.

It was like being hit with a metal rod. The braided leather cut her skin, and she cried out as pain arced through her body. "Why are you doing this?" she gasped, every word cut short with a sharp intake of air.

"I am the Executioner," he replied. "This is what I've always done."

He struck her again and again with the whip, drawing blood each time. It flecked the ironclad walls and dripped onto the floor.

She must have lost consciousness because she woke hearing her name.

"Queen Ambrose Battenberg," the creature said. His skeletal fingers held her chin. "Come back. We're not done yet."

"You know who I am?" she asked.

"I've compelled many a confession using a loaded whip," it replied. "Your friends, the fae, for example. It took a while for them to break, but the gaol's prisoners always tell me what I want to know. Like who you are, and why you're here."

"Then, what do you want from me?" she cried.

The creature drew closer and whispered, "I want to break you."

His fetid breath upon her cheek, she clenched her jaw and stared into his cold, dead eyes. She didn't see herself, like she expected. No. She saw only grey walls and barred windows reflected in those eyes.

"There's still fight left in you, girl. I can feel it." Stepping away, he reared back and lashed her again.

CHAPTER 23
DOGWOOD TREE ISSUANT FROM
SURGICAL GREENS

March 14, 1969 c.e.

6:35 pm

*L*ahar, Cerdic, and the Highlord huddled near the Tylers' living room window. Cam was in the kitchen with her mother, preparing sandwiches. Reading the newspaper, Mr. Tyler sat, his legs crossed, just across the room, occasionally looking over the edge at his unusual visitors. To his credit, he seemed to be taking it all in stride.

"I should have gone with Bo back to the ship," Lahar said. Her busy brain wouldn't stay quiet. She alternated between worrying about her ship and wanting to strangle Ambrose whenever she and Roger got back.

"Captain Lahar, we have time," the Highlord replied. "Let Roger do his job."

The phone rang in the kitchen. Everyone kept quiet when Mr. Tyler left to answer it. "This is Mr. Tyler," he said. After a brief pause, he asked, "What happened? I see. We'll be right there." He hung up the phone, his face drawn with concern. "That was Nate. Seems your Mr. Vaughn was injured. He's at the County Hospital."

The Highlord asked, "Any word about your daughter or Ambrose?"

Mr. Tyler shook his head. "No. Nate was tight-lipped about what happened, but whatever it was shook him."

"Sir, if you get me to that hospital," said Cerdic, "I can help him."

"I want to come, too," Cam said.

Holding up his hand, Mr. Tyler told Cam, "Stay here with your mother. Brie may still call or show up."

"Yes, sir," she replied. Her eyes downcast, she was clearly unhappy with being left behind.

Mr. Tyler kissed her on the forehead and said, "Everything will be all right." He turned to Mrs. Tyler and gave her a kiss on the cheek. "Battle stations, Mildred."

"You be careful," she replied, giving his arm a squeeze.

"Give me a minute to pack the sandwiches, and you can eat them on the way."

Mr. Tyler led them to a sleek two-door coupe with a long hood and short deck. Above the front grille, an emblem read, "Mercury," in fancy script. On the other side was the embossed profile of a chrome cougar. He opened the door and pushed the seat forward.

"Get in."

The Highlord and Cerdic slid into the back while Lahar walked around to the passenger side. She didn't say it, but she enjoyed riding in front. And given the close quarters, the front seat was definitely preferable.

Mr. Tyler turned the key, and the engine gave a deep growl. "Got the new 302 V8 in this baby," he bragged. "Four-barrel. Produces two-hundred and thirty horses. You step on the gas, the speedometer goes one way, and the gas needle the other!" He said it like it was an old joke everyone found funny. The silence from the three in the car was almost palpable.

He pulled out onto the main highway and said, "You don't drive much, do you?"

"We do not drive at all," the Highlord said.

Lahar ran a surreptitious finger along the Cougar's interior. It felt different than Captain Walker's truck. The comfortable leather seats, fancy dashboard, and feeling of power from the engine awoke a kind of primal desire within her. It was like when her ship *jumped,* but not quite. She wanted to go faster.

Mr. Tyler crossed the Ashley River Bridge, exited onto Lockwood, and followed it around to Calhoun Street. He turned at a sprawling brick building. A sign with glowing red letters identified it as the Oliver Krump County Hospital.

"Your friend's in the emergency room," Mr. Tyler said. He followed an arrow pointing the way to the ER and found a parking spot. "Nate's already in the waiting room."

They dashed across the asphalt and aimed for the glass door under the porte-cochere. Inside was a room filled with plastic and metal chairs. A receptionist with curly hair and a permanent smile sat behind a long counter lined with forms attached to clipboards.

Standing at the counter, Nate turned when they entered.

He motioned them over and handed the Highlord one of the clipboards. "Arthur, they'll need some information from you."

"Where is he?" Cerdic asked.

Nate nodded at a pair of closed doors and said, "Through there. The nurse came out a few minutes ago. She said Roger's wound was minor, but whatever it was that cut him was coated with poison. They have him on a ventilator."

Cerdic strode toward the double doors. When the receptionist realized where he was going, she jumped up with the smile still plastered on her face and said, "Sir, you can't go back there." Blocking his path, she gave him a once-over. "You'll have to sit down."

Nate rushed up, flashing his badge. "I got this."

The paladin ignored them both. He moved past the receptionist; his eyes focused on what lay beyond those doors.

"He can't go back there," she said, her smile slipping. "He's... armed."

"Cerdic, let the doctors take care of him," Nate urged.

Handing his knife to Nate, Cerdic pushed open the doors, and Lahar chased after him. The last thing she heard was the receptionist calling for security.

Everywhere Lahar looked, men scurried about in green clothes and green caps. Some pushed carts into curtained rooms while others, with masks tied around their necks, walked around with an air of importance. Nurses in white dresses and striped linen caps followed.

Above them, a voice called for a specific doctor to go to a specific room number. The bright lights, incessant chatter, and mechanical air set Lahar's teeth on edge.

Smelling of salt and sweat in the otherwise sterile environment, Cerdic stopped in the middle of an intersection. A nurse's station lay in front of him. Luckily, everyone had their head down despite the noise from the waiting room.

Lahar plowed into him and pushed him toward a whitewashed corridor lined with doors. "Come on," she said. "No time to sightsee."

Her sharp elven eyes picked out a man exiting a room. He made last minute adjustments to his wardrobe before striding in the opposite direction.

Casting a quick glance over her shoulder, she picked up the pace when she saw two policemen talking with the nurses and doctors. They ducked inside the room and found it filled with metal lockers.

"Why are we in here?" Cerdic asked.

Opening and closing the lockers, Lahar found a narrow door labeled "CLEAN." She'd struck gold.

"Put these on," she said, handing Cerdic the largest pair of green drawstring pants she could find, along with a matching V-neck shirt and cap. She grabbed a set for herself.

While she pulled the pants over her leathers, Cerdic glared at her and at the garment. "I don't need this." He handed them back to her.

"Put it on," Lahar said, shoving the clothes back at him. "That receptionist called out the dogs on us. We need disguises."

Cerdic's mouth fell open, and his eyebrows climbed his forehead. "I don't hide. It's cowardly. Besides, those won't fit over my clothes."

Narrowing her eyes at the knight, Lahar crossed her arms and said, "You want to find Roger, don't you?"

"Of course."

"Then. Change. Clothes," she said through gritted teeth. At the sound of barely restrained violence in her tone, Cerdic's shoulders slumped.

"Turn your back."

She complied but caught a glimpse of the knight peeling off his tunic in a nearby mirror. Unaware he was watched, Cerdic pulled off his breeches. Heat flooded Lahar's face, and she averted her gaze.

Fabric rustled, and Cerdic announced, "You can turn around now." His leather belt and pouch looked out of place against the green fabric.

Lahar shook her head and closed the space between them. Before Cerdic could back away, she gripped the leather around his waist. His stomach muscles quivered against the backs of her fingers. Staring into his eyes, she worked loose the belt buckle.

He gulped, and his face flushed red. "What are you doing?"

"You can't walk around with your pouch showing." She

grinned as his jaw dropped. "I'll hide it with your clothes in the closet. We can come back for them when we have Roger."

"But—"

"Who's the expert here? Trust me." When he nodded, Lahar handed him a mask.

He shook his head. "I draw the line at covering my face."

"You wear a helmet all the time. How is this any different?"

Cerdic stiffened and replied, "My armor bears my family crest and the crest of Carolingias. Everyone knows who I am."

Fuming, Lahar opened one of the lockers and shoved the stuff around, making noise. *"I draw the line at covering my face,"* she mimicked. Slamming the locker closed, she opened the next one. "There has to be something in here." She came out with a five-inch-long cylindrical device. "Magic Marker" was written along its side.

Though her outward appearance was confident, inside she was all knots and butterflies. She found the cap, pulled it off, and a strong chemical smell filled the air. She experimented with it on the back of the locker and smiled. "Roger would love these."

"What?" Cerdic asked, adjusting his cap.

"Nothing," Lahar said, coming at him with the marker. "Now, hold still."

Cerdic backed up with his hands spread wide.

"Come here, you big baby," Lahar said. "This won't hurt a bit."

She stepped in close, laying her hand on his chest. With her other hand, she sketched a primitive dogwood rising from a small hill over his heart and drew a big circle around them.

"There. Happy?" she said, replacing the marker cap and slipping the pen into one of her pockets.

Cerdic admired her handiwork in the mirror. "Very nice."

"Good. Now let's find Roger."

The two exited the locker room and fell in behind a trio of nurses headed back toward the ER.

"Pam said one of them was as big as a house. I can't believe he walked right in without anyone seeing him," one of the nurses said.

"Should we be worried? I mean are they dangerous?"

asked the second in a hushed voice.

"Do you think they're the ones who broke into the morgue earlier?" the first nurse added.

"I doubt it. They came in with that handsome policeman," answered the third.

"Who are they looking for?"

"How should I know?" the third replied.

The nurses split up when they arrived at the nurse's station. Feeling exposed, Lahar looked around. Cerdic was gone. She backtracked and found him in a curtained room.

A young man lay on the bed, his face contorted in pain as he fought to breathe. Wires connected to his chest and arms led to a bank of shushing and beeping machines. Behind a round, glass window, a tiny ball with a comet-like tail bounced with each beep. Running from a bag filled with clear liquid, a tube disappeared under thick bandages that wrapped the crook of his arm.

His eyes closed, Cerdic had one hand on the man's forehead, and the other on his chest. A silent prayer issued from his lips.

The lights in the room pulsed once, twice. Lahar felt it when the monitor with the bouncing ball went dark. Fresh mountain air replaced the mechanical smell, and a sense of peace filled the room. The pain on the man's face eased. His eyes flew open, and he tried to speak. Cerdic shook his head and said, "Get some rest. You're going to need it."

Sighing, the man sank into the bed and fell asleep.

Hands on her hips, Lahar said, "Roger's waiting." Visions of them being caught swam before her eyes.

Cerdic gave her a quick frown and headed out the door. Before they reached the nurse's station, a shrill alarm rang out from the room they had exited.

One of the nurses brushed past them as she ran down the hall. She called out, and others came running.

Using the chaos for cover, Lahar found a clipboard with a list of ER patients hanging on the wall. Her finger stopped when she came to room #212. Inside a little box, the patient's name was listed as "Vaughn, R. (Chas PD)". On a line set aside for comments were the initials PSP.

"Found him," she said. "He's upstairs."

Badge in hand, Nate paced back and forth in front of the reception counter. The lady with the curly hair and permanent smile eyed him as if expecting him to grow horns at any moment.

Mr. Tyler had left to find a payphone and report home. Sitting in one of the metal and plastic chairs, the man called Arthur still held the clipboard.

'*He sure is taking his sweet time filling out that paperwork*,' Nate thought. He approached Arthur and crouched in front of him. "What's really going on here?"

Arthur put aside the clipboard. His ageless, pearl grey eyes were unsettling, and Nate dropped his gaze.

Leaning forward, Arthur said, "Son, we're trying to find Brie and Ambrose."

"Yeah, but that guy with the pointed ears and silver eyes." Nate took a seat across from Arthur. "This will sound crazy, but he sank into the sidewalk. I saw it. Purple light and all."

Something sparked in Arthur's eyes.

"Who is he?" Nate asked.

"He calls himself The Archer. He's a paid assassin."

"Is he even human?" Nate gave Arthur an oblique look. '*There. I've said it.*' He expected a weight to be lifted. Instead, his gut twisted that much more.

"No. He's dærganfae. A dark elf."

"Like Lahar?"

A grim smile played across Arthur's lips. "The Celts in Ireland would tell you he's a faerie from the Unseelie Court. Completely different than Lahar, who is an elf of Gaia.

"Nate, you've stumbled upon a war between good and evil. A war we were winning. At least until Ambrose disappeared. That's why it's so important we find her."

"Why her?" Nate asked. "Seems a lot to put on that girl's shoulders."

"She's the last of the ruling family of Carolingias, one of the countries on the continent of Parlatheas. Without her, Carolingias will fall. Of that, I have no doubt."

"Wow. So, Ambrose is a queen?"

"Not yet."

"But when she does become Queen, everything will be *happily ever after*."

"Nate, that never happens. After her coronation, the true

fight begins. However, instead of it being one person doing one thing while another person does something else, we will finally present a united front. We will finally be able to push back the forces of the Dark One."

The passion in Arthur's baritone voice struck a chord with Nate. While he hadn't fully digested the events of the evening, he at least understood some of the stakes — assuming Arthur wasn't lying. He scrutinized the broad-shouldered man with close-cropped black hair and chiseled jawline. For the first time, he realized Arthur wore an iron pendant embossed with a rampant dragon flanked by a tower and an owl.

"Arthur, I promise to do everything I can to help you and Ambrose, but my loyalty lies with the Tylers and their daughters."

"Well said, young man. I expected nothing less." Looking at the double doors, Arthur said, "But to find Brie, we need Roger."

Compared to the hustle of the first floor, the second floor felt lifeless and forlorn. The stench of the sick underscored the conditioned air. Even the lights seemed sad. Lahar stopped an orderly pushing a metal cart and asked, "Room 212?"

He barely glanced in her direction. Hitching a thumb over his shoulder, he said, "Back that way."

"Bless you," Cerdic said.

Lahar hesitated. The ranks of closed doors stretching into the distance could hide any number of unknown enemies, and there were neither convenient shadows nor cover to hide behind. She was out of her element and felt exposed.

Ahead of her, Cerdic strode down the hall.

In the past, she had been the one who led the way, finding the safe route through enemies and hidden traps. Hands near her weapons, she chased after the paladin on silent feet, expecting someone to accost them with each passing second.

They passed a half-dozen doors with no cry of alarm. Suspicious, she studied the people both before and behind them. Medical staff moved about, but they had their backs turned, heads down, or were traveling away from Cerdic and Lahar. No one paid them any attention. It was like they were invisible.

Lahar tugged on the knight's sleeve. "Cerdic, are you doing this?"

"Doing what?"

He stared into her almond-shaped eyes and the innocence in them struck her. Even after working together for the better part of four years, it continued to surprise her. It gave her hope.

"Never mind," she said.

Cerdic slowed and entered a patient's room. Lying in an elevated bed, an old lady with thin white hair and deep wrinkles held a thick black book close to her breast. She whispered a prayer.

Lahar waited in the corner, fretting over the time but knowing she was powerless to move the big man any faster.

"Hello, Mrs. French," Cerdic said. He leaned over her bed and took her hand in his.

"Is it time?" she asked. A desperate hope shone in her eyes.

"Yes, ma'am. Are you ready?"

She gave him a curt nod. "Mr. French is waiting on me."

"Just relax," he said with an encouraging smile.

"Will it hurt?"

"No, ma'am."

Cerdic whispered a prayer, and to Lahar's surprise, the old woman said it with him. At the end, the woman stiffened and gripped his hand tight. Releasing her final breath, the light in her eyes dimmed and her whole body slumped.

After closing her eyes, Cerdic kissed her forehead. "Goodbye, Mrs. French."

Lahar swallowed the emotion caught in her throat and wiped away her tears. When Cerdic turned toward her, she wrapped him in a tight hug and buried her face in his chest. She felt his arms close around her and drew in some of his strength.

"How can you be so calm?" she asked.

Cerdic gave her a gentle squeeze and said, "She's with the Eternal Father. I only wish her family could have been here with her."

"At least she wasn't alone." Shivering with inexplicable

fear, she whispered, "When it's my time, promise me you'll be there."

His arm tightened around her, and one hand stroked her hair. "I promise," he replied.

The alarm at Mrs. French's bedside went off, followed by loud voices and the sound of running feet from the hallway.

"Time to go," she said. Lahar pulled Cerdic by the arm, and they darted across the corridor into another room where a young woman with honey colored skin slept on the bed. Bandages wrapped most of her body and half of her head. Along the edges, a greasy salve oozed out. Even unconscious, it was clear she suffered.

Sitting in the corner, a tall, gaunt man with pitch black skin chewed the end of a slender root. Slightly hunched, he wore a white linen suit with a lavender silk tie and dark purple glasses.

CHAPTER 24
BACK FROM THE DEAD

March 14, 1969 C.E.

7:16 pm

"*U*h been 'specting you, holy mun," said the man in the chair.

"Do I know you, sir?" Cerdic asked.

"No, but yo Miss Ambrose did. Folks 'round yuh call me Doctor Wampus."

Cerdic reached for his knife, but it wasn't there. "What did you do with her?"

Lahar closed the door. She stood in front of it, a blade in each hand.

Still sitting, the doctor removed his glasses and regarded them with cobalt eyes. "I helped her. Took de root away." His gaze shifted to the woman on the bed.

"What happened?" Cerdic asked.

"Dem fae followed yo Miss Ambrose and 'tackid us. I lost my twenty-one grams but Vie... she still fights the reaper."

"What about Ambrose?"

"Dunno. She 'scaped out the winduh wid her friend."

"Did Roger find her?"

"He duh fancy creole de police brung here?"

Cerdic tilted his head to one side, clearly confused. "I beg your pardon?"

"De man mixed race like my Vie."

"He's never mentioned having elven or dwarven ancestors," Lahar replied, "but I don't understand what that has to do with anything."

The strange man chuckled. "Uh like you, gal. You don' see de culluh of uh man's skin."

"Did Roger find Ambrose or not?"

"Can't say, but 'e find sump'n."

"He found The Archer, didn't he," Lahar said.

"I 'spec he did."

Lahar hid her knives and said, "Nate said he was poisoned. If it was The Archer, we don't have much hope. Dærganfae poison has no antidote."

"There's always hope," said Cerdic. "Roger survived it once. He can do it again."

"Maybe I kin be of assistance," Doctor Wampus offered. "But dey's a price."

"What do you want, shaman?" Cerdic asked.

"Save my Vie, en I'll help yo Roger."

Lahar turned to the man and realized there was something strange about him. She blinked a couple of times to clear her vision, but it didn't help. She could still see the outline of the chair through the doctor. "Cerdic, don't trust this ghost."

Doctor Wampus replaced his glasses and held out his hand. In the palm was a bit of wiry root. "Heal her, en you can hab de cure."

Cerdic studied the young woman. His eyes reflected the pain she felt as he took in her burns. After a moment, he said, "The Eternal Father calls to her. There's nothing I can do."

The doctor shot up out of his chair. "No! He can't hab her. There must be sump'n. I'll do anything," he pleaded. He grabbed Cerdic by the arm. His grip seemed real enough. "Don't let her die."

"What's so special about this woman?" Lahar asked, her voice filled with suspicion.

"She muh daughter."

His face stern, Cerdic said to the doctor, "Where she goes, there is no pain, no suffering. She will be young forever sitting at the side of the Eternal Father. Isn't that what you really want?"

Doctor Wampus drew up to his full height and replied, "I want her to live, to get marri'd an' have chillun, tuh see this world, and grow old befo' moobing on to de nex'. She ent done yuh."

"And what about Roger?" Lahar asked Cerdic. "Is it his time, too?"

"Very well," replied Cerdic, "but in the end, it's up to the Eternal Father. All I can do is ask."

Bowing his head, Cerdic knelt beside the bed with his arms stretched before him. He laid his hands on the woman's arm and prayed. The lights in the room pulsed and dimmed. Cerdic's presence grew. "Violet Stevenson," he called out. "Violet Stevenson, come back. Your work here is not yet done." Smoke wafted up from the bank of equipment, and Lahar's nose rankled at the sharp scent of scorched metal. The monitors squelched and went dark.

When the lights came back on, an ozone haze filled the room, concentrated near the electronics. Vie stirred and opened her eyes. Confused, she cast about until finding Cerdic. "Who are you? Where's my father?"

When Lahar looked around, Doctor Wampus had vanished.

Rising, Cerdic said, "We're friends."

Seizing his wrist, she asked, "My father? Is he here?"

Gently pulling away, he replied, "He's with the Eternal Father."

Flailing her arms, Vie clawed at the bandages covering her. "No! He can't be gone."

Cerdic caught her hands. "Look at me, Miss Stevenson. Look at me."

Peering into his eyes, she relaxed, and he let go. He helped her sit up and unwound the greasy bandages from her head and neck. "Your father loved you very much," Cerdic said as he worked. "He still watches over you."

He stopped at the tops of her breasts. Under the bandages, her honey-colored skin, while red and angry, gave no evidence of having burned. Vie ran timid fingertips over her cheek. "You healed me."

While Cerdic looked away, Lahar stepped forward and helped remove the rest of her bandages. "Tell us what happened."

Stifling a sniffle, Vie stared at Lahar's elven features in fascination. "You're fae."

"No, I'm an elf," Lahar said. "Less magic, but more deadly. I take it you saw them?"

"Yes. They stormed into my apartment after those two women. Who were they?"

"That's not important," Lahar replied. "Did you see where they went, or where they came from?"

"No. They... they threw me into the fire..."

The door cracked open, and a brawny black man wearing a high-collared shirt covered with clubs, spades, hearts, and diamonds that sprouted from ivy leaf and vine tracery entered.

Vie snatched the bedsheet over her naked body.

The newcomer's eyes grew wide. "I thought I heard voices," he stammered. Averting his gaze, he turned to Cerdic and said, "Sorry doctor, I didn't know you were here."

"It's okay, Tee," Vie said. "Come on in."

Lahar had reached for her blades but quickly put them away when she realized the two knew each other. "We were just leaving," she said.

Cerdic gave Tee room to enter and said, "Please see that Miss Stevenson is taken home."

Before they reached the door, Tee held out a leather pouch. Her strength returning, Vie sat up as best she could and said, "That's one of my father's root bags. How did you get it?"

Uneasy, Tee replied, "I seen yo pa's sperrit jus' now out in de hall. He tol' me tuh gib it tuh you, 'long with dese." He passed her two silver reales and the pouch.

"Who's the root for?" she asked.

"Nate's friend, Roger."

Lahar gave Cerdic a quick glance. He nodded back at her and said, "That's for us. Roger's our friend, too. I'm Cerdic, and this is Lahar."

Vie rubbed at her eyes and gave Tee a coy smile. "Find me a hospital gown. I'm coming with you."

Cerdic and Tee walked on either side of Vie with an arm at the ready in case she needed it. Lahar followed, her attention captured by the gown's open back. Even with it tied tight, the gown flared open with each step.

Midways down the hall was Room 212. Expecting the worst, Lahar steeled herself and opened the door.

Dressed in a hospital gown, Roger lay on the bed with wires connected to his chest and arms. A bank of machines set in the wall beeped and whirred. Similar to the first patient they met, Roger had a line in his arm that led to a bag filled with clear liquid. He was almost unrecognizable, with most of his face covered by tape where a clear plastic tube had been shoved down his throat. The tube fed into a green box that clicked in time to the rise and fall of Roger's chest.

"What did they do to him?" Lahar asked in horror.

Tee answered, "De pizen paralyzed him. He can't breathe widout de ventilator."

Cerdic laid his hands on his friend and whispered a short prayer. Afterwards, he said, "The poison has him. Tee's right. That machine is the only thing keeping him alive."

Lahar asked, "Can't you do anything?"

The look in Cerdic's eyes said it all.

"I can," Vie said, shuffling forward. "But you'll have to take out the ventilator tube."

"Cerdic just said he'll die without it," Lahar shot out. "We can't."

"Lahar, we have no choice," Cerdic said as he worked the tape loose around Roger's mouth and nose.

Vie touched Lahar's upper arm. "You have to trust me." She turned toward the bed.

Pulling a knife, Lahar snaked an arm around the woman's shoulders and pressed the blade's tip to her throat. Tee moved towards her but stopped when Lahar pressed harder, creating a dimple. "I'm not the trusting type."

Vie inhaled sharply.

Cerdic waved Tee back and carefully approached Lahar. His soft eyes bore into hers. "You must have faith."

"Did it ever occur to you that these two could be working for the Dark One? That this world is one of the planes of hell, and we're being tortured? Ambrose is gone, and Roger's attached to some infernal machine. Who's next? You, the Highlord, me? Do we fall, one by one, while those who survive watch, helpless?"

Vie stiffened. "Look, lady, I don't know what bee got up your butt. The only reason I'm here is to help. Otherwise, I'd be in my room, crying my heart out."

Cerdic placed his hand on Lahar's and gently pulled the knife away from Vie. "I know this place is strange and seeing Roger like this is a shock. It bothers me, too, but you can't strike out at innocents."

Vie ducked under Cerdic's arm as he closed the gap, still holding Lahar's hand. Swallowing, Lahar nodded toward the door and said, "Do what you must. I'll go over there and stand guard."

"Sounds like a plan," Cerdic said with an encouraging smile. He joined Vie at Roger's bedside and asked, "Can you really help him?"

Vie replied, "I'm not my father, but yeah, I think I can."

Taking the root bag from Tee, Vie opened it, and a foul

stench engulfed the room. It smelled like a mixture of raw sewage, fox musk, and cheese. Lahar gagged and covered her nose and mouth with a fist.

"Oh, My Lort!" Tee exclaimed. "Wuh is dat? It stings my-own eyes."

"You don't want to know," Vie answered. "Can one of you take that tube out of his throat?"

Cerdic shifted around and said, "I got it."

Tilting Roger's head, he supported his neck with one hand and gently tugged on the tube with the other. It made a soft wet sound as it slid out.

As soon as it was free, Vie took a pinch from the bag and put it under Roger's nose. Another pinch, a larger one this time, went deep inside his mouth. She bent down and whispered in his ear.

No one in that room understood what she said. It sounded like gibberish to Lahar's sharp ears. Doubts resurfaced when Vie straightened and Roger still lay motionless on the bed. The only sign of life was the monitor with the tiny ball bouncing steadily inside the round window.

Suddenly, Roger bucked and jerked to one side. The frantic ball bounced faster, and the comet trail became a solid line. His face turned blue, then bright red. Veins at his neck bulged almost to the point of bursting. He bucked again, snatching at the wires attached to his body, and drew in a ragged gulp of air. His chest heaved, and he began coughing. Each sounded more painful and wet than the one before, until something tore free deep inside. Making a face, Roger leaned over and spat out a thick glob of mucus. Catching his breath, his eyes darted around until they found Cerdic hovering over him.

"Welcome back from the dead," Cerdic said, the relief obvious in his voice.

Roger blinked a couple of times. "Where am I?" His voice came out a raspy croak.

"Someplace called the County Hospital."

Glancing at the wires and monitors, Roger cleared his throat a few times and said, "What is all this stuff?

Cerdic examined the medical equipment and said, "I'm fairly certain it kept you alive."

"*Hmm.* The last thing I remember was fighting The Archer. Did I win?"

"No, buh," Tee answered with a laugh. "He han' you yo hat."

"What happened to me?"

"Dærganfae poison paralyzed you," Cerdic replied. "Did you find Ambrose and Brie?"

Roger shook his head. "I followed The Archer's men to some creepy building with bars on the windows. I never saw Ambrose or her friend."

Tee looked around. The whites of his eyes were stark against his skin. "Nate and I found you out front de old jail at de cawnuh of Wilson and Magazine Streets. I know dis gone soun' crazy, but dat mun you fought, he done sunk intuh de sidewalk. How he do dat?"

The brawny man looked shaken just talking about it.

"Steady there, Tee," Vie said. "I saw them, too. They killed my father."

"Dærganfae," Cerdic said. "Evil elves. They have a lot to answer for."

"You said you saw The Archer sink into the sidewalk?" Lahar asked.

"Yaas, dey were a purple glow, en he sunk down tru' the stone," Tee replied. "Uh don' know wuh to mek of it."

Roger slapped his hand against the mattress. "I was so close. We have to go back and pick up their trail."

"Can you travel?" Cerdic asked, removing the IV needle from Roger's arm and healing the puncture in the process. Next to him, Lahar peeled off various electrodes and wires. Little lights flashed, and the monitors buzzed and alarmed.

Lifting himself up with his arms, Roger tried to swing his legs around. A helpless look overcame the thief. "Must still be weak from that poison."

"What is it?"

Roger stared up at Cerdic and said, "I can't move my legs."

The door opened and a doctor with a team of nurses pushed inside. "What's going on here?" the doctor said. His mouth dropped open when he saw Roger awake and Vie standing next to him. The nurses' chatter cut off mid-word. One edged along the wall and turned off the monitors.

Lahar gave them a mischievous smile. "Don't mind us, we were just leaving."

"But, but—" the doctor said.

Tee held up his police badge and said, "Dey with me."

"Can we get a wheelchair?" Vie asked.

"Sure," said a nurse, who dashed away.

Using his bulk to force a way through the door, Tee cleared out the doctor and nurses with a sweep of his arms.

The nurse returned with the wheelchair. Vie rolled it next to the bed and locked the wheels.

Giving her a nod of approval, Cerdic said, "Good idea." He dug his arms under Roger and picked him up. The thief's legs dangled impotently as the knight carefully lowered him.

"Damn, this seat's cold! Who came up with the brilliant idea of putting people in a dress anyways?" Roger complained. "It's slit all the way up the back."

"At least you're not wearing it backwards," Cerdic said with a straight face.

"Oh funny, *ha, ha*."

"How about your legs? Can you feel anything?" Cerdic asked, grasping the handles of the wheelchair.

"Just a tingling sensation," Roger answered. "But that's it."

"Give it time," advised Vie. "The poison hasn't completely left your system. You'll need to flush it."

"How do I do that?"

"Drink lots of water."

"*Uh-huh*, and you're going to hold me while I — you know?"

"We'll figure something out," said Cerdic.

"Hey, where's my stuff?" Roger said as they left the room.

"Nate's got dem in his car," Tee answered, "along wid dat utility belt of yo's."

Thinking of what lay ahead, Lahar motioned with her arm and said, "Tee, can you lead them out of here? I need to go downstairs and get our things."

"What about me?" Vie asked.

Cerdic replied, "Miss Stevenson, thank you for what you have done, but I think it best if you forgot we were ever here."

Tee squeezed her hand and answered, "Wait for me in yo room, and I'll help you check out."

"Don't be long, Tecumseh," she replied. Her cobalt blue eyes held his gaze for a moment before he turned away.

CHAPTER 25
GUNFIGHT AT THE O.K. PARKING LOT

March 14, 1969 C.E.

7:44 pm

*L*ahar ran downstairs and found the room where she had stashed Cerdic's clothes. She rifled the lockers with a smile. Although she and Roger rankled each other's nerves, hearing him gripe had felt like salve on a wound.

Slipping off her disguise, she swapped the green cap for the wool one and realized she had left her wide-brimmed hat in the front seat of Captain Walker's truck. There wasn't anything to do about it now.

After a quick search, she found a garment bag and stuffed her bounty inside. Giving the room a once over, she thought about the past twenty-four hours and the marvels she'd seen.

The mirror at the end of the room held her reflection, but it wasn't someone she recognized. Doubts nagged at her. Why had she agreed to come here? In her heart, Lahar knew the answer. The treasure on this trip was of a different sort, and she'd be damned if she was going to share Cerdic with her crew. Her jaw set, she grabbed the garment bag.

"You can flash that badge all you want. I can't allow this man to leave," a doctor told Cerdic and Nate. He gestured to Roger in his wheelchair. "Do you realize what you've done? This patient shouldn't even be awake, and Miss Stevenson had third degree burns over sixty percent of her body."

Overhearing the conversation, Lahar slipped into the lobby unobserved. The doctor from upstairs barred the exit. Beside him were two rotund men in uniform, their arms crossed over their chest. The Highlord and Mr. Tyler flanked Cerdic and Nate.

Nate put away his badge and read the doctor's name tag. "Doctor Jones, you don't understand. Two girls are missing. If you don't let us leave, I'll have you arrested for obstruction. Do you want that?"

The doctor's stance lost some of its confidence.

"Doctor, one of those girls is my daughter," Mr. Tyler added.

Deflated, the doctor stepped aside. "I have so many questions."

Still in his surgical greens, Cerdic gripped the doctor's shoulder and gave him a kind smile. "The answer to them all is the same: Faith."

Outside, night had fallen and the lights from the porte-cochere shined bright. Nate held the door while Cerdic wheeled Roger across the threshold.

"My car's over there," he said pointing with his chin. When Brie's dad passed him, Nate said, "Mr. Tyler, go home. The Charleston PD has this. They're scouring the city as we speak."

"Nathan, what are you not telling me? Why is this man in the wheelchair so important? Does he know where my daughter is?"

"Mr. Tyler, give us more time. I promise we'll find her."

"You've been avoiding my questions. She's my daughter, damn it!" Mr. Tyler clenched his fists.

Nate shifted closer to him and lowered his voice. "I'm not sure what's going on myself. I've seen things. Things you wouldn't believe. And somehow Brie is in the thick of it. I believe these people are her best hope."

Giving the two some privacy, Lahar, Cerdic, and the Highlord crossed the asphalt with Roger in tow. All around them, row upon row of parked cars rested in stalls marked off by painted stripes and divided by drive lanes. Regularly spaced lamps mounted on tall poles sat in bushy landscape islands. Lahar looked up. Beyond the lights, the sky was black and starless. A zing of fear shot through her chest as she wondered just how far they were from home.

A series of loud, rapid cracks cut through the night, and the Highlord fell to the ground, hard. Everyone dropped. Even Roger pushed off the wheelchair and hit the pavement.

Another staccato burst ripped the air, closer this time, and the driver's side window of the car behind them shattered.

"What is that?" Roger shouted, resting on his forearms.

"Machine guns," the Highlord gasped. Blood gushed through his fingers where he held his chest. More blood drenched the back of his clothes from the exit wound.

"That second shot came from a different direction. There's at least two of them — they're trying to flank us," said Roger.

Cerdic crabbed over. He laid a hand on the Highlord's chest and prayed. A blue glow reflected off his face as it spread down his arms and seeped into the wounds. When he lifted his hands, the bleeding had stopped.

"You're not completely healed, but you'll live," said Cerdic.

Keeping low, Lahar peeked under the car with the shattered window and saw Nate and Mr. Tyler lying flat on the ground behind a concrete planter. Another series of shots rang out. Bullets peppered the asphalt by her hand and sprayed her with dust. "That's it," she said, jerking back. "I've had enough."

"Lahar," Cerdic said with alarm.

"Don't worry. This is what I do."

"Lahar," the Highlord said, "be careful of The Archer. He uses his men to flush out his target. They're like his hunting dogs."

"Since when has he used Terran weapons?" Roger asked.

"Since now, I guess," the Highlord said. "His team is adapting."

"Bloody hell," Lahar swore. "Alright. Stay here."

Giving the cars and buildings surrounding them a quick look, Lahar tucked in her elbows and rolled sideways under the vehicle in the direction of the shooters. She came up in a tight crouch between two cars in the adjacent stall. Her ears still rang from the gunfire, and the streetlamps messed with her night vision, but not so much that she was blind.

Across the drive aisle, a man with a mossy beard and mustache wove through the parked cars with a long-barreled weapon tucked in the pocket of his shoulder. Hidden by all that hair, she almost missed that the right half of his face was pale as snow while the left half was pitch black. Where they met, the two colors fit together like cogs in a wheel or long fingers. He wore dull, black clothes, a heavy vest, and leather gloves. Using the cars for cover, the gunman crept forward with his knees bent and back hunched.

Blinding light streaked down the drive lane followed by the deep growl of an engine. Squinting, Lahar peered through the window of the car next to her. A wide truck with large tires shot down the lane. It looked like some kind of wild beast with its grill and black steel bumper guard. Atop the cab, a fully illuminated light bar cast wild shadows all about her. Lahar frowned when the gunman with the odd skin pattern signaled the driver. The truck slowed.

Lahar slithered under the next car as the truck approached. With a knife between her teeth, she rolled out from under the car and leapt toward the driver-side door as it passed. Using the runner board and light bar for leverage, she yanked on the handle and slung the door open. His black and white brow creased with surprise, the driver stared wide-eyed as she drove her knife into his neck.

Grabbing him by the collar, Lahar pulled the driver out of the cab and took his place. With a quick tug on the steering wheel, she plowed the truck into a parked car with a bone-jarring crash. Still moving, Lahar went out the other side, catching the approaching gunman with the door and knocking him to the ground.

Gunfire erupted behind her, strafing the side of the truck. Glass and bits of metal pelted her back and shoulders.

The gunman in front of her rolled onto his back and swung his weapon around. Feet spread apart, he sat up with the barrel pointed at her. She stared into that black hole, knowing there was no escape.

A loud grunt made them both turn. Cerdic held Roger's wheelchair over his head. He brought it down in a swift rush and crushed the gunman with a sickening crunch. The smell of mown grass filled the air.

Nate shouted, "Stop! Police!" The second gunman spun around. Holding his revolver with both hands and legs spread so most his weight fell on his forward foot, Nate fired. His first shot hit the man center-mass. The second pierced his forehead.

After checking to see if there were any more threats, Lahar nudged Cerdic and said, "I thought you didn't like sneaking up on people?"

"You call that sneaking?" Cerdic countered. "That chair was bigger than me."

"Maybe, but I didn't hear you challenge him. Or was that the grunting noise you made?"

Cerdic broke into a broad smile. Giving him a sideways glance, Lahar could only shake her head at the paladin's warped sense of logic.

"Everyone alive?" the Highlord asked, surveying the parking lot.

"We're good," Cerdic and Lahar said.

"Nate? How's Mr. Tyler?"

"A little shaken, but he's fine."

"These aren't dærganfae," the Highlord said, toeing the bearded gunman with his boot. "At least they die like a human."

"Probably mercenaries," Roger said, sitting with his back to a car and knees bent. Sweat dotted his forehead and his chest heaved. He took a few deep breaths, grabbed the side mirror, and hauled himself up on wobbly legs.

"Roger, what are you doing?" Lahar asked.

"The Archer's not going to wait on me to get back on my feet."

"What happens when the rush of battle is over?" asked Cerdic.

"Then I fall, damn it, or I stand," he snapped.

"Here, let us help," Lahar said.

With a tight grip on Cerdic's arm and another on Lahar's, Roger took a tentative step. Together they walked to the truck where Nate and Mr. Tyler joined them.

The Highlord knelt beside the truck driver and patted him down. After a quick search, he held a shiny ruby in the palm of his hand.

"What's that?" Mr. Tyler asked.

"Blood money," the Highlord answered.

Sirens wailed from all directions. Doctors and nurses spilled out the emergency room doors and swarmed the fallen men. Gasps and questions filled the parking lot. It was apparent by their actions that many of them thought the black and white skin was some type of intricate tattoo.

Nate ran his fingers through his hair as he stared at the carnage. "I killed a man," he said to himself. He wanted to throw his gun away and forget this day ever happened.

"We need to leave now," Roger urged.

Lahar nodded in agreement as she tugged on Cerdic.

"No," Nate said. "We stay right here and wait for the police."

"But you're the police," Roger said.

"I'm a beat cop, not homicide. S.L.E.D. will want a statement, my gun—"

Doctor Jones pushed his way past Nate and found Cerdic. "I thought you were a healer," he accused. "Those men are dead."

"Of course they are, Doctor," Cerdic said.

"But... but what you did in the hospital. And now this. How can you...?"

"Yes, Doctor, I'm a healer. I prefer peace, but I'm not a man of peace. By the grace of the Eternal Father, I'm his warrior. A protector."

There was no bravado in what Cerdic said, and for the first time, Nate felt afraid. This fight had given him a glimpse of another world and its violence. Mesmerized by the crushed mercenary under the wheelchair, he wondered at how different it was than his own — wondered at how quickly his world had flipped upside down. Sickened, he felt the bile rise in the back of his throat.

Mr. Tyler took Nate's elbow and guided him aside. "I don't know how many men we killed on our patrols," he said quietly. "Our enemy was faceless. They were targets floating above us. As a Torpedoman's Mate, I maintained the equipment. I never saw who we sank or even what flag they flew, but I did it because it was my duty to this country. I fought for a greater good. These mercenaries did it for money. They're what I call wolves.

"Nathan, you killed a man today. It will change you, but you get to decide how. Will you be the lamb, the wolf, or will you be the wolfhound?"

"What do you mean?" asked Nate.

"Take a look at Arthur and Cerdic. They're wolfhounds. They hunt the wolf to protect the lamb."

"What about Roger and Lahar?"

Frowning in concentration, Mr. Tyler replied, "They act like wolves, but they're different. I think, deep down, they're wolfhounds, too."

Nate thought about it a moment, then said, "I don't know about Lahar, but Roger's not a wolfhound. He's a lion."

Flashing emergency lights reflected off the sides of buildings as police cruisers swarmed the parking lot. Some were marked cars, others plain.

Nate waited with Arthur and Mr. Tyler near the back of the Dodge Power Wagon. Behind them, Lahar and Cerdic held Roger, each with a hand wrapped around his upper arm.

Most of the doctors and nurses had left; however, their numbers had been replaced with concerned spectators.

Doctor Jones remained behind with a handful of orderlies, who tried to control the growing crowd. He probed Cerdic with question after question. To the knight's credit, he responded to each one. Though the answers were courteous, they only further frustrated the doctor. Faith healing and hoodoo were not a part of his medical doctrine.

"I want the hospital locked down! No one leaves unless I say so!" Sergeant Collins commanded. First on the scene, he was a seventeen-year veteran with three gold stripes marking his sleeve and collar. He and his partner scanned the wrecked truck and the two bodies before putting their guns away.

"Stone."

"Sergeant Collins," Nate replied with a nod.

"How many are hurt?" the sergeant asked, studying the people around Nate while taking out a pad and pen.

"No injuries. Three men were killed."

"Who were they?"

"Looked like mercenaries, sir."

"What?"

"These men ambushed us coming out of the hospital. I identified myself as a police officer. That one over there turned on me, and I shot him."

"Who killed the other gunman and the driver?"

Lahar gave the sergeant a smile and said, "I stabbed the driver with a knife. In the neck."

"And I crushed the other man with a wheelchair," Cerdic added.

"*Uh-huh*," the sergeant said, tapping his teeth with his pen. He paused a moment. "You did what?"

"That's right, Officer," Lahar said, pointing. "He used that chair. Saved my life."

"Sergeant, it was self-defense," Nate said.

Collins put away his pad and said, "Don't go anywhere." He stepped away and pulled Doctor Jones aside.

"He didn't write down that last part about the chair," Lahar said with concern. "Do you think he didn't believe us?"

"Since when have you been worried about telling the authorities the truth?" Roger asked.

"I'm trying something new," said Lahar.

Nate turned around and asked, "I take it you've had run-ins with the police before?"

"A few," she answered.

More police officers arrived. They secured the perimeter and cordoned the area off with yellow barricade tape. Behind them came a white van and a team of crime scene investigators. While one person mapped the parking lot, a photographer walked the site, his flash going off as he recorded the scene.

A thin man in a tan suit and dark tie circled the yellow tape, talking to witnesses and writing notes. He caught the sergeant's attention and said as he approached, "Three dead outside Oliver Krump Hospital. No, wait. Gunfight at the OK Parking Lot. How's *that* sound for the frontpage headline?"

"John, don't you have better things you could be doing?" the sergeant replied.

"No way, man. Not when we have a shootout at the county hospital. Care to comment? What about their weird tattoos? Sergeant, were those men part of some new cult?"

Collins raised his hands and said, "John, give me a break. This is an active crime scene. You know better than to ask questions like that."

John wrote something down and nodded his head toward Lahar and Arthur, standing beside the truck, and asked, "What's their involvement? They look like they stepped off a pirate ship."

"Drop this one, will ya?"

"No way am I letting this one go," John said with a wolfish grin. "Sergeant, we're leading with this story tomorrow morning."

Groaning, Collins turned his back on the reporter. He cut a path through the crime scene investigators to the group. "Stone! Where's your car?"

"Over there, Sergeant," replied Nate.

"Good. Get these people to the station before that reporter tries to interview them. They're not under arrest but process them anyway. I want their statements, photos, and fingerprints on file. I'll be along as soon as I can."

CHAPTER 26
APB ON THE ARCHER

March 14, 1969 C.E.

8:12 pm

*P*erched atop the hospital roof, The Archer sighted down the length of his arrow and followed the Highlord with its tip. He was about to release the bowstring when two men in strange clothes moved forward. Fascinated, he allowed the gunfight to play out.

Their brutal weapons proved to be effective. The Highlord had fallen, but the gunmen closed too fast as they sought the easy kill. He watched as a female jumped into the truck and crashed it. The tables turned, and the hunters became the hunted.

When the Highlord rose from behind a parked car, The Archer couldn't believe it. He leaned over the parapet to get a closer look. How? He had seen him go down. Had Anshu Jezra been wrong about the Highlord being vulnerable? As much as it gave him satisfaction to know the Sha'iry was fallible, the feeling was short-lived. The hunters had failed. The Highlord was alive.

With that thought came another. Someone else was after his bounty. Even with their defeat, he was certain more mercenaries would follow.

Police arrived soon afterwards, giving him a chance to study this group with the Highlord. He recognized Roger Vaughn, who had somehow managed to recover from his poison twice. But who were the others? The female turned, and light spilled over her face, granting The Archer a moment to recognize the she-elf from the attack at the palace. His eyes narrowed. Her companion was the knight who'd thrown him from the balcony and broken his favorite bow. Now, they traveled with two Terrans, one of whom worked with the local authorities.

The Archer felt torn. With Aimsitheoir and his team missing, he had a responsibility to find them, but he also needed the Highlord dead.

Nocking an arrow to his longbow, he scoured the parking

lot. The Highlord was nowhere to be seen. Cursing himself for his introspection, he gazed at the growing crowd below him. It was time to change tactics. It was time to send a message to his competition.

The police crawled across the pavement like ants, each with a specific task. Disguised by his glamour, The Archer ducked under the barricade tape and walked unchallenged through their ranks. He stopped at a body outlined with chalk. A single hole marred its forehead.

He frowned down at the black and white face. One of Sutekh's *sclábhaí*. He could easily picture himself or one of his team lying on the ground, dead. Then it struck him. A *sclábhaí* here? That could only mean one thing: Sutekh's priest had double-crossed them.

Surrounded by humans, he recoiled at their stench. Their voices grated. He couldn't think. Their every breath drove him mad with loathing.

He found the truck and spun around, searching for the Highlord. Out of the corner of his eye, he spotted two cars speeding away from the parking lot. He leapt onto the bed of the truck to get a better view. The cars turned left and disappeared.

"Hey!" Sergeant Collins yelled. "Get down from there!"

His glamour dropped, The Archer fixed his silver eyes upon the police officer. Sergeant Collins' mouth flew open as he stepped back, ripping his pistol from its holster.

With a blur of motion, The Archer crouched and flung his knife.

Caught while raising his gun, Collins' pulled the trigger, and the bullet bit into the asphalt. Behind the cloud of smoke, he clutched the bone handle at his throat and collapsed to his knees.

The officers who stood nearby quickly gathered their wits and drew their pistols.

Leaping down into their midst, The Archer whipped out his sword. The razor edge sliced through sinew and tendon and felled every human within his blood circle like spring saplings.

"Savages!" The Archer shouted. "Tell the Highlord, this is only the beginning. By night's end, everyone in this town will know I am An Saighdeoir. *I am The Archer,* and no one takes what is mine." The elegant sword in his hand dripped with blood.

Gun blasts erupted all around. When the remaining policemen stopped firing, there was an eerie quiet as everyone sought the apparition in the black suit. However, the dærganfae had vanished, leaving behind only the bullet-riddled truck.

The Archer recalled his glamour and concealed himself from the human's primitive eyes once again. He reveled in their confusion. He savored their fear.

All except for one.

Curious, he left the chaos within the yellow tape. Still invisible, he looked over the shoulder of a thin man in a tan suit scribbling frantic notes on a small pad. The man mumbled to himself as he wrote, occasionally scratching through a word and changing it.

A chronicler. Let's see what story you have to tell.

Nate stepped on the gas. Lahar sat beside him while Roger and Cerdic rode in back. He checked the rearview mirror. Behind him, Mr. Tyler and Arthur followed in the Cougar. After three-quarters of a mile, he slowed and turned left.

With Cerdic's help, Roger took off the hospital gown and slipped on his breeches and boots.

"Sorry about your shirt," Nate said. "They cut it off you at the hospital to stitch your wound."

"Anything's better than that damnable gown," Roger groused.

Urgent voices spoke back and forth on his radio. The dispatcher cut through the others. "BOLO for a white male, approximately five feet tall with silver eyes. Last seen at the County Hospital wearing a black suit. Calls himself The Archer. Considered armed and dangerous."

Lahar sat up straighter. "What was that about?" she asked, and his two passengers in back leaned forward.

Nate shrugged. "My guess is as good as yours. The Archer? Is he the same guy Arthur told me about?"

"Yes, he's the one after Ambrose and Brie," answered Lahar. "At least he's busy chasing us and not them."

"You've seen him. He and I fought on the sidewalk, remember?" Roger added.

Nate repressed a shudder. He turned right onto Vanderhorst and took a left into a parking lot. Lit by streetlamps, the police station was an impressive three-story building with a crenellated parapet. At the street corner, a tiny turret, complete with an arrow loop, grew out of a larger corner tower. The building's limestone veneer had been scored to resemble medieval blocks.

Nate pulled into an empty space and shut off the car. Turning to Lahar he said, "The CPD put out an APB on The Archer."

"A what?" Lahar asked, her face clouded with confusion.

"An all-points-bulletin... Never mind. What can we do against someone like The Archer?"

"Nate," Cerdic said. "You must have—"

"Faith," Roger and Lahar said together. "We know."

Nate slapped the steering wheel with the heel of his hand. "I don't see how faith will help. This guy's flesh and blood." Nate inhaled sharply. "He *is* flesh and blood, right?"

"Oh yes, he bleeds," Roger said with a grim smile.

They entered the police station through a side entrance that led straight to processing. Thankfully, it wasn't busy, but there was still a crowd of people.

Nate showed the officer on duty his badge and explained, "They're not under arrest, but Sergeant Collins wanted their information on file."

"Got it," the officer replied. He motioned to the group and said, "Please form a line and follow me."

Nate left and, after a quick search, found the Watch Commander hovering over dispatch. "Lieutenant Bell, what's happening?" he asked.

Lieutenant Richard Bell stretched and everyone in the room heard his spine pop. His receding hairline gave him a tonsured appearance, and his worried expression deepened the lines on his face, adding to his years.

"Stone, you made it."

"Yes, sir," Nate said. "I have the people from the hospital. If it's all right with you, I want to wait with them until Collins arrives and takes their statement. They're my friends."

"You haven't heard, have you?"

"Heard what, sir?"

"Collins and four patrolmen were killed."

"What? How?"

"Some nut calling himself The Archer." Lieutenant Bell shook his head as he turned back toward the dispatch panel. "I can't get a straight answer out of anyone over there. I want to know how a perp can just disappear with a dozen people watching him."

"It gets worse, sir," Nate said.

Shouting erupted from the processing area. Nate and the Watch Commander, along with two other officers, ran down the hallway. At the back of the room, Lahar had a firm grip on the wool cap Beau loaned her.

"The lady does not wish to remove her hat." Cerdic stood in front of Lahar. Black ink stained his fingertips. He stared across the room at the police officer who had his hand on the butt of his pistol. The skin around the officer's eye had already begun to swell and close.

Nate jumped between the knight and the police officer. He crouched with his arms spread to either side, hands up.

Lieutenant Bell asked, "Glenn, what happened?"

"I was trying to get her photo, but I needed her to take off her hat."

"Where are the others?"

"Down the hall in the conference room."

"Lieutenant, this is my fault," Nate said. "I should never have left them alone."

"Stone, your friend struck an officer of the law," Bell replied.

Cerdic turned red and said, "The actions of your officer were unbefitting of his station. Even if Lahar is a pirate, she should be treated with respect. This man tried to feel her unmentionables."

"What?" Glenn said. "No, Lieutenant! I was reaching for her hat. She's the one that moved."

"That is of no matter, sir."

"Sir Cerdic!" Arthur said. His deep, baritone voice enveloped the room.

Lieutenant Bell faced this latest arrival and asked, "Who are you?"

"You can call me Arthur."

"Arthur, if that man is truly your friend, you'd better tell him to stand down. He's about to face a world of trouble."

"Yes, Lieutenant." Arthur entered the room and said, "Sir Cerdic, this is all a misunderstanding. The officer meant no harm. Let him take her picture."

"But, Your Majesty, Lahar's honor is at stake."

For a moment, Lahar stood frozen, her expression one of shock. Then, her cheeks flushed red, and a dark cloud of rage descended over her. Her teeth bared in a snarl, she grabbed Cerdic's arm and spun him to face her. "My honor? My honor! It's a fine time for you to start thinking of *my honor*, considering you've been my most ardent impugner of late." She poked the knight in the chest with her finger. "*You* are not my protector. I can take care of myself and my own honor."

The knight stuttered and could not seem to find a coherent response.

Lahar ripped off her watch cap and shook out her lustrous mahogany hair. With sharp facial features, almond-shaped eyes, and pointed ears, she was hauntingly beautiful, but also not human. She turned to Glenn and said, "Come on, let's get this over with."

Staring wide-eyed at Lahar, the officers at the other end of the room stood dumbstruck. Many had their mouths open.

"What?" Lahar demanded. "Have none of you ever seen an elf before?"

Mr. Tyler sat in the conference room with his head in his hands. Standing with his back to the wall, Nate felt sorry for him. He'd been there not even two hours ago.

Cap placed firmly back on her head, Lahar leaned against the edge of the table, rubbing the black smears on her fingers with a paper towel. His clothes changed, Cerdic held out a dark blue tee-shirt emblazoned with CPD on the front while Arthur removed his bloodied tunic.

Nate gasped when he saw the ragged scar punched into Arthur's stomach. Old and faded, it eclipsed the pucker left by the bullet wound. "That must have hurt," he said.

Arthur looked down with a sigh. "A reminder of a betrayal long, long ago."

"Did you kill the person who did it?" asked Nate.

"Much to my sorrow," Arthur replied. "He was my son."
The room grew quiet, and Nate regretted asking the question.

Also wearing a dark blue CPD tee-shirt, Roger sat at the head of the table. A grin spread across his face, and he said, "I wish I could have seen their faces when they saw Lahar."

"It's not funny," Arthur said. "They wanted to arrest Cerdic."

Nate replied, "They would have, too. I think Lahar's ears gave him some leniency."

Lahar fumed. "My ears are none of their affair."

"I'm just glad you set them straight with that whole elf business," Nate said with a laugh. "I still think we could have convinced them you're a Vulcan."

Joining in the laughter, Roger leaned back in his chair and said, "Nate's one of us now. What about you, Mr. Tyler?"

"I don't know what to think," he said, raising his head. "I mean, we're stuck in here while my daughter is out there somewhere." With his fists on the table, he said, "Don't you understand? There's a madman loose in the streets, and he's after my Brie. We need to get out of here!"

Lieutenant Bell entered the conference room carrying a cardboard box. Inside it were the group's photos along with their fingerprint cards and physical descriptions. He sat it down on the table and closed the door behind him.

Making eye contact with each person there, he said, "No one's leaving this room until I know what's going on in my city. I was just informed that the three body bags from the hospital shooting arrived at the morgue empty. Empty except for trace amounts of chlorophyll — plant blood. They're telling me the men you killed simply got up and *walked* out of the morgue.

"Every report from the hospital gets crazier and crazier. Some people say you're angels, but I also have a raving doctor who thinks you're in league with the devil."

Cerdic stood up. "Lieutenant, we serve the Eternal Father, not the Dark One."

"We're the good guys," Arthur said.

"I wish I could believe you."

Roger said, "Look, if we were like The Archer, would we be here?"

"That's right, Lieutenant," Nate said. "They came

voluntarily."

"Fine. You came here voluntarily. Then tell me what the hell is going on. Start at the beginning."

Arthur cleared his throat and explained, "We're from a different world, called Gaia. A mirror world, if you will."

"You expect me to believe that? Sounds like something from *The Twilight Zone* or *Outer Limits*," Lieutenant Bell muttered. "Did you lot arrive in a flying saucer?"

The Highlord shook his head. "No, Lieutenant Bell, not a saucer, a sailing ship. Gaia is a realm where your myths and legends walk the land, and guns and technology are considered supernatural. We're here to rescue Ambrose Battenberg, the Queen of Carolingias, one of our countries. During her pre-coronation vigil, The Archer attacked. We don't know how, but she ended up here in Charleston. She befriended the Tylers and, more specifically, Brie. Both young women are now missing. We've tried to find them but have so far been unsuccessful."

Roger added, "I tracked them to the salon on Beaufain. That's where I found The Archer, fought him, and Nate saved my life."

"That's why we were at the hospital," Arthur said. "We went to collect Roger and were ambushed."

"Those men who ambushed you, they worked for this Archer?" the Lieutenant asked.

Arthur replied, "That's what we think."

"Is he some kind of magician to just up and vanish with a crowd of people staring right at him?"

"He's a dærganfae. A vile assassin who detests humans," Arthur said. "He considers us animals — savages. As you probably read in your reports, he has no problem killing."

"Does he really have silver eyes?"

"Yes," Roger answered.

Arthur's ageless, pearl grey eyes became deadly serious. "The Archer is out there, Lieutenant. You can't stop him, but we can."

"Just great. So what am I going to tell the captain?" The Watch Commander stared at each one of them, looking for answers. Finally, his gaze rested on Lahar. "You're really an elf?" When she nodded, he murmured, "Who'd have thought those books my kid loves so much would have a grain of truth in them." He reached into the box and began to rip up the photos and paperwork. Taking a deep breath, he said, "You were never here. I never saw you. You find Brie; find your Queen. And this Archer — you make that cop-killer pay. You hear me?"

"Yes, Lieutenant," Arthur said with a nod.

"What about me?" Nate asked.

"Take Mr. Tyler home. Afterward, come see me. We'll need to set up a special task force after this is all said and done."

Roger exited the restroom, his expression focused as he took another careful step without bracing himself against the wall or door.

"You're doing fine," Cerdic encouraged.

Worry lines crossed Roger's forehead. "Bloody poison is still in my joints."

"Rub some dirt in it. We have work to do."

Roger took another step, lost his balance, and grabbed Cerdic's arm.

Nate and the rest of the team waited farther down the hallway. Watching the two together, he appreciated the bond they shared. As scary as their world sounded, it couldn't be all bad.

"This way," Nate said. He led them out of the building to the back of his car and opened the trunk. Inside was Roger's belt, pouches, and weapons.

Handing it to Roger, Nate said, "Here's your utility belt, Batman. Still not sure how you go around with that thing on." He reached into the trunk again and pulled out a pump action shotgun and a couple of boxes of shells. "Take this, too."

Arthur hefted it and put the stock to his shoulder. "Nice. Reminds me of the old trench guns." Everyone watched when he loaded the gun like an expert. "What?" he asked.

"Nate, you have anything in there for us?" Lahar asked.

Letting go Cerdic's arm, Roger buckled on his belt.

Meanwhile, Cerdic retrieved the haversack and opened it. He reached in up to his elbow and retrieved a broadsword with a bronze hilt. After handing it to the Highlord, he dug further, found Lahar's longsword, and handed it to her. Last, he pulled out his sheathed hand-and-a-half cruciform sword. Heavy amounts of cloth wrapped all the tips of the scabbards, giving them a bulbous appearance.

After unwrapping his sheath, Cerdic settled the baldric over his shoulder. He was adjusting the frog when, from the back of the police lot, a horse whinnied and thumped the stable wall. Cerdic whipped around, and his face lit up. "You have horses."

Nate answered, "Five of them. They're our mounted patrol. The oldest is a twelve-year-old, Clydesdale-Belgian mix, named Duke."

Like a moth drawn to flame, Cerdic handed the cloth and haversack to Lahar and headed toward the stables. While the others gathered the rest of their gear, he dashed inside.

Nate and Lahar caught up with him at Duke's stall. The knight spoke softly to the horse, and Nate had a weird feeling the horse understood. There was an intelligent light in Duke's eye that drank in everything the knight said.

"He's named after John Wayne — something about the way he walks without a rider," Nate explained.

Lahar stepped close to Nate and whispered, "Cerdic has this strange love affair with horses."

"He needs a girlfriend," Nate said.

Giving him an odd look, Lahar asked, "Who: the horse or Cerdic?"

"Maybe both," Nate said with a smile.

"We'll see," Lahar said, mostly to herself.

"I gotta follow Mr. Tyler home. What are your plans?"

"Find The Archer," Arthur replied behind him.

"Are you going back to the hospital?"

"No, I don't think so," replied Roger. "I'd like to take another look at that old jail."

"From here it might be easiest to go down King Street. If you want to go by the salon, turn right when you get to Beaufain. You can also come at the jail from the south. Go past Beaufain, turn right at Queen Street, and then turn right again when you get to Franklin."

"Sounds easy enough," Arthur said, clapping Nate on the back. "Thanks to you we're armed, and now we have mounts."

Nate's mouth popped open. "These are trained horses, they won't—"

Cerdic led Duke out of his stall, handing the reins to Arthur. Sure enough, the horse's heavy-footed trudge gave him a unique gait.

"You were saying?" Lahar asked.

Roger eyed the horse with some trepidation. "It's not natural."

"Afraid of horses?" Nate asked.

"No, it's not that. Let's just say Cerdic's horses are more *spirited*. He's worse than a ranger."

Not sure how to respond, Nate turned to Mr. Tyler and asked, "Are you ready, sir?"

Mr. Tyler looked the group over and replied, "I want to go with you."

"You were there at the hospital. It's too dangerous," Nate replied. "Let us handle this."

Arthur clasped Mr. Tyler's hand and said, "We'll find Brie. I promise."

CHAPTER 27
KING STREET

March 14, 1969 C.E.

9:41 pm

"Saighdeoir, you've failed. Again," said a voice from behind The Archer.

"I have not failed!" The Archer shot back. He stood at one of the few tables in an open room with a high ceiling. Bookshelves lined the walls, topped by busts of old men.

Darkness cloaked the chamber, but The Archer didn't need light. He leaned over the glossy oaken table with ivy carved along its edges. Sliding one book to the side, he picked up another leather-bound tome and opened it. *Histories of Charles Town Volume II* was written in fine script on the inside page.

Beside him, the chronicler from the hospital parking lot sat, his arms and legs bound to a wooden chair. His shirt had been ripped open, and his head drooped. Forming a ring beneath him, fresh blood dripped on the ebony and ivory tile floor.

The darkness congealed, and a bald man in hazy robes appeared. The long hilt of his sword loomed behind his head. "Archer, explain why you are here in this library and not out there."

The Archer slammed his hand on the table. "You and your Sutekh double crossed me, Anshu Jezra. His sclábhaí were at the hospital, and they attacked the Highlord."

"Did they succeed?" Jezra asked. His voice was cool and measured.

"No, but you knew that, didn't you?"

"Where is the Highlord now?"

"He's with the local constable. If they release him, I know where the Highlord will go."

"Then why are you here?"

"Because I can't get to them!" The Archer slung the book across the room. "His bitch Queen is with my dærganfae, trapped in that infernal gaol."

"Speak sense, fae."

"Anshu Jezra, my team are inside a place called the Old City Jail."

"That is irrelevant to our contract," Jezra said. "Your task is to kill the Highlord!"

The Archer rounded on the priest. "Have a care, Anshu! I have already lost too many in pursuit of Sha'iry goals."

"You know the consequences if you break a pact with Sutekh. Your soul will be his to do with as he pleases."

"You give me an impossible task." The Archer's quicksilver eyes glowed like twin moons in the shifting shadows. "The Highlord cannot be killed, you pompous ass. He's as invulnerable here as he is in Gaia."

"You're wrong, Archer. He can be killed. Sutekh only speaks the truth."

"I don't care what your Dark One said. I saw him, Anshu. He was injured, and he recovered like he always does. The man cannot die. Your mission is over!"

Anshu Jezra's doubt permeated the air. "Are you certain? The sclábhaí here use weapons that are alien to our world, and their projectiles are quick, even for your sharp eyes. Maybe they only grazed him."

The Archer lunged forward to grab a double fistful of the Anshu's robe, only to pass through Jezra's insubstantial image. Seething with frustrated rage, he turned and said, "It was you! You sent those men!"

"Of course I sent them," Jezra replied.

"Why? I had him."

"Did *you* shoot the Highlord?" the Sha'iry asked.

"No."

"*That* is why I sent them."

"I saw the Highlord go down," The Archer argued. "At the very least he should have been favoring his arm, or something when he regained his feet. I saw none of that."

Gazing out the window, Jezra said, "Perhaps it was the knight of Carolingias who healed him. He must be one of the Glaxons' holy warriors."

"A warrior and a healer?"

"Yes."

The Archer picked up a chair and threw it into a bookshelf with a crash. He raised his fist and struck at the air. "And you waited until now to give me this information?"

"I didn't know," replied the Sha'iry. He turned back to The Archer and said, "As long as there is life in the Highlord's veins, Saighdeoir, this mission is not over."

Breathing through his nose, The Archer forced himself to calm. There had to be a way out of this deal. A way that didn't leave him dead, or worse, a sclábhaí. "Anshu, I apologize for this display. I offer no excuses." He stared at the pile of books on the table, then reached for the one on top. It had opened to a sketch of the crenellated gaol with soldiers camped out front. "I wonder if there may be a way to use your sclábhaí and this gaol for our purposes. Drive the Highlord to this place like hounds after deer." He turned to the priest and said, "I must know more about this gaol."

"Very well, Archer, I will seek the information you desire." Whispering a vile prayer, Jezra's image drifted toward the chronicler. The index and middle fingers of his left hand stretched toward the prisoner, seeming to pass inside the man's throat. A groan erupted from the chronicler as he spasmed and tugged against the cords binding him. With a final gasp, he slumped forward, and the only sound in the room was the slow, rhythmic drip of his blood onto the tile floor.

Still facing the chronicler, Jezra said, "Master, we seek your Truth."

A deep red glow like embers in a dying fire surrounded the chronicler's body, and it twitched as if connected to strings.

"Ask your question," the chronicler said in a dry, raspy voice. The thick, rancid stench of bodies in a sepulcher filled the library.

"Tell us of the old city jail."

"The Gaol was built over one hundred sixty years ago with the blood of the innocent. It housed criminals, prisoners of war, pirates, runaway slaves, and the insane, all watched over by turnkeys whose sole purpose was to punish the prisoners for their crimes. Guilt did not matter.

"Their screams, their memories, resonate within its chambers. They feed the brick and mortar, giving the place a dark energy. Overseen by the former executioner, it is hell on earth." The body slumped forward, and the glow vanished.

Anshu Jezra rose with a faraway look, as if still listening

to the voice who spoke through the chronicler. "With foundations that share the same soil as dead slaves, derelicts, and vagrants, it's no wonder the people here are afraid of it." He fixed feverish eyes on The Archer and said, "The gaol continues to serve its purpose, feeding upon the guilty and innocent alike. You've been there. Did you feel the building watching you? Could you feel its hatred?"

"Anshu, would it work?"

"Perhaps. Before the executioner died, he made a special bargain with my Master. He is... untouchable. However, the gaol could prove useful for the task at hand, especially if you do as I say."

"What about my team? Are they already dead?"

"Oh, no," replied the priest. Were it not for his zealousness expression, one could almost mistake his tone for one of sympathy. "Your dærganfae are very much alive. Otherwise, they couldn't be punished."

Outside the library, The Archer stalked down the sidewalk. Jezra's words haunted him. What did it take to create a sentient building that took neither pride nor pleasure in its work, seeking only to strip away the qualities that made life worth living?

He thought of Aimsitheoir trapped inside that vile place. Hot blood rushed through his veins, and he swore he would tear the place down stone by stone if that's what it took to save his son.

The Archer stopped and looked around at the old buildings along either side of the street, wondering if they, too, watched him.

No. He would play the Sha'iry's game, at least until he could fulfil his contract. If he could not save his son's life, he would at least save his soul.

Taking advantage of the grassy park in the heart of the city, the four sat atop their mounts. Roger looked around even as he tried to ignore the feeling that ants were crawling up his spine.

Bounded by King Street to their left, Meeting Street to their right, and Calhoun Street straight ahead, Marion Square was a six-and-a-half-acre greenspace crisscrossed by pedestrian walkways. Centered along the southern edge rose a tall, slender monument. Atop was the statue of a man with his cloak draped over one shoulder. He glared down on the city holding a scroll in his hand.

All around, bright streetlamps and neon storefronts lit the faces of men and women heading to their destinations. More than one threw a curious glance their way. Across King Street, a valet dressed in an elaborate tailcoat and top hat exited a twelve-story hotel at the corner and gawked at them. So much for being inconspicuous. At least Cerdic would be happy.

At the southwest corner, King Street intersected Calhoun and continued south where multi-story buildings, stacked shoulder to shoulder with narrow frontage, crowded both sides. Along the right hand, parked cars squeezed the lane even tighter, and combined with the buildings gave it a claustrophobic feel.

Near the intersection, a small group of people congregated under the arched entrance of an ornate, limestone building with signs advertising live performances. This late at night, the city was mostly deserted.

"So now what?" Roger asked, cringing at the exposure.

"Do you think The Archer's down there?" Lahar asked.

"I know he is," Roger answered. He gripped the reins tighter as he thought back to his last fight. His knees felt fine now, in the saddle, but he could only hope they'd hold up when put to the test.

"What about the rest of his dærganfae?" the Highlord asked. Under him, Duke stomped the ground and let out a whinny. Patting him on the neck, the Highlord said, "Don't you think it's strange the dærganfae haven't shown themselves?"

"But they're here, somewhere," said Roger. "I tracked five of them to the city jail; I wouldn't be surprised if they're camped out there. It's their kind of place."

"What about those men from the hospital?" Cerdic asked.

Roger scratched his chin as he thought about the question. "Don't know. Probably need to expect the worst."

The Highlord scanned the rooftops. "This has the feel of a trap."

"Agreed," Roger said, and Cerdic and Lahar nodded with

him.

"Whatever we do, we need to be quick about it," Lahar said. "The *Morningstar* will not wait for us."

Cerdic took the lead as they trotted down lower King Street. He rode high in the stirrups, his sword within easy reach. Many a person stopped midsentence at the sight, and Roger hoped their CPD shirts would help ease their passage.

Like the people, the stuccoed buildings varied in color and style. Some were solid and well lived-in while others were hollowed out shells of brick braced by red iron.

Roger glanced behind him at Lahar. She kept her sharp eyes on the rooftops and abundant upper floor windows. If this was a trap, she'd be their first line of defense.

The buildings in the next block were cleaner and better maintained. Antique furniture and various wares sat behind storefront windows, arranged to be aesthetically pleasing and maximize floor space. With the stores closed, the clusters of people became more sporadic.

Beyond the next intersection, parked cars lined both sides, and Cerdic guided them down the middle. He slowed as he passed the first couple of shops.

Roger sensed it, too. Something didn't feel right.

Cerdic snapped up his fist and dismounted. Roger followed suit, using his horse to brace himself against his wobbly knees.

"Lahar, do you see anything?" Cerdic asked.

She took a moment to search the buildings lining King Street, then shook her head.

Roger pushed away from his horse and took a trembling step toward Duke. Cerdic offered a hand, but he shook his head. He had to do this himself. Concentrating on his goal, he took another step and another. Roger removed a terracotta scroll case from his belt and tied it to Duke's saddle.

"I don't like this," Cerdic said. "They could be killed."

"This was part of the plan."

"I know, but I still don't like it." With a hand on the horse's neck, Cerdic said, "Qui in Aeterno Patri confidit, custoditur." *Whoever trusts in the Eternal Father is kept safe.*

Roger struck the end of the scroll case and yelled, "Ya!" The saddle began to spew thick, heavy smoke and sent a frightened Duke galloping along with the other horses. The cloud quickly filled King Street, held in place by the humidity.

His steps becoming firmer, Roger joined Cerdic, who crouched behind a car with Lahar and the Highlord beside him.

A sudden stiff breeze whistled between the buildings, swirling the smoke. The middle of the street cleared, revealing a robed figure, the hilt of his sword prominent behind his bald head. A shadowy portal opened, and eight men with black and white faces charged forward.

Similar to the soldiers at the hospital, they wore dark clothes and gloves, but these held compact weapons with protruding tubular barrels and wireframe stocks.

"A Sha'iry. How did he get here?" Roger asked.

"Let me ask," the Highlord said. Leaping up with his shotgun, he fired. The shot passed through the cleric and shattered the rear windshield of a car across the street. The dim light in a nearby storefront glimmered through his robe.

Unscathed, the Sha'iry pointed at the Highlord's hiding place. In response, the men split into two groups, four each to a sidewalk. With a quick pull of the trigger, they opened fire with a torrent of bullets.

Lahar hunched down and clamped her hands over her ears as the noise turned deafening. Chunks of metal and brick rained down around them. Roger saw her lips move but couldn't hear what she said. The men drew closer, and their weapons became louder.

With a grin on his face, Roger pulled another terracotta scroll case from his belt, struck the end, and lobbed it high in the air. Hitting the car next to the four men coming at them along the opposite side of the street, it cracked open and exploded. Needled by shrapnel, two of the men struck the brick building and bounced off like ragdolls. The third crashed into the storefront, shattering the glass. There was no sign of the fourth gunman.

Thick black smoke reclaimed the street, and the other group of four stopped.

Sword raised high, Cerdic charged.

Ears ringing, Roger watched through gaps in the smoke as the remaining gunmen stood momentarily stunned. They came to their senses and swung their weapons around.

Cerdic dove behind another car just as they pulled their triggers. Bullets tore into the street and metal casings arced high in the air from the ejection port of their gun. He rolled to the opposite side and raced around the vehicle toward them.

With their eyes on the knight, the gunmen failed to notice the lithe elf running down the sidewalk.

Not missing a step, Lahar slung her blades. With a blur of silver, they impaled the necks of three of the men. The fourth lost his face when the Highlord shot him.

Using the low hanging smoke for cover, Roger searched one of the gunmen. Other than spare magazines, he came up empty. The body was, for the most part, bloodless except for a smear of green liquid. However, the skin seemed real enough.

Focusing on the compact gun, he grabbed the short grip behind the trigger guard. He turned it over, studying its construction, and ran a finger along the barrel. It felt greasy, carrying a thick pungent odor with a hint of ozone. Bile rose in the back of his throat, and cold sweat beaded his forehead. He felt his pulse quicken as a wave of dizziness sent the world spinning. Overcome by a sense of wrongness about the weapon, he dropped it on the sidewalk and scrubbed his hands on his pants. He backed away, eying the odd mechanical device.

"What is it?" Lahar asked, cleaning her daggers on one of the men's pants.

"It's their weapons. I don't think I can use them."

"Why not? The Highlord can show you how it works."

"Yes, you're right," Roger said, steeling himself. He reached down and picked up the weapon. Just as quickly, he dropped it and wiped his hand on the brick wall. He couldn't shed the tainted feeling from the gun.

"I can't," he said. "It feels... corrupted."

"Let me try," Lahar said. She grasped the weapon above the magazine.

Roger watched her lift it into the light and study it, just like he had, and saw the moment when the weapon's miasma assailed the elf captain.

Blanching, she tossed it aside. "Bloody hell — the Dark One's mark."

"What? Where?" demanded Cerdic.

She pointed to the grip. A forked cross had been etched into the metal, directly below the trigger guard. Roger had curled his fingers around it while examining the gun. No wonder he'd felt sick.

The knight drew his sword and smashed the weapon, destroying the symbol, grip, and trigger mechanism.

"How are we going to make it to this jail if we have to fight our way through men armed with these unholy things?" asked Lahar.

Roger shrugged. "I guess we do it our way." The Highlord picked up one of the compact guns, grimaced, and slung it over his shoulder before relieving the dead men of their ammunition pouches. "Well, maybe a slightly modified version of it anyways."

The Highlord walked over and appraised Roger.

"Majesty, their weapons are tainted," Cerdic said. "They should be destroyed."

"Not yet," replied the Highlord. "We need all the firepower we can get."

"But the Dark One's mark—"

"Needs must when the devil drives, Sir Cerdic. I have fought the Dark One for a very long time, and have learned to use his weapons against him, when necessary." The Highlord turned to Roger. "Are you ready?"

"Yes, Sir."

"Then let's run."

Sticking to the left-hand sidewalk, they dashed to the next car. The smoke from Roger's scroll case thinned, and gunfire erupted from the roof across the street, striking the vehicle windows and shops around them.

Backs to the car, they crouched with their heads down. When the gunman stopped firing, the silence screamed at them. The Highlord opened the dust cover of his carbine. Still kneeling, he turned, held the gun over the hood of the car with two hands, and sighted down the tubular barrel.

Beside him, Lahar pointed. "There," she said. Popping out from behind a parapet, the gunman had just finished reloading.

The Highlord adjusted his aim. "Got him," he said as he pressed and depressed the trigger. *Tac... Tac... Tac.* Bullets disappeared over the top of the building, and they heard a grunt as the man fell back.

"There has to be a better way," Cerdic stated. It was difficult to tell if he was more upset about releasing the horses, using unholy weapons, or that it was the Highlord doing the shooting.

"He had the high ground," Lahar said. Cerdic nodded but it was obvious these tactics did not sit well with him.

Following the sidewalk, the four moved down to the next car. It was the last one on their side of the road.

"Beaufain is ahead on the right," Lahar said, crouching. "What do we do? Turn there, or keep going? "

"What was the name of that other street?" Roger asked.

"Queen," the Highlord answered.

"I take that as a sign, Sir," Roger said.

"Sounds good. We keep moving."

CHAPTER 28
LIGHTS OVER CHARLESTON

March 14, 1969 C.E.

10:16 pm

Wailing sirens drew closer. It was a sound that was becoming all too familiar. Lahar glanced behind her and winced. The police lieutenant wasn't going to be happy with them.

On the other side of Beaufain, the only parked cars were on the right-hand side of the street. Using another one of Roger's smoke grenades for cover, the four ran across the intersection and regrouped behind the first car.

King Street bent due south, and the buildings on the east side appeared decrepit — at odds with the businesses on the west. Farther down, yellow and green lights surrounded a brilliant white canopy emblazoned with the words, "Planet of the Apes." A cluster of well-dressed people pushed and pressed against the door, trying to get inside. Even as their companions tugged them toward safety, men peered up the street, curious to see what was happening in the darkness.

"What street is that?" the Highlord asked.

"Market," answered Lahar, reading the street sign. "Do you think we eluded that Sha'iry?" As soon as she asked the question, she knew what Roger's answer would be.

"No," Roger replied. "We all heard what the police lieutenant said earlier. Those men were just like the ones at the hospital; they'll be back."

The Highlord nodded, then led them around the crowd and across the intersection. They kept going until reaching the recessed entrance of a hotel.

Lahar peeked around the corner. A deserted alleyway separated them from the next building. She waved her companions onward.

Roger and the Highlord were halfway across when the sound of running reached her ears, a mere second ahead of gunfire. Lahar grabbed Cerdic's collar and jerked him back into the hotel's entrance, while their companions dove behind a car. Staccato bursts and pinging ricochets filled the air.

Keeping low, the Highlord shot back. His compact gun sent projectile after projectile down the street.

Taking advantage of the cover fire, Lahar and Cerdic rounded the corner and put the building between them and their pursuers. The gunfire intensified, creating a lead wall. From the other side, the Highlord signaled them to go around before running for new cover.

Cut off from Roger and the Highlord, they gripped the hilts of their weapons and raced down the alley.

"We need to make a stand!" Cerdic yelled.

"Not here!" Lahar replied and pointed to a short stretch of eight-foot-high chain-link fence between two buildings.

A single security light glared down at the asphalt pavement. They both hit the fence at a dead run, climbed to the top, and dropped to its other side. Not stopping, they passed a covered dock and raced toward a row of tall, boxy white vehicles backed to the rear of the property.

More shots echoed from King Street. Lahar held on to the hope that, as long as she heard gunfire, Roger and the Highlord still lived. Heart pounding in her ears, she barely heard the rattle of the fence.

"Dive!" she yelled.

Projectiles whizzed over their heads as they landed hard between two trucks. She peeked around a tire and spotted several men approaching, guns ready.

Cerdic gave her a wide smile. "Seems like the Eternal Father is always teaming us together."

"I'm not complaining," Lahar replied. Remembering his accusation the morning they retook Battenberg Palace, she sat up and gave him a stern look. "Do you really think I slept with Jongar?"

The knight's smile faded. His eyebrows rose, and his mouth fell open. "You want to talk about this *now*?"

Lahar gave the lot a quick scan before her gaze returned to Cerdic. "It's important."

Cerdic swallowed, and she knew he'd rather be out there fighting those men than having to face her. He wiped sweat from his forehead with the back of his hand. "I don't really know what to think. I mean, the way you act when you're around him. You know," Cerdic said.

He was trying to encourage her to speak, but she was

having none of it. "What do I know?"

"All the flirting and stuff."

Her eyes narrowed dangerously, and she said, "Say it."

"Yes, I think you slept with Jongar. That's what happens when you act the wanton at every turn with him."

Lahar couldn't have been more shocked if Cerdic had slapped her.

"We all do," he added.

"You and Roger sent me to recruit him to your cause with no thought of how I might accomplish that goal." Her voice was low and laced with disgust.

A gunman stepped around the front of the truck with his weapon at his hip. He froze and slumped to the ground. Lahar's dagger stuck out from his left eye socket.

A second gunman came around the rear of the truck. He pulled the trigger just as another blade left Lahar's hand. Bullets tore into the ground then veered wildly. Already moving, Cerdic leapt to his feet while Lahar climbed to the top of the truck.

On the other side, two gunmen stood waiting. Jumping down, Lahar lashed out with two more daggers. Quick as a snake, she sliced the first one's throat, spun, and struck the other inside his armpit.

Amidst bursts of gunfire, more men rushed her. Taking advantage of the tight quarters, she stabbed the nearest gunman in the groin before attacking the next. She fought like a demoness. Chlorophyll spattered the sides of trucks and trickled down.

Lahar moved to the front and stabbed at a dark shape. Cerdic grabbed her wrist, her blade almost touching his cheek. Between the two trucks, gunmen with black and white faces lay dead or dying.

Cerdic's hazel eyes bore into hers. "We... I never meant for you to sell yourself to him or any other man."

"Well, I didn't," she snarled between clenched teeth and snatched her arm from his grip. "For your information, paladin, the price I paid for Jongar's help was forty-three lives and his brother's freedom from a Sha'iry holding cell on the west side of York."

"Forty-three... The people in the boarding house? That was you?"

"They weren't innocent citizens, Cerdic. They were

Zhitomiran soldiers, faithful to the Sha'iry, with a dozen hostages in the basement."

"You really didn't... with Jongar, I mean..."

"Eternal Father, NO! There's only one man I've ever wanted, and it isn't some Gael barbarian chieftain." Stalking away, she muttered, "Unfortunately, a pirate captain isn't good enough for you." Anger and sorrow warred in her heart. Anger that her friends thought so little of her, and sorrow for the one thing she was now certain she'd never have.

Before she'd gone two steps, Cerdic's hand closed around her arm and spun her to face him. He stepped closer and brushed her cheek with his fingertips. "Milady, you balance my soul. My heart is empty without you."

He wrapped his arms around her and kissed her. At first, it was a tentative touch as their lips pressed lightly together. But as the repressed fires within each of them flared, it sparked and the fiery passion she felt for the knight took over. The world around them faded to insubstantial shadows.

With their grease guns nested in the pocket of their shoulders, three sclábhaí crept forward. They fired their weapons point-blank at the two, a leering smile on each of their faces.

The gem at the pommel of the Cerdic's sword flashed, and a bright, golden shield enveloped the knight and the pirate, causing the sclábhaí to avert their eyes. Reflected off the night sky, the lights over Charleston concentrated into a beacon that could be seen for miles.

At seven and a half rounds per second, the sclábhaí's bullets pinged and ricocheted around the yard as the black and white creatures emptied their box magazines into the shield, then reloaded.

Three roars from the Highlord's shotgun put the hunters down.

The light blinked out, and the two pushed away from each other, flushed with emotion. Roger had to look twice at the knight. He was embarrassed, yes, but there was also a slight spring in his step. His back was straighter, and the edges of his mouth twitched as he fought to keep the smile from his face.

"Aren't you supposed to be married before you do that?" Roger asked.

"That was some show," the Highlord said, slinging the shotgun onto his shoulder and picking up the carbine at his feet.

The gunman who'd carried it crawled under the truck, leaving a slimy trail of chlorophyll.

"Where are you going?" Yanking him out by the leg, the Highlord pressed the gunman's head against the steel bumper. "Who sent you?" he asked. When the gunman didn't answer, he grabbed the man by the scruff of the neck and slammed his forehead into the truck. Getting close to his ear, the Highlord repeated his question: "Who sent you?"

The gunman swallowed and said, "Anshu Jezra."

The Highlord threw the man to the ground and stalked away. "Will I ever be rid of the Sha'iry?"

Catching glimpses of blue and red through vacant lots and alleyways, Roger followed the flashing lights on Market Street. By the looks of it, there was an army of police cruisers coming their way.

"Sir, we must leave," Cerdic said. "While I am sure they have good intentions, I do believe the police will only delay us further."

"Cerdic's right," Lahar said.

"Where do we go?" Roger asked.

The Highlord scanned the buildings surrounding them and pointed. "There."

Everyone turned. Across the street stood a vacant three-story brick building. At one time there had been a wide storefront on the ground floor. Now, it was a series of wood panels framed by granite columns. Stucco and limestone veneer had peeled away around empty fenestrations on the second and third floor, revealing weathered brick arches and rotten sills. At the top, exposed wood framing was all that remained of the parapet.

"Are you sure it's safe?" Lahar asked, giving the building a wary eye.

"No, but it'll give us a chance to regroup after that light show," responded the Highlord.

"What about him?" Roger asked, gesturing to the gunman.

"Take him with us."

Roger felt good using his legs again. He ran across the road, each step more confident than the last. Finding the construction entrance, he slid out the appropriate lockpick and had it open before the rest arrived. Keeping an eye on the street as they entered, he rushed them inside and shut the door as the first cruiser pulled into the truck lot.

A streetlamp from outside shed dusty light through an upper floor window cavity. Thick soot coated the walls, and what remained of the wood framing above their heads smelled charred. Old smoke and mildew competed for dominance, and Roger's olfactory senses served as the battleground. He held his nose, willing the sneeze to go away. It didn't, and his head nearly exploded when he didn't let go.

"That's not good for you," Cerdic whispered.

"Neither is getting caught." Roger yawned and twisted his head trying to get everything settled back into its proper place.

Holding him by the neck, the Highlord shoved their captive against a central metal column. The building shifted and dirt trickled down from the ceiling. He quickly let the man go and stepped away.

"Don't do that again," Lahar said, coughing. She nodded toward the rear of the building where a portion of bowed floor framing rested on a lone two-by-six post that, like Atlas supporting the celestial spheres, had bent to the point of buckling.

With Roger looking over his shoulder, Cerdic took strips of cloth from his pouch and knelt beside the gunman. Lahar's knife wound had left a nasty gash, but it wasn't skin she'd ripped through. His flesh and exposed innards were fibrous layers like that of a leaf or plant. Clear liquid sealed the wound and the beginnings of a scab had formed along the edges. Cerdic put away the cloth and laid his hands on the worst wound.

"What are you doing?" the Highlord asked. His voice was calm, but there was an edge to it that no one missed.

"Showing mercy, Sir." Cerdic turned to the gunman and asked, "What's your name?"

"Junopsis," the man gasped in Glaxon. His moist eyes never wavered from the paladin, and the fear inside them seemed at odds with the man who'd tried to gun them down earlier.

Man — Roger thought about that for a moment. Though their captive's basic anatomy seemed the same — two arms, two legs, and a head — the moss-like hair, elongated features, and diminutive nose, upturned and slitted, made him more humanoid than human.

Cerdic bowed his head and said a quick prayer. Blue light danced on the man's ebony skin as it stitched back together.

Roger glanced at the Highlord, a worried expression on his face. He knew they couldn't leave the man alive, but did Cerdic know that?

"Junopsis, what are you?" Lahar asked the gunman once he relaxed.

"We were *blumkinde*, but the Sha'iry call us sclábhaí."

"You're what?" she asked.

"We're slaves of Sutekh." Junopsis pulled up his pants leg and toed off his boot. A thin silver shackle inscribed with fiery runes encircled his alabaster ankle. Roger studied the writing and, after taking a moment to work it out, read, Vanity.

"It was my choice," Junopsis said, staring at the shackle. "Sutekh promised me safety and security, and in the end, I sold him my soul. I will never be free again."

"Junopsis, do you want your freedom?" Cerdic asked.

Desperate hope entered the man's eyes, and he replied, "More than anything."

"Cerdic, what are you doing?" asked Roger.

In response, Cerdic unsheathed his sword and held it over Junopsis' ankle. "Pater Aeternum, libero hic vir." *Eternal Father, free this man.*

When the sword tip touched the metal loop, a shower of white-hot sparks fountained. Cerdic pressed harder. Junopsis arched his back and his mouth opened in a silent scream, revealing bark-like gums. Lahar knelt beside him and took his hand in hers. He gripped it tight, and Lahar winced from the pressure. Through it all, Junopsis kept silent, as if he didn't have the ability to cry out.

The steaming shackle popped loose and hit the concrete floor with a metallic clank.

"Junopsis, you are a slave no longer. Through the

Eternal Father's grace, you have your freedom," Cerdic said, sliding his sword back into its sheath. "Go forth, and sin no more."

The black and white pigment staining the gunman's skin faded away, replaced by vibrant tones of blue and violet — all except his palms and wrists, which became bright yellow. His face seemed to unravel as it separated into thick layers of iris petals. Beneath them, a thin line marked its mouth.

Junopsis' black eyes went wide with rapture. An earthy scent filled the air, eliciting memories of a forest glade after a summer rain. Lahar helped him to his stalk-like feet, and he cast an eager glance toward the exit and freedom.

Roger made to stop him, but the Highlord caught him by the arm and shook his head. "You must always remember why it is we do what we do. Even I forget from time to time. It's what makes us different from the Dark One's minions."

"Quis enim te discernit?" *What makes you different?*

Everyone turned toward the voice. Even Junopsis froze.

The darkness took shape and Anshu Jezra emerged, brandishing his greatsword. Writhing script filled the fullers, except for one barren spot near the tip.

Cerdic slid his weapon free of its scabbard and moved to intercept. "Misericordia." *Compassion.*

"Misericordia," Jezra scoffed. "How hypocritical of you, knight. A warrior who's shed more blood than many of your foes."

Leading with his right foot, the Sha'iry held his sword out in front of him with both hands. Feet shoulder width apart, Cerdic faced him with his sword in his right hand, its tip tilted forward and hilt close to his hip.

Looking steadily into Jezra's eyes, Cerdic said, "I do not hate you. I feel pity for you, but that does not mean I will tolerate the evil you spread."

Jezra's face twisted with rage. "You pity *me*?" Lunging, he struck at Cerdic's chest with the long two-hander, point first.

Passing back, Cerdic turned widdershins, intending to parry the Sha'iry's weapon. The broad blade flickered as it passed through his sword.

With a snarl, the dark cleric stepped forward and cut toward Cerdic's waist.

Cerdic leapt back, avoiding the attack, and brought his

weapon down to catch the greatsword on his quillon. Once again, it passed completely through the flickering steel.

"The priest's not really here!" Cerdic exclaimed, putting distance between himself and his opponent. "He's just an illusion."

Hazy robes billowing about him, Jezra gave the knight a feral grin. He stretched forth his hand and shouted, "Columnae furoris!" A whirling mass of purplish-black fire blasted up from the ground. It struck the exposed ceiling framing and mushroomed.

Anshu Jezra motioned, and the fiery vortex began to spin. Like solar flares, tongues of purple fire whipped about. One lashed out at Cerdic and flung him backward, his blackened tunic steaming. Another arced toward the Highlord.

Roger shoved the Highlord out of the flame's path, narrowly avoiding being burned himself, and yelled, "Get out of here!"

Lahar raced to Cerdic's side and dragged him away from the raging fire.

"We go together!" replied the Highlord, pointing toward the rear of the building.

"What about Junopsis?" Lahar said, spying the *blumkinde* through gaps in the flame. He waited at the front door, indecision warring on his face, before dashing away.

"He's on his own," Roger replied.

Above their heads, the old timbers caught fire. Anshu Jezra shouted, "With your death, Highlord, I will become Maa'kheru!" He pointed and the vortex moved, spreading its damage.

The crackling of the fire grew deafening, and the surrounding air scorched Roger's lungs. Moving toward him, Lahar wrapped Cerdic's arm around her neck and supported him as they retreated. The Highlord was already near the rear of the building, holding the door open.

Last to leave, Roger rushed after them. As he passed the lone wooden post, he gave it a hard shove, and it snapped.

At first nothing happened. It was like the building had been caught by surprise. Then, it let out a loud groan, and layers of floor and roof collapsed. High above, the exterior walls teetered. Horizontal cracks traced their way along the mortar joints and loud popping sounds erupted from all sides. With a crash, the building disappeared under a cloud of debris.

Covered in dust, the four staggered out the back of the building just before it imploded. Not stopping, they ran down an alleyway beside an abandoned carriage house and jumped the fence at its end. On the other side was a two-story residence with dark windows. They crept down the gravel driveway and came to a paved lane with a coped brick wall on the opposite side. Inset in the wall was a single wrought iron gate.

"I've got it," Roger said as he picked the lock.

Using the meager light from distant streetlamps, they followed a narrow, cobblestone path under a canopy of palm trees, magnolias, and gnarled oaks. On either side, vines and leafy shrubs ran wild over disheveled gravestones, knocked sideways by thick, winding roots. Four steps in, Roger felt he had left civilization and entered a secret tropical jungle.

"Do we know that Sha'iry?" Lahar asked.

"No, Captain," the Highlord replied. "We do not."

"I don't understand how it was possible for my sword to not touch him, yet his vile magic affected us," Cerdic said in a painfilled voice.

"How bad are you hurt?" asked Lahar.

Cerdic shrugged. "Stings a bit."

"All right, let's see it," she said.

He raised what was left of his tunic and everyone winced. Beneath, his singed skin had already begun to blister and ooze.

"Heal yourself, knight," the Highlord said.

"Sir, I would rather save it for someone who needs it."

"Cerdic, don't argue. You need to heal yourself," Roger said.

"No. I'm not that hurt."

"Move aside," Lahar said, stepping past Roger. She wrinkled her nose. "You look burnt."

"I am burnt," the knight replied with a wry smile.

She took a metal jar from her belt pouch and dipped her fingers inside. They reappeared bearing a thick gelatinous glob. "Hold still," she said.

Once Lahar had slathered Cerdic's burns, the four

wound their way through the graveyard and jumped a dingy, yellow wall abutting a gothic church with flying buttresses and a square belltower in front. Across from the entry, Roger jimmied the padlock at the ornate metal gate, and they exited onto a one-way street where the narrow face of two- and three-story clapboard homes stared back at them.

Lahar pointed south to an octagonal sign at the end of the street. "That must be Queen."

CHAPTER 29
VIGILIA SECUNDA

March 14, 1969 C.E.

11:00 pm

*C*lasping her hands, Ambrose knelt on the prie-dieu with her head bowed. The candelabra on the slanted shelf lit the wheel-cross hanging on the wall in front of her. She wore her vigil robe and smelled of perfume. The hairs on her neck prickled under the silent scrutiny of her ancestors in their shadow-shrouded tombs. Close by, she heard chewing noises. Determined to ignore the distractions, she clasped her hands tighter and focused on her prayer.

Tiny, cold feet scurried across her legs, shattering her dream. The rattle of her chains and the moist woodchips against her cheek slapped her with a hard dose of reality. She was back in her cell.

The stench of rotting flesh and unwashed bodies rolled over her, and she began to gag. The sudden movement tore open her crusted lash wounds, spreading hot, stinging blood across her back.

Ambrose struggled to sit up. A wave of dizziness slammed through her, and darkness gnawed at the edges of her vision. Clutching the bars, she fought to remain conscious and forced back her nausea. Little by little, she regained control. Her pain dulled, only to be replaced by a fierce thirst. She retrieved the empty tin cup and upended it, desperately seeking a single drop of precious water. Disappointment spawned despair. The cup slipped from her fingers.

Her despair turned to panic. She tugged on her wrist shackles, but the heavy chain held tight. Changing tactics, she tucked in her thumb and tried to slide off the iron cuff. It dug into her skin, drawing blood. Crying, she heaved and tugged until her wrist was slick, but the shackle still held fast.

"Damn it!" Ambrose wanted something to throw, something to break, but there was nothing other than her cup. She swore again at the thought that she didn't know what had happened to Brie. Bowing her head, Ambrose prayed for her friend's safety. She fought back tears while recalling and focusing on York, the cathedral labyrinth, and the medallion at its center. Finding peace in that mental image, she gave silent thanks to the Eternal Father.

At the opposite end of her cage, the scraggly man with stringy hair pounced on something. She cracked open one eye, fearing the worst. Light from the hall illuminated half his face. Fresh blood covered his mouth and chin. In his hand was a dead rat. He leaned forward and offered it to her. "You have to keep up your strength," he croaked.

In the adjacent cell, the man with a boyish face rose behind her. "He's right. If the turnkeys don't get you, the rats will. Eat something."

Ambrose shuddered. As in her dream, she felt the weight of someone's gaze. Rising to her feet, she spied a dærganfae in the row of cages opposite. His quicksilver eyes fixed upon her, they glowed in the half-light.

"Here. Take it," the scraggly man said, offering up the rat.

Waving him away, she replied, "No thanks."

"Suit yourself," he said.

Ambrose leaned against the bars, letting the cold iron cool her feverish skin. Hunched over his meal, the scraggly man seemed more animal than human. "What's your name?" she asked.

He cocked his head up at her. His pale eyes grew distant, and he answered, "Kyle."

"I'm Michael," said the man with the boyish face.

In the cage next door, a roguish gentleman gave Ambrose a crooked smile and said, "Captain George Clark, Ambassador to Buenos Aires, at your service." His accent was odd, and his turn of phrase reminded her of home.

"Nice to meet you, I'm Ambrose." She looked around at the filth. "You didn't happen to find a bottle of whiskey while I was gone?"

Captain Clark stifled a laugh. The other two gave each other questioning looks. Finally, Michael said, "No. They don't let us have liquor."

She studied their faces and noticed Michael and Kyle were taller and, now that she thought about it, had more teeth.

"You're different than the others. How did you end up here?" she asked Michael.

Michael cast fearful eyes toward the gated doorway. He swallowed and replied, "I was a surveyor."

"Don't," Kyle admonished. "They'll take you."

"I don't care," Michael said. "I wasn't always like this, you know. They beat us to take away our spirit, starve us to turn us into animals, but they can't take away our memories. Everyone here has a past. It's the only thing they can't take away, as hard as they try.

"I had a wife, Kristen, and two children, Michael Junior and..." Tears brimmed, and he wiped his nose with the back of his grimy hand. He turned away and said, "I can't remember her name. I had a daughter. Her name was... Samantha. That's right: Samantha."

His face lit up. "I remember her smile. She was two when I left Atlanta." He fell silent, the pain and loss stealing his voice.

"You were a surveyor," Ambrose said, encouraging him to keep talking.

"Yes," Michael said, licking his parched lips. "I worked for the Sanborn Map Company." As he talked, the brightness returned to his eyes. "You see, it was time to update the maps."

"That's why you came to this town?"

"Yes. In 1951, I came to Charleston with a team of surveyors. We mapped building footprints for fire insurance companies, outlining streets, number of floors, building materials, you name it. Anything that could be used to assess risk.

"Three of us came to the jail. The last time the company had been here was in '37. They had labeled the place, 'County Jail — Vacant', surveyed the outside, and located one of the interior offices. Seemed regular enough. The company asked us to update the map but warned us not to go inside. We thought it odd but didn't question it."

Michael gripped the bars tight and said, "We walked the perimeter, double checking the original measurements. You know, like we were supposed to. But then Bret found an open door, and we went inside." Michael slapped the bar with the palm of his hand. "I nearly peed my pants when the door shut behind us. We hit it, kicked it. We tried everything, but it wouldn't budge. This building meant to keep us here. Eventually, we turned on each other. That's when the Executioner came."

Sliding down the bars, Michael sat cross-legged on the wood chips, his head in his hands. He let out a short laugh and said, "Funny thing is, I don't know if the company ever sent anyone to find us. I'd like to think so."

"What happened to the other two surveyors?" Ambrose asked.

"They're here somewhere, I guess. The turnkeys keep us separated."

"What about you, Captain? What brought you here?"

"Calamity, my dear." Captain Clark paced his cell, and Ambrose could easily imagine him walking the deck of a galleon. "You see, I was a privateer during the War, a gunner. Fortune shined on me and after a bit of mutiny I took control of the *Louisa*. We wreaked havoc on the high seas. British, American, Russian we plundered them all. But Lady Luck is a fickle bitch.

"The *Louisa* was damaged, and I, along with what remained of my crew, scuttled her off the coast of Charleston. Turned her own guns against her and set fire to her. Who knew they'd be waiting for us?"

The door to their room clanged open and two guards entered. One held a set of keys, the other a lantern. Behind them stalked the Executioner.

An unholy light reflected from his sunken dark eyes as his gaze swept across the prisoners. Finally, it settled on Ambrose. He drew closer, and it seemed the temperature dropped. "Why do I hear talk? Vigilia secunda is a time for sleep."

The guard opened Ambrose's cell door.

"Get away from me," she said as she rose and backed away. Her eyes wild, Ambrose tripped over the corpse. She reeled and caught herself when her back hit the bars at the opposite end of the cage.

In the corner next to her, Kyle cowered, his arms wrapped around his knees. Rocking back and forth, he gibbered. His eyes focused on another place, another time.

The Executioner stepped past the guard and examined her cage. He leveled a sardonic smile at her and bowed with an overly dramatic flourish. "Queen Ambrose, it seems we need to spend more time together." The way he said *queen* implied a profession far less honorable.

Before Ambrose could react, he snatched her by the throat and slammed her head against the bars. Stars danced across her vision, and his chilling touch seemed to drain the very energy from her.

She struggled to fight him off — to scratch out his eyes — but her movements became sluggish as a stupor overtook her.

The Executioner leaned forward and sniffed her head, drawing in a deep breath. With his free hand, he probed her scalp with his fingers. "I smell the dead on you, little queen." He sniffed her again and whispered, "It's intoxicating."

Her flesh recoiled when he pressed his skeletal body against hers.

Rattling his cage, Michael grabbed the bars and yelled, "Let her go, you bastard!"

Clubs held high, two guards yanked open Michael's cell and charged inside. Shouts and catcalls from the other prisoners filled the room.

Raising his fists in a classic boxer's stance, Michael said, "You can walk in, but you'll crawl out."

The first guard jabbed with his club.

Michael swept it aside with his iron cuff. Clasping both hands together, he pivoted at the hip and swung around with a wild haymaker. It connected with the guard's temple, and his head snapped back. Shuffling his feet, Michael swung around again and cut him above the eye with the edge of his shackle.

When the first guard fell back, the second smashed his club down on Michael's forearms. A loud *crack* cut through the clamor, and Michael held his right arm tight to his body.

More jailors burst into the room.

While the first guard crawled out, two others rushed inside Michael's cell, joining their comrade in subduing the prisoner.

"Do you see what you've done?" demanded the Executioner, grabbing Ambrose's head with both hands.

She watched helplessly while three men beat Michael with clubs. A part of her wanted to close her eyes and ignore the meaty thuds from the adjacent cell, but she couldn't. Deep down inside her, she felt that Battenberg steel begin to stiffen. Her chin rose a little, and she forced herself to watch. She pleaded with the Eternal Father. Not for herself, but for Michael. For his sacrifice.

The Executioner must have sensed the difference. He stepped back with an amused expression on his hollow face. Making a swiping motion with his hand, he said, "Stop."

The three jailors stood. Michael lay at their feet, quivering in a fetal position. His battered arms still protecting his head, he took in ragged gasps of air.

"It seems I underestimated you," purred the Executioner, eyeing Ambrose. She had stepped closer to Michael's cell and gripped the bar with one hand.

"I'm the one who was talking," she said. "Take your wrath out on me. Let him go."

"I do enjoy punishing you, little queen. You deserve to be punished, but maybe I should make an example of one of your subjects this time."

"My subjects? You have me in a cell. I am Queen of Nothing," Ambrose replied.

The Executioner gazed at the other prisoners, now crowded against their bars, watching the drama. He spread his arms wide as he addressed the room. "Ladies and Gentlemen, I present to you, Queen Ambrose of Carolingias. But your queen has rejected you. So, I ask, will you still follow her? Will you accept her punishment?"

Ambrose said, "You people do not know me. You owe me no allegiance. You are not my subjects."

Silence gripped the prisoners, baffling Ambrose.

Broken and bleeding, Michael crawled to his knees, then bowed his head. "My Queen, my life, what there is of it, is yours."

"No! You don't mean that," Ambrose said.

To her horror, Kyle also knelt and said, "My Queen." One by one, the others dropped to their knees, even Captain Clark. They accepted her — all but the dærganfae who stood back from the rest.

"You see," the Executioner said with a vicious smile. "They can't help themselves. Every person here would willingly sacrifice themselves for you."

Ambrose looked around at her fellow prisoners. "Get up, all of you! This is my punishment to take, not yours."

Captain Clark gazed into her eyes and said, "We are the

lost souls, and you have found us. There is nothing more the Executioner can do to us. We would gladly spare you our fate."

The Executioner's coal-black eyes narrowed. "You are damned to eternity in my demesne. Do you really think she can lead you out of here? She's as much a prisoner here as you are. Her fate is sealed."

"Not while she still lives and breathes," Captain Clark replied. "She's not like us, Executioner. She's not bound to this place like we are."

The Executioner leveled his hatred at the captain, but Captain Clark did not flinch. "So, I must kill her? Is that what you're saying?"

The Executioner turned when Michael said, "She's done nothing to deserve your punishments. Queen Ambrose does not belong here."

The room grew frigid. Flinging Ambrose aside, the Executioner exited the cage. He raised his arms and addressed the inmates, "I am the Hangman! I decide who lives and who dies!" He slammed Ambrose's cage door shut. "Do you need a reminder?"

He spied the dærganfae and stalked toward him.

Kyle helped Ambrose to her feet. He gibbered madly as he clutched at her. Amid his mad ramblings, she managed to make out a few words: "You must remember you're alive."

CHAPTER 30
TIGERS AND GAMECOCKS

March 14, 1969 C.E.

11:15 pm

Gazing into the darkness, Mister Smeyth leaned against the quarterdeck rail of the *Morningstar.* Captain Lahar's last command echoed inside his head. It made him afraid to look east, in case the sun decided to rise early. Counting with his fingers, he noted they'd been at dock for over nine hours with no word. All he had was the bright light he had seen to the north. Behind him, he still heard the crew gabbing about it. He took off his tricorn hat and ran a hand through his thinning hair, causing drops of sweat to trickle down his neck.

"Quartermaster."

"Aye, Mister Cavendish," Smeyth said, replacing his hat as he turned.

Mister Cavendish and Mister Mitchell stood together. Light from two stern lanterns mounted to the tafferel lit their dour faces.

"If it makes it easier for you, you can hold hands," Smeyth said. The two sea mages blanched and took an involuntary step away from each other.

"It's the ship, Quartermaster," Mister Cavendish said finally.

"Of course it is," Mister Smeyth replied. Taking in their hard expressions, he asked, "So how much time do we have?"

"It's difficult to guess. Items that use Astral magic, such as the ship's chair, are losing their enchantment at an alarming rate, while the iron dragons, which uses Elemental magic, seem to be completely unaffected."

"If we only had more time to study it," Mister Mitchell added.

"I'd say that's our problem, isn't it, Mister Mitchell?"

"Aye, Quartermaster."

"Give me something, gentlemen. Or are you saying we need to set sail and leave at once?" The words left a bitter taste in Mister Smeyth's mouth.

Staring down at their feet, the sea mage and his apprentice didn't answer.

Mister Smeyth pursed his lips. "Mister Cavendish, stay at the chair and make ready to leave."

"Aye, Quartermaster."

"We cannot abandon the captain," Mister Mitchell said.

"What would you have me do? From what you're telling me, we have no choice."

"But it's the captain."

Pointing toward the water, Mister Smeyth said, "Mister Mitchell, tell me where she is, and we'll pick her up."

When the junior sea mage didn't respond, the Quartermaster snapped, "Master Andel!"

The cabin boy popped his head above the ladder and answered, "Sir."

"Inform Captain Walker we're about to set sail."

"Sir."

"Mister Marston! Ready the rigging."

"Are we leaving, Quartermaster?" replied a long-armed man with blonde curly locks. Miss O'Brien, by her iron dragon, and Mister Bekke, in the rigging, along with the rest of the crew faced toward the quartermaster.

"Aye, Mister Marston, we are."

Pushing his chair away from the desk, Bo Walker leaned down to adjust his knee brace through his denims. Behind him, a black and white photo of Rex Enright and the 1947 South Carolina Gamecocks football team took centerstage. Beside it was a framed newspaper article from the Greenville News that read, "Tigers Upset by Gamecocks, 21 to 19, in State Fair Game." Above them both was his degree in business administration, dated that same year.

Outside the window of his office, the lantern light of the *Morningstar* illuminated the dock. He caught glimpses of crewmen climbing the shrouds and walking the yards. Turning his attention back to the desk's In-box, he eyed the high stack of papers. He rolled forward and picked up a sports magazine, turning to the article on Joe Namath and the Super Bowl.

There was a knock at the hollow metal door beside his window. Bo set aside his magazine and said, "Come on in.

Its open."

Master Andel stepped inside, and his jaw dropped as he took in the modern office. Quickly regaining his composure, he kept his eyes down as he relayed, "Milord, Mister Smeyth wanted me to tell you we're about to set sail."

Rising with a broad grin, Bo said, "So your captain was successful. That's fantastic news."

Master Andel shifted his weight from one foot to the other. "No, milord. We haven't heard from her or the others."

The smile turned to a frown. "You haven't? I thought you had 'til morning to wait for them?"

"Yes, milord, we did, but Mister Cavendish is worried we will not be able to return home if we stay any longer."

"I see," Bo said, stroking his chin. "What about your captain and the rest of your men?"

"We don't know where they are. So, we're going to have to leave them."

"We'll see about that."

Headed toward the *Morningstar*, Bo Walker lumbered beside Master Andel, Lahar's ostrich-plumed hat in one hand and rolled charts in the other. When he arrived at the gangplank, he called out, "Permission to come aboard?"

"Permission granted!" Mister Smeyth answered.

Bo pushed past all the activity and, after handing the hat and charts to Master Andel, climbed up to the quarterdeck.

"What's this nonsense I hear about y'all leaving your captain?"

"Change of plans, Captain Walker. We're heading home."

Brow furrowed, Bo said, "You can't abandon your friends. Arthur, Roger, Cerdic, and Lahar... they're still here, right?"

The look Smeyth gave Bo was the same the doctor had given him when they told him about his knee: the day they'd told him he'd never play football again.

"We don't have a choice. Captain said the ship and the crew comes first."

"To hell with that," Bo said. "You never leave an injured man on the field."

The quartermaster became red in the face as his eyes drew down on the yacht captain. "Captain Walker, you are out of line. Now get off my ship before I have you thrown off."

"At least hear me out," Bo said.

Mister Smeyth took in a deep breath, then let it out slowly. "Make it quick."

Inside the aft cabin, Bo unrolled his charts and laid them out on the table. "I say we sail the *Morningstar* to Charleston and rescue Captain Lahar and the others." Sorting the charts so the one of Charleston County was on top, he pointed to a peninsula and said, "We are here." Pointing to another, larger peninsula, he continued, "and your captain's here. Twenty miles by river, twice that if you go by the Atlantic."

Bo went to the next one, an enlarged view of the Wadmalaw Sound and the Stono River. Depth indicators gave a clear picture of the channel. "I have towboats and barges that traverse these waters all the time. I know your ship can make it."

"What about those two bridges?"

"Don't worry about them. I've swapped a favor or two with the people who work nights at the Stono River swing bridge and Wappoo Creek drawbridge. We'll need to let them know we're coming, but they won't slow us down."

"Say we do make it," Mister Smeyth said. "To what purpose, Captain Walker? Charleston's a big city. There's no way we could find the captain."

Mister Michell stepped from the corner. "Actually Quartermaster, I could locate her. She's careful so we probably wouldn't find anything in her bunk, but I'm sure we could find a hair or two in her hat."

Mister Smeyth leaned over the chart, noting the tide times and current speeds. "By my reckoning, it'll take us three hours if we go by river, as you suggest, Captain Walker. That's assuming we have the tide with us or at least not fighting us. Do we have that kind of time?"

"Mister Cavendish is the only one who could answer that one, Quartermaster," replied Mister Mitchell.

With a nod of his head toward the door, Mister Smeyth said, "Let's go ask." He led the other two outside where they adjourned to the quarterdeck.

Sitting with his hands clasping the arms of the pilot's chair, Mister Cavendish opened his eyes when the three surrounded him. "Gentlemen," he said.

THIEF ON KING STREET | 267

"Can you give us any idea how long we have?" asked Mister Smeyth.

"Nothing definite," the sea mage replied.

"Do we have three hours plus another hour to search?"

"Maybe."

"Dammit man, why can't you give me a straight answer?" demanded the quartermaster.

"It's not that simple. The tides, the wind, the stars all factor into the equation. All I can say for sure is that we're bleeding magic, and every time I try to measure how much we've lost, the rate changes. Trust me, Quartermaster, if I could give you a straight answer, I would."

"Of course, Mister Cavendish. I apologize."

"Could we use the long nines to bolster the chair's magic?" Mister Mitchell asked.

Mister Cavendish shook his head. "The two magics are not compatible."

Bo's face clouded with a mixture of concern and confusion. "I'm not following everything y'all are saying, but if there's any chance at all, you need to take it." He looked around and found the crew watching them. Turning back to the quartermaster, he continued, "Look here, I know these waters. I know them like the back of my hand. I can get you to Charleston Harbor."

Miss O'Brien stepped away from her iron dragon and said, "Mister Smeyth, it's your decision, but I say we find the captain while we still can."

"Even if it means we may be trapped here?"

"Yes," she replied with hands on her hips and chin jutted out, daring anyone to challenge her.

When no one did, Mister Smeyth nodded toward her and said, "Captain Walker, the ship is yours."

Bo clasped the quartermaster's hand and shook it. "As long as y'all handle the sails, I can navigate her."

"Do you need anything?"

"Just a marine radio and navigation lights." Seeing their blank faces, Bo said, "I have some handy if you don't."

With his brand-new Motorola on a squat table beside him, Bo took the wheel. "Quartermaster, let's weigh anchor!"

Mister Smeyth repeated the order, and the brigantine floated away from the pier. Inky waters sloshed as they came about. Overhead, the copper sails billowed and snapped to attention. They emitted their soft chime, and Bo caught himself gazing at them. The exhilaration of commanding such a magnificent ship flowed through his veins and made him long for the open water. Instead, he shouted, "Kill the lights."

The ship went dark.

"Navigation lights!"

A diffused red glow lit the port side hull followed by a diffused green glow on the starboard. The colored lights reflected off the faces of the twenty crew members as they watched the world glide by. No one said anything. No one had to. The aroma of the sea and feel of the ocean breeze lent peace to the moment, a feeling that couldn't be reproduced anywhere else.

His eyes adjusted to the darkness, Bo Walker turned the ship's wheel and let muscle memory take control.

CHAPTER 31
THE GAOL

March 14, 1969 C.E.

11:30 pm

*K*eeping to the sidewalk, Roger led the Highlord, Lahar, and Cerdic down the righthand side of Archdale. He stayed close to the clapboard homes, using the cars for cover when he could.

At the intersection with Queen Street, he held out his hand and signaled everyone to hide. Ahead, headlights from a car driving down Queen intruded on the sleeping neighborhood. Fortunately, Archdale was a one-way street, going the wrong way, and the car drove past them. Following the red brake lights, the four crept around the corner and tried to avoid the radius of light surrounding the streetlamps.

As they passed several more of the narrow-faced residences typical of the city, a gentle breeze wafted over them, carrying the earthy scent of irises. Roger let Lahar catch up to him and asked, "Are you wearing perfume?"

"No," Lahar responded.

"Well, it smells like it."

Lahar sniffled. "I don't know what it was about him, but I can't smell anything since we helped Junopsis."

He glanced at Cerdic, then back to Lahar and leaned in close to whisper, "You think he pollinated you?" Her silence spoke volumes, and he knew Lahar wanted to smack him.

Finally, she said in a measured tone, "You think you're funny, but you're not."

He couldn't stop the grin that covered his face as he backed out of her immediate reach. "I'm not funny. I'm hilarious."

Lahar stalked away, and Roger could almost see the heat rising from her. She paused under a tree with a broad canopy. Like many of the trees planted between the curb and the sidewalk, its roots had buckled the stone pavers and made walking precarious. Roger's grin widened when Lahar placed a hand on the tree and surreptitiously sniffed her sleeve.

In front of her, a sign mounted to a fence proclaimed, Charleston Home for Children. Set apart from the other homes with a yard teeming with flowering plants and shrubby trees, the building looked worn and tired. It had the feel of an older grandparent whose time was nigh but still had work to do. From the roof patches and wall repairs, the people who maintained the home for children were fighting a losing battle.

"Bluestone. It's everywhere," the Highlord whispered.

"What?" asked Roger.

"Something Nate told me while we were at the hospital," answered the Highlord. "He said The Archer sank into the sidewalk. Do you think that's how they travel? I mean there was bluestone all over the palace in York and the church undercroft."

Roger looked down at the interlocking pavers at his feet and half expected a dærganfae to jump out of one. He rubbed his chin. "Perhaps so. I never made that connection."

"One thing's for sure," Cerdic said. "If that's how the dærganfae are doing it, we're ripping all that bluestone out of there."

"I'm sure the Lord Steward will love that," Lahar laughed. "First thing that happens when we get back, we start tearing the palace apart again."

"True. It will give Sir Jeffrey something to complain about," Cerdic said.

There was still no sign of pursuit. They dashed across Logan Street, passing several apartment buildings with cars parked in front. At the last one, cold fingers of dread clutched Roger's heart.

Ahead was the tenement housing project he'd seen before encountering The Archer. Veneered in brown brick, the short side of the two-story building closest to them bore four dark windows, two above and two below. The long side, which led away from them, had two covered entrances lit by wall mounted sconces.

Roger stepped over the metal fence guarding the property from pedestrians and peered around the corner. Three other identical buildings flanked a grassy quadrangle bisected by a sidewalk. Diagonally opposite, a fourth building, with two stories above a raised basement, was of older, grander construction, perhaps the home of the housing manager.

At the far end of the quadrangle, the octagonal wing of the gaol stared back at him above a low, grey border wall braced by regularly spaced piers. He could practically feel the evil leaking from the cracked concrete parging and barred windows. Looking around, it amazed him families could live so close to such a thing.

Lahar joined him, and a soft gasp escaped her. "Ambrose is in there?"

"Yes," Roger answered with certainty.

"How are we going to get her out?"

"Pick the lock, I guess."

"*Uh-huh*," Lahar said, her words thickly laced with doubt.

Careful not to make any noise, the two scurried along the long wall. When they reached the second entrance, with its covered stoop, they eased past a dark window and crouched behind a wide bush planted at the corner. A patch of grass and sidewalk separated them from the next building.

"This doesn't feel right," Lahar whispered. "It's too easy."

"The Archer?" Roger said, peering around and trying to glimpse any movement. He scanned the nearby rooftops and trees but didn't see anything. If The Archer was here, he'd have no trouble finding a place to ambush them. "You sure? I mean, if he were here, wouldn't he have already attacked?"

"He's waiting," Lahar said.

"Waiting for what?"

"How should I know?"

"Well, I don't want to make it easy for him. We need to keep moving," said Roger.

The two retreated the way they came and collected the Highlord and Cerdic. This time, they went around to the other side of the brick building. A tree-lined sidewalk led from covered stoop to covered stoop, dimly lit by copper sconces mounted beside each of the entrances.

"Lahar?" asked Roger.

"Looks clear to me," she answered.

Using the building to conceal their passage from the openness of the quadrangle, they again came to the corner and patch of grass with its intersecting sidewalk.

"Why do all these buildings look the same?" Cerdic whispered.

"Cost," answered the Highlord. "It's cheaper to build using materials in bulk."

Lahar gave the two an incredulous look and said, "Will you focus? Ambrose—"

"And The Archer," interrupted Roger.

"I was getting to him, if you' let me finish. Let's not get sidetracked. Time is short." Turning away, she muttered under her breath, "Why is it I'm the only one who wants this expedition over? I don't even like her."

"We apologize, Captain Lahar," the Highlord said. "It's difficult to ignore this world we're in."

The four dashed across the short gap between buildings and again held tight to the brown brick. Ahead, tall oaks and a low grey wall marked the end of the tenement housing. Light from a lone sconce fought valiantly against the dense shadows around it.

A blade in each hand, Lahar took the lead. Cerdic slid free his sword, while the Highlord raised his carbine and opened the dust cover. Putting a little distance between him and the other three, Roger crept through the shadows, watching for signs of danger from both behind and above. If The Archer was here, he was just as likely to be on the roof as anywhere.

With a flurry of footsteps, a sclábhaí in combat gear rushed from the shadows, gun raised.

Expecting the worst, Roger looked on wide-eyed. Bunched together as they were, there was no way any of them could have dodged away in time. Someone was going to get hurt.

The sclábhaí's trigger finger twitched but he didn't fire. Instead, he gave Lahar a quizzical look.

Faster than the eye could follow, Lahar had the sclábhaí's back against the brick, her blade pressed hard against his throat.

Three more sclábhaí advanced from a gap within the gaol's border wall, their carbines tucked into their shoulders. The two in front bore long wounds with fresh scabs.

Lahar locked eyes with her captive. "Drop your weapons," she hissed.

Panic marred the sclábhaí's features. He tried to swallow, but Lahar's knife prevented it.

"We can't," the rearmost sclábhaí replied in a strained voice. "Friend of the *blumkinde*, we do not want to hurt you, but our master makes us. Please... run..." Straining against himself, he raised his gun and pulled the trigger. The muzzle flashed with each shot.

Green chlorophyll sprayed the wall when Lahar sliced through her captive's throat. Not stopping, she leapt toward the other sclábhaí.

The two in front collapsed, shot in the back.

His gun barrel still smoking, the last man standing ejected the box magazine and inserted a new one. "Go now," he said through a clenched jaw. "Wounds shock us, but they don't stop us."

Cerdic grabbed Lahar by the elbow, and with Roger and the Highlord, they ran in a crouch through the gap in the border wall. Gunshots echoed over their heads as the sclábhaí behind them fired his weapon. Other sclábhaí converged on their position, only to be mowed down.

Roger looked over his shoulder and caught sight of two sclábhaí gunning down their benefactor. His body jerked left and right as if punched, and he finally dropped to the ground.

From the quadrangle, sclábhaí rushed to the border wall. Firing over the top, they tore up the ground behind the four Gaians.

Using the oak trees for cover, the Highlord squeezed the trigger and returned fire. When the carbine clicked, he ejected the spent magazine, slapped in another one, and continued firing.

Except for an old prisoner transport wagon with black iron bars, the yard beside the jail looked clear. "Let's go that way!" Roger shouted above the noise and gestured with his chin. His companions turned and nodded their agreement.

With the Highlord laying down cover fire, the four ran past the octagonal wing and crouched behind the convict cage. On the other side was a double door that accessed the ground floor of the east wing.

North of them, near where the salon had burned down, a loud explosion rocked the city, and a cloud of flame rose into the air. Another explosion lit the night sky to the north and east of their position.

Streetlamps at the front of the jail illuminated black and white faces. They waited across the street in an apparent attempt to contain them if the four breached the border wall.

"Bloody hell, they're everywhere," Lahar said, her back to

the cage.

"Why do I feel like we walked right into a trap?" asked Roger, beside her. Gunfire from the south pinged off the metal bars, drawing sparks.

"Because we did," the Highlord answered as he slid in his last magazine. "Anshu Jezra must have used Ambrose for bait."

"Can we get inside?" Cerdic asked, studying the defenses. "With those thick walls, we could hold them off."

"But for how long?" asked Lahar. "We have to be on the *Morningstar* by sunrise, or we don't leave at all."

"Cerdic, grab this wagon and roll it over to that door," the Highlord said between bursts of gunfire. "Once inside, we can take stock of our situation."

Cerdic sheathed his sword and gripped the frame with both hands. Not turning, the wheels simply skidded across the dirt. Cerdic reversed direction, then shoved it forward. A screech of metal-on-metal cut across the yard, and the rusted axles broke free with a lurch. Gaining speed, he rolled the convict cage closer to the jail. Beside him, the Highlord took aim and fired from the corner, while the others crouched, using the cage for cover.

Eyeing the wooden door and the three-story gaol with its cracked façade, doubt crept up Roger's spine. "Are you sure about this?"

After cocking the transport wagon at a diagonal, Cerdic laid a hand on the jail wall. "The gaol *is* evil, but if Ambrose is inside, we must rescue her."

The Highlord's carbine clicked again, and he tossed it aside. Unslinging the shotgun from his shoulder, he pumped the slide action and aimed.

Bullets peppered the iron cage and the jail, and everyone ducked. Sheltered behind the eastern border wall, four sclábhaí took turns firing and reloading.

"Unlock the doors, Roger," the Highlord urged. "We have no chance at all if we remain out here."

Amidst shotgun blasts and chunks of dirt and brick raining down, Roger picked the lock and opened one of the double doors. Inside, another pair of doors barred the way. Lined with iron, these had a more intricate locking mechanism. Closing his eyes, Roger blocked out the noise and focused on the lock.

The gunfire from the sclábhaí grew frantic. Lahar let out a curse when a bullet grazed her thigh. Another furrowed Cerdic's upper bicep.

"Got it!" Roger shouted, pushing the second pair of doors open.

All four rushed inside the jail, and Roger slammed the doors behind them. Light from the streetlamps outside filtered through the barred windows, revealing a bleak cellar. Partially below grade, a short ramp sloped from the door down to the dusty floor. To their left, empty rooms disappeared into the darkness. Straight ahead was a wall of solid black.

"I see nothing in front of us," Lahar said. "It's as though the world ends here."

But then the void advanced. Before they could react, it embraced them, its cold arms reeking of death.

The Archer walked down the middle of Magazine Street. His inky cloak concealed his features as he surveyed the jail and the team of sclábhaí collecting their wounded. To the north, more explosions rocked the city, and the firelight reflected in the low hanging clouds gave the city a sinister glow.

The mission was over. Despite the sense of closure, the feeling was bittersweet.

"The reign of the Highlord is finished," declared Anshu Jezra from the shadows. "Without him, Gallowen and Carolingias will fall. By Sutekh's will, today has been an exceptionally good day. Wouldn't you agree, Saighdeoir?"

"We didn't kill him," The Archer replied.

Anshu Jezra waved his hand airily. "It is of no matter. He is as good as dead. In fact, it's better this way. The Executioner will punish him, and those with him, for eternity. Could you ask for anything more?"

The Archer eyed the barred windows. A niggling of doubt formed in the back of his mind.

"Your services are no longer required, Saighdeoir," said Jezra. A cunning look came over the cleric. "And you must not attempt to free your fae. They are now inmates of the jail. Go home."

"You forget, Anshu. There is the matter of the contract."

"Your work here is done."

The Archer shook his head. "If your trap fails, my dærganfae will not be forced to become sclábhaí. I want to hear you say the contract is complete, Anshu. I want to see you destroy the document, freeing my team and me."

The Sha'iry's shadow image glared at the dærganfae assassin. He produced an ebony scroll case and unscrewed the embossed gold cap. Extracting a roll of heavy parchment, he held it up so The Archer could see the thirteen bloody thumbprints at the bottom. The flowing script glowed cherry-red.

"Your contract with us is complete." He rerolled the scroll and gestured with his hand. It floated up and passed through a portal. "Take it back to where the bargain was first made."

"But that's on Bhfolach Abhaile, my home world!" The Archer said with a snarl.

"Place it on the Altar of Sutekh," Jezra continued.

"What about my son?" The Archer asked.

"That is up to the Executioner."

"That's not good enough!"

"Saighdeoir, D'yakon Sagart Olc is expecting you. Do not make him wait or we may think of another task for you to perform." The Sha'iry spoke every word with fatalistic certainty, like the tolling of a death bell.

"Yes, Anshu," the Archer said, taking the parchment. By the time he had secured it, the cleric's image had vanished.

CHAPTER 32
VIGIL... COMPLETED

March 15, 1969 C.E.

12:00 am

Standing in front of the dærganfae's cell, the Executioner motioned toward a guard, who left the room and returned moments later with a length of rope: a noose with six coils tied at one end.

The Executioner took it and gave the fae a calculating look as if measuring him. Older than the ones Ambrose remembered seeing in the vault below the church, this dærganfae had translucent skin which exposed tendons and faint blue, throbbing veins.

"There's a science to hanging someone," the Executioner explained. "You see, death at the gallows comes in three forms: apoplexy, asphyxia, and — sweetest of all — the snap of a man's neck. That was the holy grail. That was what every executioner wanted. Tables, published by the military, listed the proper length of rope needed based on a person's weight. The lighter a person, the longer the drop required to break their neck."

He eyed the hook embedded in the shallow brick vaulted ceiling before tossing the rope inside its crook. A guard entered with a three-legged stool and placed it underneath the hook. Another carried a short table that barely fit through the narrow door. Behind him came a third with a set of wood steps. When finished, the makeshift gallows took up most of the central aisle.

Moving to the metal column, the Executioner adjusted the height of the noose up and down before tying it off to an iron ring riveted to the flange.

At the Executioner's signal, two guards moved swiftly into the dærganfae's cell, brandishing clubs. They fell on the prisoner and dragged him out. He fought every step of the way until one jabbed him in the stomach with his club. Outside the cage, a third guard grabbed the dærganfae and, with the help of the other two, manhandled him onto the stool.

Ascending the wood steps like a judge about to proclaim sentence, the Executioner placed the noose around the dærganfae's neck and tightened it such that the knot rested just behind the fae's left ear.

"How do you like my handiwork, little queen?"

Speechless, she watched the proceedings, unable to fully comprehend the madness she witnessed.

"I've killed hundreds. Black, white, red, men, women, it didn't matter. They all met the same fate," the Executioner said. His fingers gently caressed the noose before he stepped off the table. "I was sought out for my expertise, and on the gallows, I became a god."

"You were a drunk," Captain Clark said. "They'd drag you in here days before a hanging and stuff you in a cell just to sober you up. You were human... once."

"I am a god! I punish lawbreakers!"

The building rumbled and shifted on its foundations. Dirt and grit fell from the ceiling.

Ambrose blinked. For a second, the room was empty. There were no prisoners, no cages.

The dærganfae came to his senses and reached for the noose around his neck. With a smirk, the Executioner kicked the stool out from under him.

"No!" Ambrose shouted.

The dærganfae fell and the rope went taut. He dangled there, convulsing.

The Executioner watched the fae's throes, his full attention on the other's suffering. That's when Ambrose realized he had done it on purpose. The Executioner had never intended on killing the fae. This was another one of his tortures.

Her scalp itched as she focused on the bars. *She was alive.* The itching sensation became a burn, and to her surprise the bars became transparent. The men around her became apparitions, ghosts trapped in the aether.

Electric light from outside revealed an empty room. She drew in a ragged breath. No more shackles. No more cages. Even her wounds had vanished. She stepped forward, passing through the space where bars had been just a moment before.

Frowning, Ambrose stared hard at the room's open door. She could run, flee, and never look back. All she had to do was step through that door. But what about the others trapped here? What about Brie?

Steeling herself, she concentrated on the room.

Feeling like her scalp was aflame, Ambrose reappeared in the central aisle, outside her cage. Everyone and everything had a semi-solid cast to them. Everyone except the Executioner and the old dærganfae, who fought against the noose around his neck even as he dangled.

An eerie calm settled over the room as the cages filled with prisoners became solid again. Ambrose's shackles fell to the floor with a metallic clang, and all eyes turned to her. Pleading hands reached for her through the bars.

Even though she didn't have a key, Ambrose broke the aethereal lock and opened her and Kyle's cage, followed quickly by Captain Clark's.

The guards rushed her, clubs held high.

With a fury fueled by an eternity of torments, the freed inmates attacked and clawed at the jailors. Ambrose dashed around the far side of the cages, breaking locks and pushing open doors as she went. More inmates entered the fray. Shouts from those still in their cages urged the others on. They shook the bars, and the cacophony became deafening.

Letting out a low groan, the jail shifted, and the ironclad door slammed shut.

Suddenly, the Executioner stood before her. His mouth contorted in a vile grimace, he lashed out with the back of his hand and sent her crashing to the floor. "You have no power here, woman! This is the land of the dead!"

Ambrose scuttled back and bumped against the cold fireplace in the corner.

The sounds of fighting diminished as the Executioner stepped toward her. "You will beg... you will cower before me. I will flay the skin from your corpse every night, and you will know Hell."

With a feral snarl, Michael leapt upon the Executioner's back and grappled him to the floor, biting and punching.

A manic look in his eye, Captain George Clark beat the Executioner with a short club, struck Michael, then hit the Executioner again, bits of gore and hair clinging to the polished wood.

The jail lurched and mist rose from the floor. Michael jerked back just as Captain Clark landed another blow. This one hit concrete. The Executioner had disappeared.

"Where did he go?" Kyle asked fearfully from the crowd of prisoners, some of whom had started back toward their cages. It was as if, now that the fun was over, it was time to go home.

Horrid sounds of the dærganfae struggling against the noose cut through the shuffling. Her jaw set in determination, Ambrose climbed to her feet. The inmates parted as she made her way to the center of the room and the metal column.

"Anyone have a knife?" she asked, looking at the rope. Not waiting for an answer, she said, "You. Grab his legs," as she fought the knot.

When the knot came loose, the dærganfae fell to the floor, coughing. Ambrose knelt beside him and removed the noose. He gave her a questioning look and tried to form words. His neck was raw and bleeding, and she could only imagine the damage done. She clasped the aethereal shackles and broke the pin binding them together.

"Why?" asked the dærganfae in the barest of whispers.

"No one, not even a dærganfae assassin, deserves to die in this place."

The dærganfae rubbed his wrists. He gave her a hard stare, and she wondered if she'd made a mistake. The ring of prisoners around them gave her some assurance, but dærganfae were notorious killers, and she had just set one free.

"Queen Ambrose, there are those who would consider your actions a sign of a weak ruler. I see it as one of strength." With a dip of his head, the dærganfae said, "I am called Saoi, the Elder, and I am at your service."

Ambrose grabbed his hand and helped him to his feet. Looking at the other prisoners, she said, "Let's get everyone out of here."

Sir Cerdic Uth Aneirin felt his sword slip from his grip. He jerked awake and waited for his eyes to adjust. Recognizing the musty smell, he grimaced at the thought of being trapped in the old city jail. His alarm grew when he realized he was alone.

At some point he had dropped to a knee, but all he could

recall was the void that swallowed them. He could barely make out the block walls and dusty floor in the electric light that filtered through the barred window. He was on the ground floor.

Retrieving his sword, he bowed his head and prayed, "Pater Aeternum, defende nos in proelio." *Eternal Father, defend us in battle.*

Limned by holy light, the paladin stepped into the central hallway and climbed a short flight of concrete stairs. He passed through a thick doorway and under a three-story lightwell to a tiled foyer with a tin-plated ceiling. Thick cobwebs clung to the plaster walls.

Silence blanketed the jail.

To the right and left, closed doors led to other parts of the building. Straight ahead, the glimmer of streetlamps shined through dusty windows flanking the jail's exit.

A single flight of cast-iron stairs cut back toward the lightwell and accessed the second floor. Gripping the handrail, he took the stairs, one tread at a time. Zephyrs slid across him, leaving him feeling cold and clammy. Visions of jailers leading prisoners up this flight of metal stairs appeared in front of him. Uncomfortably aware of the second-floor guardroom windows at his back, he fought against the rising panic with a prayer on his lips.

At the top, a wall of rusted bars waited for him, the gate open. On the other side, a hallway ran past cast-iron stairs leading to the third floor and stopped at another thick masonry wall and arched doorway. To either side of him, a single ironclad door accessed the west and east wings.

A clank of chains startled him. It had come from behind one of the doors. He placed a hand on its surface. Evil coated the door like ectoplasmic slime. With the hilt of his sword held tight, he wrenched back the bolt and tugged on the handle.

Giving it another try, Ambrose shoved against the stubborn door. The previous attempts had proven that her ability to unlock doors and shackles was limited. It seemed the building itself was trying to keep her captive. If she died here, there'd be no escaping the Executioner.

Captain Clark, Kyle, and some of the others had also

tried, but they, it seemed, were bound by some aethereal law that made the walls and doors of the old jail solid.

With a stomp of her foot, she glared at the door. Desperate, she lowered a shoulder and pushed with everything she had.

The door flew open. Ambrose stumbled forward. A strong arm caught her, and she found herself pressed against a muscular chest covered in the singed remnants of a cotton tunic.

"Ambrose!" Cerdic exclaimed with a broad smile. "Thank the Eternal Father, I found you. Have you seen the others?"

Ambrose frowned. Although happy at finding Cerdic at the door, she was having trouble distinguishing between the aethereal world and the living world. She gripped his arm like an anchor and returned his hug. Relief flooded through her when he didn't fade away like some dream-spawned apparition. Collecting herself, she let go and after a moment realized Cerdic couldn't see the men and women pressing behind her, including Saoi.

"Others?" she asked when she found her voice.

"The Highlord, Roger, and Lahar. We all came to rescue you. They should be here somewhere."

"How did you get here?"

"Long story," he replied. A worried light crept into his eyes. They lingered on her bald scalp and tattered clothing, and she knew he wanted to ask her about it. Instead, he said, "You're here, but you're not. What happened?"

"We're trapped. I think I can free myself, but there are those with me who can't."

Cerdic scrutinized the empty room behind her and said, "Pater Aeternum, Si ergo inveni gratiam in conspectu tuo, ostende mihi faciem tuam, ut sciam te, et inveniam gratiam ante oculos tuos." *If I have found favor in your sight, please show me now your ways so that I may know you.* The holy light surrounding Cerdic filled the threshold, and the faces of inmates appeared within its limits.

Bathed in the glow, Ambrose felt warmth seep into her bones. However, those behind her shied away. The light, though comforting and inviting, also revealed the truth. It revealed how far they had fallen under the cruel ministrations of the Executioner. A tentative hand touched her shoulder, and she turned to find Kyle staring wide-eyed at Cerdic, tears streaming down his cheeks. Others crowded forward, seeking the promise of solace.

"Flectere si nequeo superos, Acheronta movebo," a voice hissed from the third floor. *If I can't move heaven, I shall raise Hell.*

Cerdic whipped around, sword ready.

Standing on the landing, the skeletal form of the Executioner peered from the edge of darkness. Frigid cold seeped out of the walls as guards with short clubs in hand approached from the southern octagonal wing. More charged up the cast-iron stairs from the ground floor, their booted feet pounding on the metal treads.

"Cerdic!" Ambrose shouted. "Watch out! It's the Executioner! He controls this place."

"Et super hanc petram stamus contra malo, et portæ inferi non prævalebunt adversus eam," Cerdic said to the figure on the third floor. *And on this rock, we will stand against evil, and the gates of hell will not prevail against us.* His voice rang out, and with it, the glow around him became brighter. It expanded and filled the hallway, and the guards fell back.

Fleeing, the Executioner's screams of rage followed in his wake. In response, the massive structure around them shook. Brick and mortar became fluid as sand streamed from the ceiling and walls.

"The building's collapsing!" Captain Clark cried out.

"My Queen, I must get you out of here," Cerdic said, clearly torn between his duty to his queen and his absent friends.

"No, Sir Cerdic, we free these people, once and for all."

CHAPTER 33
GHOST TOWER

March 15, 1969 C.E.

12:40 am

*T*he building trembled again. Barely keeping her feet beneath her, Ambrose raced across the hallway and threw open the door to the other cell room. Beside her, Cerdic's light caught the edges of the cells. Peering through the curved recess in the barred gate, she spotted a couple of dærganfae. She didn't see Brie or recognize any of the prisoners who stared back.

"Brie, are you here?" Ambrose shouted as she opened the gate. She stepped aside, and Captain Clark and several other inmates rushed past. He carried a ring of skeleton keys and started unlocking cages. Shouting as they came, guards poured through a gap in the north wall.

Cerdic grabbed Ambrose by the arm and said, "We can't do anything for them until we find the Executioner."

Moving to the third floor, Ambrose discovered two more rooms filled with caged prisoners and the remaining dærganfae, but no Brie. At the north end of the hallway, a barred wall prevented anyone from falling into the lightwell. Opposite, a ghostly oil lamp lit the guardroom through the third-floor window. The guards pointed and waved their short clubs at them; however, they had no access to the cell room floor. They filed into the adjacent rooms, and Ambrose could only guess they had entered the square towers flanking the jail's main entrance.

"Have at 'em, lads," Captain Clark shouted from below. In answer, strident yells and meaty thuds erupted.

Michael and Kyle, each holding a ring of keys, joined her at the doorway. "Go. Find your friend. We'll free everyone on this floor," Michael said.

Ambrose faced the octagonal wing and her heart lurched. Something in that direction cast a shadow of fear, and she found her resolve wavering.

"My Queen, what's wrong?" Cerdic asked as he followed her gaze.

"The south wing is where the Executioner tortures people."

Captain Clark climbed the metal stairs. In one hand, he carried a short club; in the other, he carried wrist shackles. His eyes scanned the floor for more guards, even as the fighting continued below.

"Are you alright?" Clark asked.

Ambrose nodded and replied, "I'm looking for a friend of mine."

The glow surrounding Cerdic intensified when he and Ambrose took a step toward the southern end of the gaol. It revealed a wispy stair, leading up.

"There's another floor," Ambrose gasped.

With a cry of warning, Michael yelled, "Don't go up there. Those who do, never return. When they originally built the gaol, it had four floors, and the southern wing bore a two-story tower. They say an earthquake struck down this place, destroying the tower, along with most of the city. It's not a place for the living."

Cerdic cast a determined eye on the stairs. "Evil hides in shadows where it thinks the light of the Eternal Father cannot reach, but His light always exposes the truth."

Ambrose wondered at the paladin's words. His whole manner was one of intense focus and faith. How could they even consider climbing those aethereal stairs to nowhere? The Knights of Carolingias were renowned for their bravery, but she had heard her father tell stories of their foolhardiness. Honorable to a fault, they often charged into the lion's den without consideration for their lives and the lives of those around them.

"My Queen," Cerdic said, "if we go, we must go together."

Ambrose pictured Sir Baldwin facing Archbishop Letizia. Now that she thought about it, he had demonstrated the same intense focus and faith she saw in Cerdic, only his faith had been in her.

"Lead on, Sir Knight," she said finally. "Where you go, I shall follow."

Ambrose breathed a sigh of relief when the aethereal treads and risers, revealed only by the glow surrounding the knight, bore their weight. Cerdic smiled grimly and gripped his sword tighter.

"Et detraxero te cum his qui descendunt in lacum ad populum sempiternum. Collocavero te in gaia novissima sicut solitudines veteres, cum his qui deducuntur in lacum, ut non habiteris: porro cum dedero gloriam in gaia viventium," he said. *Then will I send thee to the abyss to join those who descended there long ago. Your building shall lie in ruins, buried beneath the ground, like those in the grave who have entered the world of the dead: You will have no place here in the land of the living.*

The goofer dust in Ambrose's scalp burned as they ascended, and she felt lightheaded. Inside the cell rooms, filthy soldiers in faded blue and grey uniforms huddled in overcrowded cages. The stench of rank bodies made the ghostly floors and walls seem solid. "Brie!" she shouted as she opened their cells.

After everyone was set free, Cerdic aimed south down the hallway and led Ambrose into the octagonal wing. A malignant feeling of hate beat against them with each step.

Like a castle donjon, clockwise stairs climbed into the misty ceiling. Focusing on Cerdic's back, Ambrose didn't look down as she followed him up the steps.

At the top, the knight pushed through a door that should have led to the gaol's roof. Instead, they found themselves in a tower room. Darkness flowed through eight arrow-loop windows like aethereal fog and pooled in corners. As it moved and shifted, Ambrose caught glimpses of shackles hanging from the brick walls.

"Executioner, release my friends!" Cerdic shouted. "You have no reason to hold them."

"They have killed. They have lied. How can you say I have no reason to hold them? They belong here with the other criminals. An example must be made of them."

"Scriptum est enim: mihi vindictam ego retribuam, dicit Pater Aeternum," Cerdic replied with narrowed eyes. *For it is written, "Vengeance is mine, I will repay," saith the Eternal Father.*

A portion of the darkness parted and revealed the Executioner holding Lahar by the throat. Her head lolled to one side, but her features contorted as though she fought an internal struggle.

Leveling the tip of his sword at the Executioner, Cerdic

said, "Wretched creature, let her go. Now!" He took a step forward.

"Eques sanctus, stay back. If I snap her neck, she becomes mine forever."

Cerdic seemed frozen. Concern for Lahar filled his eyes even as his lips drew back in a grimace.

The Executioner laughed, and the glow around Cerdic shrank. "You have no power here. The Dark One gave this place to me. Not even your precious Eternal Father can sever our pact."

"It's not your pact I want to break," Cerdic hissed.

The burning sensation from the goofer dust flared sharply. Screaming in pain, Ambrose fell to her knees and pressed her hands against her temples. Taking in deep breaths of air, she fought against the pain, redirecting it toward the tower walls.

All around her the shadows thinned, and the tower began to look different as if a gauze curtain had lifted. Its walls became semitransparent, and beyond them the aethereal world lay open.

Doctor Wampus stepped forth, as through a doorway. "Gal, oonuh in deep," drawled the ghost, helping her to her feet.

Captain Clark charged up the tower stairs, followed by Michael, who carried the noose from the second floor in his hands. Arrayed behind him, Kyle and the other inmates filled the stairwell.

Rage contorted the Executioner's gaunt features, and his thin lips drew back in a feral snarl. "What is this? Back to your cells!" His voice boomed like thunder in the close confines.

The newly freed prisoners cowered before their gaoler, but Doctor Wampus straightened to his full height. "Un Moses said tuh de Pharaoh, 'Leh muh people go!' I's come fuh dem what you un dis building done took bedoubt jus' cause."

"They are all guilty!" the wraith shouted. His claw-like fingers remained clenched around Lahar's throat. Her skin had taken on a pale blue tinge.

Mumbling words meant only for the Executioner, Doctor Wampus removed his glasses and fixed his cobalt eyes upon him.

Ghosts pressed in from all sides, and shadowy hands reached for the Executioner. Each time one touched him, he grew less substantial. Aethereal mists billowed about his feet and began to climb his legs. Panic-stricken, the Executioner flung Lahar at Cerdic and fled to the tower's upper level.

Cerdic eased Lahar to the floor, trembling fingers desperately searching for her pulse. "Pater Aeternum, quaeso ne a me Lahar auferas." The glow surrounding the paladin brightened. In its warmth, color returned to Lahar's cheeks, but she remained unconscious.

"Holy mun, she gwine uh live. Right now, you gots work tuh do. I'll look attuh yo lady," Doctor Wampus said. His long, bony finger pointed upward where the Executioner had fled. He turned to Ambrose. "Gal, you hab a part tuh play, too. You's a Queen. Yo 'thority mo powerful dan de Executioner. Is up tuh oonuh tuh see justice served tuh de Jack Ketch."

The tower stairs let out into a space that resembled a sepulcher. Growling like a beast guarding its prey, the Executioner drew back his flail in preparation to strike one of the figures lying at his feet — Brie, Roger, and the Highlord.

"Begone, knight. You have no authority over me," snarled the emaciated figure.

Cerdic leveled his sword at the Executioner. "Release these people and seek the Eternal Father's forgiveness."

The Executioner spat at Cerdic even as he shied away from the cruciform sword.

Cerdic pressed forward. "There is no escape. You have only one chance for redemption. There will be no other." The steel in Cerdic's voice matched his blade.

"The Dark One cannot be defeated. He will strike you down and feed your souls to the fires of Hell."

"Vengeance does not strengthen my arm," Cerdic replied. "But I will not suffer the evil you have done to these people. Criminals or not, they deserve to be judged by the Eternal Father. You have kept them from that judgment."

"*Hah!* You wish to execute the Executioner. I am the gaol, and the gaol is me! I cannot die!" With that, the Executioner lurched forward, forcing himself onto Cerdic's sword. The unholy light in his eyes intensified as he struck Cerdic with his flail and dug his bony fingers into the paladin's chest.

Face contorted in pain, Cerdic tried to back away, shake the creature from his sword, but it wouldn't let go.

"'E draw him strengk from de prisoners and dese walls!" Doctor Wampus shouted up the stairwell. "Take him 'thority, gal!"

Images flashed through Ambrose's mind — not only of the things she'd experienced within the City Jail, but also of the people suffering in Carolingias under the unjust rule of the Sha'iry. Like those evil priests, the Executioner served the Dark One. Although she took no satisfaction in the task, she knew that evil could only thrive when those who serve goodness failed to stand against it.

"Executioner!" she shouted. When the creature met her gaze, she continued, "You have taken upon yourself roles which you were not granted. You have tormented and tortured the unjustly imprisoned. You denied swift justice and the Eternal Father's judgement to the guilty."

The Executioner laughed and stepped away from Cerdic. The paladin's sword passed through him as if it were insubstantial as mist. "Who are you to accuse me, little queen?"

Ambrose drew herself up to her full height and lifted her chin to glare down her nose at the evil wretch. "I am Queen Ambrose Battenberg of Carolingias. By the authority granted to me by my subjects and the Eternal Father, I grant pardon to every prisoner within these walls."

"No! They are mine!" cried the Executioner.

"Furthermore, you stand accused of dereliction of duty, heinous acts of cruelty, and consorting with the Dark One. For these crimes I find you guilty, Jack Ketch."

The ghastly creature seemed to shrink in upon himself, losing his monstrous aspect as he became more emaciated.

"You are no longer Executioner here," said Ambrose.

Baring his teeth, the deposed executioner leapt at her, flail in motion.

Michael charged forward and dropped the executioner's noose around the wraith's neck.

The flail turned to dust as it pattered harmlessly on Ambrose's skin. Startled, the Executioner looked down at his empty hand as if seeing it for the first time. He reached up to brush fingertips over the noose around his throat. Though it seemed impossible, his countenance grew paler. "No!" he cried out.

Michael shoved his former tormentor to his knees and gave a short bow to Ambrose. "Your Majesty, what would you have us do with him?"

"Give the rope to me, Michael." Ambrose took in the crowd of ghosts at the head of the stairs. "You are all free to leave this place. May the Eternal Father grant you peace."

Captain Clark stepped forward and bowed. "Thank you, Your Majesty. By your leave, we'll stay to see justice served."

She granted the captain's request, and turned her gaze to Cerdic, who held his sword ready.

"What is your command, Ma'am?"

"Pray," she replied. "Pray for the many souls held here too long, and for this wretched creature who walked willingly into the darkness." Gripping the noose with both hands, Ambrose sinched the knot until it pressed tight against the former executioner's skin. "Earlier, you said death at the gallows comes in three forms: apoplexy, asphyxia, and the snap of a man's neck," Ambrose said and jerked the knot even tighter.

The Executioner wailed when wisps of smoke rose from where the rope touched his flesh. His skin blackened and burned as the noose dug deeper. He writhed and clawed at the rope, but it would not come loose. If anything, it seemed to grow tighter of its own accord. The now pitiful man emitted a final cry as the noose closed, and the Executioner's head came free and tumbled to the floor, staring blindly. The unholy light in his eyes slowly dimmed, then snuffed out.

Raising his sword in salute, Cerdic said, "The Eternal Father's will be done."

'Guilty,' an ominous voice rumbled.

Roger blinked awake. A hard concrete floor pressed against his cheek, and his body felt cold and stiff. Beyond the ghostly shapes surrounding him, narrow windows revealed an infinite blankness. His colorless surroundings reminded him of stories he'd heard about the aethereal realm. Fearing he, too, was dead, he closed his eyes to pray, but the words would not come.

Cerdic's voice cut through his despair. Roger reopened his eyes to find the ghosts gone, and color returned to his sight. Lying next to him was a tall, slender woman with tousled golden-brown hair obscuring her face. She wore a loose-fitting, tie-dyed dress that seemed out of place in the ancient tower.

A few paces away, Cerdic sheathed his sword. At his feet was a cadaverous body. Unseeing eyes from a decapitated head stared up at the knight, and it sent an involuntary shiver down Roger's spine.

"Where are we?" the Highlord asked, rising.

"The gaol, Your Majesty," Cerdic answered as he stepped away from the corpse.

"I don't recall seeing a tower like this," Roger said, climbing to his feet. "Where was it?"

"It doesn't exist. At least not anymore," replied Cerdic.

"I hate it when you're cryptic," commented Roger, knocking the dust from his pants.

"Queen Ambrose, you seem... different," the Highlord said, eyeing her bald scalp. "It's good to see you."

"Highlord," Ambrose responded, "you shouldn't have come."

"I told him the same thing before we left York," Lahar snarked as she climbed the stairs, "but he and your knight champion insisted. Now, let's get out of this place and find the *Morningstar* before we're all trapped in this accursed world."

Turning toward her voice, Cerdic stumbled.

The Highlord caught Cerdic's upper arm to steady him. "Are you alright?"

"Yes, sir, or at least, I will be." Visible through his tattered shirt, the marks of a lash and deep, angry scratches faded to white scars.

Nodding to the corpse on the floor, the Highlord said, "I take it he's the one who had us trapped."

"Yes, sir. We've passed into the land of the dead. The exit's that way," Cerdic replied, pointing.

Ambrose let out a gasp and crouched beside the sleeping woman. "Brie! Is she—?"

Cerdic knelt beside her and touched the young woman's exposed shoulder. "She'll come around," he answered. "We just need to give her time."

With Lahar's help, Cerdic stood. She was about to turn away, but he caught her with a hand on her bicep. With his other hand, he caressed her cheek. "I'm happy to see you awake."

Staring into his eyes, Lahar grabbed his hand at her cheek and gently pushed it aside, but she didn't let go. "I was worried when I didn't see you, but I knew you wouldn't be far."

Roger coughed, and the two stepped away from each other. He scooped up Brie, and they went downstairs where Captain Clark, Michael, Kyle, and Doctor Wampus waited.

Captain Clark asked the paladin, "What now?"

"Captain, you know the answer he's going to give," Lahar said with a glint in her eye.

"I guess I do."

Cerdic bowed his head, and said, "In sudore vultus tui vesceris pane, donec revertaris in gaiam de qua sumptus es: quia pulvis es et in pulverem reverteris." *By the sweat of your brow, you will eat your food until you return to the ground, since from it you were taken; for dust you are and to dust you will return.* Facing the Captain, he continued, "Seek the Eternal Father and ask to be forgiven."

Captain Clark doffed an aethereal wide-brimmed hat and said, "What a grand final adventure." Placing it back on his head, he said even as he faded away, "We sail on the tide, and where the sea takes us, only the wind will know."

Michael and Kyle each wrapped Ambrose in a hug. "I will wait for my wife at Peter's Gate," Michael told her. "I just hope they have a bench where I can sit." The two walked toward the tower wall and vanished. Next came Doctor Wampus, who took Ambrose's head in his hands and touched his forehead to hers. Next, he grasped Cerdic's hand and gave it a firm shake. "May I pass f'um oonuh sight, but not oonuh memory."

After the doctor had faded away, the Highlord said, "Ambrose, Cerdic, it's time to go."

They continued down the stairs to the third floor and the land of the living. Colors became sharper, and Roger looked down at himself. Everything he had worn prior to entering the jail had returned, including his pouches filled with his alchemical supplies. Ambrose was no longer barefoot and wearing her white gown. Matching Brie, she wore tennis shoes and a tie-dyed sundress that was most un-queen-like. The doors to the cell rooms stood open. Now empty, the building was diminished — less imposing. The evil that had filled its walls had fled, hopefully never to return.

At the second floor, Saoi stood with the other four dærganfae, the horrors they had experienced still fresh in their expressions. The largest of them slid free a curved longsword with a silver and gold filigreed hilt.

"Trodaire, stand down," said Saoi. "Can you not feel it? Our contract with the Sha'iry is no more."

"Dærganfae!" Cerdic yelled. His eyes filled with madness as he leapt forward, his blade brandished.

Ambrose grabbed his arm and quickly put herself between him and the fae. "No!" she said, leaning into him. "They are to go free as well."

"But Lord Alfonso... Sir Baldwin," Cerdic stammered.

"No," Ambrose said, softer this time. "There has been enough blood spilt within these walls. Let our last memory of this place be one of peace." She released his arm as she said it, but kept her eyes focused on his.

Lowering his sword, he said, "Yes, my Queen."

Lahar and Roger exchanged glances. It seemed the young Queen had changed a lot during her stay here. He felt strange seeing the dærganfae. They had fought for so long, the very sight of them sent his adrenaline rushing. He gripped Brie tight, ready to run if necessary.

"The Queen is right," Saoi said. "There has been too much bloodshed."

"But An Saighdeoir?" a slim dærganfae asked.

"He will respect our decision even if he doesn't agree with it," Saoi replied. Turning to Queen Ambrose, he said, "We know your companions by reputation. Let me introduce mine. I am Saoi, the Elder. This is Trodaire, Aimsitheoir, Gadaí, and File our inquisitive scop." As he spoke, each one bowed his head toward the queen and to the Highlord.

"Queen Ambrose, we beg a favor," Saoi said. "Let us come with you."

Ambrose's eyes widened at the request, but she quickly recovered.

"How did you reach Terra?" Roger asked.

"Once, ages past, we traveled the Secret Ways, and the Terrans worshipped us," Saoi replied. "The Ways were sealed, and now, they remember us only in myths and tales to frighten their children. An Saighdeoir had a key that opened those ancient Ways, but he would never use it to help the Queen. His lust for Battenberg blood has consumed him."

"So why do you help us?" Lahar asked.

"Queen Ambrose saved us. We owe her a life-debt we must repay before returning home. It is a matter of honor."

"I see," Ambrose said.

"Captain Lahar, would your ship have room for five more passengers?" the Highlord asked.

Lahar's lips pressed tight together, and her face became pinched. Roger wanted to say something but held his tongue. Ruled by her heart, the elf captain would not easily be swayed with reason, especially coming from him.

Finally, Lahar nodded and said, "They can come, but if they fall behind, I'm not waiting."

"Understood, Captain," Saoi said.

Retracing their steps back to the cellar, the group raced up the short ramp and outside. Happy to be out of the building, Roger didn't even mind the sirens wailing in the distance.

Still in Roger's arms, Brie sucked in a ragged breath of fresh air. At first, he saw only grey walls and barred windows reflected in her eyes. When she blinked, brilliant sapphire replaced the grey, and he felt his heart skip a beat.

"You can set me down now," she said.

His mouth suddenly dry, he lowered her to her feet, but kept an arm around her slim waist while she regained her balance. He swallowed hard and cleared his throat. "I'm Roger."

"Brie," she replied, still dazed. "How did I get here?"

"I'll explain on the way," Ambrose said.

Brie looked toward the voice, and her whole face lit up with a smile. "Ambrose!" she cried, pulling away from Roger to hug her friend. "Are these some of the people you talked about?"

"Yes," Ambrose answered. "This is the Highlord of Gallowen, Sir Cerdic Uth Aneirin, one of the few remaining Knights of Carolingias, Captain Lahar, and you've already met Roger Vaughn." Brie moved toward each one, and as she did, Ambrose warned, "Watch out, she's a hugger." Brie ignored the offered hands and wrapped each one in a warm hug.

"And these," Ambrose added, "are Saoi, File, Gadaí, Trodaire, and—"

"Aimsitheoir, Milady" the last dærganfae responded with a low bow. Between the cut of his features and the long recurve bow he carried, he appeared to be a younger version of The Archer. He wore an inky cloak that hid everything except for a single quiver filled with black fletched arrows on his hip.

Once Brie doled out her hugs, Cerdic asked, "Where to?"

Lahar scanned the area and said, "We go west."

Her arm wrapped around Ambrose's shoulders, Brie said, "Let's aim for the Yacht Club. I can call my dad to come pick us up."

The Highlord nodded, and with the dærganfae following, the group raced across Franklin Street and shot down Cromwell Alley.

CHAPTER 34
TRAPPED

March 15, 1969 c.e.

1:30 am

*F*earing an ambush, the Gaians and their companions
wound through alleys, between residences, and along
narrow streets. Traffic was nonexistent this deep in the
night, but Cerdic still felt uncomfortable with all the
sneaking around.

Lahar must have sensed his thoughts. "We're not
sneaking," she said. "We're walking quietly so we don't
disturb anyone. That's being polite."

Cerdic's mouth dropped open and his eyes went wide.
Despite the darkness, he knew she could see the red creeping
up his collar.

"Cerdic, you read like an open book. I doubt you could
conceal a thought if you tried."

"Probably not," Cerdic replied sharply. He tried to keep
his expression impassive, but like planning before a battle, it
seemed to always go awry after the first punch.

"Don't be angry. I was only teasing."

"I'm not angry," Cerdic said, the red on his neck rising
higher.

"How long have you two known each other?" Brie asked.

"Four years," Lahar answered.

"Have y'all fought the whole time?"

"Fought? You mean with each other? Or did you mean
anything that stands in our way?" Lahar asked.

Brie shrugged. "Each other, I guess."

"We don't fight," Cerdic proclaimed. He was sure his tone
held the proper amount of firmness and brooked no
challenge. It had put many a soldier in their place, but for
some reason the two women gave him a look of sympathy.
Shaking his head, he quickened his steps.

"Does he always run away like that?" Brie asked behind
him.

"No, not always," Lahar replied.

He could feel her eyes on his back and wondered what

life would be like once they returned home. Lahar was not someone you introduced to your parents. But that's just what would have to happen if their relationship were to continue.

Would his family accept her? A pirate? Swallowing, he gripped the hilt of his sword. *They'll have to.*

Turning his eyes to the Queen, he wondered at the change that had been wrought by this place. She had matured and found her courage. Ahead of him, she and the Highlord talked policies and politics. It seemed Carolingias would be in good hands, after all. The Eternal Father had a way of pulling everything together.

Cerdic had a feeling of déjà vu when they turned down a newly constructed road and saw the County Hospital in the distance. Stockpiled with construction material, the area around them was a testament to the amount of improvement planned by the city. New roads, new bridges, and infilled inlets: he expected the west side would be unrecognizable in a few years.

Across the street, a four-story building with a gabled roof overlooked a treed parking lot on one side and a marina on the other. Cerdic inhaled the salt air and caught the pungent tang of marsh and mud. Wispy fog had rolled in from the harbor, and the streetlamps radiated an eerie glow. From the looks of it, docks were under construction as well.

Several metal huts huddled behind a chain-link fence, guarded by a whitewashed block building bearing a faded military crest with a crown over anchor flukes and "MINE FORCE U.S. ATLANTIC FLEET" in the shape of a U. On the building's porch, an arow pointed to a glass door that read, Dockmaster. Beyond it, the marina's southernmost point held a variety of fishing boats and yachts.

"There's a phone," Brie said, pointing to a strange rotary device with a handheld receiver. Sheltered by the porch roof, it was illuminated by a security light.

She picked up the receiver and flicked a lever a few times. "No dial tone," she said.

"Do they have one in there?" Roger asked, nodding to the glass door.

"They're closed," Brie said, reading the hours posted beside it.

Roger smiled. "Only for some."

Blockading the entrance to Rutledge at Calhoun with a line of bright orange flares and their police car, Nate and Tee directed traffic with their flashlights. At the other end of the block, two more officers did the same. Together, their blue lights illuminated the six columns supporting the entrance to the Charleston Museum.

Between the cruisers, water sluiced across the pavement even as firemen collected their hoses and other gear. They worked around the steaming remains of a burnt-out car.

Nate had radioed for a tow truck, but the fire chief wanted to hold off on leaving until they could survey the area and make sure a fiery spark hadn't found purchase somewhere. So, firemen searched house to house, while he and Tee waited.

Before midnight, the two had been called in along with every able policeman in the county. Four cars in total had been firebombed, all within the confines of the peninsula, and all in front of public places.

Assigned to the one at the museum, they'd arrived on the scene to find four gunmen in combat gear ready for them. Similar to the ones at the hospital, two had been armed with German assault rifles; however, there were two others who carried close quarter M3 grease guns with its distinctive barrel. Instead of attacking, the strange men established defensive positions across the street from the museum.

Using the homes for cover, the hostiles seemed determined to hold their ground, their shots meant to keep the two police officers pinned down. Nate called for reinforcements while Tee tossed several canisters of tear gas into their midst, filling the street with a noxious cloud.

Two other units arrived, and the gunfire intensified. Flanked and outnumbered, the hostiles had dug in further.

Then, at the stroke of midnight, an odd shadowy portal appeared on the sidewalk. Opening up with their automatic weapons, the gunmen charged from their hiding places and ran toward it. At Lieutenant Bell's direction, all units had closed in, but the black and white-faced men had vanished.

Nate wanted a cigarette. His hands still shook. He thought of Cam and unwrapped a stick of gum.

"Want one?" he asked Tee.

"Naw, buh," his partner replied.

Static from their radio preceded Lieutenant Bell's voice. "1-Echo-25. 1-Echo-25."

Half in, half out, Tee sat in the driver's seat of the cruiser and unclipped the receiver. "1-Echo-25 here."

"We have a possible 10-31 near the Yacht Club. I want you to check it out. Use caution."

"1-Echo-25. Acknowledged."

"You driving?" Nate asked, sliding into the passenger seat.

Closing his door, Tee grinned, and his white teeth shone in the darkness. "Of co'se." He looked over his shoulder as he backed the cruiser, turning the steering wheel, and put the car in drive. Leaving the other police unit, he pulled onto Calhoun, leaned forward, and switched off the rotating top light.

"What happened, Anshu Jezra? Where are my dærganfae?" The Archer asked as he stepped through the gaol's open door. Peering down the empty hallway and into the adjacent rooms, he clenched his longbow in a tight fist.

"I don't care for the tone of your voice, Saighdeoir," the Sha'iry replied from the metal stairs.

"What does my tone have to do with anything?" The Archer snapped. "The Queen and the Highlord escaped *your* jail. You let them go. Your Sutekh let them go. Yet here I am, again, suffering your recriminations while breathing the air of this dismal realm. Why did you insist I return?"

"There were complications," replied Anshu Jezra with a sneer.

"What complications?" The Archer asked.

"Your dærganfae helped them escape."

In one fluid motion, The Archer unsheathed his sword and pointed it at the priest. "Do not toy with me, Sha'iry. There is nowhere in Gaia or Terra you can hide from my vengeance."

With his eyes fixed on those of The Archer, Anshu Jezra stepped forward, allowing the blade to pass through his image. "Your *son* was seen leaving with the Queen and the Highlord along with the rest of your dærganfae. It seems the renowned loyalty of your kind is but a mere myth. Bí Gan Staonadh — the Way of the Dærganfae — is that what you call it?"

The Archer tamped down the fear in his heart. As subtle as it was, there was no mistaking Jezra's threat toward Aimsitheoir. His hatred redirected, The Archer met the priest's glare and asked, "What do you want of me?"

"Find the Highlord and kill him."

Sheathing his sword, The Archer asked, "Do you know where they are or where they're going?"

"Pardon the intrusion," a sclábhaí said from the cellar. "The police just sent someone to investigate prowlers at the marina."

Jezra gave The Archer an evil sneer and said, "Sutekh provides the way."

As they stepped out of the dockmaster's office, bright headlights flashed from a single car heading their way.

"Looks like a police car," Lahar announced, squinting.

"You think its Nate?" Brie asked with a hopeful expression.

"I can't tell."

The police car was about to turn in to the parking lot, when gunfire erupted from behind a cluster of trees. Throwing sparks, bullets peppered the hood and front quarter panels.

"Sclábhaí," Saoi hissed. "Anshu Jezra must know where we are."

Three of the five dærganfae unslung their longbows and nocked arrows. The other two, Saoi and Trodaire, unsheathed curved blades.

"Go," Saoi said. "We'll hold them off."

"Come with us," Ambrose said.

"No, Milady, we owe you a life debt."

"Saoi, dying here serves no purpose."

Looking frantic, Brie stepped toward the police cruiser. Roger snatched her back just as the gunfire turned on them. Bits of asphalt flew into the air. Beside them, Trodaire went down, followed by Gadaí, their bodies shredded. With smooth, fluid motions, File and Aimsitheoir loosed their arrows and fired again.

"Run!" the Highlord shouted. He sprinted in a half-crouch toward the docks.

Heart beating counterpoint to the staccato of gunfire raging overhead, Cerdic fought the urge to fall flat on the ground. He and Lahar leapfrogged with the three dærganfae from column to tree to construction vehicle.

When they had shots, Aimsitheoir and File fired arrows at the Sclábhaí. Cerdic was glad it slowed their advance, but the two dærganfae's supply of arrows was quickly dwindling.

The direction of the gunfire changed. The Sclábhaí were trying to get in front of them.

More headlights lanced across the lot and with them came the wail of sirens.

"Can you drive one of those boats?" the Highlord asked Brie, nodding toward the white yachts tethered to the array of docks.

In a daze, she looked around. Ambrose grabbed her shoulders and gave her a gentle shake. "Brie."

Brie blinked owlishly as she stammered, "Those men... they're trying to kill us."

"Yes, and they're going to keep trying. Can you pilot one of those boats?"

Brie turned toward the dock and replied, "A small one. Not the larger ones."

"That's our plan," the Highlord announced. "Pick one you're comfortable with, and we'll get out of here."

"Can you do that?" Ambrose asked Brie.

Brie nodded and pointed toward one at the far end. "We'll need a key. I just hope it has fuel."

"I can handle the first part," Roger said. "The second part's out of my hands."

"One problem at a time, thief," the Highlord said.

Nate assumed a prone position on the pavement and fired his revolver.

On the other side of what remained of their car, Tee blasted away with his .44 magnum. His cannon boomed with each shot and probably had as much of an intimidation factor as the actual bullet.

With lights flashing, police cruisers screeched into the parking lot. Behind them came the dark blue riot control van, and before long, they had the parking lot and building fronts lit up like it was the middle of day.

"Is dat Brie?" Tee asked.

Nate peered past the car's undercarriage and replied, "Looks like it. What's she doing here?"

"Getting' shot at," Tee said.

"Cam's gonna kill me." Knees bent, the two eased forward in a standard cover formation.

Caught amid the trees between the police force and docks, the gunmen seemed to be waging a war on two fronts.

Nate took aim and shot one in the chest. The man spun to the ground, then got back up. Tee fired, and half the man's face vanished in a green mist.

"You have another one of those cannons?" Nate asked, kneeling behind a shrub.

"Not on me," Tee replied, firing again.

"One thing about it. When you shoot them, they tend to stay down."

"Dat's de point."

They continued through the parking lot. Somewhere along the way, they lost sight of Brie and the people with her. Nate crouched as he reloaded and said a silent prayer.

"Police!" Lieutenant Bell announced using a bullhorn. "Drop your weapons! We have you surrounded!"

CHAPTER 35
SHOWDOWN AT THE YACHT CLUB

March 15, 1969 C.E.

2:30 am

*L*ast to enter the marina, Cerdic vaulted over the short fence and raced down the concrete and steel dock. Sporadic gunfire chased him. He glanced over his shoulder and caught glimpses of the black and white gunmen behind him.

Brie motioned toward the boat she'd selected. All things considered, Cerdic thought she was holding up well. It's not every day you're shot at by minions of the Dark One.

When the shooters reached the fence, Roger slung one of his terracotta scroll cases. It exploded in a giant fireball that engulfed the bank.

A sense of unease overcame Cerdic. He whipped around as Anshu Jezra emerged from the rippling wave of heat.

Shrouded by hazy black robes, his bald head seemed to float. Wielding his greatsword in front of him, he said, "Et sectatio malorum mortem, quia ego sum malum. Ego mors tua." *He who pursues evil will die, for I am evil. I am your death.*

"I'll deal with this," Cerdic stated as he slid his sword free. "Get to the boat."

Brie led Ambrose and the others along the pier — everyone except the Highlord, who unsheathed his broadsword and remained at the paladin's side.

Sword held in his right hand and down to the right, Cerdic said, "Go, Your Majesty. Keep Queen Ambrose safe for me. I'll delay him as long as I can."

Scattered along the shore, several sclábhaí edged their way past the smoldering fence and raised their weapons. The others turned to fend off the approaching police.

"The Eternal Father be with you, paladin," the Highlord replied, then raced after their companions. He leapt into the closest boat, then scrambled out the far side into another craft whose gunwales practically kissed those of the first.

"Your weapon cannot touch me, Knight of Carolingias,"

Jezra said. "Your pitiful sacrifice will be for nothing. The Highlord will die. I have foreseen it." He snarled as he brought his sword down in an overhead cut.

Stepping forward, Cerdic raised his sword in a two-handed parry. The phantom sword passed through Cerdic's weapon without a sound. Barely avoiding the attack, Cerdic pivoted and made a horizontal stomach swipe at the cleric.

Jezra laughed as the blade merely caused his image to flicker.

With his arm across his chest and his sword pointing down and to the left, Cerdic grabbed his blade by the ricasso with his left hand and pulled it into its scabbard position. From further down the dock, he heard the Highlord shout out orders and saw File and Aimsitheoir take up firing positions with their longbows.

Reversing his grip on his hilt, Cerdic made a diagonal slash from low left to right.

Jezra again let the blade cut through his image. "Impotent fool. Beg Sutekh for mercy!"

With the momentum of his sword carrying it past his right side, Cerdic raised the hilt, swiped in the other direction, and advanced.

This time Jezra jumped back, putting enough distance between them to raise his sword. Instead of attacking with it, he cried out, "Ignem defanatum!" The runes along the fuller glowed, and blue-black flames swept up the blade.

Letting the blade drop to his right, the cleric grabbed the fiery steel with his right hand and held the hilt with his left. In one smooth motion, he lunged forward and punched Cerdic in the stomach with the pommel.

The paladin fell to the deck, feeling as if he'd been crushed by an elephant. He fought for the air that had fled his lungs while crawling backward.

Throwing off waves of searing heat, the blue-black flames spread along the Anshu's robes. The steel edge of the dock became red hot, and the ropes tethering the boats melted with a sizzle.

"Mortem quæretis, et non invenietis: mori desiderabitis, sed mors fugiet a vobis," Jezra hissed, the point of his fiery sword poised over Cerdic's heart. *You will seek death, but you will not find it; You will long to die, but death will flee from you.*

Jezra gasped and his image flickered as Lahar stabbed him in the back. Her longsword's dark blade shimmered with an eerie, multicolored aurora, revealing the silver cord that connected the priest's aethereal form to his physical body. Crouched behind him, she prepared to strike again.

His right hand on the fiery blade and left hand on the hilt, Jezra spun clockwise. The ring of steel cut through the night as he parried Lahar's blade just above his quillon.

With her blade still pressed against his, he pushed the tip of his weapon upward with his right hand. Taking a step forward, he swept her sword aside and shoved it away.

Cerdic winced as he realized Lahar's sword was out of position, exposing her body.

Releasing the blade, Jezra raised his right hand, palm out, and blue flame spat forth.

"LAHAR! NO!", Cerdic roared. He surged to his feet, and a bright, golden shield enveloped him and Anshu Jezra, snuffing out the blue flame and severing the silver cord. Rather than killing the priest, it drew his body to Terra in a sudden rush of air.

Jezra's hazy robe faded away, revealing his leather armor and vest. Stunned but still on his feet, the Sha'iry pivoted, leading with his sword.

Cerdic swung his blade, right to left.

Jezra executed a sloppy parry, stepping back as he did.

Reversing his attack, Cerdic bloodied the priest along his ribs. Not letting up, he planted his left foot on the priest's instep and shoved.

"Quoniam brachia peccatorum conterentur, confirmat autem justos Pater Aeternum," Cerdic said. *For the arms of the wicked shall be broken, but the Eternal Father upholdeth the righteous.*

Falling back, Jezra eyed the cruciform sword in Cerdic's hand and fear crept into his eyes. He threw out an arm to catch himself while holding up his weapon with the other.

Both hands on the hilt, Cerdic brought down his sword in a mighty cleave and struck the flat of the greatsword a foot above the quillon.

The blade cracked.

Blue flames flared then retreated, as if the weight of the priest's evil drew them to the pit of his soul. They consumed Anshu Jezra from the inside, slowly at first, but then quicker and quicker as if starved. His eyes remained fixed on Cerdic's as his flesh melted, until all that remained was a black smear.

The golden shield winked out.

Kneeling, the knight touched his sword to his forehead and prayed, "Pater Aeternum misereatur animae tuae." *Eternal Father have mercy on your soul.*

Rising from his prayer, Cerdic moved to Lahar, who lay on her side, propped on one elbow. Other than her shirt having a hole burnt along the midriff, she appeared in good health. At her feet, the circle of concrete within the shield had turned varying shades of pink and begun to crumble.

"Now!" The Archer ordered. As one, the remaining sclábhaí on shore charged.

"Cerdic! Lahar! Let's go!" the Highlord shouted.

Looking their way, Cerdic saw that everyone else had made it to the boat Brie selected. He helped Lahar to her feet. Too far to jump, they ran in a half-crouch along the top of a steel rib protruding through the failing concrete. Losing his balance, Cerdic lurched and stepped clear through the weakened deck. Before he could fall, Lahar yanked him back with a grimace, and the two leapt to safety.

Bullets tore into the wood planking when Cerdic and Lahar turned down a narrow dock.

Near the end, Aimsitheoir helped Brie and Ambrose board a twenty-six-foot-long cuddy cabin. Cerdic and Lahar dropped to a low crouch when the young dærganfae went wide-eyed with panic.

Behind them, The Archer raised his longbow. The sclábhaí came up, forming a line.

"Move, Son!" The Archer shouted.

"No, Father!" Aimsitheoir cried out.

Fired in rapid succession, two black-fletched arrows streaked through the air: one toward Ambrose and the other toward the Highlord.

The Highlord spun in time to catch the poisoned arrowhead in the shoulder and collapsed onto the dock.

Aimsitheoir knocked Ambrose into the boat, taking the arrow intended for her in the heart.

The sclábhaí charged, firing their carbines as they closed on their targets. All around Cerdic and Lahar, bullets tore through bulkheads and cabins, shattering glass and throwing splinters.

The Archer stood stunned, his longbow at his side.

Brie plucked Aimsitheoir's longbow from his lifeless hand and snatched the arrow from his chest as she scanned the chaos around them. In one swift motion, she nocked the arrow, drew, and sent it into the shifting shadows.

Amid gunfire and flying shrapnel, the black fletched arrow, still bearing the blood of the fae who sacrificed himself for Ambrose, disappeared inside the folds of The Archer's cloak. Even with all the noise, everyone heard the splash when The Archer fell into the water.

Not slowing, Cerdic slung the Highlord over his shoulder and dashed aboard the boat while Lahar found the key hidden in a lockbox. Handing it to Brie, she said, "Get us out of here."

Brie had the engine primed and motor started even as Roger cut the mooring lines. She backed the fishing boat out of its stall and, pushing down on the throttle, steered it clear of the marina.

"Can you do anything for the Highlord?" Lahar asked Cerdic.

Inside the cramped cabin, Cerdic had a hand on the wound and a prayer on his lips. Blood seeped between his fingers, but, with time, it slowed and stopped. The dærganfae poison was another matter altogether. "I don't think so," he replied.

Tears coursing down her cheeks, Ambrose grabbed Saoi by the shirt and asked, "Is there anything you can do for him?"

His eyes still on Aimsitheoir's body, Saoi answered, "No, Your Majesty. Where we come from, surviving the poison is a rite of passage. There is no cure."

"What about Doctor Wampus' daughter, Vie?" Cerdic asked. "She may have something that could help."

Lahar gave the paladin a bleak look. "We don't have time to find her."

"But we can't let him die," Cerdic protested.

"We're not," she replied. "We're taking him home."

CHAPTER 36
DESPERATE ALLIES

March 15, 1969 C.E.

2:45 am

*L*it with green and red lights, the cuddy cabin sliced through the still water of the Ashley River. Overhead, wispy clouds obscured the stars. Behind them, the sclábhaí had faded away to be replaced by policemen with bright flashlights.

Brie wanted to relax, but her eyes remained fixed on the Coast Guard Station at the end of Tradd Street. Abuzz with activity, she watched a white utility boat with a red and blue racing stripe leave its mooring and head toward them. At forty feet long, the steel-hulled vessel was almost twice as big as they were and had a machinegun mounted on its forward deck.

"What do you want me to do?" Brie asked. Her mind raced with ideas, but they all ended with her having to face her father.

"Can we outrun them?" Lahar asked.

"Remember what the Highlord told us," Roger answered. "We may outrun them but not their radio."

"What do I do?" Brie asked.

Roger laid his hand over hers and backed off the throttle. "Let's draw them in."

"Roger," Lahar said, her voice filled with suspicion.

He threw her a devil-may-care smile and said, "I have a plan, but I'll need your help."

Brie studied them, wondering which of the two was the bigger pirate.

With Saoi behind her, Ambrose said, "Maybe those sailors can help the Highlord."

"I doubt it," Lahar replied. "Cerdic's keeping him alive, but just barely. I'm afraid if Cerdic stops praying, even for a moment, the Highlord will die."

"Can't we tell them that?" Brie asked, nodding toward the Coast Guard vessel.

"Can we take the risk?" Lahar countered.

Her face clouded, Ambrose asked, "Roger, what did you have in mind?"

Floating in the dark water, Roger led Lahar and File toward the Coast Guard vessel.

A sailor shined a handheld spotlight on the cuddy cabin, revealing Ambrose and Brie standing near the ship's wheel. The girls threw a hand in front of their eyes, and Brie cut the engine. Saoi lounged on a bench, his glamour disguising him as a young man. The door to the cabin was shut tight.

With the aid of the bright spotlight, Roger watched the vessel come alongside. A sailor in a light blue uniform and cap threw Brie a line.

"Officer, what can we do for you?" Brie called.

Roger could see the hesitation in the sailor's face. More importantly, he was glad to see she had all five of the sailors' attention. Standing at the rail, one asked, "Did y'all just come from the marina?"

"We passed it and saw all the bright lights," Brie replied in a slurred voice. "But we came from farther upriver."

"Miss, are you stoned?" The sailor gave an exasperated sigh and climbed aboard the smaller craft. "I apologize, but we need to search your boat. If we find any drugs, they will be confiscated, and you'll be arrested. Are you the owner?"

Near the rear, the sides of the Coast Guard vessel were lower to the water and had regularly spaced stanchions to support a cable rail. At the back, a barren flagpole canted at an angle. Careful to avoid both the rudder and propeller, Roger grabbed hold and pulled himself out of the cold water.

Without a sound, he crept across the deck. A sailor, wearing a white hat with gold trim, watched the proceedings through the windscreen from behind the steering wheel. In his hand, he held the receiver to the radio.

Roger pressed his knife to the man's throat. "Put that thing away," he hissed. After a brief struggle, Lahar pinned one of the remaining sailors down on the forward deck with her knee on his spine while File held the man with the spotlight.

The captain placed the receiver back in its carriage. "You're making a big mistake, buddy."

"We'll add it to the list," Roger quipped. "Now, tell them

to stand down."

"Johnny, Thad," the captain called.

The sailors on the cuddy cabin turned. The taller of the two crept his hand near his holster. Saoi leapt up from the bench and grabbed his wrist. "Easy," he said as he disarmed him and his partner.

"We're exchanging boats," Roger announced.

"You'll never get away with this," said the captain. "We have stations up and down these waters. Where will you go?"

"Don't worry about that," Roger replied. "Just do as I say, nice and easy, and no one gets hurt."

Brie and Ambrose tied up the officers while Cerdic brought the Highlord out of the cabin. They transferred over to the Coast Guard vessel, then sent the mariners to the smaller boat, where Saoi bound them together.

Once everyone was aboard the larger ship and the two vessels disconnected, Roger asked Brie, "You can drive this thing, can't you?"

Brie looked over the console and throttle and gave him a quick nod.

"Hang in there," Roger said, giving her a reassuring squeeze on the shoulder as he moved to help Cerdic. "We're almost out of the woods."

Roger held the cabin door for Cerdic and joined him as he passed. Though still cramped, the Coast Guard vessel had a roomier cabin than the previous boat. Together, they laid the Highlord on one of the berths and adjusted him so that at least he looked comfortable. When finished, Cerdic knelt and bowed his head.

The engine growled when Brie shifted the throttle. "Where to?"

"The ocean. We need to go south," Roger answered as he rejoined the others on deck.

"Hold on," Brie said through clenched teeth. Whitecaps spread in a V as they turned east and rounded the end of the peninsula.

Lahar rifled through the charts and found one of Charleston Harbor. She oriented herself and helped Brie navigate the channel. "According to the chart, Fort Sumter lies straight ahead, with Morris Island to the right and Sullivan's Island to the left." Beyond it was a dark void that could have marked the ends of the earth.

Teeth chattering, Roger wiped saltwater from his brow and looked over Lahar's shoulder. They needed a chart that would lead them to Captain Walker and the *Morningstar*.

"I hope you disabled their radio," Roger said to Saoi.

"I did, but we left the boat undamaged."

"At least they don't have the key," Ambrose said with a grim smile as she tossed the tiny metal object into the water.

The faint outline of Fort Sumter grew more distinct. Lahar scanned for channel markers. "Where's that spotlight?"

"I have it," File answered.

"Shine it over there," Lahar said.

The bright light hit the dark water and the green panel glowed. Brie adjusted course, and File searched for the next marker.

From behind Fort Sumter, a massive black shape slid into the channel. All at once, its lights flared to life, revealing a white steel-hulled ship with the distinctive red and blue racing stripe. Over eighty feet long, it was unlike any ship Roger had seen before. Instead of a machinegun mounted on the forward deck, this one had a small cannon. The black barrel rotated and aimed straight toward them.

Brie cut the wheel and banked hard left.

"Surrender or you will be fired upon!" an electronic voice stated. The cannon belched flame and water sprayed high into the air ten yards from their position.

"Oh, God," Brie repeated as she gripped the throttle. "We have to give up. There's no getting out of the channel now. Not with that ship guarding it."

"Don't worry. That was just a warning shot," Roger said, eyeing the ship.

"You mean they meant to miss us?" Brie cried.

Lahar shouted, "Roger! This was your plan?"

"How was I to know Momma Bear guarded the pass?"

She rolled her eyes at him. "Do better. We don't have long before the *Morningstar* leaves for Gaia."

Boats with sirens and flashing blue lights seemed to fill the harbor.

Brie continued turning the wheel, and their boat shot up the other side of the peninsula. "You do know the Navy Base is up this river, don't you?"

"Well, don't go that way," Roger said. "Turn around."

Overhead, a line of fiery orbs streaked toward the ship's white hull and exploded at the waterline. The ship rocked and became lost inside a cloud of steam.

"Again, Miss O'Brien!" Mister Smeyth cried out.

The iron dragons spoke, and another barrage of fiery orbs lit the night sky. Again, they hit the water, and the steam grew thicker.

"Quick   Cap'n!"   Mister   Smeyth   yelled   from   the quarterdeck. "We won't be able to hold 'em off for long."

The *Morningstar* glided between the smaller craft and the Coast Guard's ship. With no lights, it was as if a ghost ship had emerged from the depths.

Lahar let out a short laugh and called, "Mister Smeyth, you and the crew are a sight for sore eyes! Get us out of here."

Brie's mouth dropped open at the sudden appearance of the tall ship. Roger helped her aim the steering wheel toward the portside hull and let off the throttle. "It's all right. They're on our side."

"It's a... it's a pirate ship!" Brie stammered.

"Privateer," Lahar corrected. Cupping her hands around her mouth, she said, "Mister Smeyth, the Highlord's hurt. Have Mister Mitchell help us. We're abandoning this boat."

"Aye, Cap'n!"

Brie switched off the engine in a daze. Roger grabbed her by the waist and said, "Hold on."

Suddenly, the boat lurched and rose out of the water. To be more accurate, the water under the boat lifted the hull until the deck was level with the *Morningstar*.

Everyone scampered over the side and into the arms of waiting crewmen. Once the last person crossed over, Mister Mitchell, who stood at the rail, swiped horizontally with his right hand, and the modern boat plummeted.

Roger and Brie followed Lahar up the ladder to the quarterdeck and stopped short. The last person he expected to see was Captain Walker at the wheel. He held Lahar's wide-brimmed hat in his beefy hands and offered it to her. "Your hat, Captain," he drawled.

"Thank you, Captain Walker," Lahar replied, putting it

on.

"The ship is yours," he said.

Lahar took the wheel and peered out toward the horizon. Searchlights leading the way, boats of varying sizes swarmed in for the kill.

"Your orders, Cap'n?" Mister Smeyth asked.

"Take us out of here," she answered.

Still looking like a corpse, Mister Cavendish closed his eyes, and the copper sails snapped into position. The lanterns at the yardarms sparked. The *Morningstar* rose, dripping saltwater from her keel.

Captain Walker and Brie both wore expressions of wonder and awe as the ship sailed over the harbor, gaining altitude as it sped away.

"Captain, perhaps you can drop us off at the Morris Island lighthouse," Captain Walker suggested. "We can use the gallery." The large man pointed a meaty finger toward the slender shape at the end of a dark jut of land.

"Mister Cavendish," Lahar said, adjusting the wheel.

"Yes, mum," he replied.

The ship changed course and aimed straight for the lighthouse. Below them, faces stared up from the Coast Guard ship, some afraid, others amazed.

"Get ready," Lahar said to Brie and Captain Walker. "We won't be able to stop, but we should be able to slow enough for you to jump."

Captain Walker stretched his knee. Beside him, Brie gazed about and nodded.

"You'll do fine," Roger said with a smile. "Just don't look down."

Brie bit her lip and gave him a skeptical look.

"Be safe," Ambrose said as she wrapped her in a tight hug. "Thank your family and tell them goodbye for me."

"I will," Brie said, returning the hug. "Goodbye."

"Captain," Bo Walker said with a nod.

"Captain," Lahar replied, touching the brim of her hat.

"Take care of Cerdic," he said.

She smiled. "I will."

Brie and Captain Walker followed Mister Smeyth to the main deck where a portion of the starboard bulwark had been removed. The lighthouse drew closer and closer.

A cannon shell from the Coast Guard ship exploded

above them.

"Miss O'Brien, return fire!" Lahar shouted.

"Beg your pardon, Captain, but we don't have the angle. We need to come about."

Lahar swore and started to adjust the wheel. Roger gripped the rail and said, "Lahar, you can't. We're almost there."

Another shell burst, closer this time.

"Mister Vaughn, remember your place." Lahar looked up at a sailor in the rigging and said, "Mister Marston! Add more sail!"

"Aye, aye, Captain!"

The *Morningstar* sped up even as gunfire struck the hull.

The lighthouse came alongside.

Timing their jump, Brie and Captain Walker launched themselves from the deck.

Cannon fire struck the port side.

Captain Walker landed hard on the metal gallery. He let out a bellow of pain as his knee buckled underneath him, and he rolled to the lighthouse wall.

Brie fell short. She hit the railing, bounced, and slipped down. Catching the lip of the rusted deck in a death grip, she dangled one hundred and fifty feet above the eroded base.

"No!" Ambrose cried. "We have to stop!"

Lahar was already turning the wheel so the ship would veer away. "We can't."

Another cannon blast tore through the stern.

Roger climbed up and balanced on the ship's taffrail. He gave Lahar and the Queen a hasty salute.

Lahar nodded toward him and said, "Good luck, thief."

"Good luck, pirate," Roger replied before leaping.

Brie held on by her fingertips. Caught in gravity's tireless pull, her body grew heavier. Panic seized her heart. She knew she was going to die. With the inevitability of fate, the galley's metal rim slipped out of her grip, and she screamed.

A hand clamped around her wrist, jerking her to a stop.

"I've got you," Roger said with a grin, and pulled her to safety.

Holding on to one another, they watched as the

Morningstar continued its climb toward the stars. With a wink of lightning, the ship seemed to stretch before disappearing.

CHAPTER 37
YORK

April 30, 4208 K.E.

4:30 am

*P*raying to the Eternal Father, Cerdic knelt on the aft cabin floor with his hands pressed to the Highlord's chest. In his heart, he knew he was losing the battle, but he refused to give up, even with the gunfire and cannon blasts.

He felt the ship rise as if riding a tidal wave, similar to the last time it *jumped*. His heart pressed against his throat as they plummeted into the cosmic wave's trough, but they never hit bottom. Instead, they flew faster and faster.

At some point, Cerdic felt a change in the Highlord. He was no longer responding to the prayers. Still, the paladin continued. A tear leaked from the corner of his eye, and he felt an emptiness within.

"We're home," Lahar said, laying a hand on his shoulder. He gripped it tight and used it as an anchor against his emotions. "I lost him," Cerdic whispered.

Lahar knelt beside the weeping paladin, and said, "You didn't lose him. He wasn't yours to lose."

Cerdic looked into her eyes, not understanding.

"Remember when we were in the hospital?" she said. "You told me it's up to the Eternal Father. Death calls to each of us at one time or another."

"But this is the Highlord."

"Exactly. Healing prayers don't work on him. This is between him and the Eternal Father. If it's his time, there's nothing you or I can do."

Cerdic rubbed his nose with the back of his hand and sniffed. "When did you get so smart?"

"I listen." Lahar helped him to his feet and said, "Let's move him to my bunk. It'll be more comfortable than the floor."

Cerdic lifted the Highlord while Lahar opened the door to her quarters.

"Perhaps we're not too late after all," Lahar said, a hint of wonder in her voice.

Cerdic looked down.   Under his shadow, weak sparks flickered and danced in the blood on the Highlord's chest. Laying him on the cot, Cerdic searched for signs of life. "He's not breathing."

"Leave him," Lahar said. "He'll have to make this journey on his own."

Cerdic gave the Highlord one final look before exiting the cabin. "How's the ship?" he asked after a moment.

Closing the door, she replied, "That bloody cannon tore holes in my ship. We'll have to dry dock in order to repair the hull."

"I'm sure the Queen will accommodate you."

"She'd better."

Cerdic and Lahar rejoined the others on the quarterdeck. The *Morningstar* lay anchored along the shore of the Isura several miles south of York.   To the east, false dawn illuminated the lower rim of the horizon, but night still dominated the sky above them.   Sailors wearing fur-lined jackets adjusted the sails and checked the rigging and yards for damage.

"How's the Highlord?" Mister Smeyth asked.

Cerdic sucked in a deep breath of cool air and replied, "It's in the Eternal Father's hands now. Where's Roger?"

"Stayed behind to save the Queen's friend," Smeyth replied.

"I see," Cerdic said.

Ambrose gazed in the direction of York. Saoi and File remained beside her, conversing in hushed tones.

"Captain Lahar," she said as she turned away from the rail. "We have no idea what to expect when we arrive in York. You may want to drop us off here."

"Is that wise?" Lahar asked, looking toward Cerdic for support. "Wouldn't it be better to gather your forces before going ashore?"

"Captain, I mean to take back our kingdom once and for all."

"My Queen," Cerdic said, "wait."

"We are not waiting another minute!" Ambrose exclaimed.

"If I learned nothing else from friends and enemies over the years, it's to never go into a fight without a plan — it gives

318 | McDonald & Isom

you a far greater chance of success," Cerdic explained.
"We've already done this dance once. We had a plan then,
plus the element of surprise, and we only barely prevailed."

She glowered at him, brows lowered and an obstinate set
to her jaw. After a long moment, she ground out, "What do
you have in mind?"

"First, send runners to Camber and Jongar. Have them
meet us at the docks," Cerdic answered. "Then, send File or
Saoi with a note to the Lord Steward. Let's hope he's still on
our side."

"Mister Cavendish, how are you holding up?" asked
Lahar.

"Tired, mum."

"Mister Smeyth, how are you and the crew?"

"The same, Cap'n. It's been a long day."

She slapped the quartermaster on the back and said,
"We can sleep when we're dead. For now, there's work to do.
General quarters if you please, Mister Smeyth."

"Aye, aye, Cap'n." Mister Smeyth turned to the crew and
bellowed, "You heard the Cap'n! Battle stations!"

Sailors rushed across the main deck as they took their
positions.

"What colors do we raise?" the quartermaster asked.

"Carolingias, Mister Smeyth," Queen Ambrose replied.

"And mine," Captain Lahar added.

With the metallic squeal of a rope and pulley, the flag of
Carolingias, a silver dogwood tree issuant from a mount vert
on an azure field, rose to the top of the mainmast and
snapped in the breeze. Next, a black flag bearing a stylized
ship's compass in white, rose to the top of the foremast.
Under the compass was the motto, "Ante Ferit Quam
Flamma Micet." *Strike before the flame glimmers.*

The *Morningstar* weighed anchor and sailed upriver.
Cerdic gripped the rail, thinking of the fight to come. Too
quick for his liking, she rounded a bend, and York came into
view. Still sleeping, the city had the appearance of a
wounded veteran who dreamt of better times — a time before
the war.

The tall ship glided into an empty berth, and the portside
kissed the dock. The gangplank slid into position, and

Queen Ambrose, still in her tie-dyed sundress and white tennis shoes, led Cerdic and Saoi past a hungover stevedore. Behind them came Miss O'Brien and three handpicked marines, bearing crossbows. With her plumed hat set at a jaunty angle, Lahar brought up the rear.

A crowd gathered around the bald Queen. The flabbergasted dockmaster bowed three times before sputtering, "My Queen, we didn't expect you."

"Who's in charge?" she asked.

"Don Esteban, with the support of the Archbishop and the other ambassadors. He took over the palace the day after you disappeared. He has men taking 'inventory' of the foodstuffs in storage."

Ambrose swore and clenched her fists at her sides. "Of course, he does." Ignoring the rest of the dockmaster's statement, she asked, "What of Camber, Jongar, and the knights?"

"And Phaedrus?" Cerdic added.

"The priest was thrown into the dungeon the very morning you all disappeared. Camber has taken refuge in Jongar's camp here in town. Sir Julius and Sir Martyn are trying to keep the peace, but I'm afraid Camber and Jongar are too much for the young knights. Rumors of rebellion are spreading."

"And the Bluebloods?"

"Undecided, my Queen. Many are openly skeptical of Don Esteban's claim on the throne, but I think their resolve is wavering, especially since the Archbishop supports him."

"We'll see about that," Queen Ambrose said. "Spread the word, dockmaster: the Queen has returned."

Sunrise painted the morning's clouds in fiery orange and red, a harbinger of the conflict that lay before Ambrose and her allies.

Camber and Jongar approached the docks together, their soldiers following. When Camber spotted Queen Ambrose, he rushed toward her, armed with his rakish smile. Seeing the crowd behind her, he stopped, and his face became uncertain.

"Ambrosia?" Camber asked.

She threw her arms around the rakehell and buried her face in his chest. "Did you miss me?"

Holding her tight, he whispered, "You look different."
"Lass, where's yer hair?" Jongar exclaimed.
Cerdic coughed and murmured, "My Queen."
Giving Camber a quick kiss on the cheek, Ambrose said, "I plan to take back the palace. Are you with me or against me?"
Each gripping the hilt of his weapon, the two men — one a highwayman and the other a barbarian — knelt and bowed their heads. "My Queen, we're with you."
"Then rise and join us."

Cerdic looked around at the gathering mob. No, it wasn't a mob. These were his countrymen. These were Carolingians. Whatever they knew or suspected of Ambrose's recent past, they didn't care. She had lived as a commoner, suffering under Sha'iry rule the same as them, and now they were willing to follow her as the last Battenberg and their rightful Queen.

He walked with her, and the crowd behind them continued to swell. Word spread like wildfire, and men and women bearing what weapons they had at hand joined the march on the palace.

Speculation was rampant. Some even said the Queen had tamed the dærganfae. While much of what was said wasn't true, it added to her mystique, especially after her abrupt appearance at the docks with a shaven head and wearing strange clothes.

They passed the inn where Roger had stayed. Christopher rushed out carrying the flag of Carolingias. Though torn and tattered, the crowd cheered when they saw it. He raised it high and found a spot next to Miss O'Brien.

Ahead, the palace loomed like a fortress. They'd stormed its walls before and defeated the evil that had taken up residence there. This time was different. This time, it was a usurper with the support of the church, his church. As he marched, Cerdic felt divided. *Was he a knight of Carolingias or a knight of the church?*

Setting aside the fatigue that threatened to sap his strength, Cerdic marched past the statue of King David. When they entered the barren dogwood grove, a fresh breeze swept through their ranks. Along both sides of the lane, green leaves suddenly sprouted, and white blossoms opened. A collective gasp erupted from the crowd. Many gripped their weapons tighter as they turned their eyes toward the dozen Espian soldiers in red and gold surcoats standing guard behind the hastily repaired gate, each armed with a tall halberd. In front of them, Sir Martyn blanched at the sight of the senior knight but stood his ground.

"Animam meam convertit. Deduxit me super semitas justitiæ, propter nomen suum," Cerdic prayed. *He restoreth my soul: he guideth me in the paths of righteousness for his name's sake.*

Beside him, Ambrose gave the armed men a stern look. She turned to Cerdic and had a fierceness in her voice when she said, "You know who I am and where I come from. I am the rightful heir of Carolingias and intend to take the throne — the throne Don Esteban now holds. Sir Martyn has chosen his side. Who do you choose, Sir Cerdic?"

Cerdic gazed toward the palace and then back to the queen. In a voice loud enough for Sir Martyn to hear, he replied, "I choose the Eternal Father."

"That's not an answer," she said.

"It is my only answer," he replied, softer this time. "I am guided by my faith."

"What does your faith tell you now?"

"The dogwoods have blossomed for the first time since your uncle's death. I see that as a sign our path is righteous. Now, Archbishop Letizia and Don Esteban must make their choices. It is they who have turned away from those who are suffering, barricading themselves behind walls of stone."

Ambrose nodded her acceptance of his answer, then said to Jongar, "Hold their attention."

"Aye, lass," the kilted Gael answered, the relish of impending battle shimmering like fire in his eyes.

"Christopher, furl the colors for now," Ambrose directed as she stopped and let the crowd flow around her toward the gate.

She watched Sir Cerdic wrap a cloak about himself to hide his tattered clothing. After Lahar stepped in to help, he was concealed well enough to be lost in the crowd and not be recognized.

The crowd surged forward, stopping at the gate, and began taunting the Espian guards. More soldiers in red and gold hustled out of the palace gatehouse.

"Are we hidden?" Ambrose asked Lahar.

The half-elf squinted, searching the front of the mob. "As best I can tell from this angle." She looked down at the youthful queen. "I recommend we leave now."

Ambrose nodded solemnly and, her voice barely audible above the growing cacophony, said, "Sir Cerdic."

The knight led the Queen, Lahar, Christopher, Miss O'Brien, and the three marines around the east side of the palace. Separated by a hedgerow and a grassy strip twenty paces wide, they followed the street as it paralleled the low stone wall topped with sharp spikes.

Shaded by two pollarded willow trees, Ambrose caught a glimpse of the servants' entrance. Despite being frightened, she wanted her home back. She wanted to be Queen, and the feeling lit a fire inside her.

"There!" hissed one of Lahar's crewmen as two guards came into view through the bars.

"Miss O'Brien, if you will," Ambrose requested.

At Lahar's confirming nod, the gunny and her three crewmen raised crossbows. "Fire!" she hissed loudly, releasing her own bolt as she did.

Three of the four bolts struck true, and the two red and gold-clad guards dropped like puppets with their strings cut.

Camber, Saoi, and Mister Mitchell, along with six soldiers wearing scarlet sashes, exited the alley across the street.

"Just like old times," Camber said, gripping the base of the spikes.

Ambrose paled slightly as her motley group climbed the fence and rushed across the flagstone concourse to the postern gate. Knocking in triple sets of three, the group waited breathlessly. *If their message failed to get through or—*

The banded wood door swung open, revealing Sir Jeffrey, the Lord Steward. "Your Majesty! I was worried you would not make it."

"Then we both worried unnecessarily," Ambrose replied as she led her group past him.

After dragging the dead guards inside, Camber

instructed two of his men to don their uniforms while Cerdic and Lahar hid the bodies in a side room.

With a snick, the two posing as guards closed the door behind them, muting the sudden, mob-sized roar of rage that echoed down the street.

"My Queen," the Lord Steward said, "you must stop Don Esteban. He aims to have himself crowned king of Carolingias. Tonight."

Lahar gave a contemptuous snort. "What a lovely nest of vipers!"

"What about Phaedrus?" asked Cerdic.

"Guest bedrooms, first floor. His is the room with the guard outside." He looked at the Queen with a mix of fear and awe. "Your dærganfae... was a surprise. He just vanished into the floor."

"Never mind about that. Where is the Archbishop?" Ambrose asked.

"With Don Esteban in the throne room."

"And between us?"

Sir Jeffrey smiled grimly, "A smattering of guards. However, the upper floors are mostly empty. Fortunate for us, Don Esteban doesn't have enough troops to cover the whole palace. At least not yet. Word is he's asked for reinforcements."

"Sir Cerdic," said Ambrose.

"Yes, My Queen." Before the knight carried out the unspoken command, he gave Christopher a hard look. "Stick with the Queen, no matter what."

"It's clear," Lahar said, peering around the corner into the hallway.

They rushed up a narrow set of servants' stairs that emptied into the second-floor ballroom. Their boots thudded dully in the cavernous room as they crossed it and huddled behind a pair of double doors.

Crouching, Camber peeked outside and waved everyone into a wide corridor that ended at another pair of doors.

"That's the dining room," Ambrose whispered. "We can use it to access the east wing drawing room, and from there, the Grand Hall."

Lahar resumed the lead and hastened down the corridor. Everyone held their breath when the half-elf opened the doors, revealing a long room dominated by a heavy oak table capable of seating thirty-four guests. The crystal chandeliers sparkled, a testament to the diligence of the Lord Steward.

They passed through another set of doors and out the east wing drawing room where File waited for them. A pair of Espian guards lay dead at his feet.

"My Queen."

"Good work," she replied with a nod.

As they approached the throne room and could see the gallery, Cerdic made eye contact with Lahar and nodded to the far side. Ambrose smiled at the look of concern the two shared for one another before Lahar and her five pirates crawled across the south end of the Grand Hall and towards the west wing.

The knight glanced at Ambrose and, at her nod of confirmation, strode towards the grand stairs.

"Saoi," she whispered. Using their glamour, the two dærganfae disappeared.

"Unfurl the colors, flagbearer," she commanded.

Christopher did so with alacrity, though she noted his hands shook.

"Queen Ambrose seeks an audience with Archbishop Letizia Trastámara of Peninsular Espia!" Cerdic announced from the gallery overlooking the Grand Hall.

At the top of the stairs, Ambrose stood squarely in the center of the landing, flanked by Cerdic on her left, Camber on her right, and Christopher directly behind with the Carolingian flag.

A dozen olive-skinned women with long, dark hair and tight-fitting scale armor the deep blue of lapis lazuli split into two squads and headed for each base of the curved stairs. They carried long ranseurs with a sparkling sapphire embedded at the intersection of the spearhead and the crescent-shaped blade.

When Cerdic and Camber passed Ambrose to take up positions mid-way down the stairs, he murmured, "Don Esteban is a coward."

The caballero stepped out from behind the Archbishop. "We will not entertain armed rebels and false Queens. Lay down your weapons and leave this place."

Cerdic narrowed his eyes at the Espian. "Ambrose is the true Queen, and you know it. Why do you stand against us?"

One of the Espian guards mounted the stairs, and the creak of crossbows from the gallery answered.

"I'd step back if I were you," Camber said, a promise of violence thick in the growl of his voice.

On the rostrum in ornate robes of office, the raven-haired Archbishop watched events unfold, her face an emotionless mask. A dozen monks in brown cowls and tunics guarded her. Heavy maces set into loops hung from the knotted, silk ropes at their waist.

Cerdic eyed the throne room, and visions of the Sha'iry came back to him. It was weird how things had come full circle. Similar but different. He wondered if Archbishop Letizia realized she stood just as Maa'kheru Bolezni had before he fell.

"Welcome back, Ambrose Battenberg," Archbishop Letizia said. Her voice was pleasant, but her eyes spoke differently.

"You have overstepped, your Grace," Ambrose said.

"Who are you to treat with me? Just because you look different and call yourself Queen, does not make you the Queen."

"I am a servant of the people," replied Ambrose. "Nothing more."

"Ambrose Battenberg, you have been found weak and wanting. You have none of the traits required to be a ruler."

"Weak and wanting, you say," Cerdic replied. "Your Grace, Carolingias has been weak and wanting for some time, but there is a strength here. A strength that is just now blossoming. Ambrose has survived her vigil, and she is the rightful heir to the throne."

"Sir Cerdic, you sound like that half-elf duende."

"Thank you," replied Cerdic.

Ambrose cut in between the two and said, "I am the last bearer of the Battenberg name, a family that has ruled Carolingias for generations. It is true both Don Esteban and Sir Cerdic are my cousins, but their kinship is several generations removed. It is also true I did not want to be Queen, but I will hide no longer. I mean to take my place as Queen of Carolingias and, to the best of my ability and the Eternal Father willing, rule this country with a just hand."

Dropping their glamor, Saoi and File bowed. Archbishop Letizia took an involuntary step back, and the monks in front of her closed ranks.

"Your Grace, we owe Ambrose our lives," Saoi said. "I speak for my dærganfae clan when I say that an alliance between our peoples can only be had if she is Queen."

Archbishop Letizia pressed a hand to her chest as she studied the two dærganfae and the young queen.

"Though we are prepared for battle," Ambrose said, squaring her shoulders, "we did not come here to fight. We came here to show you our solidarity and our resolve." She paused and looked Letizia in the eyes. "The choice is yours."

Red in the face, Don Esteban sneered, "Archbishop Letizia has no authority here. She has no choice to make. You are not, and will not be, Queen."

The Archbishop gifted Don Esteban a look of such venom that he should have died on the spot, but then she turned back to Ambrose. "In this matter, the church must remain neutral, Ambrose Battenberg."

Her head came around, as did others, at the rising sound of violence coming from the Quadrangle.

"Duellum! A trial by combat," shouted Don Esteban. The corner of his mouth turned up in a cunning smirk as he eyed Cerdic's haggard appearance. "Your champion, Ambrose, against mine. Winner takes the throne."

"I accept," Ambrose stated flatly as she strode down the stairs with Cerdic at her side. Behind them came Camber with his four soldiers. Reaching the bottom, she waited for the scale-clad guards to retreat. When they did, the center of the room cleared and out stepped a knight who wore a woman's lace scarf tied around his rerebrace.

"Sir Julius?" Ambrose gasped.

Cerdic glared at the young knight. "Why do you do this? Ambrose is the true Queen, and you know it."

Julius glanced at the crowd. His eyes focused on the Carolingian flag in Christopher's hands. "I'm trying to keep the peace," he replied in a meek voice.

"Then keep it. We are not here to fight you. There has been enough bloodshed," Cerdic said. "The Queen has come home."

"Perhaps, but I swore allegiance to Don Esteban, so we will fight," he replied grimly.

"Don't do this," Cerdic whispered. "Yield."

Julius shook his head. "I cannot."

The scrape of steel on leather filled the quiet room when Cerdic unsheathed his sword.

A commotion broke out in the hallway beyond the throne room. When it ended, the doors opened to reveal Phaedrus and Sir Jeffrey. The half-elf priest presented Cerdic with his shield and helped strap it to his arm.

"Pater Aeternum, in te confido; non erubescam." *Eternal Father, in you I trust; let me not be put to shame; let not my enemies rejoice in my defeat.*

Lifting their weapons, the two knights saluted one another and took up a defensive stance.

Julius circled sunwise. When Cerdic didn't mirror him, only turning to face him squarely, he was a bit thrown off and reversed course, circling widdershins around the room. Still, Cerdic only shifted in place.

Thinking he saw an opening, Julius closed and brought his blade down heavily from above. Cerdic blocked it with his shield, and a flurry of attacks ensued, each one parried or blocked.

A sudden hammer blow, several times the force of previous attacks, struck squarely at the center of Julius' shield. He hopped backwards, out of range of a follow-up.

"Yield!" Cerdic ordered.

Julius shook his head. He squared his shoulders and, leading with his shield, once more began circling.

Again, Cerdic only shifted in place.

"You fool, look at him. He's hurt!" shouted Don Esteban. "Finish him!"

Julius considered the Don's words, but he knew Cerdic, having sparred with him before, and knew the senior knight wouldn't go down easily, even without armor. He circled back widdershins and closed half the distance.

Cerdic leapt forward. His raised sword crashed down.

Julius brought up his shield at a cant, letting the blade slide past. Before he could counterattack, Cerdic smashed his shield against Julius' chest and face. Blood dripping from his chin, the younger knight staggered back.

Shoving up and to the right, Cerdic's shield edge

slammed into Julius', throwing it wide.

Cerdic plunged his sword through the opening. There was a screech of metal on metal and the tearing of mail links when the tip of Cerdic's sword stabbed outwards through Julius' tabard.

With a roar, Cerdic lifted the smaller man into the air, the guard of his sword caught in the chain protecting his foe's armpit. He held the man aloft for a moment before hurling him to the floor. The crash of plate armor on stone was deafening.

"Yield!" Cerdic bellowed, kicking away Julius' weapon.

Silence reigned.

It took several seconds for the stunned man to recover. No one moved while he did. When he finally regained his senses, he was on his back, holding his shield.

Cerdic stood over him, sword poised to strike.

His resolve shattered. He lowered his head to the floor and whispered, "I yield."

As Ambrose stepped past Camber to address Archbishop Letizia, Don Esteban shrieked, "No! I will be king!" and lunged at Ambrose.

Jumping in front of her, Christopher shouted, "My Queen!" and blocked the Espian's dagger with his body.

The boy fell at her feet.

His eyes glazed, Don Esteban simply stood there, gurgling, with Camber's rapier lodged in his lung.

Staring the Espian nobleman in the eye, the rakehell sneered as he twisted his blade and then withdrew it.

Kneeling in a growing pool of blood, Ambrose held Christopher's limp body. Tears streaming, she said, "Camber, help me."

He turned his attention to her, and she saw the bloodlust in his eyes dim. He nodded, put away his sword, and offered her the red sash from his waist.

Pushing past Camber, Letizia knelt and placed her hands over the boy's wound. "Queen Ambrose, the Eternal Father can heal him."

CHAPTER 38
CORONATION

May 23, 4208 K.E.

12:00 pm

Still undergoing repairs from the dærganfae attack and Sha'iry occupation before that, Daventry Cathedral held bright streamers from every pinnacle and spire. In the street out front, the people of York gathered around the Queen's procession for the coronation.

Four tonsured priests in white cassocks waited within the pointed arch framing the entrance. Wearing a long, flowing white dress traced with silver and blue, Ambrose took Sir Cerdic's arm and stepped from the carriage.

Lining the sandstone plaza, Camber and Jongar, along with a dozen soldiers in blue and silver livery, brandished their swords in an arch. Ambrose crossed under the glittering blades, remembering the last time she had been here with Sir Baldwin.

They entered the cathedral and passed under the thin stone ribs that met in a point a hundred feet above the nave. Sunlight streamed through the stained-glass windows onto oak pews filled with foreign dignitaries, Carolingian representatives from both near and far, and those people who had helped her get here, including Christopher and his mother. In the back, Lahar and her crew seemed ill at ease. Taking up several rows in front of them sat a mix of Camber and Jongar's men. Ambrose hid a smile at their mention of an after-coronation party.

Maintaining a regal pace, Ambrose saw where scaffolding filled the north transept and wood planking replaced the medallion at the center of the octagonal labyrinth. At the eastern end of the sanctuary, long, narrow windows set into seven polygonal apses gave the rostrum a radiant glow. The largest held the cloth-covered altar table and crown.

Before the altar, Archbishop Letizia took her place with Phaedrus serving as her assistant. Ambrose fought against another smile, watching the two having to work together.

Sir Cerdic guided her down the central aisle and stopped

at the front row of pews. She stood beside him for a moment, thinking of Brie, Doctor Wampus, Michael, Kyle, Roger, her family, even the dærganfae — all those who had stood by her side.

Behind her, Camber and Jongar led the honor guard inside the cathedral. Ambrose dipped her head, said a quick prayer, and proceeded to the altar alone. She felt the presence of her kinsmen and wasn't sure if it was the ceremony giving her goosebumps or the goofer dust rubbed into her scalp.

Archbishop Letizia and Phaedrus stepped around to the front of the altar table and genuflected before the wheel-cross. Rising, the Archbishop moved to stand before Ambrose while Phaedrus lifted the crown and joined them, a step behind.

"Your Majesty, are you willing to take the oath?" Archbishop Letizia asked.

"I am."

"Will you solemnly promise and swear to govern the Peoples of Carolingias according to law?"

"I solemnly promise to do so."

"Will you exercise justice with mercy?"

"I will."

"Will you, to the utmost of your power, maintain the Laws of the Eternal Father?"

"I will."

Ambrose bowed her head while Archbishop Letizia took the crown from Phaedrus.

Placing it on Ambrose's head, Archbishop Letizia raised her voice and proclaimed, "By the Will of the Eternal Father and the People of Carolingias, I proclaim you, Queen Ambrose Battenberg."

Cheers and shouts erupted within the cathedral.

"Please turn and accept your people."

Ambrose faced the crowd with tears brimming in her eyes. Blinking them away, she said, "Sir Cerdic, please step forward." She took his sword by the hilt and, after he knelt, tapped him on the right shoulder with the flat of the blade. Raising it over his head, she tapped him on the left shoulder. After giving him back his sword, she said, "In recognition of your valiant services, I pronounce you the Queen's Champion. Rise, Sir Cerdic Uth Aneirin. Please accept the gratitude of your Queen and your friend." He rose and she kissed his cheek.

"Roger Vaughn and Christopher Inman," she said when Cerdic stepped away.

Beaming, the boy leapt to his feet and practically ran down the aisle. A strong hand caught him before he reached the transept. He looked up and met the Highlord's timeless gaze.

"Easy there," the Highlord said.

Walking together, the two stood before the Queen. She and the Highlord exchanged short bows, then Ambrose turned and retrieved a medal from Phaedrus. "Your Majesty, since Roger Vaughn cannot be here today, will you accept this token of my friendship in his place?"

The Highlord smiled. "I will."

"Christopher Inman, you have shown bravery above and beyond the call of duty and, in so doing, you saved both my life and my crown. Our country needs more brave young men like you."

"Thank you, ma'am. I mean, Your Majesty."

"Christopher, please kneel." The Highlord offered her his sword. After tapping Christopher on the right shoulder with the flat of the blade, she raised it over his head and tapped him on the left shoulder. "In recognition of your valiant services, I pronounce you the first Knight of the Golden Stag. Rise, Sir Christopher Nicholas Inman." He rose and she kissed his cheek.

Ambrose waited with the Highlord while Christopher resumed his seat beside his mother. Gazing across the pews, Ambrose said, "Captain Lahar."

Sheathed in black leather, Lahar strutted down the aisle. Ambrose saw her glance toward the Aneirin family, and the worried expression that followed.

Taking two folded flags from the Highlord and handing them to Lahar, Ambrose said, "In recognition of your valiant services, I pronounce you and the crew of the *Morningstar* Ambassadors of Carolingias and Gallowen. Please accept my gratitude and the gratitude of the Highlord."

Taking the flags, Lahar bowed to them both and headed back down the aisle.

Ambrose waited for Lahar to resume her seat, then let her gaze drift across the crowd, making eye contact here and there. A hush fell over the room. "My fellow Carolingians and honored guests," she said, "now we are faced with the arduous task of repairing our country even as war threatens our western borders. The forces of the Dark One have advanced while we fought amongst ourselves. We have all seen the power of the Sha'iry. We have cowered in fear of it, but when ruthless evil threatens to engulf us, it becomes the duty of all to stand against tyranny. We must join together and affirm that Parlatheas does not belong to any one people, but to all intelligent beings. Faith and Freedom shall be our beacons of hope. To this end, I pledge to join with the Highlord to form a Confederation of Nations — an alliance that will bring down the forces of the Dark One. Let us show our children that we are not cowards who stand idly by while others fight our battles for us, that we will not lie down to be trampled under the heels of evil. No! We must show them we are lions, and that through the Eternal Father's grace, good will always triumph!"

CHAPTER 39
A NEW HOME

March 17, 1969 C.E.

5:30 pm

*R*eaching up, Roger removed the simple wooden placard with a haint-blue hand and replaced it with a new, hand-painted plaque emblazoned with a V. Written inside the letter was ROGER VAUGHN, Consultant.

"I still don't know why you chose this for your office," Brie said through the open door. Barefoot, she wore cut-off jean shorts and a green and white tank-top that read, "JETS." She sat on the leather couch, rifling through the magazines.

"You heard Vie. She didn't want it."

"Roger Vaughn, consultant," she said, leaning back. "What's that supposed to mean, anyways?"

Roger peeked into the quaint foyer and replied, "It was Nate's idea. He says the police may want me to assist this new task force they've created, especially if they're faced with something weird. It got me thinking. Maybe other people could use my help."

"Sounds dangerous to me."

"Possibly. I figure it will earn me a keep until I find a way home." Roger stepped inside. His eyes slid over Brie's bare legs before he jerked them up and stared at the encaustic painting of concentric blue and yellow circles on a red field that dominated the wall behind the couch. "I'm not sure if I'm ever going to get used to that thing." '*Or the way you dress*,' he added silently.

"Give it back to Vie if you want. Let her decorate her new home with it."

Roger laughed, picturing Vie's face. "Me carrying that painting is the last thing she wants to see right now. I'm telling you. She wants to put her father's office as far behind her as she can."

"That's a shame. The doctor wasn't as bad as he pretended."

Roger caught the sadness in her voice and asked, "So, you don't mind working for me?"

"No. Not as long as I can still finish school." Rising off the couch, she stood in front of Roger and continued, "And I get to help you."

"That's the general idea," Roger said. He frowned at the narrow hallway and the closed door of his new bedroom. This was his new home, and he'd have to get used to it.

"I mean it, Roger. I want to learn as much as I can about where you're from."

"Like you said, it may be dangerous," Roger answered. "Although from the way you handled yourself at the dock, I expect you could take care of yourself if the need arose."

"What makes you say that?"

"At the marina, you shot The Archer with his own arrow. I saw it happen, saw him fall, but I still can't believe it. It was an impossible shot."

Brie watched him, head canted to one side. Finally, she said, "I don't know what came over me. Don't get me wrong, I've been part of an archery team since I was a Brownie in Girl Scouts. It was the only sport I was any good at, but I never shot anyone. That man, The Archer, chased Ambrose and me all over town. He was going to kill my friend." She shrugged. "I guess I'd finally had enough."

Roger nodded. "I can understand that." Silence settled between them, and he turned toward the front of the building, where he'd set up his office with a simple desk and two chairs. Centered between the lead-paned windows looking out over Church Street, a narrow door led outside to a wrought iron balcony. He stared out a window and said, "I wonder why Doctor Wampus didn't use this room for his office."

"Probably too public. You can see out, but people can also see in," Brie replied.

"Makes sense, I suppose."

They heard a car pull up and Nate's and Tee's voices.

"Y'all home?" Nate said. "Mrs. Tyler wanted us to swing by and make sure you're not late. We tried calling, but you don't have your phone set up yet."

Roger gave his office the onceover before following Brie outside.

"Where are we going?" Roger asked, locking the door.

"Mom and Dad's," Brie replied with a sly smile. "They've invited you all over for some Irish fare. It's supposed to be an authentic Saint Patrick's Day dinner."

"Sounds fun," Roger said, coming down the stairs. "Maybe on the way, you can tell me who Saint Patrick is." In the parking lot, he shook Nate's and then Tee's hand.

"Settled in yet?" Tee asked.

"I'm getting there," Roger replied, glancing back toward the building.

"Come on," Brie urged.

Roger slid into the passenger seat of the Metropolitan. He thought about the Highlord, Cerdic, his family, and friends back on Gaia. He missed them, but for the first time he felt content. Oddly enough, it felt like his life was finally moving in the right direction. Maybe he'd spend a little time here before finding a way home.

Brie goosed the engine and jumped the curb. Just like that, his feeling of contentment was gone.

Thank You for Reading!

We hope you've enjoyed our first foray into Urban Fantasy with Roger Vaughn and his friends as much as we enjoyed bringing it to you! No author would be where they are without readers, so please accept a HUGE thank you for taking a chance on our endeavor. Whether you loved it, hated it, or landed somewhere in between, it would be of immense help to us, as well as other readers, if you would take a moment to leave a review on Amazon and/or Goodreads. Even a single sentence will mean a lot.

We love to hear from readers! Feel free to drop us a line at mcdonald.isom@gmail.com. Let us know what you loved (or what you hated). If you have questions about the story, we'll do our best to answer them. For more information about cultures, countries, creatures, and races of Gaia, visit the glossary on our website, www.mcdonald-isom.com. You can also find us on Facebook, @McDonald.Isom.author.

There are more adventures yet to come!

Behind the Scenes

How did a story set during Gaia's Plague War become an urban fantasy, set in 1969 Charleston, SC? Well, we're glad you asked. We already knew when Roger's sons were born on Terra. From there, it was a matter of working out what year Roger and Brie met and how he ended up on Terra.

Like other tales set in the world of Gaia, Thief on King Street has its roots buried deep in our college era D&D campaigns. Roger Vaughn, Cerdic Uth Aneirin, Lahar, and Phaedrus were integral in saving the nation of Carolingias and its reluctant Queen apparent, and we've tried to stay true to that adventure. However, as writers, we frequently ask ourselves, what if? What if that adventure was the genesis of Roger Vaughn and The Archer's enmity? What if *this* was how Roger met his Terran wife?

If you had not already guessed, writers are rather like magpies. We collect bits of interesting information and hoard it away for later use as the occasion arises. Several years ago, a contractor invited Jason to tour the Old City Jail in downtown Charleston with him. About the same time, Stormy was reading Six Miles to Charleston (SC): the True Story of John and Lavinia Fisher. Jason's intriguing visit, his numerous photos, and Bruce Orr's book inspired us to research the jail's long and sordid history. That research led us to the South Carolina Historical Society archives, where we read John Blake White's description of John and Lavinia's hanging and the executioner employed for the task. We asked ourselves, what if the Old City Jail was not only haunted, but had gained an evil sentience? What if an executioner who enjoyed his job a little too much made a deal with the Devil to continue his work for eternity? I think you can see where this is going...

Because so much history informed and inspired the Terran portions of Thief on King Street, we wanted to give you a bit of "Fact from Fiction."

Facts:

The 1908 Police Station: R. Thomas Short, architect, designed the facility located on the corner of St. Philip and Vanderhorst streets. The building had a castle-like appearance, including the corner tower and turret. Charleston's central police station remained here until 1974, when they moved to Lockwood Drive Extension.

Antonio de Erqueta: Assayer for Spain, he ran the mint from 1651 to 1679. His mark "E" can be found on many of the silver reales — "Pieces of 8" — with their distinctive Pillars of Hercules over the waves of the Atlantic Ocean design.

Captain George Clark: A privateer during the War of 1812, Captain Clark mutinied and assumed the command of the Louisa in 1818. Under the flag of Buenos Aires, they wreaked havoc on the high seas until their capture in 1819. George Clark was hung in Charleston for piracy in March of 1820.

Charleston County Hospital: Originally the Charleston County Tuberculosis Hospital, it began operations in 1953. With a wing dedicated to TB patients, its primary focus was caring for Charleston's indigent population. Purchased by MUSC in 1985, the facility was demolished in 2001. The name in our story, Oliver Krump, is a purely fictional addition.

Hoodoo: Equal parts belief system, magic, and shamanic medicine native to the Gullah and Geechee cultures of the Carolinas and Georgia. Goofer Dust is but one of many "tools" in a Root Doctor's repertoire. There are many great books on the subject, written by members of the Gullah/Geechee community, anthropologists, and botanists. We strongly encourage you to research and explore the fascinating history of this culture.

Magnolia Cemetery: Still in operation today, the expansive cemetery contains a wide array of funerary monuments and markers dating from the mid 1800's to modern times. The receiving tomb is a real building on the property, though the doors have been removed and its walls stabilized.

The Market Hall and Sheds: Today, the open-air market in Charleston is a popular spot for tourists and locals alike, offering a wide array of arts, crafts, clothing, food, and souvenirs. It was listed in the National Historic Register on June 4, 1973.

Morris Island Lighthouse: Today, the lighthouse is accessible only by water. Save the Light foundation held fundraisers in the early 21st century to build a coffer dam around the lighthouse foundations to prevent the sea from claiming the structure. The park at the far east end of Folly Beach provides free, unobstructed views of the lighthouse. There are also boat and helicopter companies which provide 'drive-by' viewings. At this time, there are no tours which go inside the lighthouse.

The Old City Jail: Built in 1802 and decommissioned in 1939, the jail originally consisted of four stories, topped with a two-story octagonal tower. It lay vacant under the ownership of the Charleston Housing Authority. Later, the American College of the Building Arts purchased the property and taught aspiring historic preservationists joinery and other "lost" arts. In more recent years, the property was purchased by a development company with plans to convert it into offices and an event center.

Sandborn Map Company: Founded in 1866, this company created lithographic maps of towns and cities in the United States (roughly 12,000 total) for use by fire insurance companies to assess liability. Although the last maps were published in the late 1970s, they are still available in various historic archives and through your local library.

Fiction:

Captain Thomas Richards and Rowanoake: Based loosely on Lieutenant Richards, one of several men who sailed alongside Blackbeard, escaped death on the gallows, and disappeared from history. Our Captain Richards was one of the eight founders of Rowanoake and ended up losing his head to the Highlord. The idea that there was a portal between the lost colony on Roanoke in North Carolina and Rowanoake the city state in Gallowen is purely fictional.

Dærganfae: there is no evidence that fae, unseelie or otherwise, have ever visited South Carolina.

Doctor Wampus: to our knowledge, there is not, nor has there ever been, a root doctor who called himself by this name. However, the courthouse scene in which Brie and Ambrose first see the Doctor is based on an actual event which took place in Beaufort County.

The Highlord and King Arthur: In our original D&D campaign, The Highlord of the Confederation of Nations was a man of mysterious origins. Like King Arthur of Welsh legend, he was unkillable. To give the Highlord more depth and a greater purpose, we decided to make his connection to Arthurian legend more obvious in this novel. Aside from his name, there are several clues within the narrative: he was from Terra, Britannia called him home in times of need, and the old scar inflicted by his son. Although *Le Morte D'Arthur* makes mention of Arthur's final resting place ("Hic jacet Arthurus, Rex quondam, Rexque futurus." *Here lies Arthur, the once and future king.*), older Welsh legends and "Englynion y Beddau" (*The Stanzas of the Graves*) point out that, although one can locate the graves of many heroes of legend, Arthur's remains a mystery. "Anoeth bid bet y Arthur." *The world's wonder [difficulty]: a grave for Arthur.*

About the Authors

Jason McDonald: An engineer by day and world builder by night, Jason is an advocate for using both sides of the brain. With his stepfather as a guide, Jason traveled the worlds of Edgar Rice Burroughs, Robert E. Howard, and J. R. R. Tolkien at an early age. As he grew older, he discovered Dungeons and Dragons and the joys of creating his own campaigns.

During all this, Jason graduated from Clemson University and embarked on a career in structural engineering. Now, he owns a successful engineering firm, where he continues to design a wide range of projects. His attention to detail and vivid imagination help shape the various adventures that challenge his characters.

Stormy McDonald: Coming from a family of storytellers — traditional, oral storytellers, that is — it's little wonder that Stormy is driven to weave words as well. She can't remember a time when she didn't love books — from the feel and smell of the pages, to the information they hold, to the tales that they tell — but storytelling is a labor of love, which doesn't always pay the bills. A ridiculous variety of side jobs have supported her writing habit, including waitress, security guard, library minion, salesperson, hairdresser, handyman, engineering drafter, and small business owner.

Alan Isom: Alan's adventures with literature began as they should: with Tolkien's *The Hobbit*, read to him as a child by his father. His love of fantasy and science fiction eventually led him to RPGs — most notably Dungeons & Dragons — where world building became a fascination.

After majoring in Physics at Furman University and Civil Engineering at Clemson University, he became a licensed engineer and now works for an international Engineering-Procurement-Construction company. Alan also served as a soldier with the Army National Guard. Each of these careers, as well as a multitude of hobbies, helps bring depth and creativity to the characters and worlds he brings to life.

Printed in Great Britain
by Amazon

11319063R00205